A COMPANY OF FRIENDS

Talog was warming toward his companions, especially the healer Lysandra. She had the Hand of the Divine upon her—even if she knew it not.

It was part of his training as a Guide to read the clues others revealed about themselves. Many things about his companions still puzzled him, however. Why were Renan and Lysandra not Joined—because she was a healer? Little as he knew about Upworlders, it was plain that they had the same feelings for each other that meant a male and female of the Cryf would go to the Guide to say the words of Joining.

But Renan and Lysandra each tried to hide their feelings from the other. To Talog, it made no sense.

THE
THIRTEENTH
SCROLL

REBECCA NEASON

ASPECT®

WARNER BOOKS

A Time Warner Company

WARNER BOOKS EDITION

Cover design by Don Puckey
Cover illustration by Daniel Craig
Hand lettering by Carol Russo

Aspect® name and logo are registered trademarks of Warner Books, Inc.

Warner Books, Inc.
1271 Avenue of the Americas
New York, NY 10020

Visit our Web site at
www.twbookmark.com

For information on Time Warner Trade Publishing's online program, visit www.ipublish.com

 A Time Warner Company

Printed in the United States of America

First Printing: June 2001

10 9 8 7 6 5 4 3 2

This book is dedicated
To my mother
Shirly Matilda
1923–1999
Who instilled within all her family
a deep and abiding love for the written word,
and who was truly
"One of a kind."

THE
THIRTEENTH
SCROLL

Prologue

Old King Osaze was dead, only a month dead, and already the kingdom of Aghamore was near to erupting in violence. The King had left no bodily issue to inherit the crown, and now each of the Barons who ruled the eight outer provinces thought himself the best allied—by family and wealth or by strength and greed—to lay claim to the throne.

The Church, whose power in Aghamore rivaled that of the Barons, supported the late King's nephew, Anri. But the people thought Anri too young and untried, not a leader to inspire confidence or imbue the kingdom with an aura of strength in the minds of their enemies. Yet even he was preferred to the threat of civil war.

The Barons knew Anri for what he was—greedy in his tastes, perverse in his pleasures, and interested in the throne of Aghamore only for the riches it could provide. Unlike the people, the Barons thought civil war was preferable to Anri.

The specter of that threat hung like a shadowed veil across the kingdom. As the throne remained unfilled, the people of Aghamore looked with desperation to the Church, praying that it would find the means to exercise its authority in the matter of the succession and control the Barons' predilection for war.

It was, therefore, on Ballinrigh, Aghamore's capital, that the eyes and the hearts of the kingdom were fixed.

In that great city, the law of the land still held sway and the people still walked the streets in safety, going about their daily business while waiting to see which way the winds of change would blow. But such was not true away from the larger cities. All through the eight provinces that encircled Urlar, Aghamore's central province, bands of soldiers roamed through towns and villages, sought out hamlets and farms, conscripting every able-bodied young man into service of the Barons. Rather than be pressed into the army and forced to fight a war no one but the Barons wanted, many men fled from their homes to hide out in the forests and hills until the dangers of the conscription gangs—or the war—had passed.

With the law's attention focused elsewhere and so many men either in the army or in hiding, outlaws were growing in numbers and boldness. They marauded unchecked, taking whatever they wanted wherever they found it.

In the Fifth Province of Camlough, in the once-prosperous town of Scorda, Lysandra lay on her bed sobbing, crying with all the passion of her seventeen-year-old heart. Her mother sat next to her, trying to give her comfort. But Lysandra wanted none. She wanted life as she had planned it.

"You can't ask Ultan to stay," her mother said gently. "Not when the conscription gangs have reached Lamford already. They could ride into Scorda any day."

"But why now?" Lysandra still sobbed. "Our wedding is only a week away. It's not fair."

Her mother's low chuckle made Lysandra furious. She sat up quickly, trying to glare—but her blue eyes were too swollen and red. Her puffy, tear-streaked cheeks made her look like a cross and fretful child.

"Oh, Lysandra," her mother said, reaching out to softly wipe away the tears that still lingered on her cheek, "no one, in any place or at any time, has ever said life was going to be fair. Life isn't *fair*—life simply *is*."

"But—"

"No, Lysandra," she continued, taking her daughter's hands into her own, "you're not a child anymore to think life must behave a certain way just because you wish it so. Life comes when and as it will, and we—especially we women—must make the best of it, without ever giving up hope that all will eventually be well."

There was scant comfort in her mother's words, but there was truth and, still heart-sore, she slowly nodded. Her mother gave her a smile and brought a handkerchief out of her apron pocket to dry Lysandra's eyes.

"That's better," she said, her tone turning brisk and matter-of-fact, a tone Lysandra knew well. "Now go splash some cold water on your face and comb your hair. Go to Ultan as a strong, courageous woman. Show him that he can leave here knowing that you will be all right until he returns."

Lysandra blew her nose. "Where will he go?" she asked.

"Well, if he leaves now," her mother replied, "he will have time to join with the other men who are going into the Great Forest—as so many have already. I swear Scorda will be a sad and empty place with so many gone. But"—she sighed—"better they go like this, on their own terms, than be forced away."

The net under which Lysandra had so neatly bound her hair this morning was hopelessly askew. She yanked it off and with quick fingers, gathered her wheat-colored hair back into a single braid that fell nearly to her waist. Then Lysandra's mother pulled her into a quick hug.

"I promise you, Lysandra," she said, "all this will pass more quickly than you think. You and Ultan have a long life ahead of you—and it will be made all the sweeter because of your separation now."

The smile Lysandra gave her mother was still forced and a little crooked, but, at least for now, her tears were spent. There were more tears to be shed, but they would wait until after Ultan had departed.

"Do you know where he is?" she asked, her voice still wavering slightly.

"He's with your father down at the stables. Your father's lending him one of the packhorses—but I know he's waiting for you."

Lysandra nodded as she took a deep breath. Then, giving her mother one more quick embrace, she left their home in the back of her father's wool-and-dye shop and headed for the stables that served this part of the town.

She gave barely a glance to the long, twisted ropes of brightly dyed wool that hung in the shop's window, nor did she stop to look at the other shops as she passed. The weaver next door, with the lengths of beautiful cloth; the seamstress's window, full of coats and dresses; the cobbler's shop, with the giant wooden boot over the door; and, across the street, the ironwright's shop, standing next to the silversmith's whose window display of platters and goblets, buckles and jewelry always caught the morning sun—all those and more were as familiar to Lysandra as her own home. She gave them no more thought than she did the sound of neighbors' voices or the playful barking of some of the town's dogs. Her mind was filled with only one thought—*Ultan.*

She walked briskly, her mind so busy with thoughts of

him that at first she paid no heed to how the noise behind her had changed. Dogs now barked fiercely and over them, Lysandra heard the sound of galloping hooves—far too many to be a casual ride.

Her first thought was of the conscription gangs. She started to run. *I've got to get to Ultan,* her thoughts now came in a whirl, matching the rhythm of her feet. *Tell him to get away. It's my fault—he should have gone yesterday or last week . . . he only stayed for me . . .*

She threw a glance over her shoulder. Just then, the first scream hit her ears. Lysandra's stomach contracted in true fear—for this was no conscription gang. These riders, at least twenty strong, rode behind the most dreaded man in the province, perhaps in the kingdom.

They rode with Black Bryan.

Black Bryan was a bull of a man, with coal-dark hair and eyes to match. It was said that he used to be a blacksmith until ruinous taxes had claimed his smithy. Having lost his means of honest living, he now took what he wanted. The law had been after his gang for more than five years, but they remained elusive and unstoppable.

And now into Scorda they rode, knowing they could take what they wanted and caring nothing for the screams or the lives of those in their way.

Black Bryan stayed on his horse while his men fanned out in search of plunder, some on horseback, some already pushing their way into shops and houses. Lysandra saw all this in a scant moment. Her one thought was to reach the stables, now closer than her home. If she could get to Ultan and her father, she might be safe.

The air around her rang with the wails of children and the screams of women. Such violence was inconceivable in this town, this place filled with her childhood memories of sunlight and laughter. *This cannot be real,* her mind cried.

But it was. Lysandra heard the hoofbeats. They were close—too close. Her heart was pounding more wildly than the horses' hooves, pounding with the fear of an only half-recognized premonition, as she slipped into a small alleyway to hide. But it was too late; she had been seen. She was trapped with no way to escape the four men who had leapt down from their horses and were closing in upon her. Their eyes shone with a light that left Lysandra little doubt of their intent.

"No," she heard herself say as she slowly backed away. "No, please—let me go."

The men kept coming. One of them laughed. "She's a pretty one, don't you think, m'lads?" he said.

"Aye, right fair—and ripe for the pickin' too."

Lysandra started to scream. But her fear meant less than nothing to the men. Her helplessness fed their lust as they grabbed at her, easily holding her arms though she struggled with all her strength. One man grasped her bodice, ready to rip it apart. Suddenly, he was hit from behind. He stumbled, his fingers slipping from her as he turned toward his attackers.

In that same instant, through her screams and her fear-blurred vision, Lysandra saw what he saw. It was Ultan— the boy she loved, the boy she planned to marry. Her father was with him. Her mother, too, suddenly appeared, running from the other direction, come to find her and fight for the safety of her only child. Ultan wielded a length of board; Lysandra's father grasped a hayfork, and her mother clutched a kitchen knife. Lysandra knew they would be no match for the swords of the men who held her.

"No!" she screamed again, renewing her struggles. She

kicked, she hit, she tried everything she could to break free and save those she loved.

But the men were too strong, their reflexes too swift. While two still held her, two turned on her family. Lysandra saw the quick parry and thrust of their swords flashing in the sunlight. She saw the looks of surprise, terror, and then death, come to the faces first of Ultan, then of her parents. She saw the blood gush and flow, staining the clothes, their bodies deep crimson. She saw their bodies crumple to the ground. She saw all that was life and love to her die.

She saw . . .

The men turned back around. The swords in their hands still glistened, wet and red. In horrified fascination, Lysandra saw the blood run down the blade, drip by drip, onto the ground. She tore her eyes away and looked into their faces again. She saw how the violence had only sharpened their lust.

Suddenly the world spun around her. It went black as Lysandra's body crumpled, unconscious, in the grip of her attackers.

When, at last, consciousness returned, Lysandra did not know how long it had been. She knew only that she was alone.

The pains in her body told her that the men had carried through their intent. But at least they had left her behind and not dragged her off for further violation at the hands of their leader.

Lysandra could smell the blood and death that lay only a few feet from her; she could hear the cries, the wails of sorrow and agony from elsewhere in her village. With them, the horror of the day flooded her anew and made permanent wounds upon her soul.

She crawled toward the bodies of Ultan and her parents. Although the pain each movement cost her assured her that consciousness had indeed returned, her world remained in darkness.

Lysandra was blind.

Chapter One

Deep in the heart of the Great Forest, twenty-seven-year-old Lysandra knelt in her garden, feeling the warmth of the spring sun upon her shoulders. At that moment she felt wrapped in peace. But it was a peace that had come hard-earned. Time had taught that such moments were to be cherished but never trusted; security was more delicate than a butterfly's wing—and even more easily destroyed.

She had been in this cottage for almost nine years now. It was a place she had come across by accident, an old hermit's home standing alone and abandoned deep in the forest. She had at once sensed an affinity for the place; her own heart had felt just as empty as this house, just as overrun by brambles and weeds as its garden.

For the first few days of her blindness, Lysandra had stayed in her family home. Although the villagers were kind in their pity of her, she could not stand the silence of the house that had once been filled with her mother's singing and her father's hearty laughter.

And there was Ultan's death, the death of her love, of her future. Without him, her heart felt as empty and bare as the void her eyes could not see. The only thing that filled them both was the memory of blood and fear.

The memory of death.

The decision to leave Scorda was not one she made consciously; reasonable thought would have told her that, blind now and needy in her infirmity, she must remain where life was familiar. But Lysandra could not stay in that empty place that had once been her home. As she packed those few belongings she could comfortably make into a bundle and headed for the door, leaving felt as inevitable as her next breath.

She did not care where she went as long as it was far away from the reminders of what she had lost. She wandered, somehow finding her way to the Great Forest. She fully expected to die there, of loneliness and starvation. She accepted that fate without care or regret—perhaps, even, with eagerness.

It was instinct that kept her alive as she learned to rely upon her senses other than sight. Touch and hearing kept her from falling down ravines or stumbling into brambles; smell and taste told her what food she had found; and it was the feel of the sun and the sounds of the birds or crickets that separated daylight from the night.

But time did not matter. She ate when she was hungry and found food; she slept when she was tired, beneath some tree or in the shelter of a thicket. None of it mattered to her. Though she walked and moved and breathed, life was only a façade; she felt as dead as her murdered family.

Lysandra had no sense in which direction she wandered or for how long, but she kept herself away from any human contact. Twice she stumbled upon a crofter's home whose goodwife took her in, fed and cleaned her, and for pity's sake offered her a place to stay. But these acts of kindness only deepened the wounds upon Lysandra's heart until she ran from them, back into the forest and her solitude.

Spring became summer, that faded into autumn. Rumors spread throughout the Province of the crazed woman roaming the forest. She was crazed then—crazed with the pain of her grief and her loss, crazed with guilt that she should live while those whom she loved had given their lives to save her.

If only she had not screamed . . .

If only she had been stronger . . .

If only was the voice of her madness . . .

Lysandra waited for death to claim her and bring welcome reunion with those she had lost. But it was not death that came to her during those timeless months. Instead her mind began to open in a way so new, so unexpected, it was nearly incomprehensible.

Slowly, creeping on her almost unawares, vague shapes began to form, filling her mind with outlines and patterns that at first it refused to recognize. This was not vision as she had known before; to her eyes the world remained in darkness, a void unfilled and unfillable. But into her mind now came images cast in auraed shapes of shadow and brightness.

This new way of seeing was not easy, nor did it come all at once. It was like the morning sun burning through a thick bank of fog—slowly, revealing not only an object before her, but its intent, its inner nature. She could *see* which plants would harm her and which would nourish, which animals feared her, which were curious, and which might do her injury.

At first, in her heart-numbed state of grief, she felt neither surprise nor fear at this new *Sight*. She felt nothing, remembered nothing; she merely existed from moment to moment, day to day, not dead but neither truly alive.

She spent that first winter sheltered in a cave she shared with a young female fox. It was there, during the long, snowbound days, that her sanity began to return—and with it came the first puzzled wonderment at the images filling her mind.

Lysandra was sitting across the fire from the vixen when the spark of true awareness glimmered, changing into a spreading dawn that came upon her so gently, she was not certain when, between one breath and the next, the darkness had ended and the light of Self began again. But it was the fire that first caught her attention. She knew, in some vague way, that she had kindled and maintained it this night as on countless nights before. Yet she had no more direct memory of the action than she had of taking shelter within this cave.

She felt the fire's heat—and then, suddenly, she realized that within her mind she *saw* the dance of light and shadow that was its flame. Across the fire, the vixen regarded her calmly. Now, her wonder growing with each passing second, Lysandra considered her companion and found she *saw* much more than the outlined shape of the animal; this was far less distinct than her physical eyes would have seen. Instead, Lysandra *saw* the acceptance that shone from the fox's eyes, and from this she knew they had spent many weeks learning to live together.

And even more amazing, Lysandra found that by concentrating, by listening beyond the silence, she could share the fox's feelings. They were not thoughts; at least they did not mirror the individual patterns of human thought. But she knew that the fox's wariness of the fire mingled with its comfort in the warmth. Accepting the fire was part of its acceptance of her.

From that moment, Lysandra never again sank into the blackness of unremembered days. It was now she truly began to wonder at this new *Sight*. What was it exactly and from whence had it come? Was it a gift from the God in whom she was no longer certain she believed—some Divinely ordered recompense for all she had lost?

For this, as for so much in her life now, she had no answers. A part of her, the larger part, did not care. To question was to invite again the grief-filled darkness that still hovered somewhere close. Instead, throughout the winter, she and the fox continued to share their cave while Lysandra learned to choose *life* again. She knew that the person she had been before, the girl to whom laughter came easily and who believed in love and happy endings, was dead. She had died in that alleyway in Scorda and was part of the dreams that had been buried along with her parents—with Ultan. She could never be resurrected.

Yet this realization was not only one of endings. With the acceptance of youth forever gone, with the choice of the new life waiting, Lysandra knew herself reborn; though she wore the same body, this new Lysandra had a very different soul.

Like all the newly born, each moment held things she must learn if her new life was to continue and she was now glad of the long winter months. Her time in the cave gave her an opportunity to explore the range of her new *Sight*. She found it was not like physical vision, full of countless hues of bright and muted color. Color in Lysandra's world was more felt than seen, though on rare occasions it would still manifest with sudden and surprising clarity, granting her a glimpse of the world as she used to know it. The first time her *Sight* expanded, showing her the vixen in the full beauty of her winter coat, it took Lysandra several seconds to realize what was before her.

The vision did not last long, and the brilliant detail of it was almost blinding. But in those few seconds, Lysandra saw again the colors of earth and stone, of flame and fox, of the winter night's darkness outside the cave's opening and the golden glow of the fire's radiance within. Then, as this revelation of her world began to fade, there came a long awe-filled moment when the two manifestations of *Sight* blended, when color and clarity melded with aura and pattern. It was a marvel that almost reawakened the depth of her failed faith.

Then the moment passed, leaving Lysandra to question again the nature of this *Sight*.

Those brief glimpses of color returned upon occasion, but never for long or by any reason Lysandra could find. Nor was her *Sight* always with her. Sometimes she existed in true blindness once again, as if to remind her of the darkness out of which her new life had been born— and in which a part of her soul still existed.

When spring came again and the vixen moved on in search of territory and a mate, Lysandra was sorry to see her go. The fox had been a good companion, and Lysandra would miss her silent presence and the lessons of existence she had taught.

Soon Lysandra also left the cave. For a while she resumed walking through the Great Forest. But this time her travels were different because *she* was different. With the fox as teacher, she had learned to be her own companion. There were no more dreams of the future. She had learned to live each moment for what it was, and to accept what it—what she—was not. As the forest and its creatures cycled forward into spring, Lysandra, too, moved on into the life that must be lived by the woman she had become.

She found it here in this cottage, where over the years she had become a healer. The animals came to her and, like the fox, seemed to know that she was someone they need not fear, whose touch and voice were soft and whose actions were only for their good. This pleased Lysandra in a way that went far beyond words. Her devotion to these creatures grew, became her focus, and filled her hours with purpose.

In one section of Lysandra's garden, she grew the food to keep her alive, for she would eat no animal flesh. But most of the beds were filled with healing plants that she tended carefully. Eventually, people in the area also came to know of her healing touch. Crofters and gamekeepers, shepherds and farmers, would occasionally show up at her door, sometimes bringing their animals to her, other times in need of care for themselves or their families. Lysandra did what she could for them, accepting payments of eggs or cheese or bread, of wool or cloth, if they chose to offer such. But she never asked for payment or turned anyone away for the lack of it.

Also over the years, as she learned to use her *Sight* to heal, she found that other . . . gifts . . . were occasionally present, as well. As with the vixen that first winter, she could often feel the emotions of her patients. With the animals, emotions were simple, primal—fear, confusion, pain, or relief. But with the nearness of humans came a jumble of thoughts and emotions that bombarded her mind, destroying her hard-won peace.

She was always glad when they left her; she was happier with the birds and beasts. They were friends Lysandra never tried to tame. She fed those who came to her hungry, healed those who were sick or injured, and let them go again in their own time.

There was one exception—a wolf she had found, injured, as a small pup. From the first moment she started to care for him, the pup had touched her heart as nothing had in many years. His trusting nature, the eager way he responded to her nearness, the unquestioning love he gave her was a balm more potent than any medicine in her cupboard.

She named the pup Cloud-Dancer, partly for the softness of his thick silver-and-white fur, whose beauty she had seen only upon occasion, and partly for his habit as a pup of dancing on his hind legs, front paws lifted as if trying to reach the clouds. Now, at two, Cloud-Dancer rarely left Lysandra's side, except once a day when he needed to hunt. He always returned to her swiftly—and never did he make a move toward any animal in her care.

She had come to rely upon his presence and his instincts, especially in those times when her *Sight* left her. Over the last two years this bond of trust between them had become so strong, that when her need for true vision was great Lysandra could put her hand on Cloud-Dancer and see through his eyes. Like her inner *Sight,* this, too, was an odd sort of vision, a world of strange perspective seen in tones of sepia, gray, and muted pastels. But, also like the *Sight,* her understanding of it had strengthened with use and familiarity.

But Cloud-Dancer was more than just a companion and another pair of seeing eyes. Although Lysandra cared about all the creatures of the forest, it was to Cloud-Dancer alone that she gave the only love she had to give.

But the reawakening of her heart came at a price. Life

in her cottage moved in a rhythm of simple actions and simpler pleasures, an easy cadence built slowly through the years. On days like today, kneeling in her garden in the warmth of the sun, feeling Cloud-Dancer's nearness soft but ever-present in her mind, the life and dreams of her youth seemed like parts of a fairy story she had once heard before falling asleep—lovely but unreal.

Yet now that her heart had its own beat again, however soft, into moments of deepest silence a half-and-best-forgotten voice sometimes whispered. It brought back moments and memories out of her long-dead past—thoughts of home and family, abandoned yearnings for love, marriage, children.

She had a home, she told herself each time; she neither wanted nor needed another. Her children were her plants, the animals she cared for; her family was Cloud-Dancer. These were enough.

But, despite her brave resolve, the whispered memories still returned.

Lysandra stood and stretched the ache of the garden hours out of her back. The days were lengthening as summer slowly approached, and sundown was still two hours away, but it was time to go inside and close down the day.

As Lysandra headed for the door, Cloud-Dancer came to walk beside her, brushing her thigh as he always did. The walkway to her house was so familiar she needed neither his guidance nor his eyes to find her way, but she reached down and gently ran her fingers through his fur to signal the gratitude she always felt for his company.

At the door, she stopped. Over the years, Lysandra had developed one final ritual, performed each evening before going in for the night. She turned back toward the forest and closed her eyes. She waited until her mind and body stilled, until all she could hear was her breath and the sound of her own heartbeat. When at last that moment of perfect stillness enveloped her, Lysandra opened her mind and embraced it with all the eagerness of a lover.

The quickly cooling freshness of the spring air blew across her cheeks, and Lysandra sent the full awareness these years had developed in her outward to soar upon it. Her questing thought touched the wings of the nearby birds in flight, rustled new sprung leaves, brushed across the creatures of the forest. Her mind reached out, ever farther . . . listening for the cry of anyone, animal or human, who might need her help.

All remained silent . . . and in that silence was her rest, her peace, her home. All was well. With a soft smile, she once more touched Cloud-Dancer, then put her hand to the door latch and went inside.

Two hours later, she sat in her chair before the fire. Contentment had settled over her like a soft, warm blanket. Outside, the occasional cry of a night bird heralded the deepening darkness. Lysandra sighed and, closing her eyes, rested her head against the warm fleece that covered her chair. Soon she would go to bed.

Oh, but that means I have to move, she thought sleepily. *It would be so easy just to drift off here, by the fire . . . it's so warm here. . . .*

Suddenly, her tranquility shattered and flew into a thousand fragments.

All day long she had felt the presence of . . . something . . . flitting around the edges of recognition, elusive yet insistent. Now it cut through Lysandra's sleepy peace like a sword slicing a remnant of tattered lace. Heart pounding, she sprang to her feet.

What are you? her mind cried. *What do you want? Tell*

me or leave me alone. But still it refused to be pinned down or give itself a name.

Cloud-Dancer whined, responding to her turmoil. She put her hands out for him and he was immediately there, warm and soft, a touchable comfort.

Lysandra rubbed him gently behind one ear. "I'm all right," she said to him. "We're both all right, aren't we, boy?"

Her voice was low and soft, and she felt his ears perk forward in response to it. As always, his eagerness touched Lysandra's heart. She knelt beside him, putting her arms around his neck and resting her cheek atop his head.

"Yes, we are," she whispered her own answer. "We're all right just the way we are."

In spite of the brave assurances she gave herself, she knew that some small corner of her heart now held a new and unexplained foreboding. She feared that somehow the world outside her forest, the world she did not wish to enter again, was about to find her.

It was deep in the night when the dream came, full of vivid color that even in dreams now took Lysandra by surprise.

She saw only a pair of eyes, the deep brown of newly tilled earth, sparked with flecks of green and gold, and soft as the eyes of a fawn. They were looking for something . . . for her? She felt that she was being sought, being called, but not in a voice heard with her ears. This call was one she felt in her bones.

Lysandra shook herself awake, away from the disturbing feelings of need that filled the dream. Was it her need . . . or someone else's? She did not know—nor want to.

She felt Cloud-Dancer's reassuring weight upon the

foot of her bed. Through the bond they shared, Lysandra knew he was awake and watching her, made wary by her second burst of agitation. Like her, he, too, was used to the undisturbed routine of their lives.

"It was just a dream," she said to him—to herself. "Dreams mean nothing."

But as she lay back down she wondered how much truth those words held.

It was easy to dismiss the dream the first time it happened, but not the tenth or the fifteenth. Night after night those eyes invaded Lysandra's sleep—always looking, always searching.

Night after night she felt as if her name were being called, though in truth she heard no word. It became impossible to shake off the feeling. It lingered as she rose each morning and set about her tasks in house or garden. She felt as if those eyes watched her from every bush and shadow, as if every breath of wind among the trees whispered her name.

Then it began to interfere with her work as healer. A shepherd brought a sick ewe to her. Lysandra could tell he was young by the sound of his voice, though, oddly, she could feel none of the tumbling mix of thought and emotions that were always part of human presence. But Lysandra, concentrating upon the ewe, spared this absence barely a thought—for she suddenly faced a new and far more frightening lack.

For the first time since the beginning of her *Sight*, Lysandra received no impression when she touched the animal.

Her *Sight* was never a constant thing, present or absent for reasons she understood no better now than she had at its inception. But it was always there for the animals. *Always.* And so she waited, ignoring the shepherd as she bent all of her will upon the ewe.

No *Sight* came to show her what was wrong.

At this continued darkness, the foreboding that had become her ever-present companion sent a sudden burst of panic through her. Her fingers trembled slightly as she took the ewe's head gently between her palms and held it, once more ordering her mind to stillness.

She slowly exhaled, determined to help the ewe. Whatever her own sudden affliction, she would not let this animal continue to suffer. She was a healer, she told herself; she could rely on her other senses and on her past experience.

As other healers do, she reminded herself firmly.

Still, the panic turned to bile in her throat as she began to run her hands across the body of the ewe, trying to be sensitive to any signal of movement or breathing. She was so intent upon her patient that she had almost forgotten the young shepherd's existence until she realized he was asking her a question.

"So, who do you think'll get the throne this time?" he asked.

Lysandra looked up, slightly confused. "Get the throne? We've King Anri, don't we?"

"Gor . . . you do live cut off 'ere. Anri's been dead these seven months, since Michaelmas. I say good riddance— and I'm not the only one neither. Most of Aghamore's glad to see the last of 'im. There's some what say 'e was poisoned, to get 'im off the throne, you see."

"Why would Aghamore be glad to have no King?" Lysandra asked, still bewildered. She knew—too well— what it meant for a kingdom to have no ruler. It meant lawlessness and the suffering of innocents while those who were supposed to look after the common good turned their attentions to gaining power any way they could—and the common good be damned.

"Right ruinous, Anri was," the shepherd was saying. "I mean, 's'truth a King's got to have 'is pleasures—everyone knows that. But weren't the old taxes enough to pay for 'em? They was for ol' Osaze, and 'e weren't no hermit from what I 'ear. But Anri—'e raised taxes again and again 'til I knows some folks what couldn't pay and they lost everything to the tax collectors, dirty vultures that they are. Even so, I 'ear the treasury's all but empty. Anri spent it on his 'favorites,' didn't he? And not women what could become 'is wife, neither, if you take my meaning. I'll wager the Church'll be more particular who they support this time, seein's how they's the ones what put Anri on the throne."

"You're rather young to have such strong opinions, aren't you?" Lysandra asked, a bit amused by his vehemence. "You can't have been more than—what, four or five?—when King Osaze died."

"Six I was," the shepherd replied, just a little indignant. "But I got ears, 'aven't I? And eyes? I 'ear people talk. I see what's what around me. You'd 'ave to be a blind fool—"

The shepherd stopped, embarrassed. "I . . . um . . . I'm sorry. I didn't mean—" he quickly stammered an apology.

"It's all right," Lysandra gently assured him. "My blindness is a fact I long ago accepted. And it's true . . . I am isolated here. I have little interest in who is on the throne or what is happening away from this forest."

That said, Lysandra turned her full attention back to the ewe. Still no *Sight* had come, nor had her tactile examination revealed anything to cause the ewe's symptoms. Yet the animal's distress was quite real. Confused, frustrated, and more than a little frightened that her *Sight* should so completely abandon her, Lysandra made a bold decision. There was one final thing she could try; it was difficult and something she attempted only in rare cases, but the truth was she did not know what else to do.

Lysandra closed her eyes and drew one more deep breath. Then, as she slowly exhaled, she forced every fear and feeling of failure aside, opening herself to the ewe and its pain, willing herself to be one with the animal and to take its distress into herself.

But, though Lysandra was willing, though the gates of her mind were open and her instinct for self-protection suppressed by her commitment to healing, she could not create the necessary bridge. Her inability to help the ewe made her want to weep.

She knew she needed to be alone. The sudden possibility that she might now face a future in true and complete blindness was too frightening to imagine and too real to be ignored. She needed solitude to think.

And, perhaps, to find a new path through the threatening darkness.

With a deep sigh, she sat back and lifted her hands from the ewe's body. "I can find nothing physically wrong," she told the shepherd. "I would guess that something is stalking your herd and has frightened her badly. Sheep will manifest their fright in illness sometimes. They can even be frightened to death. I suggest you keep her close to you for these next few days. Touch her, carry her, let her feel the constant safety of your nearness—and keep more vigilant watch than usual. It's the time of year when many predators are giving birth and have new, hungry mouths to feed. If she's not better in a few days, bring her back and I'll look at her again."

"Right," the shepherd said, gathering the ewe up into

his arms. "I've brought you a pot of cheese and some bread. Is that enough?"

"More than enough," Lysandra said. "I don't deserve any of it. I didn't *do* anything."

"You deserve your pay, same as the rest of us," he replied firmly. "But you'd best pray a new King gets settled quick-like, and that 'e's better than the last, before the tax collectors find you, too. Though 'ow they'd tax bread and cheese, I don't know. But sure as sunrise, they'd find a way."

When the shepherd left, taking with him all the energetic convictions of his youth, stillness settled again in Lysandra's garden. But her mind was filled with the shepherd's news and with the emotions they set to whirl within her.

The King was dead, the throne empty again . . . well, what had that to do with her? With her *Sight* gone—for how long or if permanently, she did not know—she now had problems of her own.

Yet, even as that thought came, she knew it was why the dream was calling her.

Chapter Two

Many miles away in Aghamore's Third Province of Kilgarriff, Baron Giraldus DeMarcoe stalked the battlements of his fortress. Impatience marked every line of his body and pounded through his restless footsteps. He was not a man who liked waiting, as those who dared to try his patience soon found out.

The woman behind him was another matter. She was a study in stillness. Only her eyes moved as they followed his pacing. The dark blue gown, the color she habitually wore, draped around her without a ruffle of movement; her dark hair fell straight and unbound, making her look like a pillar of shadow.

This was Aurya, Giraldus's lover, advisor—and sorceress.

Aurya carried the name Treasigh, but that was her mother's name. Her father's identity was unknown by the world. Some said that even Aurya did not know; others claimed she was the spawn of none less than the devil himself. Her past was shrouded in dark and mystery and Aurya kept it that way—even from Giraldus.

"Where is he?" Giraldus demanded, turning toward her suddenly.

"It is not yet even noon," Aurya replied. "You only

make the hours longer with your pacing. Patience, Giraldus."

"Patience be damned," he countered curtly. "I'm risking everything on this venture—more than you, more than Elon. If we lose, it will mean not only the crown, but this province as well. Unlike the late King, *I* have a large family, and there are plenty of others just waiting for the Barony to be passed. I still say a clean win on the field of battle is the better way to claim the throne than whatever it is Elon's message said he was bringing."

"Do you truly think Elon would be bringing it, were he not convinced of its importance?" she asked. "We've taken a long time to cultivate this partnership. You've played every turn just right. Don't let your impatience get in the way now."

Aurya watched as Giraldus tried to make up his mind whether to preen at her compliment or be annoyed by her admonition.

"I still don't like all this *waiting*," he said finally, "all these plots and counterplots. I'm a man of action, Aurya— as you well know. I have to *do* something, not wait around for the next bit of information like a lapdog waiting for a morsel of food to drop from his master's hand. I've paid the bishop a small fortune in gold for his ... services ... and I'll not be treated with such disdain."

A sharp burst of breath escaped Aurya. She was not impatient with waiting, but she did sometimes become impatient with Giraldus's impatience.

"Elon will be here. Today. When, I don't know—but he *always* keeps his word, especially for the amount of money and the promises you've given him. You might not be High King yet, but you are ruler of this province. If you're so anxious to be busy, go ... *rule* ... something. Just *quit pacing*."

Aurya watched the flush creep into Giraldus's cheeks. No one else would have dared speak to him in such a manner. But she did not care what others dared; her rules were her own, and even Giraldus had to play by them if he wanted what she offered.

And he did; he always did. Since the moment they met at the Summer Faire here in Adaraith, Kilgarriff's capital city, almost nine years ago, Aurya had known that Giraldus wanted her. She had made certain that he did. Although she was barely eighteen and not long on her own, she already knew her powers and how to use them to her advantage. Even joining the Faire by erecting a small booth and passing herself off as a fortune-teller had not been for the few meager coins she had earned. It had been a trick to get her where—and who—she wanted.

But it was not magic she had used on Giraldus, except the magic of being young, beautiful, and intelligent. She had used that intelligence to make certain her beauty was seen just enough to weave its own brand of ensorcellment. When the young and vigorous Baron Giraldus, then twenty-five, opened the Faire, she had been in the forefront of the crowd. Quickly disappearing after she was certain he had seen her, she carefully planned her days so she was close enough to be often glimpsed, but never near enough for more. She counted on Giraldus's curiosity and his hunter's instinct to do the rest.

By the fifth day of the weeklong Faire, she received an invitation to the Baron's fortress. By the end of the summer, when she was quite certain he had fallen in love with her, she finally let herself be wooed into his bed. Since then, they had been rarely separated.

Her beauty had ensnared him, but it was Aurya's intelligence and fire that kept him. From her low beginnings as the daughter of a woman she still thought of as a contemptible fool—so meek and compliant, unwilling to stand up and name her child's father so that he might share her disgrace, always at church, on her knees and begging for forgiveness—Aurya had found her own way in life.

And now she was the Baron's consort. Giraldus had hesitated only once in their relationship and then only briefly—when he had discovered her hatred of the Church and her use of magic. She had left him then, the first and only time. It had been less than a week before he was after her, unable to stand their separation. When she returned to his side, she convinced him that her magic was a tool she could use in his favor.

They had been together less than a year when an assassin managed to enter their bedchamber. He had made it past Giraldus's guards, but he could not sneak past her magic. Caught in the web of protection she habitually set over them each night, the assassin had raised an arm to strike—and found himself unable to move.

Giraldus would have turned the man over to his guards and had information tortured out of him, but Aurya considered torture clumsy and unreliable; too often the subject died before everything could be gleaned. Instead, she asked Giraldus to give the assassin to her. An hour later, she knew everything the man's mind had held—and he was by then a mindless, helpless threat to no one.

The assassin had been sent by Giraldus's cousin, Tyrele, who was next in line for the Barony, should Giraldus have no children. Aurya's revenge on Tyrele had been as slow and deliberate as her action against his ill-fated tool had been swift. She could have killed him with any number of spells, but that would have been too easy. She wanted him to suffer, and she wanted others to realize what could happen to anyone she considered a threat . . . and she wanted Giraldus to see her powers at work.

Tyrele died a slow, agonizing death of the plague, his swollen and disfigured body covered with unburst pustules and twisted in fever and pain.

After that, Giraldus made certain Aurya was part of every occasion, whether he was negotiating a trade agreement within his own province, settling disputes over lands and borders, or simply hearing the petitions brought to him by the townsfolk. Most often, her presence was enough to ensure that events went the way Giraldus intended; it was rare anymore that she had to take a more . . . active . . . role.

Throughout the nine years they had been together, she and Giraldus had many an argument—in the privacy of their own bedchamber. But they had only one true disagreement; it was ongoing—and its subject was marriage. Even after all this time, he refused to accept that she hated the entire notion.

She stayed with Giraldus because she had chosen him as the means to the end she meant to have. She had come to his bed shortly after Anri came to the throne, and for the ensuing years she had been content to be the Baron's consort, using her magic to prevent conceiving a child. She would bear no man's name, be no man's possession, nor be bound by any ties other than her own purposes.

Now that the throne was empty again, Aurya had set her sights higher—for both of them. How long after that she would be able to keep both her freedom and her childless state, she did not know. But she intended to try.

Now, on the battlements, they stared at one another, close to an argument again. Such a look from Giraldus would have had his courtiers and advisors stammering to apologize and his servants scrambling in fear.

Aurya did not flinch.

It was Giraldus who finally looked away. He raised one eyebrow and gave her the slightest of bows. "I'll leave you then," he said, his voice now filled with sardonic humor, "and do my *pacing* where I will. But if Elon is not here by nightfall, I'll have his hide—and yours."

Aurya knew he did not like to be bested by anyone— even her. But as he strode away, she nearly laughed at the emptiness of his threat. Competent leader, fierce warrior—and acceptable, even accomplished, lover—Giraldus might be. But he did not have the ability to stand against the powers she could summon. She knew it . . . and so did he.

Once Giraldus had departed, taking his frenetic energy with him, Aurya closed her eyes and let the welcome silence envelop her. She did not need her powers to know that Elon would be here within the hour. She could have said as much to Giraldus, but he needed to learn how to *wait,* how and when to let things come to him. In all their years together, it was one thing she had never been able to teach him.

But Elon—he was a different matter. Bishop of Kilgarriff, sometime Suffragan to the Archbishop and of the College of Bishops for all of Aghamore, Elon was a man with a powerful presence. He, she was certain, knew both how to wait and when to act. His greed was outshone only by his ambition, and Aurya had but to wait in stillness to sense him.

They were of a kind, she and Elon. Both accepted whatever life had to offer—and forced from it whatever it dared to withhold. They had recognized this in each other the first time they met, as if they were somehow related.

Elon could well have been her father, Aurya had often thought. Silver now frosted his hair, but Aurya could see that it had once been as dark as her own, and his eyes were just as blue. But then—she told herself just as often—dark hair was common enough in Aghamore, and her mother's eyes had been blue.

Yet this feeling of kinship with Elon remained. Although the identity of her father was a secret Aurya's mother had taken to her grave, Elon did not strike Aurya as a man who would let an inconvenient vow of chastity bar him from something he wanted.

Blood relation or not, he was a useful man to have on one's side. *And I intend to make certain he* stays *on our side,* Aurya thought as she walked slowly toward the edge of the battlements to look calmly toward the direction from which Elon would come.

It had been her idea to initiate contact with the bishop; without her guidance, Giraldus would not have had the patience for the subtle games they had played during those early months, each wondering if the other could be trusted. Now, over a half a year later and with Elon considerably richer, that delicate balance of trust had been established. Giraldus wanted the crown, Elon wanted the Archbishop's mitre—and she was the connecting force between the two.

It was with an eye to both prizes that, when the bishop sent his message saying he was bringing something they must see, Aurya carefully concocted a plausible reason for his visit, one that could be seen and approved by even their harshest critics. She was not such a fool as to think she was without enemies among the people of Kilgarriff. But what she planned would silence many a disapproving tongue—and give Elon an excuse for any other such visits he might, of necessity, make.

As long as he does his part, I'll protect his reputation, Aurya's thoughts confirmed, knowing that such careful preservation was even more a hold over Elon than was the gold he had already received. *He'll wear the Archbishop's mitre soon enough—as long as when Giraldus makes his move for the throne, there are no surprises from within the College of Bishops.*

As she stood at the edge of the battlements, a slight breeze ruffled her gown until sunlight caught the silver threads woven into the midnight blue cloth, giving each movement a whisper of brightness. It was cloth that was made only for her and she rarely wore anything else. Its dark richness made her skin look like cream, deepened her eyes from mere blue to sapphire, and brought out the blue-black highlights in her raven hair.

She closed her eyes again and waited. Soon her mind, already disciplined to quiet receptiveness, grew even more still. Here was the place where power abided; here was the inner realm from which magic could be called forth.

Aurya waited until she could clearly sense the presence of he who was coming. It was like a pale blue light shining in the darkness, hidden from the naked and untrained eye but plain to those who knew how to *look*.

Then she withdrew her mind from these inner realms, back into the common world, with all its light and noise. She felt the power within her recede. Then, allowing herself a small smile of satisfaction, she turned to descend the stairs. It was time to alert Giraldus and walk out to the courtyard. She wanted to be there when Elon rode through the gates.

As usual, Aurya's timing was perfect. She and Giraldus had just taken their places on the great arched porch when Elon rode under the portcullis. His purple robes—the bishop's cassock, cincture, and mozzetta, and the amethyst-encrusted pectoral cross he habitually wore—

were overlaid by a black fur-trimmed cloak that billowed out behind him like a dark specter riding his tail.

His horse, lathered from the long, hard ride, responded eagerly to Elon's tug upon its rein. It stood with sides heaving while Elon dismounted and threw the reins in the direction of a stableboy.

Aurya, standing immovable at Giraldus's side, met the bishop's gaze. Again there was the feeling of affinity. She gave him a small nod of greeting, which he returned with a nod and a smile just as slight.

Giraldus, however, was not a man for such subtleties. He stepped forward, voice booming.

"Welcome, my lord Bishop, welcome. We have been awaiting your arrival most eagerly."

"No doubt," Elon replied dryly.

Giraldus knelt to kiss the bishop's ring, either not hearing or choosing to ignore the sarcasm in Elon's voice. But Aurya heard it and understood. Her lips twitched a little in a self-congratulatory way that was too brief to be a smile as she, too, took a step forward, ready to turn Giraldus's loud gruffness to their advantage.

It was as chatelaine of the fortress she greeted the bishop, but she made no move to kiss his ring. She had never hidden who and what she was, and to the Church those who practiced magic were declared anathema. They were cut off from the sacraments—including Holy Matrimony, Aurya was pleased to think—until such time as they renounced their powers and did suitable penance for their disobedience.

Aurya had no intention of doing either. She did not repent of her powers; she gloried in them—and she had no more liking for the Church than its representatives had for her. Except Elon. He possessed a power all his own: the power of deception.

The bishop had made it very clear that gold was not his only price for helping put Giraldus on the throne. Elon did not care about Aurya's magic, how much or against whom she and Giraldus used it, as long as in the end the Archbishop's crozier was in his hand and the golden triple-crowned mitre upon his head. As Aurya and Giraldus were using him, so the bishop was using them.

Self-serving as it was, Elon's aid suited Aurya's purpose completely. With Elon as Archbishop, she might indefinitely forestall both the marriage she did not desire and the public renunciation of magic necessary for that marriage to take place. Once Giraldus was crowned High King, she would formally be named his Chief Advisor and head of his Privy Council. Then, though he wore the crown, *she* would be the true power in Aghamore—as she was now in Kilgarriff.

"Welcome, my lord Bishop." Aurya spoke loudly enough for the many listening ears to overhear. "It was kind of you to come here in person to answer my questions. I had expected you to send someone with less pressing duties."

"I would not send someone else on such an important mission," Elon said, taking his cue from her. "Holy Mother Church has no more important business than to bring one of her lost children home."

There, Aurya thought, *that will give the gossiping tongues something to wag about—and Elon an acceptable reason for being here. All is going exactly as I planned.*

Aurya stepped to the side to let the men precede her into the fortress. There was a cold luncheon set out for them in the main hall and she, herself, would make certain the best wines were served. Nothing must go wrong this day as they began their final journey toward the throne.

*   *   *

It was late before they got down to their true business. All through the afternoon and early evening, they had kept up the pretense for Elon's visit. But finally, after Giraldus had sent away the last of the servants, Elon pulled out the true reason for the message he had sent.

It was a scroll, yellowed with age, and Elon handled it as gently as the precious relics of a saint.

"This scroll is from the writings of Tambryn," he said, "his thirteenth and last."

"I thought Tambryn and his writings were condemned by your Church." Aurya's eyes narrowed; the Church had condemned so much of the old lore and ancient truths.

"That is true, m'lady," Elon agreed. "Nonetheless, I have been studying his words for many years. I have seen what my brother clerics refuse to admit—that what Tambryn prophesied is true. It is how I know that Giraldus will come to the throne . . . *if* he can find and destroy the one person who stands in his way."

"Who is this person?" Giraldus demanded.

"A child, my dear Baron, a child you must find and . . . remove. That is why I have brought this scroll to you. You are fortunate that Lady Aurya is so learned. Given her other . . . studies . . . she should be well able to read this rather archaic language and understand its images. At least, you had best hope. Prophecies, by their very nature, are filled with images and subtexts often difficult to understand, and even those who study such things cannot always agree about their meanings. Tambryn's are even more so. As I said, I have studied these scrolls, this one in particular, for more than a decade, and I still cannot say I fully understand it.

"Nevertheless, this scroll contains your greatest hope for success. If you fail to destroy the child of whom Tambryn writes, then our mutual goal will be lost. It will be the child and not yourself who will be next to wear the crown of Aghamore. Or so Tambryn says," he added with a slight lifting of one shoulder.

Aurya found her fingers itching to take the scroll from the bishop's hands. The Writings of Tambryn were as famous—or as infamous—as the man himself. Six centuries ago he had been a monk. Some stories said he had risen high in the Church and was in line for the Archbishop's mitre.

Then his visions had begun.

Like nearly all mystics, Tambryn was convinced of Divine revelation so, being a learned man, he wrote everything down and presented it to his beloved Church. At first, his visions were indeed heralded of Divine origin. But when they began to make statements the Church did not want to hear—to tell of the Church's greed, its perversions, its often-cruel demands in the guise of false, pietistic words and to predict its eventual downfall—Tambryn's writings were banished. The man himself was declared a heretic, in league with the devil, and his visions changed from being a "gift from God" to the work of hell.

Some said he went into the Great Forest, other rumors claimed he left Aghamore completely; all agreed that he lived out the rest of his days in hidden solitude and died a silent, unmarked death. The Church searched the land, gathered up every copy of his writings it could find, and sent them into the flames his body had escaped. But for six hundred years tales had persisted that some of Tambryn's writings had survived.

Aurya had never hoped to see them. Yet here they were—and being given to her by a bishop. She almost laughed aloud at the irony.

"Oh, we shall succeed, Bishop," Aurya said softly. "We

shall succeed. You just be certain of your part. We must know we can count on you when the time comes."

"Have no fear, m'lady," Elon said as he laid the scroll in her hands. "Already the seeds have been planted and are being nourished. Baron Giraldus's name is being whispered among the people, and not only in this province. Soon, the College of Bishops will meet to take up the question of the succession. You may trust that at the right time and in the right way, the name Giraldus of Kilgarriff shall be part of those proceedings."

"What of Aurya?" Giraldus demanded. "Does she have any support yet to become my wife?"

Elon shot Aurya a quick glance. "Alas, no," he said apologetically, "she does not—though our little ruse of earlier today might well change all that. It was most astutely played, m'lady," he added, looking at her.

Aurya inclined her head in acknowledgment, but Giraldus was not satisfied. "If they want me, they'll have to accept Aurya. I'll not give up one to gain the other."

Aurya gently laid a hand on Giraldus's arm. "Peace," she said. "If we all play our parts well, there will be no need for such talk. Never fear—I shall remain by your side, as I ever am."

Giraldus's high temper was, as always, mollified by her words. He put his hand atop hers and looked at her with an adoration Aurya often found disturbing. Useful, but disturbing.

Obviously, the bishop did as well. He cleared his throat purposefully and Aurya turned toward him, not ungrateful for the interruption.

"I'm afraid, m'lady," Elon said, "that though the deception today was most astutely played, it will not be enough to carry the Baron to the throne. The people of Kilgarriff may accept you as the Baron's consort—but the people of the kingdom will not, and neither will the Church. We must all continue in the roles established today, and build upon them, but after this last decade of uncertainty, neither the people nor the Church will accept a King who cannot produce a legitimate heir. A *legitimate* heir. If Giraldus is to be High King, you must at least appear to renounce your powers and to marry. Or, Giraldus must marry someone else. . . ."

The bishop raised his hands slightly, as if handing her the choice of which future she would have.

"I'll not marry elsewhere," Giraldus said before Aurya could reply, almost shouting at the bishop. "It'll be Aurya or no one."

"Without marriage, there will be no crown," Elon returned, his voice as soft as Giraldus's had been loud, and just as emphatic.

The contrast was not lost on Aurya, nor did she miss the hopeful light that sparked in Giraldus's eyes. It made her angry—the entire subject made her angry, but especially that Giraldus would be so *happy* to see her forced into marriage when he knew how she felt.

But after marriage comes the crown, a voice inside her whispered. That might—*might*—make the marriage tolerable, as long as it was on her terms from the beginning. But, thankfully, she did not have to act on that decision today.

She laid a hand on Giraldus's arm. "Let us see to one thing at a time," she said. "You may, of course, my lord Bishop, embellish our deception as the situation demands—but do not give too much of me away."

Elon inclined his head toward her in a gesture of agreement and acceptance. Then he met her eyes and gave a little half smile that communicated his understanding quite well.

"Let us see what Tambryn's scroll has to tell us," Aurya continued. "Perhaps it will be enough to secure all our futures without too many sacrifices from anyone."

Trying not to let her fingers tremble or show the eagerness she felt, Aurya stood and, to all appearance calmly, began to uncurl the scroll across the table before them.

Chapter Three

Aurya had read the Thirteenth Scroll of Tambryn four times and still she was not certain she grasped its full meaning. It was not just the archaic language in which it was written; she could read the *words* easily enough. It was the meanings within and behind the words that perplexed her. Tambryn had written in the poetic language of dreams and, as with all such prophecies and visions, how much was to be taken literally and how much was allegory was her quandary.

The Thirteenth Scroll, she thought as she sat back and rubbed her tired eyes. *If they're all like this one, no wonder Elon said he'd been studying them for years. Prophecies aren't supposed to be so . . . difficult . . . at least not the others I've read. They're supposed to instruct and guide. They can't do that if no one can understand them.*

It could take a lifetime—or more—to understand all the hidden meanings in Tambryn's words.

Aurya did not have a lifetime to study the scroll or to search for the key to unlock its mysteries. Now that fair weather had arrived, campaigns could soon be launched, and Giraldus was not the only Baron who thought to occupy the throne of Aghamore. And who else besides the Barons, she wondered, might also have set their sights upon that prize? Events would soon begin to move swiftly—and so must she.

Once more she rubbed her tired eyes. Her entire body was craving sleep, but that was a luxury she could ill afford. One thing was certain, and Aurya had known it without these writings—the longer Giraldus waited before making his bid for the throne, the more likely he was to fail.

Moving the candles a little closer, she used her belt knife to trim their wicks for a brighter flame. Then she pulled paper and pen in front of her and began making a list of the things she *did* understand in the scroll—which would, she hoped, begin to clarify the many things she did not.

Days passed as Aurya studied the scroll to the exclusion of all else. She kept her chamber door locked except when she opened it to call for food. If she unlocked it, she knew that Giraldus would be at her elbow, distracting her with his impatience and wanting to know what she had learned before she was ready to share it.

She begrudged even the demands her body made for food and rest. But by the morning of the sixth day, she had a workable knowledge of Tambryn's prophecy. There were still many undeciphered mysteries, but what she did understand made it clear that she and Giraldus faced something far more dangerous to their plans than all the other Barons combined. This . . . *child*, if she and Elon read the prophecy correctly . . . must be found and destroyed.

Now.

All through the past night she had been trying to understand one thing. It was perhaps the most perplexing of all the scroll's mysteries. *Prophecy's Hand*: references to it appeared constantly. Sometimes Aurya thought it must be a person, but at others she was just as certain it must be a talisman of some sort that conveyed unusual powers.

And it could only be used by the one born to wear the crown.

That will *be Giraldus,* Aurya vowed as she forced her exhausted, cramped body out of the chair in which she had spent too many hours and hobbled to the door. *While I've breath in my body, it will be Giraldus.*

She had no sooner drawn back the bolt than the Baron himself burst through the door, filling the room with the restless energy she was too tired to face right now.

"It's about time you let me in," he began. Then his expression darkened at the sight of her weary eyes and the wan pallor that tinged her skin.

"You'll do neither of us any good by wearing yourself out this way." He reached out to stroke her hair.

"Ah, but I have," Aurya said, turning away, back toward the table.

"You've finished with the scroll, then? You know what it says?"

"Enough of it to know that Ballinrigh may be our final goal, but it is not our first."

"Where, then?" Giraldus demanded. "The *throne* is in Ballinrigh. What benefit can there be in going elsewhere?"

Aurya sighed, trying to curb her exhaustion-born irritation.

"Patience," she said. "How many times have I told you the value of *patience*? The best way to gain a thing is not always by laying siege to the front gate."

Aurya could see the flush rising in Giraldus's cheeks, as it ever did when he grew angry. But she had no energy for this either.

"Please, Giraldus," she said, "I promise I will explain more after I have rested. For now, be content to know that *I* know."

Giraldus opened his mouth to speak. But before he could, Aurya held up a hand and shook her head.

"Go," she repeated, pointing at the door. "Have the kitchens start gathering provisions for two weeks, perhaps three. We will leave soon—but right now I must sleep. I can't think anymore."

Giraldus stared at her a moment longer. Then, like any good soldier, he recognized the time to retreat. At the door, however, he stopped.

"Do not rest overlong," he commanded. "I'll not have another gain the crown because you were sleeping."

Aurya laughed. "I promise you," she replied, "that will not happen."

And as he closed the door, she hoped that she would continue to feel as confident as she had just sounded.

Nights wore into days into a week as Lysandra discovered anew how very fragile was her peace. Day after day, she tried to forget the news the shepherd had brought; night after night, the dream that was calling her returned, until sleep became a time of dread. She felt as if her entire existence now whirled somewhere between memory and premonition, and she was trapped at the mercy of both in a place where no mercy existed.

She tossed again upon her bed, trying to find her way past the discomfort that had little to do with her body. But tonight, all the memories of who she had been, of what she had once felt and hoped and wanted, refused to let her rest. She did not want to venture back into the world, where all the things from which she had fled, all the loves and hates, the beauty and the ugliness of human life, would assault her.

Again her memories whispered; again came the feeling of being summoned from her solitary life. Again her heart asked the question, what could she, one blind woman, do?

Perhaps, came the answer, *she could save one person, one life, from suffering what she had suffered. Perhaps that was enough.*

With that answer, Lysandra knew she had no other choice but to fulfill the persistent call of her dream. Once her decision was made her inner battle ceased. The voices stilled, the memories—and the storm of emotions that came with them—all abated. With her acceptance, Lysandra's mind was suddenly made silent and free.

That night, she slept the first dreamless sleep she had known in weeks.

It was nearly dawn when she heard Cloud-Dancer's low growl. It brought Lysandra awake with a start. Her *Sight,* which for the many days of her turmoil had been elusive, was fully upon her from the moment she opened her eyes. This time it was rich with color; the images were sharp and clear.

As always, the presence of color surprised her, and it took her a moment to realize that her room was bathed in an odd, eerie light. It came in through her bedroom window, turning the room a soft, luminous green, as if all the plants in her garden had started to shine.

Lysandra sat up quickly. Cloud-Dancer, who usually slept curled next to her feet, was standing in front of the window, hackles raised. Suddenly, he raised his head in a long, plaintive howl.

Lysandra jumped from her bed. This was a sound he almost never emitted and it drove every other thought from her mind. Nothing mattered except Cloud-Dancer as she knelt beside him.

"What is it, boy?" she asked softly, forcing herself to keep calm as she ran her hands over his body, checking for anything that might be causing the pain she heard in his cry. But as Cloud-Dancer continued to howl, neither her fingers nor her renewed *Sight* could find anything wrong.

Lysandra felt fear closing in, carried on the love she bore him. "What is it, boy?" she whispered again. "Show me what's wrong."

She knew he could not understand her words, but she prayed he would sense their meaning through the bond they shared. If he did not, if she failed to help him as she had failed with the ewe . . .

Cloud-Dancer's howling ceased and he began to tremble beneath her hands. Lysandra was becoming desperate, in a way that both instinct and experience told her would do Cloud-Dancer no good. She forced herself to sit back on her heels and release her touch on the wolf. Then she took some long, slow breaths to calm herself so her own fear would not prevent her from helping him.

Cloud-Dancer began to howl again. The light from outside had grown brighter. The green was almost rich enough to touch. It pulled Lysandra's *Sight* from Cloud-Dancer to the window.

Then Lysandra *saw* him—a man in worn, much-mended monk's robes. All around him, coming from him, was the light that filled her garden and poured in through the window. Nor was this light static; it pulsated in time to Lysandra's own heartbeat.

He stood, unmoving, at the end of her garden. In his hands he carried something Lysandra could not quite make out. She concentrated upon it, feeling that it was important—but both its identity and its purpose eluded her.

Then Lysandra *saw* his eyes.

They were the eyes she had seen so often in her dream—and yet they were different, too. Older, sadder, they were the eyes of someone who had seen too much and laughed far too little.

Although he still did not move, and no sound was uttered, Lysandra could feel that he was calling her. She felt herself start to rise, ready to leave the house and go into the garden. But even as she did so, he vanished. Her *Sight* did not fade; all was as clear to her in the moonlight as to a sighted person in the light of day, but he was no longer there . . . and with his passing the green light also disappeared.

To Lysandra's relief, Cloud-Dancer stopped howling. She again put her hands on his fur and found that he no longer trembled. His hackles were down and his muscles relaxed; his posture was neither threatened nor threatening. Finally, Cloud-Dancer shook himself and went to the foot of her bed, as if to say all was well and it was time to go back to sleep.

Lysandra almost laughed aloud with her relief that Cloud-Dancer was all right—but what was it he had sensed that caused his strange reaction? And who, or what, had she glimpsed in the garden?

She knew there would be no more rest for her that

night. "Sleep if you want to," she told Cloud-Dancer, stopping to pet him. "But you gave me quite a fright."

She gave a small smile as, leaving the bedroom, she heard Cloud-Dancer jump on the bed. She wished she could do the same, but instead she headed for the kitchen and placed some fresh wood onto the well-banked fire in her stove. Once the wood caught flame, she moved the ever-ready pan of water onto the heat.

While she waited for it to boil so that she could cook her breakfast of porridge and tea, she went to the back door and opened it. She stood in the doorway, breathing in the cool air and listening to the calls of the night birds and the rustling scurry of nocturnal creatures. Everything seemed normal, undisturbed by the strange presence that had been there such a short time ago.

Once more, Lysandra stilled her thoughts and with her *Sight* searched her garden. There was no trace that anyone had stood there—no trampled leaves or newly smudged dirt along the paths. Nor did any internal resonance remain. Lysandra extended her *Sight* as far as she was able and still found nothing.

Whatever had once been there was gone, leaving her with only more questions.

Chapter Four

Like all the bishops of Aghamore, Elon Gallivin, Bishop-ordinary of Kilgarriff, had two residences—one in Ballinrigh and one here, in Ummera, the cathedral city of Kilgarriff. Ballinrigh was where he stayed when either the business of the court or the Church required his attendance—but it was in Ummera he kept his secrets.

The Bishop's Residence in Ummera was palatial. It had been enlarged several times over the last three centuries and its heart, the oldest part of the building, had been built during a time when the Church's hold in Aghamore was not yet strong and persecution came often and without warning. It was filled with hidden rooms and secret passages. Through the years, as the Church's position became more secure, those rooms fell to disuse and were soon forgotten—until Elon discovered them again.

Only two of his servants knew of their existence and Elon's use of them. One of those servants had been dead these last two years. The other, Thomas, had been with him for nearly a quarter century, since Elon's rise in the Church demanded he employ a staff. Thomas was the one person whom, for various reasons, Elon trusted with his life.

That was what he was doing by giving Thomas this

knowledge. Had his brother bishops found out the contents of the secret rooms, his life within the Church would have been over—and his physical life might well have been forfeit. Elon would have been burned as a heretic and blasphemer, an agent of the devil sent to poison the Church from within.

Even knowing this, he could not keep away. The writings of Tambryn, though proscribed by the Church, were nothing compared to many other books and scrolls in Elon's collection. Tambryn's words had been banished because they held things the Church did not want to hear. Tambryn had offended too many people in positions of authority—but his "heresy" had been only a lack of prudence. He dared to tell the truth.

The other writings Elon owned were the works of countless minds and hands, meticulously gathered from every land possible, spanning many centuries and many faiths. These were the gateway to magic and to arcane knowledge, to the occult—to power that fascinated Elon.

When he returned from his visit with Aurya and Giraldus, Elon gave orders not to be disturbed and hurried to his secret library. Aurya fascinated him in the same manner as did the writings he had collected. Although she could only guess at her parentage, he knew she was his daughter.

He had carefully searched the records of the province to find her mother, Aileen. From parish records, he knew there was magic in her maternal ancestry; a century before, her grandmother's grandmother had been driven from their village under the accusation of witchcraft. This information, coupled with the fact that Aurya's mother had been an only daughter, the last and seventh child, born on the night of a lunar eclipse, meant she met all of the requirements of the ritual Elon was set upon attempting.

Whether she possessed magic herself was something Aileen's unprepossessing nature would not allow her to explore. The *potential* was there and that was all Elon needed; already downtrodden by a domineering father and six older brothers, she was far more easily controlled than Elon had expected. That she also possessed a gentle beauty added an unforeseen pleasure to his task.

It took but little attention from him for the affection-starved Aileen to lower her guard without even realizing she had done so. Then, using the power of his voice, he had entranced and then seduced her, taking her to bed at a precise time and day and dedicating the act to an ancient god in order to conceive a creature of magic.

And it had worked. It was this fact, and not any form of fatherly affection, that fostered Elon's fascination. For all the Church's claim that no other gods existed, *this* had worked. Aurya was, in every way, a creature of magic. Elon sometimes felt as if the magic in her radiated all around her, making even his old bones tingle.

Although Elon made use of many hidden rooms, each having its own purpose, this library was his favorite. Tonight, a lamp burned on the table, casting shifting shadows through the room. The room was without window or chimney, yet somehow the air was not stagnant; in some places it felt as if the air was actually moving, as if that place contained another entrance or unseen portal. Although he had searched, Elon had found no hidden doors or air shafts—nothing to explain the freshness of the air he breathed or the drafts he sometimes felt upon his skin.

He did know, however, that the house had been erected over a place the ancient religion of this land had dedicated to its god of divination. Just as there were places in this room where moving air could be felt, there were others that sent a chill down his spine.

The lamp gave enough light for him to find what he wanted. Open before Elon was a tome from the ancient land of Kaitrue, half the world away. It told of the dark god Leshtau and his consort Parumia. Together they ruled the underworld, gathering living souls to be their minions here on Earth. It was from this book that Elon had taken the ritual when he seduced Aurya's mother. Now he searched for a way to bring the daughter as much under his control as the mother had been. If something in their plan went awry, he wanted to be certain he had the means to protect himself.

Gingerly, Elon turned the time-brittled pages, concentrating as he scanned the faded ink. It had taken him years to learn this language, and still he was not certain he understood all of its nuances and applications.

But he knew that Aurya's will was too strong and her magic too powerful for her to be entrapped by a simple trick of voice. He found the pages for which he was searching, the words just following the ritual he had used all those years ago on Aileen. Now he began to read more carefully, his mind translating it into the familiar.

". . . and in the child of this union the strength of Leshtau will be found. Mortal concerns will trouble it not. Power shall rain from its fingers; the mighty darkness of Leshtau shall fill its soul.

But beware, for such power as Leshtau gives can destroy the weak-hearted and all those who have called his power forth. Be therefore warned. Do not call upon Leshtau with less than a heart of mighty courage. Once called forth, the power of Leshtau cannot be banished. Take care, then, to control what has been created.

Yes, Elon thought, control was what he wanted.

If thou wilt control the creature of this union, it is a fearful undertaking. Leshtau requires sacrifice of soul and

*of blood; and let the sacrifice be made in this manner
and none other. To falter in the sacrifice is eternal death
and pain in the belly of the all-consuming Leshtau.*

Elon's heart was pounding now, and his mouth had
gone dry. He took a sip from the goblet of wine at his
elbow, both intrigued and repelled by what he was reading. But he could not turn his eyes away. Blood sacrifice
was one area into which he had not delved. The idea now
captured his imagination. What would it be like, he wondered, to hold a living creature in his hands and know its
life or death was solely his undertaking?

Could he do it? Did he have the courage to plunge a
knife into a living breast, to feel the blood run body-hot
upon his hands and give sacrifice to this god who claimed
all dark power as his own? The question raised a hunger
for arcane power that was like a living, gnawing creature
inside his belly.

But this hunger was not an answer of itself. So far in
his life the only power close to magic he had exhibited
was the ability to use his voice and entrance those who
were weak-willed or already predisposed to believe in and
follow him. Blood sacrifice to summon and then control
dark power might well need a magic he did not possess.

Or it might give it, a little voice within him whispered.
The channel to all you desire might be on these next pages.

Late into the night Elon studied the text, but nothing
he found assured him that without already wielding magic,
he could either summon or command the power of which
it spoke. Yet he could not give up on the idea. He had
many other sources through which he could search; somewhere within them, he would find the secret that would
allow him to manipulate even Aurya, should the need
arise.

Finally, his eyes now gritty and refusing to focus, he stumbled to his bedchamber and threw himself, still fully clothed, across the bed. But sleep eluded him. His mind was churning with all he had read and the many possibilities stretching before him.

He had long ago realized that he lacked the type of faith he saw in his brother clergy. Their simpering timidity nauseated him. What they called humility, he called the lack of courage to *live* . . . and to accept the consequences. He had entered the Church not for any true vocation, but as the only path to power, to education, riches, and authority open to him as a younger son of a merchant. Such a practice was not uncommon, and Elon's keen mind and sharp wit had quickly realized that if he played the game carefully, he would eventually gain everything he craved.

He did acknowledge the existence of God—perhaps of *all* the gods. He also believed that the Power of Darkness, and its minions, was present and active in this world. Experience had shown him that in the eternal battle between the Light and the Dark, Darkness most often won. In *this* life, anyway . . . and this life was all Elon cared about. His immortal soul, if indeed he had one, did not concern him. He wanted power now, while he could make it serve him.

When at last he arose, bleary-eyed and irritable from lack of sleep, he had made a reluctant decision. To learn the way of the blood sacrifice, to perfect and understand its many nuances, would take time he did not have. If one Baron did not rise supreme—and quickly—Aghamore would surely erupt in civil war. Now that Elon had so firmly thrown his support behind Giraldus, he intended to make certain that Kilgarriff was the next High King and ruling House of Aghamore.

Of course, Giraldus was a warrior, a formidable one, and in such a war he might well be the victor. *But men are killed in wars,* Elon thought as he finished his breakfast and went into the official study to begin the work of the day. *And Giraldus is not invincible.*

But Giraldus was not the problem. It was Aurya—beautiful, powerful, and stubborn Aurya. If he was not going to try the dark ritual, he must still find some way to ensure his control of her. Even after they found and destroyed the child, she could still cost them the throne, and if she continued in her refusal to at least publicly conform—in private she could do as she wished, as he did—she could put them all in danger.

He hoped he had made that clear enough the last time they had met. Of course, he had tried to say it in temperate, if logical, terms so that her inflexibility did not ruin everything before it had begun. Years of dealing with royalty and Ruling Houses had taught him that necessity—and though Aurya was not royalty yet, she certainly had the temperament for it.

Yes, the time to act was *Now,* as soon as was possible. When Aurya and Giraldus returned, he must have found a means of mastery—and if other spells failed, the blood sacrifice would be waiting.

Seated now at his desk, he surveyed the pile of correspondence before him and curled his lip in disdain. These letters, petitions for some gift or favor, were generally ones his secretaries had sent on to him because they required his personal attention. This morning, however, he was in no mood for such trivial duties. He wanted to return to the ancient writings and to the search that had so fascinated him last night.

Elon was about to summon his secretary and make

some excuse—*perhaps illness,* he thought—when there was a knock on his office door.

"Come in," he called, wondering who would be disturbing him at this hour of the morning. He did not usually receive visitors until afternoon. Elon recognized the young monk who entered as one of the Archbishop's many clerks.

"Brother Naal," he said as he rose, employing the talent for remembering names that always worked to his advantage. "What brings you here?"

The young monk kissed the ring Elon held out to him. His surprise that the bishop had remembered him showed on his face.

"'Tis my parents' anniversary and His Holiness the Archbishop gave me leave to go visit them," he said. "His Holiness asked only that I deliver this letter on my way."

The monk reached into one of the deep pockets of his plain brown habit and brought forth a letter. Elon looked at the crest that had been pressed into the hot wax seal. Beneath the official crest was a smaller indent. It was the Archbishop's private seal and meant this letter was from the Primus's own hand.

Elon made no move to open it. Instead he again held out his hand so that Brother Naal could kiss the ring and be dismissed.

"Thank you, Brother," Elon said to the monk as he genuflected. "If I might also ask a favor of you. . . ."

"Anything, Your Grace," Brother Naal said.

"Then after you have seen your parents, will you come back here on your return journey to Ballinrigh. I might have an answer that needs to be taken to His Holiness."

"It will not be until tomorrow, Your Grace."

"Perfect," Elon replied. "Until tomorrow then, Brother.

Tell your parents I will ask a special blessing upon them in today's Mass."

"Oh, thank you, Your Grace," Brother Naal said, his face beaming with true delight. "I know that will please them greatly."

What can the old fool want now? he wondered as he sliced open the letter. Because they carried the Archbishop's personal seal, letters such as this demanded his immediate attention—but they were often filled with such trivialities that Elon had grown to hate opening them. He heaved a small, impatient sigh as he unfolded the letter and scanned it.

This one was not so trivial. He was summoned to Ballinrigh for a special meeting of the College of Bishops concerning the succession. This he had been expecting, but underneath the official wording of the document, the Archbishop had written a personal message in his wavering, spidery hand.

I have heard a strange tale, my son, it began, *that you have been visiting an enemy of the Church. I'm certain there is a good reason, but remember St. Paul says we are to avoid not only evil, but also the* appearance *of evil. Send word to me as soon as you reach Ballinrigh. I will make certain we have time to talk privately. I want to put this matter to rest before the meeting begins.*

Elon sat back in his chair and stared at the letter. He had no doubt to what visit it was referring. *So,* he thought, *someone has been carrying tales. I wonder who—and to whom else they have been talking.*

He did not fool himself by thinking he had no enemies; power always came at a cost. He was glad anew that in their correspondence, Aurya had arranged their plausible—and *witnessed*, yes, that was the important part—reason for the visit. He now had something that would satisfy even the Archbishop.

The meeting of the College of Bishops was set for four days hence; to get there a day early, he would have to leave tomorrow. Disappointed, Elon knew he would have to postpone any other, more interesting . . . activities . . . until his return. But he would take some of his books with him and when not otherwise occupied with official business or the Archbishop's requests, he would continue his search.

We'll leave tomorrow after Brother Naal returns, Elon's thoughts continued. *Then he can travel with us—and take a report about our piety back to the Archbishop, and to whomever else has employed him.* Elon grinned sardonically. *That was, no doubt, part of the Archbishop's plan. Well, let the little monk report every detail. He shall see nothing from me or mine that is the least bit questionable.*

He would let his houseman, Johann, see to the packing, and his body servants would know what clothing, both personal and religious, must be taken. But there were some articles he would trust to only one other set of hands but his own. Tonight, when the rest of the household was asleep, he would have Thomas help him with the books he would take with him. He could trust Thomas to see them safely, and secretly, stored, and just as safely unpacked in Ballinrigh.

His own life was embarking on a journey far more important—and more dangerous—than this trip to Aghamore's capital. What he was doing was a gamble. But if he played it right, he could win everything. If he played it wrong . . . he could lose far more than his office.

Elon smiled again. *That is what makes it worth doing,*

he thought. A life safe and secure, going through the same motions throughout endless days of boredom, was only death while still breathing. Elon knew what he wanted. He wanted it all—to *have* it all, *feel* it all, *be* it all . . . and *risk* it all. Win or lose, only by this would he be satisfied.

Aurya slept nearly twelve hours. When she awoke, she was both ravenous and clearheaded. Her certainty had not left her after all. She and Giraldus would succeed; he would be King, and she would be at his side—directing, advising, *ruling* the man who ruled the kingdom. Elon's words about the need for marriage ran briefly through her mind, causing her to frown. But she dismissed them just as quickly. Time enough to think on them later, once they had taken care of the child—and only if she was certain there was no other way to succeed.

Ah, yes, she thought as she stretched beneath the covers, her smile returning, *success is the best revenge*.

It was all her revenge on all those who had made her childhood years a time of sorrow and loneliness . . . or had until she discovered her gift. It was magic that became her true and faithful companion—and she needed none other.

She stretched again, knowing she should rise, bathe, and dress, so that she and Giraldus could begin their final preparation to depart. But the cradling comfort of her warm bed held her. Surely, after all her hard work of the last few days she could allow herself a few extra moments of luxury. Once they rode away from this fortress, who knew how long it would be before she again had such an opportunity. She snuggled farther down into the bed and engaged in her favorite—and very private—pastime of picturing what her life would be like when she and Giraldus had gained the crown.

It was daydreams that had gotten Aurya through her childhood. They were her companions when the cruelty of other children became too much to bear; they were her comfort when her mother, consumed by the guilt of conceiving a child outside of holy wedlock, turned away from Aurya as the proof of her sin.

It was her dreams that led Aurya to wander the hills outside the town—and in those hills she had met Kizzie. Some called Kizzie wild, others said she was mad, but she was the first one to recognize Aurya's potential.

Kizzie. Once more Aurya smiled as she pictured the old woman's coarse gray hair, forever coming free from Kizzie's attempts to bind it, giving her a wild, unkempt look that fed the rumors about her madness.

Aurya had heard the tales of Kizzie long before they met, but it was from Kizzie that she learned the truth. The old woman was not mad at all. She had once been one of the goodwives of the village. She had once renounced her powers in order to marry—but when he had died young in a hunting accident, Kizzie had been left penniless. Her only choices then were to live as a poor widow begging alms from the Church, to take the veil as many widows did to ensure a future of food and housing—or to return to the Earth-magic of her youth and live in the ways of her ancestors.

Kizzie chose the latter almost fifty years before Aurya was born. By the time twelve-year-old Aurya stumbled upon Kizzie's little hut in the hills, Kizzie was old and grizzled, bent with age, but content with the life she lived.

Even in that first meeting, Kizzie acted as if she had been expecting Aurya. And it was under Kizzie's tutelage that Aurya felt first the stirrings of magic within. She left her mother and her unhappy life and went to live in the hills with Kizzie, for already at that age Aurya possessed the strength of will to do what was needed to get what she wanted. From Kizzie, she wanted to learn.

Soon it became obvious that Aurya's powers would soon be far greater than Kizzie's had ever been. Aurya did more than learn—she had *absorbed*, soaked in every last drop of magic and learning her mentor had to teach and wanted more. Still she stayed, for it was from Kizzie that Aurya had her first taste of approval, the first feeling of belonging her young life had ever contained.

Aurya stayed until the old woman died.

She was then seventeen, a young woman full of promise yearning to be recognized and expressed. Yet, even with Kizzie gone, Aurya did not leave her mountain home immediately. Instead, she cast a spell of protection over Kizzie's body and waited three nights, until the full moon of the winter solstice when the power of the Great Goddess whom Kizzie had served would be at its height.

Aurya laid Kizzie out on a pyre of rowan branches, a tree sacred to the Goddess. She felt her heart racing as she prepared herself to dare an incantation such as she had never tried before, even when Kizzie was alive to guide her. This was the magic of the old ways. Aurya did not know if she had the power to succeed on her own— but she did possess the courage to *try*.

Raising her arms toward the ether, the spirit realm, she first drew her mind inward to find her silence, as Kizzie had taught. When the stillness had come, and she felt the first stirring of magic, she began her incantation, calling on forces she did not know if she could control.

But youth dares where age will not. Her voice was low and uncertain at first, her command of the language stilted,

but even from the first utterance she knew she would—
she *must*—continue.

"*Ignus. Incendium Sanctore. Meus iplore cura. Ele-
mentus numen, tuus ipse convocare. Tuus ipse convocare
ut serva. Tuus ipse capere ut arbitera. Incendiu Sanctus,
Exire.*

With each word her voice became stronger, more certain, and with that certitude she felt those first stirrings
build and become the fire upon which she was calling.
She had only to stretch forth her hands . . .

Flame flew from her fingers like streamers of molten
gold. It enveloped Kizzie's body, burning it as easily as
a bonfire consumes a brittle twig.

When Aurya lowered her arms, all that was left of
Kizzie's body was a pile of ash. Now Aurya would complete the ritual she had come here to perform. She gathered the ash up as best she could into a small mound at
her feet. She then walked withershins around the mound
three times, chanting as she stepped.

"To the Heart of the Universe I give thy heart. To the
Breath of the Universe I give thy breath. To the Soul of
the Universe I give thy soul."

At the head of the circle, Aurya stopped again. She
bowed to the four directions, the four pathways of powers. First to the northern quarter, the place that held and
gave forth the Powers of the Fire; then West, to the Powers of Water. Still traveling withershins, she bowed to the
South, the place of Earth. Finally she bowed to the East
and the Powers of the Air. Then, raising her arms once
more, she cried out the final words of command.

"Receive thy servant. Now."

Though the night was calm and still, around Aurya a
wind gathered. From all four corners it came and met as
a swirling tempest that encompassed the pile of ashes,

lifting them higher and higher, gathering them up, then sending them outward to be scattered throughout the four quarters.

Aurya watched, exalted at what she was seeing—at what *she* was doing. Here, at last, she found the sense of fulfillment that had eluded her until this moment. Her father's identity did not matter; her mother's rejection did not matter. Even Kizzie's death—though for that, at least, Aurya felt a twinge of grief—no longer mattered. She had her purpose and knew who she was at last.

Aurya was so filled with exultation, she almost did not notice when her arms began to tremble. Then, with what seemed impossible speed, the trembling spread through her body. Her arms came down of their own accord, and she collapsed, spent, upon the ground.

The wind stopped. Aurya lay in silence, hearing only her own heart beating wildly. She could not move; she barely had the strength to breathe. Yet she was happy . . . no, more than happy, much more. She had honored her teacher in the way she knew Kizzie would have wanted, and that in itself pleased Aurya. But she also knew that this night she had crossed over the threshold. No one could hurt her now—not in body or in spirit. She would learn to master the power she had now tasted until no one dared stand in her way.

This older Aurya had learned. She was a master now, self-taught and self-proclaimed. Yet she knew that in the silent depths of her soul, she still yearned for *more*.

Suddenly impatient, she pushed back the cover under which she lay. She would gain only more *nothing* by staying in her bed.

She had to call twice before a servant answered, bleary-eyed and only half-awake. "What time is it?" Aurya demanded.

"Near two hours past midnight, m'lady," the girl answered. "Everyone be sleeping—even Lord Giraldus."

Aurya tapped her foot while she thought. She was awake now and eager to get under way.

"Fill my bath," she ordered. "Then rouse the household—including Lord Giraldus. Tell him to come here. Then go to the kitchen, wake the cook, and get the fires stoked. There'll be no more sleep here this night."

"Yes, m'lady," the girl answered softly.

Aurya heard the weary edge to her voice but chose to ignore it. They could all sleep their lives away once she and Giraldus had departed. Until then, there was work for them to do.

Finally, her bath was ready. Aurya dismissed her servant to carry out the rest of her instructions, then lowered herself into the steaming water. Giraldus, she knew, would not be pleased at being roused from his bed, but his mood would improve once he heard what Aurya had to tell him. Many of the things that had perplexed her tired mind now, after her long sleep, seemed clear. She knew where they were going and what they would find when they got there.

Lying back in the water, surrounded by the warm, rich scent of ambergris, the only scent she ever wore, Aurya laughed out loud. It would all be hers—soon the entire kingdom would be at her command and hers for the taking. At that moment she saw only success ahead.

"I'm glad *you* can laugh at such an hour," came Giraldus's voice behind her.

Aurya did not bother to turn. "I have much to laugh about," she replied, "and so do you."

"Now is not the time for riddles, Aurya," Giraldus

growled. "You may have just awakened from full, restful sleep, but I have not."

Aurya could not help but laugh again, and this time she did turn to face him. "More than restful, Giraldus. It was enlightening. I understand it—the prophecy. I know where it wants us to go."

Aurya watched the grogginess leave Giraldus's eyes and his face light up at her words. "As simple as that?" he said. "Just follow the scroll's instructions?"

"As simple as that," she answered. "Tambryn's prophecies are gone, his writings banished and destroyed. Were it not for Elon, *we* would not have them. But we do—we alone, of all the kingdom. With them to guide us and the courage to do what we must, we will succeed. *You will be King* . . . and I know you do not lack courage for that."

"Or anything else," Giraldus assured her. "Come, my heart, and show me. I am now as eager to hear what you have learned as you are to tell it."

Aurya rose and stepped from her bath. Then, after toweling off quickly and wrapping herself in a warm dressing gown, she led the way back into their chamber to call for maps so she could trace for Giraldus the trail that they must follow.

Chapter Five

It did not take Lysandra long to gather her provisions. Although she did take a few supplies from the cottage larder, she knew how to live off the land, and so the main weight of her bundle consisted of a change of clothing, an extra cloak in case the nights turned cold, a small paring knife, and a larger dagger. With these latter she could easily harvest the plants and roots on which she would live. She also included a large assortment of dried herbs, a few small pots of prepared medicines, and strips of bandages. The herbs all had properties she might well need—and many of them made excellent teas.

Finally, Lysandra brought out her mother's jewelry. She did not remember gathering it before she left Scorda, but she remembered little of that time. Nor had she brought the pieces out to admire or remember, let alone wear, in all the years since.

Now, Lysandra was glad of them. She would need to pay for food and lodging, and her mother's jewelry could be traded or sold. *It's not much,* she thought, trying to be practical. She fingered each piece, trying to guess its worth.

There were five rings, three of gold and two of silver. One of the gold rings was set with a garnet, her mother's birthstone—as was the largest of the three brooches. Of the other two, one was silver filigree and the other was heavily enameled. There were also a few unadorned chains and one from which a large, tear-shaped freshwater pearl was suspended, four hair clasps, silver—of knotwork design—and two carved-bone hair combs. It had been her father's pride that, as a dyer and seller of dyes, he had been prosperous enough to buy such things for his wife.

Well, that doesn't matter now, she told herself. Still, she put the combs aside to keep. Her mother had worn them so often . . . and besides, Lysandra did not think they would be of much value to sell.

But where am I going? she asked herself. It was all so confusing, like trying to put a puzzle together with no picture as a guide, and the pieces just seemed to get smaller and smaller. Lysandra sat in her favorite chair, a steaming mug of tea in her hands, and closed her eyes. She opened her mind, and her soul, to be as receptive as possible. In slow, deep breaths, she inhaled the scent of chamomile and wood betony, one of her favorite herb mixtures. It rose from her cup and filled her senses with warm, soothing fragrance. Soon she could hear her own heartbeat, feel each breath as it entered and escaped her body.

And in this stillness, she waited.

It did not come as *seeing,* as with her moonlit vision in the garden. Nor did words come into her mind. Yet, suddenly, between the space of one breath and the next, a deep certitude filled her. She *knew.* She must go to Ballinrigh, to the capital city of Aghamore, and somewhere amid the crowded houses and tall spires, the city noises and the crush of people, she would find the object of her search.

Lysandra still abhorred the idea of rejoining the world,

of again being around people with their whirling jumble of thoughts and needs. Yet it seemed there was no other way to end the dreams and visions that plagued her. But through whatever awaited, her one true goal would be to return here—to come *home*—to this place, this life, that had given her back the will to live.

The warmth of the sun coming through the windows told Lysandra that the day was bright and fine. She finished the last of her tea and reluctantly put the mug aside. She wished she could convince herself that the decision she had made was wrong, that she did not really have to leave at all. She was no adventurer, to go wandering the kingdom. She wanted to believe that everything she had experienced over the last weeks was the product of an overtired mind giving too much freedom to her imagination.

But all that she had felt and seen and heard defied logic. Though she hated to admit it, what she was doing was not only *right*, it was the only thing that could be done.

Cloud-Dancer came over and laid his head across her knees. It was the signal to go outside they had established when he was still a pup. He gave a single plaintive whine, as he did when nature's call was urgent. This time, however, Lysandra knew it was *her* call to which he was responding.

"All right," she told him as she ran her fingers through the ruff of thick silken fur that covered his head and neck, "we'll go."

At her words, he stepped back. Even without her *Sight* she could picture him—the eager stance of his body, ears forward and tail high, the happy half-open way he held his mouth in the excited lupine version of a grin.

Lysandra would trust his instincts; he would never

knowingly lead her into danger. But it took all of her resolve to walk away from her chair and over to the door, to swing her bag onto her shoulder and wrap her fingers around her walking stick.

She wished she could share Cloud-Dancer's joy for the adventure ahead. Instead, she continued to stand in the doorway, nearly paralyzed with the dread of going forward. The battle raged within her, between the fear of going and of staying, between the known and the uncontrollable.

Lysandra held herself still a moment longer. Slowly, her *Sight* came to her and gifted her with a last look around the interior of her small cottage. Though she already knew it as well as life within her own skin, her heart memorized anew every part of it, as if afraid she would never see it again. Then, finally, she stepped out and firmly closed the door.

I will not think of what I am leaving, she told herself, *only of where I am going.* Still, when she reached her garden gate, she could not help but repeat the process. Her heart embraced every stand of flowers, clump of herbs and vegetables that fed her, the little table where she spread out crumbs for the birds, the stone bench where she so often sat in the warmth of the sun. All these, like the forest beyond, were so much a part of her that the thought of leaving them was like losing an arm or a leg— or her sight.

Then, with a flash of memory so intense she automatically took a step backward, her mind filled with the vision of the man in the worn monk's robes. Once more it seemed as if her garden was shaded in moonlight through which rich green light radiated. As if to spur her on her way, Lysandra felt an urgency coming from the man and from the odd cylindrical object he carried.

Once again she saw the man's eyes, so full of pain and pleading. For an instant they reminded Lysandra of the eyes of all the sick and injured animals she had helped over the years.

But with that thought came the memory of the young shepherd and his sick ewe. Would she be just as ineffective this time? But if so, why would she feel this need to go? she wondered. If she was going to fail, why not stay here and let someone else answer this call?

The intensity of the man's gaze doubled, trebled, telling Lysandra that this was more than a memory. He opened his mouth; though her ears heard no sound, his voice filled her—mind and body—telling her that she could do what must be done.

Lysandra bowed her head in defeat.

Then, with a sigh, she turned away from this place that had healed her heart and given her a life once again and began her journey into the unknown—heading north to Ballinrigh.

Studying Giraldus's maps and marking out their journey had not proved as easy as Aurya anticipated, even with Tambryn's scroll in hand. Aurya thought she had understood the many veiled phrases and metaphors, so that his directions would be easy to place on a map. But it took her two full days to accomplish what she thought would take only a couple of hours.

While Aurya was busy with the maps, Giraldus worked on arranging the business of the province to his satisfaction. After taking care of the needed correspondence, rendering judgment on some of the court cases and appeals awaiting his word, Giraldus summoned his council. Together they examined some of the province's pending trade agreements to be certain that his absence of a few weeks would not jeopardize the welfare of his people. Finally, Giraldus ordered Maelik, his Master Sergeant-at-Arms, to keep the army drilled and at battle readiness.

Then, nine days after Elon had put the Thirteenth Scroll of Tambryn into her hands, Aurya and Giraldus were finally under way.

The route they were to follow was convoluted, and the reason for its many detours was unclear to Giraldus. But Aurya insisted they stick to the course, no matter how puzzling the guidance seemed, certain that a mystic of Tambryn's great power had a reason for every twist and turn within his words.

She and Giraldus traveled alone and without pomp or insignia. This was a point of contention between them, for even when traveling with his army Giraldus was used to a degree of comfort and the deference due his rank. But Aurya did not want them recognized. It was important, she told him time and again, that they draw no attention to themselves; Giraldus was not the only Baron with an eye to the throne, and spies could be anyone, anywhere. Her reasons made sense to Giraldus, and so he accepted the small unadorned tent and lack of embellishments, finding his comfort at night in the warm closeness of their bodies while they slept.

Each night when they made camp, Aurya would again pull out Tambryn's scroll and study. By the third night, Giraldus was becoming bored with her lack of conversation. She was always something of a mystery to him, and never one to easily share her thoughts and feelings. But now her complete absorption in the scroll made Giraldus feel superfluous, even more cut off from her than ever before.

Although he had never shown much interest in her mystical studies or working of magic—except in its outcome—Giraldus decided to start discussing the scroll with her. *Perhaps,* he thought, *if she reads me more of it, we can use this time traveling to better our union. Maybe if I take more than a passing interest now, she'll soften to the idea of marriage.*

He had been delighted when Elon told Aurya what he had been hesitating to say. He knew how she felt about marriage, and he accepted some of the reasons, even if he did not agree with them. Her illegitimate birth and unhappy childhood with a mother too crushed by her own guilt to care for her child, the life of her old teacher and what widowhood would have meant for her if she had stayed within society—Giraldus knew all these things.

In their early years together, he had tried to convince Aurya that their marriage would have been different, that she need not fear the loss of her *self,* her independence. But to receive the Sacrament of Holy Matrimony, she would have to come into the Church—and to do that, she would have to deny the part of herself she held most dear. Accepting that, Giraldus had ceased mentioning marriage.

But now, with the throne as the prize, the subject had gained a new and vital importance not even she could deny. It was for this, more than the belief in any mystical revelation, that he had agreed to this journey. By the time they returned to Adaraith, with or without this child she and Elon thought so important, Giraldus hoped to have found a way to convince Aurya to marry him.

And to give him an heir. Giraldus had often thought that having a child, being able to give it the love she had been denied, would soften the hard shell of protection Aurya wore around her heart.

With that thought in mind, he sat down near her, in the warmth and light of the small fire over which they had cooked their meal, and asked her to tell him more about what she was reading. He did not miss her look of surprise, and he smiled; surprising Aurya was not easily accomplished. Still smiling, he brought the skin of wine from among their provisions, poured, and handed a goblet to her.

"The time of the House of Baoghil is over," she said, accepting it and still looking a little bemused. "That much is quite clear. Anri was the last King of that line. But the future . . . there are several references here that could be interpreted any number of ways."

"What references?" he asked, trying to sound enthusiastic.

"Well, here," Aurya said, unrolling the scroll to the section she wanted, "Tambryn writes of the rise of the Third House. That, of course, is Kilgarriff—unless the Houses were numbered differently six hundred years ago."

"They were not," Giraldus replied. "Kilgarriff has always been the Third House, the House descended from Lihadanes, the third son of Liam Roetah the Builder, first High King of Aghamore. All of the Houses are numbered in the birth order of the sons of Liam. That doesn't change no matter how many years go by."

Aurya nodded. "Well, Tambryn views the rise of the Third House with alarm and warns that it must be guarded against," she continued. "He says that unless the Third House is stopped, it is from Kilgarriff that the next High King will arise . . . and that's you."

"And what is supposed to stop us—the child of whom you and Elon spoke? I hardly think that *I* need fear a child, no matter what anyone's prophecies say."

"But the child will not be acting alone, if I read this correctly. There are also several references to the Fifth House, and to the Ninth—Camlough and Rathreagh. The scroll says help must arise from the Fifth House . . . and that the Ninth House holds both threat and salvation."

Giraldus's well-intentioned patience shattered. He stood and threw down his cup. The wine still within it went flying, splattering into the fire with a hissing sound.

"Why didn't you tell me this before?" he demanded. "We're off chasing down some *child*, while the very scroll you and Elon say we must follow warns us of enemies. Oran of Camlough is no fool to be dismissed, Aurya, and neither is Hueil of Rathreagh. They are both warriors with well-trained, formidable armies. If they're on the rise, then I still say we'd be better off heading for Ballinrigh with *our* army at our backs. The *throne* is in *Ballinrigh*. While we're off trying to find this child, what do you think the others will be doing? Just waiting around peacefully until we return? No—they'll be getting ready to march. We should be doing the same."

"If you believe that, why did you agree to this journey?" Aurya asked quietly, very quietly.

Giraldus was not fooled. He had learned, long ago and the hard way, that a soft tone often masked Aurya's most extreme anger. But this time he did not care.

"I accepted Elon's help, and paid him well for it, so he'd win the bishops to our cause. That's what will gain us the throne, not this business with ancient scrolls and heretical prophets. But I thought you'd told me everything and that this child was our only real threat. That's why I'm on this accursed journey, that and . . ."

Giraldus glared at her across the fire for a moment, then turned and stalked off.

It's for you, he had not said, but he had meant. His anger was because he knew that *she* knew it, too.

Heaven blast her, he thought as he stormed away,

breathing hard with his fury. *Why can't she do* anything *like a normal woman?*

He walked until the darkness hid him and the light of the campfire was barely a glow behind him. He needed some time alone. Being with Aurya always befuddled his thoughts. Her nearness, even after these nine years together, was like a sweet wine, too easily consumed in excess, robbing him of both strength and reason.

He found a log and sat alone in the dark, where he could think clearly. He felt his anger begin to dissipate, but he did not want to let it go. He reminded himself that Aurya *owed* him for the life of comfort and privilege she enjoyed. She should be subservient, grateful, and gentle. Even though she was not legally his wife, she lived as such, and as such she should honor him. Furthermore, he was a skilled warrior; she should trust him to provide for her, not the other way around.

Yet, even as he thought these things, he knew he loved Aurya's fire and her intelligence. He just wished that sometimes she would . . . *Oh, hell and damnation,* he thought with a sigh, as he started back to the camp. He would go apologize for this fit of temper and, now that the subject had been opened, he would make certain that there were no other surprises left unsaid.

Then Giraldus smiled, for tonight beneath their bedroll they would make up their differences—and at *that* part of a woman's nature, Aurya excelled.

He stepped back into the circle of firelight, expecting to see her still studying her scroll. But Aurya was nowhere in sight. Her bedroll was gone, one of the bags of provisions, her horse . . .

"Blast her stubborn, heartless—" Giraldus cursed as he gathered up their remaining travel-fare to follow her. But which direction? *She* had the map; *she* was the one with the hopefully discerned knowledge of their destination.

Continuing to curse under his breath, Giraldus saddled and loaded his horse as quickly as he could. He spared a brief thought to wish it were daylight so that Aurya's trail might be more easily seen, but even in the darkness he was certain his tracking skills would find her.

Once the saddlebags were packed, Giraldus took one of the burning branches from the fire and, using it as a torch, began to search for signs of Aurya's departure. Finally, he found what he was looking for: a hoofprint on the ground and some bent and broken branches where horse and rider had pushed through.

Giraldus hastened back to what had been their camp. He quickly kicked dirt upon the remains of the fire, then threw himself onto his horse and sped off in pursuit of the woman who angered and frustrated him, who often confused him—but whom he truly loved.

Aurya had not ridden slowly, as if hoping he would catch up. She was moving as quickly as the darkness would allow. It took Giraldus nearly an hour to find her. Grabbing her reins to pull her horse to a stop, he was not certain whether he wanted to pull her into an embrace, glad of her safety and their reunion, or pull her across his knee and spank her like a worrisome child who had run away.

He did neither. He sat glaring at her over the heads of their animals, panting with the effort to not scream at her for her idiocy. And he waited. This time *she* must make the first move toward reconciliation or, by heaven, he would leave her now and not look back. . . .

"You want to take your army and storm the capital," she said at last, her tone cool and uncontrite, "then go.

I'll find the child myself. If after so many years you have such little confidence in me or in what I tell you we need to do, then—"

"Ever since Elon put that cursed scroll in your hand, you've cut yourself off from me. How can I have *confidence*, as you call it, if you won't *tell* me everything? You give me information by little spoonfuls, like I'm some child or idiot who can only take so much. Well, I'm sick of it, Aurya."

His outrage seemed to take Aurya by surprise. She recognized, *finally*, that this was more than a tantrum or a bout of the impatience she was always rebuking him over, impatience that was an offshoot of their contrasting approaches to life.

"Well, what am I supposed to do—you've never shown the slightest interest in my studies before. But, you're . . . right," she added slowly, "and I'm sorry, Giraldus. I shouldn't exclude you when you are interested."

This rare apology from her melted the last of his anger. He dropped the reins of her horse and moved his in closer, so that he could take her hand.

"Aurya," he said softly, "come, let's make camp again. I do trust you, and I know we share the same vision of the future. All I ask is that you trust me the same way."

Giraldus was delighted that Aurya not only let him take her hand, but then squeezed his in return. She leaned toward him, turning her face up for his kiss with a demureness that made him realize he could never have left her. He would go anywhere with her, follow whatever plan she devised—if only she would act like this more often.

"After we have made camp," Aurya said once the kiss had ended, "I'll tell you everything you want to know of

Tambryn's words. Then you will see why it is the child that is important to us."

"Yes," Giraldus replied, "I want to hear it all—and let this be the last time there are secrets between us."

Later that night, as they lay entwined in each other's arms, Aurya smiled into the darkness. She was pleased with herself; she knew she had played Giraldus in just the right way. Her timing had been perfect.

She had known that, at sometime during their journey, his years as a warrior, his habit of leadership and custom of receiving obedience, would cause him to balk. She had not expected it quite so soon or over a matter that she considered trivial. But since it had come, at least she had the intelligence to make use of it. And now, more than ever, he was hers—heart and body, mind and will.

It had cost her so little; she almost laughed aloud. She would tell him all he wanted to know—she would even read the entire scroll to him, though she knew that he would soon lose interest. Eventually, when it was her magic rather than her intelligence that was needed, she would make him part of that, too.

Oh yes, she had a special part for Giraldus to play when magic became necessary, as she knew it would. Magic could be difficult, draining, even dangerous to the wielder. But with Giraldus nearby to act as a reserve of energy, usable at her request, she knew there was little she could not do.

It was all coming together just as she had planned, despite what the bishop had said about her needing to become more . . . acceptable . . . in order to be Queen. That was what Giraldus wanted, she knew. He had said little about it since Elon had raised the subject, but Aurya knew

Giraldus well enough to be certain it was never far from his thoughts. He was but biding his time.

And so was she. After they had found and destroyed the child would be time enough to decide the question of marriage. As she had tonight, she would know how and when to act; she would make certain then, as she had now, that everything worked the way *she* wanted.

Regardless of what Elon, or the Church, or anyone said, Giraldus was hers. So was the crown. So was Aghamore.

Smiling still, Aurya closed her eyes and welcomed sleep. She wanted to dream of the future.

Chapter Six

With Cloud-Dancer by her side, Lysandra traveled through the Great Forest. Despite the many superstitions about the place, all the stories she had heard as a child, Lysandra knew no fear. For almost ten years she had lived deep in the heart of this forest and had found nothing but beauty and safety.

The inner *Sight* that had first come to her among these trees stayed with her now. It was as if the forest itself held the magic of this Gift. Whether that was true or not,

Lysandra did not know; she accepted it with gratitude, for it made the journey easier.

She gathered the food to sustain her as she traveled. It was plentiful this time of year, as the warming of the air and the soil triggered the growth of tender shoots and succulent mushrooms, and new growth showed her where edible roots lay buried. Each day she gathered a little more than she needed to add to her bag of provisions, knowing that these extra portions might save her from starvation somewhere on the long, unknown journey ahead.

She also added to her supply of medicines, especially when she chanced upon a stand of white willows. Their bark, brewed in a tea, reduced both pain and fever better than any of the herbs she grew.

By day the wolf left her side only to hunt. At dusk, Lysandra carefully made a fire, for the nights were still chill, then laid their bed on piles of fir needles and bracken to insulate them from the damp of the ground.

The trek through the forest took nearly four days, then another to walk around Crooked Lake, from which the province took its name. On the other side, they crossed into the central province of Urlar. Here, where the ground leveled out, towns sprinkled all the roads to Ballinrigh. To get to the kingdom's capital, Lysandra had no choice but to follow the roads, but she did her best to avoid the towns and human contact for as long as possible.

She planned, however, to stop in Granshae—the third biggest city in the province, and only twenty miles from Ballinrigh. It would have taken Lysandra and Cloud-Dancer too long to circumvent it—and she needed to find a shop that would buy her mother's jewelry.

Still, Lysandra dreaded it, and she stood for several minutes outside Granshae's walls. Even out here the presence of so many people pounded at her in a cacophony of minds and emotions she had not endured since running from her home village a decade before.

She did not like it; she did not want it; she could not avoid it.

Steeling her mind as best she could, she laid her fingers on Cloud-Dancer's head, running her fingers deeply into his fur for a stronger contact. Then, using his vision for guidance and his presence to give her strength, Lysandra headed for the city gate.

Walking into the town of Granshae was like walking into a wall of both internal and external noise. More than ever, she relied on Cloud-Dancer's instincts to guide them through the moving maze of people. Even with his vision to orient her, Lysandra found the onslaught of human presence overwhelming. All the people's voices, their loud, quick actions and even quicker thoughts that darted and flashed both around and through her, made Lysandra feel dazed. She held on to Cloud-Dancer ever more tightly. People passing them began to take notice that it was no ordinary dog by her side and to give Lysandra a wide berth, but she could still sense the startled thoughts and whispers that swept through the crowd.

"Come on, boy," she said softly to Cloud-Dancer. "Let's find what we need and get out of this place."

Continuing to share his vision, she began to examine the storefronts as they walked down the straight main road. At last Lysandra saw a store where she might be able to sell her meager supply of possessions.

The window of the shop displayed a myriad of goods, the majority designed to catch a woman's eye. Hopeful, Lysandra entered. She had only taken a few steps when a man's voice shouted from the back of the store.

"You—girl," he boomed, his voice stern, "no animals in here. Leave your dog outside."

Lysandra kept walking, silently using the language of touch to signal Cloud-Dancer. She needed the man behind the counter, whom she hoped was the owner of the store, to see both her blindness and her need for Cloud-Dancer's presence. This would be a trial run for what she was certain to face in Ballinrigh.

Through Cloud-Dancer's eyes, Lysandra could see the man. He was portly and florid, with a bulbous nose and big muttonchop whiskers that added even greater dimension to his already rotund face. He stood with his hands on his hips, staring angrily. He opened his mouth to bellow at her again.

Then, as Lysandra watched, his expression changed. Though he remained wary of Cloud-Dancer's presence, he had now taken note of Lysandra's sightless stare. The anger in his eyes slowly changed to pity. He cleared his throat as Lysandra and Cloud-Dancer neared, and he looked decidedly uncomfortable. But he stood his ground, not backing way from the sight of the wolf.

"What are you doing with that animal, girl?" he asked sharply. "Is it maging you've used to tame the wildness from him?"

Lysandra saw the man's fingers flash in the ancient sign to ward off evil, and she almost smiled. His thoughts were easy to hear as he wondered if she was a witch with her familiar.

She rummaged deep inside her bundle until she found the little packet of linen in which she had wrapped her mother's finery. She placed the package on the countertop. Then, silently signaling Cloud-Dancer to sit, she released her hold on him and reached to untie the cloth.

As soon as her fingertips left Cloud-Dancer's head, his vision left her mind. She was plunged into complete and immediate darkness. For one brief instant, she felt a wave of panic. She fought it—and won—but her fingers still trembled slightly as she untied the knot and spread the jewelry on the counter.

"I want to sell these," she said. "I thought you might buy them, or tell me someone who will."

Lysandra's hand quickly dropped back to Cloud-Dancer's head. She rubbed him affectionately behind one ear and opened her mind to the gift of his vision.

The storeowner was eyeing the jewelry before him, picking up one piece then the next to examine them closely.

"Where did you get these, girl?" he asked. "Are they stolen? I'll have nothing stolen in my store."

"I didn't steal them. They belonged to my mother."

"If she wants them sold, why didn't she bring them here herself? Did she think a blind girl would trick more money out of me? I'll tell you now, girl—pity is pity, business is business, and I'll not mix up the two."

"My mother is dead," Lysandra stated matter-of-factly, "and my father . . . and I don't want your pity," she added as she reached to scoop up her possessions.

She did not want the storekeeper's pity—just his money in a fair price. It seemed, however, she would have to go somewhere else. Then, just as her hand touched the corner of the linen, the man stopped her.

Despite his statement, his face did wear a look of pity. "I'll buy your baubles," he said, "and for a good amount. I'm an honest businessman, and to my mind that works in both the selling and the buying."

Lysandra could feel there was no deceit in the man; he meant what he was saying and was proud of the honesty he proclaimed. Lysandra nodded, accepting his word.

"How much then?" she asked.

"Well now, these are all of an older style—but they're

well made and of quality materials. I'll give you one gold angel and two silver sovereigns for them."

Lysandra considered. It was a good sum; a silver sovereign was worth twenty silver pennies or one hundred copper ones, and a gold angel—that was worth one hundred silver pennies or twenty-five gold ones. It seemed a fortune—but would it be enough to buy food and lodging in Ballinrigh?

She drew a deep breath. "All right," she said aloud, "I'll take it . . . and, thank you."

The man before her began rummaging through a drawer behind the counter. Lysandra could hear the chink of coins of different sizes, weights, and metals. Finally, he held them out to her.

"I said I'm an honest man and I meant it," he began, "but there's many you'll meet who won't be. You'd best memorize the feel of these coins well, so you know what you've been given and what's due you in return."

He placed one, then another of the coins into Lysandra's outstretched palm, pointing out their differences. She ran her sensitive fingers over them, feeling the size and weight, tracing the images on their fronts and backs.

"Do you know the feel now, so that no one can fool you?" he asked.

"I do," Lysandra replied with confidence.

"Then put them somewhere safe, girl, where clever fingers can't steal them. As I said, there are many about with dishonesty in their hearts—and not all of them travel as outlaws."

"How can I thank you for *your* honesty?" Lysandra asked. His kindness was an unlooked-for boon.

"No need, no need," the shopkeeper replied gruffly. "In my day a man was *expected* to be honest, in all his dealings. You could count on a man's handshake same as a contract, and his word was a sacred vow . . . and to cheat someone afflicted—you'll pardon my bluntness, 'tis but the truth—was nothing less than a sin against society and before God. All that's changed these last years, and there's no telling where it'll end. You best keep that in mind."

Thanking the man again, Lysandra left the store. She felt somewhat better, more prepared for what might wait ahead.

On her way through the town, she stopped at a vendor's stall and spent some of her new money on supplies, things it was too early to harvest from the land but that would keep her a few days when she reached Ballinrigh.

The road beyond Granshae was a busy one, and at night the other travelers made camp wherever they stopped. But Lysandra and Cloud-Dancer left the road to find a wilder place to rest, in quiet and in peace, glad to be under trees once again.

Cloud-Dancer ran down a rabbit for his supper; Lysandra nibbled on the fare she had just bought. Then, with a small fire beside them for warmth and a pile of bracken underneath their bedding to keep them from the damp, they settled to their rest.

At first her sleep was peaceful, with neither dreams nor memories to plague her. Then suddenly, a snarl close to her face shattered her slumber.

Lysandra's eyes flew open—but not to darkness. In the full impact of her *Sight*, she was confronted with Cloud-Dancer standing over her, teeth bared and hackles raised. For one brief instant, her heart thumped wildly against her chest.

Then she *saw* that he stood not in the attitude of attack, but of protection. Everything else around them was silent. No night bird called or leaf rustled; even the fire gave forth no crackle of ember or flame. The silence was filled with eerie anticipation.

Slowly, Lysandra turned in the direction of Cloud-Dancer's stare. There, amid the trees just beyond the small circle of light given off by her lowing campfire, stood the vision from her garden. The green aura that encased him sent out flares like tongues of flame—deeply brilliant green flame.

Lysandra found it at once beautiful and terrifying. Gently, she put a hand on Cloud-Dancer, to reassure them both that they were real, that all—she hoped—was well. Then, slowly, she raised herself to her knees, facing her vision.

This time she *saw* him in greater detail. He was dressed in an old, much-mended monk's robe, of an Order she did not recognize. And he was old, ancient to her eyes. His beard, which reached to the middle of his chest, was thin and scraggly with age, as were the wisps of hair that only partially covered his head. His forehead and eyes were lined with furrows.

But his eyes captured and held her. They were kind eyes, full of both sorrow and compassion, and as their gazes locked, Lysandra understood that he knew much about her she had yet to discover. She understood, too, that in some undiscerned way, he was trying to help and guide her.

In his arms she *saw* that it was not one object he carried, but several in a bundle. Try as she might, she could not bring them into focus. It was as if they were something she was not yet meant to see; though all else before her was clear, these objects were wrapped in a fog that wavered and shifted before her eyes.

Lysandra felt an urgent need to get closer to this man— even, perhaps, to touch him. She wanted to see what he carried, to talk with him and hear his voice. Yet, just as before when he stood in her garden, as soon as these thoughts entered her mind, he began to fade.

Lysandra scrambled to her feet, but the man held up a wizened hand to stop her. As she watched, he became more and more dim. The green aura around him began to sputter like an untrimmed candlewick. Then, just before he vanished completely, he reached into the midst of the objects he cradled and retrieved one. He held it out toward Lysandra.

Of its own accord, her hand reached toward it. She could not touch it, but the man seemed satisfied. A slow smile spread across his vanishing face. Somehow, without words spoken, Lysandra felt his assurance within her mind, telling her that soon she would understand.

Then he was gone.

Though the vision was gone, Lysandra's *Sight* remained, clear and full. Off in the east, she *saw* the first streaks of golden dawn washing the sky. Around her, birds gave their first, tentative awakening calls to herald the day. A new day, one more full of promise than Lysandra had felt since she began this journey. Today she would reach Ballinrigh and, if her vision's promise was to be believed, soon she would understand.

But understand what? she wondered again as she put her arms around Cloud-Dancer's neck and hugged him close for comfort.

"It's almost over," she said to him, hoping that her words were true. "And once it is, then we can go home. Right, boy?"

As if in agreement, Cloud-Dancer licked her cheek and leaned into her. They sat there together, letting the world slowly lighten around them.

Chapter Seven

Bishop Elon entered the capital city with all the pomp and ritual his Office demanded. The journey here had been excruciatingly slow, but summoned to the Archbishop's presence and certain of spies set to undermine all his plans, he knew all proprieties must be strictly and carefully observed. It was a game he played well, though his spirit sometimes chafed with impatience.

Upon his arrival in Ballinrigh, Elon sent a note to the Archbishop, via Brother Naal. Elon knew that the young monk would be questioned regarding his impressions of traveling amid Elon's retinue. The bishop had carefully arranged all facets of this journey with just such a report in mind, and he wanted it delivered while it was still fresh in Brother Naal's memory.

Having done all he could, Elon now awaited the Archbishop's summons.

It had come this morning as a casual handwritten invitation to dinner. Elon was not fooled by the friendliness of the words on paper. This was an inquiry of conduct and nothing less; he only wished he knew who, besides the Archbishop, would be attending, which of his enemies had been whispering in his superior's ear.

He dressed with special care, wearing his second-best

cassock of purple watermarked silk and matching mozzetta. His best one, the one with the gold buttons, he would save for High Mass in the cathedral, which he hoped to be asked to concelebrate. With the entire College of Bishops sitting in attendance, only a select few would be granted such an honor—and Elon planned to be one of them. This act of recognition before his peers was the first overt step on his journey to the Archbishop's triple mitre.

He smiled to himself as he looked in the mirror, making a slight adjustment to the wide cincture that girded his waist. He was pleased by what he saw. The long, straight line of the cassock accentuated his height, as well as the broad shoulders and narrow hips he still possessed even though he was nearing sixty. He had not allowed himself to grow fat. The people of Aghamore, so used to looking at bishops either portly or fragile, could look at him and see a man of vigor, a man fit and strong enough to be their leader.

For one last adornment, Elon added his pectoral cross, made of gold, amethyst, and onyx. Fittingly attired to show the prosperity of his see, he grabbed up his long black cloak and left for the Archbishop's residence.

He arrived precisely on time—a half hour earlier, it turned out, than the other guests who were to join them.

"I thought we might use this time for a private talk," the Archbishop said after he had shown Elon into his personal study. It was a cluttered, informal room in the back part of the house, rather than the richly furnished official room in which the Archbishop received Kings or supplicants.

Archbishop Colm apBeirne had always been a scholar. Open books, half-rolled scrolls, and papers were scattered like fallen leaves over desk, carpet, and chairs. But the well-trimmed lamps and the bright fire in the fireplace kept the room from looking gloomy. Instead, it had a homey feeling, as if to say that the occupant was always happiest here.

Before the fire sat two winged-backed chairs, mercifully cleared of the clutter that covered nearly every other available surface. On a little table between the chairs, a decanter of chambried wine waited next to two crystal goblets.

"Please, please, have a seat, Elon," the Archbishop said, absently waving toward a chair and using Elon's familiar name void of title. "We'll not stand on ceremony here, in this room, eh? This is not an inquiry, just a talk."

As he spoke, he poured them both a glass of wine. Elon noticed the slightly palsied shake of his hands and how the Archbishop's body bent forward, stooping unconsciously toward the fireplace, as if his old bones were seeking the heat. To a person of Elon's temperament, his movements were aggravatingly slow, and it was all Elon could do to make himself sit still, to keep smiling and not take the decanter from the old man's hand and complete the task himself.

Finally, the Archbishop slowly lowered himself into the remaining chair. He took a sip of wine and closed his eyes for a moment.

"Ah, the heat feels good, doesn't it?" he said.

Actually, Elon was beginning to feel the room was too close and overheated. "Yes, Your Eminence," he said nevertheless. "A fire is always a welcome comfort."

"More so at my age, I daresay," the Archbishop replied, opening his eyes.

Elon could see there was a bit of a sparkle in them; the old man, for all his physical frailties, still possessed a sharp mind and a wry wit. Elon reminded himself to tread carefully and not underestimate his opponent—especially not when he hoped to turn opponent into ally.

The Archbishop studied Elon for a moment. The younger man did not flinch under the scrutiny. This was a game of nerves, and Elon knew he played it well. Too bold, and he would appear offensive, belligerent; too timid, and the Archbishop would think he had not the stuff in him to stand beside Kings.

The Archbishop, the Primus of the Church in Aghamore, was the spiritual ruler of the Kingdom. He must be willing to give deference and obedience to his sovereign in all things temporal—so long as they did not compromise the spiritual well-being of the souls within his care. For that, he must have the courage to stand by his convictions even in the face of royal anger.

All this, Elon knew he could do. For this he had trained all his adult life. He knew the canons and bylaws of the Church and the spiritual precepts on which those were built, knew them as well as he knew his own mind. Outwardly, in every way that would matter to this kingdom, Elon could fulfil the role of Archbishop better than any other man in Aghamore.

As for what he *believed*—ah, that was a different matter entirely.

The scrutiny of the old man's gaze went on for a long, unspoken moment. Had it not been for the intelligence in Colm apBeirne's watery eyes, Elon might have thought the old man had drifted off in some senile playground of the mind. But Elon would not make the mistake so many did and think that the Archbishop's wits were as atrophied as his muscles.

"Tell me about the Lady Aurya," the Archbishop said

without preamble. The abruptness of the question was meant to catch Elon off guard.

But Elon knew the ploy; he used it often himself. Get your opponent somewhere comfortable, let him relax— then strike, suddenly, when it is unexpected. Silently, he acknowledged a well-played opening move.

"Lady Aurya is not at all what I expected, Your Eminence," he began.

The Archbishop held up a hand. "Let us not be so formal, Elon," he said. "Here we talk openly, brothers in the service of Our Lord and His Church . . . perhaps, I hope, even as friends. If we keep throwing titles back and forth, we'll never get anywhere."

The second move, Elon thought. *Break your opponent's train of thought early. Reinforce his sense of security. Very good . . . well played indeed.*

With a tiny nod that appeared to be deference to the old man's wishes but was, in fact, an acknowledgement of strategy, a move within a move, Elon continued.

"I went to see Lady Aurya at her own request. As she is the consort of Baron Giraldus, I thought I must go myself, to find out why she would send such a request—for his sake, if not for hers. Her . . . attitude . . . toward the Church is one she has never hidden."

"It is a godless union they share," the Archbishop said sternly. "Did you not think that by such a visit you might seem to be condoning her unholy use of magic? It is the devil's tool, and those who use it are fallen from Grace."

"I thought only that here might be a penitent in need of spiritual guidance," Elon replied.

There, he thought, *the seeds Aurya so thoughtfully laid can now be harvested.*

The Archbishop nodded. "Such a thought does you

credit," he said. "And is that how you found Lady Aurya? Penitent?"

"I found her angry at first, from the many exaggerated rumors spread about her," Elon answered, somewhat truthfully, for the best lie is a carefully selected portion of the truth. "But I believe she is a lady who has been much maligned by such tales, many of which she lays firmly at the Church's door. Finding spiritual guidance has not been easy, it seems. Many have turned away from her because of these tales of her 'unholy practices,' as you call it. Rather than chance encountering her anger, they have condemned her without hearing, without trying to answer her questions that might lead to her repentance. That, too, is why I put aside my other business for the day and went to see her myself. Should she return to the Church, I know Baron Giraldus will as well—and two souls will be saved. Is that not our highest duty?"

Move and countermove, Elon thought. With this last question he had backed the Archbishop into a corner.

Again, the old man nodded. "It is indeed. And I hoped—nay, I was sure—your reason would be one such as this. I am glad to have it confirmed and to know my faith in you is not misplaced. But remember, there are many in this world who do not look with the eyes of charity. They seek always to find fault with those who lead. As shepherds of this flock of human souls, we must have a care that the *appearance* of our actions does not lead others onto a path of destruction."

With the Archbishop's words, Elon knew he had won, though not a *complete* victory. There still remained some little question in the old man's mind and Elon would have to find a way to set it to rest if he was to gain Colm apBeirne's support.

But now was not the time. The next move was his, but

it must be subtle and come at an unexpected moment. It was his turn to catch his opponent off guard.

For now, he changed the subject. "The College meets tomorrow," he began. "Have you heard anything to indicate a favored candidate for the throne?"

Colm sighed. "Nay," he said. "We are indeed a house divided on this subject. Each bishop favors his own Baron as the best qualified, the strongest leader . . . and truth be told, there's not much difference between any of them. The people, I think, just want to see the matter settled before Aghamore erupts into civil war."

"Whom do *you* favor?" Elon asked. He kept his tone casual, but inside he felt his muscles tighten. The Archbishop's answer now would name the one who posed the greatest threat to Elon's plans.

But the old man raised his hands in a gesture of bewilderment. "That, I cannot answer," he said. "It is clear that the House of Baoghil is ended and by right, each of the Barons is equally in line of succession. But who would be best for this kingdom? That I do not know, not this time. I thought I knew last time with Anri, but I was wrong, and the people of this kingdom paid the price. If only . . ."

These words were spoken softly, as if to himself, but they were not lost on Elon. The implication was clear: If only the problem of Aurya did not exist, then Giraldus would have the Archbishop's support for High King. And Elon intended to make certain the problem was either controlled or removed—at least long enough for Giraldus to be crowned. The artful deception that they so publicly played out during his last visit to the Baron's fortress would continue to serve them well, though Elon knew that any embellishments must be carefully considered and even more carefully added. Then, once Aurya and Giraldus returned, he had no doubt that her own intelligence would convince Aurya of the necessity of formalizing both her relationship with Giraldus and her public image of religious contrition. Once that was done, there would be nothing in all of Aghamore that could stop them, no one could stand in their way.

Elon wanted to shout out loud. Instead, he hid his feeling of triumph-glimpsed behind an expression of concern, one he had carefully developed over the years.

"If only?" he said to the Archbishop, opening the door for further confidences, and inviting the Archbishop to confirm what Elon believed he had meant. But the Archbishop was too experienced to make such a slip again.

He shook his head. "Nothing, my son," he said. "Just an old man's meanderings. When you get to be my age, life is full of 'if-onlys.' Let us speak no more of it. How are things in Kilgarriff? What do the people there say about the succession?"

"Like the people everywhere, they are worried that Aghamore has no King—many of them have lived through such a time before. And, like the people everywhere, they would like to see their own Baron on the throne. They know him to be a good leader and a strong warrior who could protect this kingdom from civil war, or from invasion—both of which they fear will happen if the throne remains empty much longer."

The old man nodded. "I, too, fear such things. Tell me, Elon, do you have plans to meet again with Lady Aurya?"

Elon shook his head. "She and Baron Giraldus have undertaken a retreat, a pilgrimage you might call it—a time of withdrawing from cares and demands of the kingdom to consider the things we talked about during my visit."

The Archbishop's face lit up at the news, both pleased

and astonished. "I should like to have heard that conversation," he said. "The Spirit must have truly been guiding your words to have had such a profound effect. Can you tell me more of what was said?"

"Alas, I cannot," Elon replied. "Most of our discussion was 'Under the Stole,' and so I may not divulge it even to you. As for my words and their effect—I believe it was only because I found receptive hearts awaiting."

The clock on the mantel sounded the hour. The Archbishop looked up at it sharply, then sighed as he put his empty wineglass aside.

"The other guests will be arriving," he said, "and I should be there when they come in. We must return to the front of the house before Gregory comes looking for us. Thank you, Elon, for indulging an old man's need for good company and quiet conversation."

"I have enjoyed it as much as you," Elon replied humbly.

Indeed more, he thought as he stood. He put out an arm to help the Archbishop to his feet, pretending at the same time to take little notice of the arthritic manner in which the old man moved.

When the succession was settled, Elon was certain, Colm apBeirne would retire. He would want to be away from drafty cathedrals and long hours at court, retired to a place where he could spend his last years sitting before a fire with his books. Between now and then, Elon would do whatever it took to make certain to be the one named as his preferred successor.

Then, with Giraldus on the throne and the retiring Archbishop giving his approval and backing, the College of Bishops would have no choice but to place the golden triple mitre on Elon's head. With that certainty filling him,

Elon walked by the old Archbishop's side, heir-apparent, into dinner.

Elon enjoyed his evening at the Archbishop's residence. The game was still going on, he knew, with the other guests unwittingly serving as part of the players. In attendance were Bishop Sitric of Lininch, Bishop Tadhg of Farnagh, Aileen, Abbess of the convent attached to the cathedral, and Bishop Mago of Tievebrack.

Were these his biggest rivals? Elon wondered. Did they have aspirations as high as his own, or were they happy as little more than sheep themselves, never caring to become the shepherd? Only time would tell him—but before the College of Bishops was dismissed a final time, he intended to know it all.

For the rest of the evening, Elon appeared relaxed. It was a careful façade, but an effective one. Even while he smiled and pleasantly chatted on inane topics in which he had no interest, his mind was watching, measuring, looking for openings he might later exploit. By the end of the dinner, he realized that any serious threats would come from other quarters.

As Elon rode home in the formal carriage he kept here in Ballinrigh, he finally permitted himself the triumphant smile he had kept hidden all evening. He had played the game well, and he knew it. If this evening had been a test, then he had more than passed . . . he had excelled.

Elon Gallivin, Archbishop of Aghamore—yes, he liked the sound of that.

Chapter Eight

Footsore and weary, Lysandra approached the great walled city of Ballinrigh, the capital and heart of Aghamore. In this city stood the great cathedral and its library, which housed all the records of the kingdom. Here, like a walled city within a city, the High King's palace lifted its cream-colored turrets toward the sky.

It was near dusk by the time she reached the city gates. The bright energy of the morning had long ago left her, as had the *Sight*. Now, feeling the long journey in every muscle and relying once more upon Cloud-Dancer's vision to guide her, Lysandra faced an obstacle she had not expected . . . the gatekeeper.

"You, girl—I'm talking to you," he snarled, stepping in front of her. "I said you can't bring that beast in here."

Crossing his large, hairy arms over his chest, he glared at her in self-important anger. For a moment Lysandra just stared back at him, letting her sightless eyes do their own talking while she searched for the right words. She found herself too tired for eloquence.

"But . . . but I must," she stammered. "He's my guide. I . . . I need him."

She kept her voice soft and meek, an easy thing to do in her present condition. Her weariness draped her like a cloak, and, after so many days on the road, she could only guess at the picture she presented. Nor did she, for pride's sake, try to present any other. She would gladly sacrifice her pride in order to keep Cloud-Dancer by her side.

Her helpless attitude was having some effect. She could feel the gatekeeper's resolve wavering.

"He's well trained," she continued. With a gentle move of her hand, Cloud-Dancer immediately sat, proving her words.

"What be your business in Ballinrigh, then? Where be your people?"

Here was the tricky part, Lysandra realized. She did not want to lie, but how could she tell him what she did not know herself?

"My family is dead—killed by outlaws. Black Bryan," Lysandra said. Still watching the gatekeeper through Cloud-Dancer's vision, Lysandra saw by the look that flashed across his face that he knew the outlaw's reputation. She pressed on.

"I'm here searching," she continued, still the truth. "The cathedral has copies of all the kingdom's records, and I must have family somewhere."

Still she knew she had not lied—not exactly. She had not said she was *going* to the cathedral.

"If there's a fee for bringing my . . . dog . . . into the city, I have money," she said eagerly. Fishing into the small purse she had made of the linen that once held her mother's jewelry and tied around her neck for safety, she drew out one of the silver sovereigns.

A look of greed blossomed on the gatekeeper's face. Seeing it, Lysandra knew she had won. She carefully kept the triumph from her face and voice as she held the coin out to him.

"Please," she said, her voice pleading. Suddenly, all of

her weariness overwhelmed the spurt of hope she had just felt. Tears, born mostly of exhaustion, welled in her eyes. The sight was too much for the gatekeeper. He took the coin and quickly pocketed it.

"All right," he said. "But if there be any trouble from that beast, I'll deny that I was the one what let you enter. I'll not forfeit my job here for his sake—nor yours neither."

"Thank you," Lysandra said humbly. "And there will be no trouble. That I can promise."

In this she spoke only the truth. At another silent signal from her fingers, Cloud-Dancer stood and stayed by her side as they walked through the gate. It was nearly dark now, and Lysandra knew that at any moment the gate would be pulled closed behind her. But before she passed completely through, she turned back toward the gatekeeper once more.

"Please," she said softly, "where do I go to find lodging?"

The man considered for a moment. "Go straight ahead five blocks, then turn right. Another three blocks and turn right again. At the end of that street you'll find an inn— The Crowing Cock. It be not fancy, mind, but it's clean. The innkeeper be named Gavin and he likes animals. He'll likely let your beast in there."

"Thank you," Lysandra said again. Then, drawing a deep breath, she and Cloud-Dancer at last entered Ballinrigh.

They followed the directions the gatekeeper had given. Tired as she was, Lysandra was forced to deal with the onslaught of city-minds all around her. This was far worse than the town of Granshae had been; she felt as if she was walking through a mire that dragged at her, slowing her mind as well as her body. So many people, all living their separate lives filled with hopes and fears, loves and hates, anger and laughter.

Lysandra was glad it was nighttime, when most people had withdrawn behind their closed doors. Weary with traveling, she did not think she could have faced this city amid the tumult of midday. At least now she would have some rest to strengthen her before tomorrow when, she knew, she must begin her earnest searching for why she had been drawn here.

Her mind was so intent on shutting out the mental noise that she did not feel the approach of the two men behind her. Suddenly, beneath her hand, she felt Cloud-Dancer's hackles rise. He emitted a single, low growl. This sound penetrated the mental and emotional fog that had encased Lysandra. Suddenly, she *saw* again.

She turned just as the men were nearly upon her. In that brief instant she recognized them as men she had seen upon the road. They must have been at the gate at the same time she was and seen the coin she gave to the gatekeeper.

Cloud-Dancer, who had been so well behaved at the gate, did not look docile now. Lysandra lifted her restraining hand; it was all the permission Cloud-Dancer needed. He bared his teeth in a warning snarl and again emitted his low growl. The men hesitated briefly.

With her *Sight*, Lysandra scanned the area, looking for an exit or a place of safety for herself and Cloud-Dancer. A few yards away was a small church. The outside was unimpressive—a poor neighborhood parish in the great cathedral city—but a light shone in its windows.

The man on the left took a couple of steps to the side, trying to draw Cloud-Dancer's attention away so his companion could reach Lysandra. But the wolf's instinct of protection was too strong to be fooled by such simple tactics. Seeing it was not working, the men rushed forward together, more intent on the possible gold in Lysandra's purse than fearful of their own safety. Their eyes were more than greedy—they were desperate.

But they were no match for Cloud-Dancer's fury. As the men made their rush, the wolf leapt toward them, biting and snarling. In the same instant, Lysandra made a dash for the church. She heard one of the men cry in agony just as she reached the door. There were more snarls, more cries, all jumbled into a single crescendo of conflict . . . then the sound of limping, running feet slowly dying off in the distance.

Lysandra called Cloud-Dancer to her and, dropping to her knees, threw her arms around his muscular neck. He had just saved more than her coins; had she been alone, such men would not have hesitated to take her body—or her life.

With that thought, Lysandra began to shake. She could not find the strength to stand. She could hardly make her hands work as she reached for the latch of the church door, but she knew she had to get inside. She needed time to sit where it was quiet and safe. Only then would she find the strength to go on.

From her knees, she finally worked the latch and fell through the door as it opened. She lay panting on the floor for a few seconds, suddenly close to tears of weariness and relief.

She had not been inside a church since the day she stood beside the coffins of the three people she had loved best in the world. She had thought never to enter one again. But, surprisingly, she found that she wanted to remain here.

Walking from the narthex into the nave, she took a seat

in the back pew and slowly let her *Sight* extend to brush lightly over her surroundings. The place was small, and the shadowed corners were dimly lit in the wavering light of votive candles that burned before cushioned prayer stations and statuaries of patron saints.

On one side was a statue of the Virgin. She stood with willowy grace, her arms gently outstretched as if waiting to embrace the supplicant kneeling in prayer at her feet. Long years of candle and incense smoke, and of loving hands touching her motionless robes, had given a golden patina to the once-white stone from which she had been carved, softening her appearance and yet, somehow, making her even more ethereal.

The other was a statute of Saint Anne, the mother of the Blessed Virgin. She had an older but very kind face and stood holding a white lily, symbol of her daughter. Saint Anne was the saint most often invoked against poverty and a fitting patron for a poor city parish.

The statues, like the rest of the church, showed their age. Though the parish was obviously poor and refurbishments rare, it was a place where care had been taken with such things as were here. The frontal on the altar, though somewhat threadbare, was clean and precisely hung; the pews, where hands and bodies had over the years worn away the finish, had been cleaned and polished with beeswax that added its sweet scent to the room. The floors were swept and the candles new. The air held a hint of old incense, as if over the years it had been absorbed by the wood and stone. It was pleasant to breathe, like a whisper of spice barely tasted on the tongue.

Lysandra sat back and closed her eyes, breathing in deeply, taking in the atmosphere of human care and divine peace; this church felt like a spiritual home.

A little sound, a shuffling of feet across the floor, disturbed the silence that cradled Lysandra's thoughts. Suddenly she knew she was not alone. Yet she felt no threat—nor was Cloud-Dancer wary; relaxed and content, he sat by her side, leaning familiarly against her legs as if they had been sitting in the sunlight or before the fire at home.

Lysandra's blind eyes could tell her nothing, but her *Sight* explored the shadows by the altar. There to the left, by the little door that led into the sacristy—that shadow held a physical presence. Like Cloud-Dancer, she could sense nothing sinister. In fact, she sensed nothing at all except silence and peace.

Someone *was* there; she knew it as a certainty—and yet, throughout the last decade of this often useful, often unwanted sensitivity to the thoughts and feelings of others, she had rarely been near another human without hearing something, some echo of their mind.

But from this person there was still nothing. It was as if a shield was dropped between them, a barrier of protection. *For whose benefit?* she wondered.

Shadow within shadow moved. A moment later a man stepped out into the softly flickering light. Suddenly, Lysandra's *Sight* blazed to new clarity, as if the candle flames were tiny suns, illuminating the room with the brilliance of midday. As the man walked from within the sanctuary of the altar toward her, all the color and detail that had once been such a rarity to her *Sight* came upon her again.

Lysandra let her *Sight* extend to envelop him. He was a priest, dressed in the long black clerical cassock that was the basic garb of his Office. He had left a neat pile draped over the altar rail as he passed, and Lysandra saw that they were the vestments he would don before service.

Although she could not feel his mind—a sensation that

was both welcome and disconcerting—she could *see* him clearly. He was perhaps ten years older than she, the first strands of silver sprinkled among the dark brown hair at his temples. His eyes, deep brown with tiny flecks of green and gold, were full of gentleness and compassion. His face was clean-shaven, his lips full and drawn back in a small smile, the kind that invited confidences without fear of recrimination.

He slid into the pew in front of Lysandra, turned so he could face her. "Hello," he said. "I'm Father Renan. That's a beautiful animal. What's his name?"

Father Renan spoke as if the sight of a wolf in his parish was commonplace. It startled Lysandra—but not as much as the sound of his voice. It was familiar, yet Lysandra knew she had never met him before.

"This is Cloud-Dancer," Lysandra answered as her hand slid down his shoulders. Her *Sight* told her of Father Renan's reaction to Cloud-Dancer; by her touch, she was trying to feel the wolf's reaction to the priest.

Cloud-Dancer sat peacefully. His ears were pitched slightly forward, but with an attitude of listening curiosity, even eagerness. He seemed completely at ease with this man's presence.

In fact, Lysandra realized, Cloud-Dancer was exhibiting less wariness than he ever showed around anyone, save herself; gatekeepers or shepherd boys, Cloud-Dancer always gave off a feeling of watchfulness, a vigilance in her protection that Lysandra had come to trust. But here, with Father Renan, the wolf was silently telling her of his total acceptance. Lysandra knew she could trust this priest as well.

"He's quite beautiful," Father Renan was continuing, though he made no move to pet the wolf as he might a family dog. "Now that I have met your companion, will you tell me your name, too?"

"Lysandra," she answered him. "We did not mean to disturb you. There were . . . men . . . outside."

Lysandra was uncertain what to say; she was no longer used to small talk. But she knew she wanted to hear more. With each word, Father Renan's voice became more familiar; and she was certain that if he spoke long enough she would know where she had heard it before.

"No need for apologies," he said. "You are, of course, welcome here. What good is a church if no one enters? And I am always glad to see a new face among our small numbers."

Father Renan's voice was pleasant, light, as if he was truly glad to see her. Although a part of Lysandra was glad to be here, *Surely,* she thought, *I wasn't drawn to Ballinrigh just so I could sit and make idle conversation.*

From the way he was watching her, Lysandra had the feeling Father Renan knew something she did not. Before she could say anything else, however, he rose.

"Evensong will start soon, and I must finish getting ready," he said. "Please stay. We'll talk more after the service."

Before Lysandra could reply, he turned and went back to the altar, leaving her still wondering who he really was and why she was here.

While Father Renan busied himself at the altar, Lysandra looked again around the little church. The clarity of her *Sight* was failing; colors were turning to indeterminate shadows, details giving way to misty outlines. With a sigh, she accepted the change.

Then, as the first of the parishioners came quietly through the door, outlines were swallowed by darkening fog. Blindness came to her again. She did not try to change it by borrowing Cloud-Dancer's vision. As her *Sight* withdrew, she felt a need for the darkness, a need to have external distraction cease so that she could find herself again.

Only half-listening, she heard other feet shuffle through the door, some pausing at the statue in the narthex as she had done, before coming into the nave and finding their places to sit or kneel. Lysandra smelled the odor of bodies coming from their day's labor, heard the whisper of personal prayer.

Finally, Father Renan turned toward the congregation. His voice, full and melodious now, began the first chant of Evensong.

> *"The Lord is in his holy temple; let all the earth keep*
>   *silence before Him.*
> *"Let my prayer be set forth in thy sight as incense;*
>   *and let the lifting up of my hands be an evening*
>   *sacrifice. . . ."*

The evening Office continued. Lysandra's eyes were closed as the ancient words and chants washed over her. Their timeless simplicity filled her soul, and carried her, floating, to a place were questions no longer existed and answers no longer needed to be found. The parishioners chanting, soft and uncertain even in their familiarity, held together by the confident thread of Father Renan's voice.

Father Renan's voice . . .

Suddenly Lysandra *knew*. This was the voice she had heard in her dream, night after night, sometimes as soft as a breath, sometimes loud with urgent pleading. Father Renan's voice . . .

It was all too strange. Lysandra wanted to get up, leave this church and this city, to turn her back on whatever perverse fate had governed her life thus far. But she could not make her body move.

Evensong is not a long service. It is a gentle closing down toward sleep, a time of quiet thanksgiving for having made it through the demands and confusions of another day. Even with Father Renan's homily, the last prayer was soon said, and the people began to leave the church with the same respectful silence they had entered.

All through Evensong, Lysandra had tried to *sense* Father Renan. The other people around her were easy to understand. She felt emotions; she knew who was here from devotion and who from habit. But Father Renan remained as closed to her as if he were not there. Only his voice confirmed his continuing presence.

Lysandra had found the service refreshing to her tired spirit, and although most of the thoughts and emotions around her had been focused on the single, peace-filled purpose of worship, she was glad to have the people go. Now, perhaps, some of her questions might be answered.

As the last of the congregation exited, a state of nearly perfect silence descended on the church. The thick stone walls blocked the noise from the city and the only sound within was that of Father Renan finishing his post-service ablutions at the altar.

Lysandra put her hand on Cloud-Dancer's head to borrow his vision. When the moment of transition passed, she saw Father Renan coming down the central aisle. He still wore that half-expressed smile on his face. Now it broadened slightly as he again slipped into the pew in front of her and turned around to face her.

"I'm glad you stayed," he said. "I believe we have things to talk about."

He knows, Lysandra's thoughts exploded in glad circles.

"My rectory behind the church is small, but it's clean and well provisioned, thanks to the generosity of the people who worship here. Let us go find something to nourish our bodies before we fill our minds."

"Please," Lysandra began, not wanting to wait a moment longer. "I need to know."

"And so you shall," Father Renan replied, his voice both patient and encouraging. "But what I must tell you will take some time. It is best done where we can be comfortable."

Lysandra could tell there would be no rushing Father Renan in his tale. She stood, ready to follow the priest. After so long, she told herself, what was a few more minutes, even an hour's further wait?

It is an eternity, her heart cried as she and Cloud-Dancer walked behind Father Renan toward the little set of rooms he called home.

Chapter Nine

Aurya and Giraldus had left the province of Kilgarriff. They were passing through the northern portion of Urlar, carefully avoiding the larger towns where they might be recognized, on their way to the mountain passes between Urlar and Lininch. Aurya was certain that their final destination was to be Rathreagh, the northernmost province of Aghamore, and there were certainly more direct routes. But she was carefully following the directions from the scroll and was just as certain it was directing them to Lininch.

Or so she hoped. The words of Tambryn were often ambiguous at best. Using all her past experience, she thought she understood most of them and kept any doubts she still felt to herself.

They had taken rooms in the little town of Wexlay. Aurya sat with the map of Aghamore spread out before her . . . and once more Giraldus was arguing about her decisions.

"I don't understand you," he was saying, his voice a snarl of impatience. "First you say we must hurry to find this . . . this . . . Wisdom-something—"

"Font of Wisdom," Aurya supplied quietly. Giraldus just grunted in response.

"Whatever," he said with a dismissive wave. "And you say we must go north—but you're taking us a damnedably roundabout way to get there. If we must go with such haste, then let's go *directly*."

"No," Aurya said with a sigh. She would *again* try to explain.

"Tambryn gave these directions for a *reason*, Giraldus," she said, trying to sound more patient than she felt. "I don't know what the reasons are—yet—but there must be something we're supposed to find or do by going this route, something that will make a difference."

"What could we possibly gain by going into Lininch to get to Rathreagh? I still say it doesn't make any sense."

"Make sense or not, it's the way we're going," Aurya

snapped, finally losing the fragile hold on her temper. She closed her eyes and breathed in deeply, slowly . . . once . . . twice . . .

Once she felt herself becoming centered again, she opened her eyes and looked again at Giraldus. "We must go into Lininch, to Yembo. The scroll clearly states that we must find *'the water that runs between the tall hollows where the children sing.'* Think, Giraldus—Yembo is known for the river that flows through the heart of the town. Every year in the spring, when the birds return from their winter lands, Yembo holds a festival at the entrance to the city. I've been there and seen it. The Eastern Gate of the city, that they call the Water-Gates, are built over where the river flows into the harbor. The Gates form a great arched bridge and on either side are tall, carved columns, hollowed to make homes for the returning birds. At the base of the columns, the city meets for the opening of their spring festival. The biggest event is the city's children's choir. They sing at dawn on the first of May. We *must* get to Yembo, and we must get there in time for the festival."

Giraldus did not look pleased as he headed for the door. "If you're wrong," he said, his hand on the latch, "it had better not cost me the throne."

He jerked the door open and left, pulling it shut with a slam behind him. Aurya was glad to see him go. The downstairs of this inn was a public house, and there he could drink himself into a better humor while she studied the scroll and the map in peace, trying to be certain she had missed nothing.

Although her words to Giraldus had sounded sure, the truth was that this was one of the places in the scroll that Aurya was working on guesses and probabilities. She was taking them by the only route she could connect with the descriptions in the scroll. The festival at Yembo was famous throughout Aghamore, but had it been so during the time of Tambryn? If not, was the description based on some vision of the future the prophet had seen?

Or could she be reading it all wrong? As Giraldus had said, it did not make sense to travel this far out of their way.

Aurya unrolled the scroll and laid it out on the same table as the map. Using her finger to follow the words, she read them aloud, pronouncing each one carefully.

They were to cross the *"heart of the flower"* to the *"farthest high paths."* She was certain that meant Urlar; the eight outer provinces encircled the capital province like the petals of a flower and they were heading toward the mountain passes. But then came several phrases that made no sense, beginning with and containing several of the ubiquitous references to "Prophecy's Hand."

". . . Prophecy's Hand shall point the way, and the Three Sisters shall be found. The Three Sisters looking west face not the path but mark the hidden. So shall Prophecy's Hand again reveal; the forgotten shall be remembered. The unspoken must be heard and with Prophecy's Hand unite.

"Find then the water that runs between the tall hollows. . . ."

Here, Aurya once more felt she understood what Tambryn meant. She sat back and closed her tired eyes. *Prophecy's Hand*—it was always Prophecy's Hand that confused her. If only she could find some clue to tell her what, or who, it was, perhaps then the rest of this passage—and all the other oblique places within the scroll—might become clear.

And, perhaps, she told herself, she would not understand until she actually arrived where she was meant to go and saw the things about which Tambryn had written. Either way, they were going to Yembo.

Aurya got up and paced the room. She had ordered a flagon of wine sent up with their meal earlier. Now she stopped and poured some for herself. The feeling that there was something she had failed to see or do nagged at her.

Aurya drained the cup, grimacing at its inferior quality, and poured herself another. This room, while not elegant, did boast the comfort of its own hearth, with chairs set before it. She added more wood to the brightly burning flames and centered one chair before the hearth. She would use the fire as a focus while she attempted a Far-Seeing over time and distance. She hoped her magic would reveal what she was missing and show the future of their travels.

She took one more sip of the wine then put the cup aside. She would need it later. What she was attempting took both strength and courage. Once she entered the tangled skein of lives and times, she might lose the single line that was herself and become endlessly trapped in the etherworld. But with everything they planned depending on this journey, Aurya was willing to face the danger.

Aurya closed her eyes; she had never let fear keep her from what she wanted. She took a deep breath, slowly to the count of four, held it . . . exhaled just as slowly, and held that as well. She did this three times. Then, with the fourth breath, she felt herself enter her quiet place within, the place where the external world stilled as if it stopped between seconds, and where magic reigned.

Aurya opened her eyes. The fire before her still burned, but its crackle and dance had been slowed, silenced. She stared into the flames, seeing but not seeing, letting her eyes focus both within and beyond. Soundlessly, she began to chant, her lips forming the words only her mind spoke.

> *Magda, Queen of Darkness and Light; Mother of Time, enfold me.*
> *Anu, Weaver of What Is to Be, take my hand; show me the path I must follow.*
> *Teslaigh, Reiba, first to bring light to the mortal world, I call on ye for aid;*
> *Guide me in my quest and lift the veil from my inner eyes.*
> *Let my eyes become as Your eyes; lift the darkness that shadows the future.*
> *In Your wisdom and Your power, show me all that I must do;*
> *Then will I vow myself Your servant eternally, body and spirit.*

Aurya did not have long to wait before she felt the first stirring of those presences on whom she had called. They were ancient forces, gods and goddesses served by the Kings, sages, and sorcerers who had once been mighty in this land—before the Church had come to convert the people and banish the old ways.

When Giraldus is King, she promised herself— promised the ones *she* still served—*it will be as it was before.*

Aurya felt the shift within herself that told her the magic was building. She whispered the names of power once again: *Magda . . . Anu . . . Teslaigh . . . Reiba . . .* She felt first emptied then filled again. Before her eyes, the fire grew dark. Then slowly . . . slowly . . . a spark of light began at its center. It expanded, became a bright tunnel down which her awareness flew.

In her peripheral vision, distorted images formed and passed dizzyingly. Seen and not seen; stretched beyond recognition. Spinning. Sliding. Twirling. Aurya's stomach lurched dangerously close to emptying itself. Still the images sped by.

Then, by the force and strength of her will alone, she finally managed to focus on the path ahead. She wanted to shut her eyes, too, but she dared not. Down the tunnel she sped, riding on light and thought, on will and breath.

The light exploded, shooting outward like shards of splintered glass. Each piece was a new destination, a possibility of fate discarded. Aurya was not interested in possibilities; there was only one outcome she wanted to see.

She was still chanting the names of the old ones under her breath, still calling on the ancient gods to help her. Now, as the sensation of rushing forward began to abate, her words slowed. Though her lips moved, no sound passed them.

Slowly, new images began to form within the window in the flames. They were hazy at first, indistinct like a painting viewed from afar. With each passing second they became clearer until at last she recognized the figures.

But not the setting. She saw herself and Giraldus in a place of stone and of treasure, where gold and gems mingled with granite and limestone to form walls that looked unhewn. It was a place of both wildness and beauty, each strangely augmenting the other.

She had the feeling that she and Giraldus were not alone, but she could not make out who, or what, surrounded them. The people or creatures were indistinct splotches of darkness amid the surrounding light. And they were closing in. . . .

The vision stopped. Abruptly, she was back in her chair, staring at the flames. But the spell was not broken. Before she had time to do more than draw a breath, the sensation of fleeing forward began again. This time she was prepared; this time her stomach did not twist and turn.

Again she saw herself and Giraldus. As the vision cleared, she saw they were on horseback. Behind them rode a force of arms, though how many she could not see. They were approaching the great cathedral in Ballinrigh. The bells of the cathedral were clamoring wildly; she could feel the ringing like the pounding of her heart.

What does it mean? her heart asked the powers she had called upon. But no answer came, leaving Aurya to draw her own conclusions. Were they coming to the cathedral in triumph? she wondered. Were they there to claim the crown—or to attack?

Still no answer came—and the vision disappeared.

This time the spell also snapped, breaking like a frayed thread. To Aurya, it came like a physical blow. Her head jerked back as if someone had slapped her. Lights exploded behind her eyes, and, for a brief moment, her mind reeled.

Then it was over, the sensations gone, and she was left panting in her chair.

Aurya was thirsty, as she had known she would be. She picked up her wine cup and drained it, no longer caring if the wine was good or bad. Then she rose and began to pace the room, glad that no one was there to witness her agitation. She was dissatisfied with the revelations her spell had wrought. More than that, she was angry. She had called on the old gods, honored their power—why had they chosen to show her such obscure and meaningless moments?

"The Great Ones guard their secrets," she remembered old Kizzie telling her, *"and they do not give them up easily. What they reveal will be of their choosing, not yours. You must learn to look deeply into the heart of each vision and understand what they are telling you. Such meanings are not always easily understood. Patience, child—always remember patience."*

But try as she might, Aurya could not find any answers in these visions. And, although she often lectured Giraldus on the need for patience, just as Kizzie had once lectured her, that virtue was eluding her right now. She needed to know. *Now.*

Aurya stopped pacing. She refilled her wine cup a third time, emptying the pitcher. With a deep breath, she forced the thoughts of the future from her mind and turned instead to the past, to Tambryn and his scroll, and to the one other thing she might try in order to find her answers—if she dared.

This conjuring would be far more difficult. The future, especially the near and personal future such as she had just viewed, was a thread of time still bright with use. With the gift and the proper training, it was easily found and followed. At any fair there were gypsy women who claimed to see the future and would tell you, for a price of course, what lay ahead. It was a role she had played herself in order to meet Giraldus. She, therefore, understood better than most that the majority of these "gypsies" were fakes, performers who based their "predictions" on the experienced understanding of human desires rather than true magic. But Aurya also knew that there were, occasionally, true seers among them whose visions of the future could not be dismissed.

But to go back into the past, either to let one's spirit walk among the long-dead or to call the spirit of one of them forward—that took true magic. Aurya only dared it because need demanded no less. To visit the past, especially a past six centuries distant—to find that one silver thread amid the tangled weavings of existences already spent and follow it back to its source—that was a profound magic Aurya had never tried.

If something went wrong, her spirit could become trapped in the past, unable to find its way back to the present life. Or, if her spell was not precise, her skill not equal to or greater than the spirit she now thought to Summon, what awaited would be worse than death or oblivion. Her body, her will, her powers, could be overpowered by what she had conjured and compelled to do its bidding here. Her body would live on as before, but without a consciousness or mind to call its own.

Taking a sip of her wine, Aurya went back to sit before the fire. She closed her eyes and concentrated, going through the spell she would use to be certain she remembered it all. When at last she felt ready she went to the door and opened it, listening. Finally, she heard Giraldus's voice, one among many, raised in an old drinking song. She smiled; when Giraldus reached this stage, it could be safely assumed he would be hours yet in his cups.

Satisfied, she closed the door and locked it. She could not risk interruption. Then she went to the table and cleared it, rolling up both the map and the scroll. The map she put aside; the scroll she kept with her to use as a guide. She then turned the chair away from the fire and pulled it up to the table. Finally, she found a single candle in its holder by the bed, brought it to the table, and lit it.

When the candle was burning brightly, Aurya extinguished both the lamps in the room. All was ready for her to begin.

She took a seat in the chair at the table. Closing her eyes, she again began her slow breathing to center herself and call forth her magic. Once she felt that inner door open, she opened her eyes and focused on the candle. Without moving her sight from the tiny flickering flame, she reached to her belt and drew out her small dagger. She passed it through the candle flame, keeping her breath slow and steady as she softly began to chant in the old tongue.

"Tan ac dur, tan ac dur . . .

*

"Fire and steel, fire and steel;
Power to burn, power to kill;
I summon thee, I gather thee;
All power unto myself . . ."

*

She said the words three times, once with each pass of the blade through the flame. The candle was a small fire, its flame symbolic, but touched by the magic she was summoning, its heat was magnified far beyond its size. Aurya felt herself start to sweat as the dagger blade began to glow.

The third rotation completed, she drew another deep breath . . . then laid the hot blade to the palm of her left hand and sliced quickly and cleanly.

Burning pain seared through her as her flesh separated and blood began to flow. Moving quickly, she used her own blood to draw a circle on the center of the table. Inside the circle, she drew a pentagram, each point of the five-pointed star touching the outer circle. At the center of the star she drew another circle; its center became an inward-closing spiral. Aurya then lifted the candle from its holder, dropped some hot wax onto the very center of that spiral, and placed the candle there.

She held her hand above the candle so that her blood dripped onto the flame. She had no fear of it extinguishing—inside the circle, only magic could put out that fire. As the smell of burning blood began to swirl about her, Aurya began her incantation.

"*Middyr*," she called to the ancient god of the underworld. "I give Thee blood to pay the passage from Thy dark world. Blood and fire to feed Thee. Let Thou one specter pass and come again into this world. Guided by this flame, which blood has consecrated to Thy service, I call forth Tambryn to stand before me, held within this circle of blood."

Aurya took the scroll and laid it across the pentagram inside the circle.

"To the words his hands created, I summon Tambryn's spirit. By this circle bound; by blood and fire captive."

As Aurya watched, the air before her began to shimmer and stir. *It is working*, she thought jubilantly. Soon she would have the answers to all the hidden messages in the scroll. With the path made plain, the objective clear, nothing would stand in the way of the throne.

The disturbed air began to coalesce into the outline of a man. Before Aurya's eyes, the outline became more and more substantial. And it began to glow—first soft, and then the brilliant green of a woodland glade in summer sunlight.

The glow took Aurya by surprise. No reference to this Working had mentioned such a thing. Then she noticed an aroma filling the room. It was sweet, like flowers and growing herbs, with no stench of decay, no smell of the blood or the fire.

Now she was truly bewildered. She had prepared herself for the sight of death, the smell of rotting flesh. Instead, as the specter before her continued to solidify, she saw one who though old, exuded health and vigor, and who smelled of lush growing things.

"I come to your Summoning by my own choice, not yours," the image spoke to her, startling Aurya further. Its power to speak was supposed to be under her command.

"Are you the one whom history calls Tambryn the Seer?" she asked.

"Tambryn was my earthly name," he replied. "I was called many things—Seer, prophet, heretic, healer . . . and others. They do not matter now."

"Then, with the fire and blood by which I called thee forth, I now bind thee here, a spirit to serve the living. By fire and blood, I order thee to give me the answers I desire."

The spirit of Tambryn began to laugh. "I warned you that I came not at your Summoning. Your power cannot hold me. I came to teach you the price of your arrogance."

Tambryn waved his hand. On the table the candle toppled, hitting the scroll. The ancient parchment immediately caught flame. Aurya scrambled to put it out, smothering it with her hands and shirt. Though the flames burned her fingers, she did not dare pull away. If the scroll was lost, so was the crown.

Again she heard Tambryn's laughter. She looked up and saw his specter dissolving into the air, and she knew there was nothing she could do to stop him.

"Blind eyes see clearer than a darkened heart," he said, his voice still strong, though his image was almost gone. "And Prophecy's Hand lights the flame of Truth."

Then there was silence. It was more than silence, it was emptiness. Aurya felt as if, for the present at least, all the magic in the room—in her—had been drained away.

With the candle out, the only light in the room came from the fire. Aurya relit the lamps, grimacing as her burned fingers and sliced palm struggled with matches. She could do nothing to banish their pain now, not until her magic returned.

Once the lamps were lit, she wet a towel from the pitcher of washwater in the corner and wiped the table clean. Then she turned the chair back toward the fire and sat, needing to think.

She reviewed the steps she had just taken, trying to understand what had just happened and how the Summoning could have failed so miserably. She could find no mistakes; every word and action was performed exactly as it should have been.

Why then? she wondered again. *How did I fail?* She knew of nothing, neither history nor legend, that called Tambryn a worker of magic—and yet he had just shown a power few sorcerers could have claimed.

And what did his final words mean? she also asked herself. *What are these blind eyes and what do they see? And what is this Prophecy's Hand?* It was the same title used in the scroll, and it was just as frustrating—no, more frustrating to hear it from Tambryn himself and still not understand.

The charred scroll lay on the table. Aurya rose and went to it. Slowly, carefully, she unrolled it to examine the damage. The outer edges were burned away and there were holes where sparks had eaten into the parchment. But they had not penetrated all the way. The inner two-thirds of the scroll, including most of the directions she needed, was untouched.

Aurya breathed out a deep sigh of relief—and she could feel her magic returning. She still had what she needed to make certain Giraldus became King . . . and no spirit from the netherworld was going to stop her, no matter how powerful it might be.

Chapter Ten

L ysandra sat at the small kitchen table, talking with Father Renan. He had fed Cloud-Dancer, who now slept contentedly on a rug before the hearth, and the two of them had also finished their supper. So far, nothing of import had been revealed. In fact, Lysandra had done most of the talking, prompted to tell her tale by Father Renan's questions.

She found herself telling more than she had planned. By the end of their meal, he knew not just about her past, but about her dreams and her *Sight*, and about why she had come to Ballinrigh.

Finally, Lysandra had nothing more to say. Suddenly, Father Renan rose and left the room, leaving her bewildered.

A few minutes later he returned. "I have something to show you," he said, "something important. Give me your hand."

Something to show me? her thoughts sneered. *He can't show me anything.*

Then she realized that she was being petulant, her

thoughts peevish. But she was *tired*, physically and emotionally. She was tired of this journey and all the uncertainty; she just wanted to know what she had to do so that she could go *home*.

She held her hand out to Father Renan. He took it in his own and started to guide it toward something on the table. Instantly, Lysandra's *Sight* flooded her. There was no gentle lifting of fog this time, no slow lightening of shadows. Its force stunned Lysandra, leaving her breathless.

Father Renan placed her hand upon a scroll. As her fingers touched it, her *Sight* focused upon it. *This* was what all of her dreams and visions had been about—*this* was why she was in Ballinrigh.

"This is the Thirteenth Scroll of Tambryn," Father Renan said as he carefully unrolled the parchment. "It was written in his own hand over six hundred years ago. It is very rare—and very important."

"Who is Tambryn?" Lysandra asked. "I've never heard of him."

Father Renan chuckled mirthlessly. "Few people have anymore," he said, "and of those who have, few will speak his name."

He ran his fingers lightly, gently, across the parchment. For the first time there was a little chink in his well-armored emotions, and Lysandra could feel how much this scroll meant to him.

"Tell me about him," she said.

Father Renan did not speak at once, but sat as if trying to decide where to begin. Finally, he shook his head.

"Tambryn's story is a long one," he began, "and, perhaps, best kept for another time when the hour is not so late. In short, he was a monk, a man holy and true. He began his life as a Religious as an herbalist and healer.

But then, shortly after he turned thirty, his visions began. At first, he was proclaimed a Seer with the gift of divine prophecy—until he offended the wrong people. After that, he was named a heretic. But he escaped his captors and fled—no one knows where. The rest of his visions, if there were any, are lost to us. His writings were burned by those who did not want the people to learn the truth in Tambryn's words. Very few copies now survive . . . this is one of them."

"How did you get it?"

"That's not important," the priest replied. "What is important is the words this scroll contains."

As Father Renan spoke of Tambryn, the carefully maintained wall around his mind continued to slip little by little, giving Lysandra the barest glimpse of the man underneath. With her question, however, it snapped firmly back in place. On the one hand, it was a relief to be around a person whose inner thoughts and emotions did not constantly pound at her, disquieting each moment. But this unyielding control also made Lysandra wonder what Father Renan was hiding.

"Why is this scroll so important?" she asked him. "What does it have to do with me?"

Once more Father Renan ran his hand over the scroll, as if drawing some strength from touching it.

"Because," he said at last, "I believe you are the one whose coming was foretold. I have waited and watched carefully . . . and from the moment I saw you enter the church, something told me that my waiting had ended. You are the Prophecy's Hand whom Tambryn's writings say will find the Font of Wisdom. Together you will bring Aghamore back from the precipice of destruction before all is lost to darkness and evil."

Lysandra felt a shock run through her, a current containing both recognition and disbelief. She jerked suddenly to her feet, knocking her chair over.

"No, you're wrong," she said, backing away. She did not want to hear this; she just wanted to hear that she could go home.

"Am I?" Father Renan answered. "Tambryn's scroll says that Prophecy's Hand will be one who has lost everything to the instruments of destruction and who has walked in darkness, as one dead. Yet out of this death, a new life is born, so that Prophecy's Hand can *'Look through the Eyes of Blindness with a Sight that is more than seeing. Prophecy's Hand will know the ways of the wild ones and dwell among them. They will be both guide and companion. Only Prophecy's Hand can unlock the Font of Wisdom that will be the salvation of Aghamore.'"*

Slowly, Lysandra shook her head. Her stomach contracted into a tight and painful ball, and the sudden lump in her throat made it difficult to breathe. She wanted to reject everything she was hearing—but her heart and her *Sight* told her it was all true.

"I don't understand," she said. She wanted to run away, but instead she began to pace. The movement helped her think. "I'm no Seer. How can I be this Prophecy's Hand when I have no gift of prophecy?"

"You may have gifts you've not yet realized," Father Renan said softly. "But the scroll does not say Prophecy's Hand will have the gift of prophecy, only that it will deliver *this* prophecy into action.

"'. . . And so shall the way be shown by the clear, unsighted vision of Prophecy's Hand. Inner Sight shall know what eyes cannot see. The Font of Wisdom found, unlocked, then Truth embraced shall set free all that has been bound . . .'"

The scroll's words rang in her head. *Unsighted vi-*

sion . . . Inner sight . . . She could not deny these had been her reality for nearly a decade. But what was she supposed to do? What could she do, even with her *Sight*, one woman alone?

"What is this 'Font of Wisdom'?" she asked. "How is 'Prophecy's Hand' supposed to unlock it?"

"I don't have all the answers, Lysandra," he said to her. "I have studied Tambryn's words half my life, and until I saw you I didn't understand much of the description of what Prophecy's Hand was to be. Tambryn's prophecies often become clear only at the moment of their fulfillment. Or so it seems. But everything I do understand says that the Font of Wisdom is a child who must be found—and soon, before another King occupies the throne. If this latter is allowed to happen, it will mean the end of Aghamore.

"But as to how the child must be found and what will 'unlock' the Font of Wisdom—I'm not sure. There are directions here in the Thirteenth Scroll that indicate a journey north. But it also says that only through the *'blinded Sight of Prophecy's Hand can the Font of Wisdom be seen.'*"

Lysandra put her hands to her head, trying to stop her whirling thoughts. She must decide what to do, but she could not—not right now. She was too tired. She had wanted Ballinrigh to be the *end* of her journey, not the beginning of a new one.

Father Renan came over to her. He put his hands on her shoulders in a gentle, comforting touch.

"Have you found a place to sleep yet?" he asked. She shook her head.

"Then stay here," he offered. "The guesthouse is small and not lavishly furnished—but it is clean and warm. You and Cloud-Dancer could be quite comfortable there."

The offer was more than welcome, Lysandra realized. It was a prayer answered before it was voiced. "Thank you," she said.

Father Renan smiled. "I'll show you there so you can rest," he said gently. "A tired body often makes the mind see things as darker and more difficult than they are."

The priest retrieved Lysandra's bag. Cloud-Dancer had been lying next to it, silently watching Lysandra's movements. Now he rose and followed Father Renan. When he brushed against her, Lysandra's hand automatically came down to rest on the top of his head.

"I've never heard of a wolf so tame," Father Renan said, his voice filled with both marvel and admiration, "or of an animal and master being so close."

"We are both family and pack for one another," Lysandra affirmed, "though I doubt the men he ran off tonight would call him tame."

Father Renan chuckled. "Then I shall have to be careful to remain in your good graces."

He led the way across the small churchyard to a little freestanding house. Once they were inside, he turned his attention to starting a fire. With her *Sight*, Lysandra looked around her temporary residence, quickly memorizing its furnishings for the time when her *Sight* again faded. It was, as Father Renan had said, a small house. The main room, in which they stood, opened onto a cooking area to her right. To her left was a half-closed door into the bedroom.

The fire started with a blaze of light and heat. Father Renan stood, dusting off his hands on his cassock, leaving handprints that he completely ignored as he turned to her.

"There," he said, "that will soon put this place to rights. I'll bring some food over from the rectory. There's a garderobe through the bedroom and a personal midden—and the fire heats a small cistern, if you want to bathe."

"Thank you," Lysandra said. "This is far more than I expected."

"As I said, it's nothing fancy—but you'll be warm and safe here. I'll return in just a few minutes with those provisions, then I'll leave you so you can rest. We'll talk more in the morning, or whenever you're ready."

He left, and stillness descended. The only noise was the sound of the fire crackling on the hearth. It was a homey sound, full of comfort for both body and soul, and Lysandra felt some of the tension within her drain away. She went over and stood before the fire, letting the heat of it lick her legs, slowly travel up and warm the rest of her body.

There were two large chairs positioned a comfortable distance from the flames. She sank into one and let out a deep sigh of relief, of gratitude, of being safe within walls after so many days of travel, of finding a haven—for however brief a time—such as she had not thought a city like Ballinrigh would offer.

And the enticement of a bath, of hot water and being clean from the dirt of her travels—ah, that thought made Lysandra smile. It would take a while for the water to heat; while she waited she could close her eyes and absorb the silence, the peace.

Lysandra awakened to her own heart beating wildly, as if in panic or flight. She opened her eyes. All around her, the room seemed shrouded in a thick, swirling fog. The only light came from the embers of the dying fire and the half-full moon shining through the window.

Lysandra knew the dimness before her had nothing to do with the hour. Her *Sight* could make midnight bright as a summer day. This fog was trying to tell her something, as was the sense of fear and foreboding coursing through her body and mind. She forced herself to take a couple of deep breaths, trying to get past the grip of sensation and open herself to its meaning. Why was she so panicked? She was still in the guesthouse, safe and warm; there was no threat, no harm within these walls.

Then she realized it was not for herself that she was afraid. *Who then? Cloud-Dancer? Father Renan?* But no—they were safe; she knew with perfect certainty that her fear was not for them either.

Her *Sight* began to expand in a way it had never done before, taking her with it. Lysandra felt as if she were flying, and wondered, briefly, if she were still dreaming.

But this was too real to be a dream—and she found herself too stunned to be truly afraid. It was unlike anything she had ever experienced. How could she be sitting in her chair and yet be unconfined in her body?

A sense of urgency began to tug at her mind, pulling her along to newer and greater heights. She was higher than any bird could have flown, with all of Aghamore displayed beneath her like a patchwork quilt smoothed across a wide bed.

Across the kingdom a gathering fog swirled—sometimes thick and impenetrable, other times as barely a wisp. Here and there, bright lights shone like beacons or like stars come to Earth; the greatest of these lights was far to the north, where the land's end of Aghamore met the sea.

But a bitter darkness was also present. It sent swirling ribbons of danger inward, like fingers grasping through the fog. The darkness had the taint and smell of evil. Some of it, too, came out of the north—but the greater darkness was gathered in the west, pouring out over the land in a foul and steady stream. If it was not stopped and soon, it would extinguish the lights, and all hope would die in Aghamore.

In an instant, Lysandra was back in her chair. All sense of Far-Seeing vanished. With it, her *Sight* went, too. She was left within her physical blindness, made all the more complete because of what she had just experienced.

She called for Cloud-Dancer, not knowing that he was already standing by her side until she felt his head press itself beneath her fingers. She welcomed his presence and his comfort. As she ran her fingers through his fur, a certainty she did not welcome filled her.

"We have to go, don't we?" she said to him.

Cloud-Dancer pressed against her. He laid his head on her lap in silent reassurance. At least she would not be going anywhere alone.

But where was she going? Father Renan had mentioned north, and so had the vision she had just witnessed—but north was a big place in which to look for a single child. Father Renan had also said that the scroll contained directions . . . but she could not read them; the words she had *seen* meant nothing to her.

Lysandra found herself wanting to scream her fury at God or the Fates or . . . whatever . . . that found it such a cosmic joke to send her on a quest where her only guide was something she could not understand.

Then Cloud-Dancer turned his head and licked the palm of her hand. The gentle action made Lysandra smile. Then she sighed, realizing that her anger could neither help her nor change the course of what was to come.

She put her arms around Cloud-Dancer's neck and laid her head on top of his, sitting there for a moment and letting the last of her frustrations drain away. Tomorrow would take care of itself. Tonight, she had comfort, and she intended to avail herself of it. The embers of the fire were still warming the water. She would have a bath and sleep in a bed—and then tomorrow, clean and rested, she would leave Ballinrigh for the road once again, trusting in whatever had brought her thus far to guide her once again.

In the morning, Lysandra awoke shortly after dawn. The daylight noises of the city were already building, filtering in through the windows and walls of the little guesthouse. It was noise such as she had not heard before, even on market day when she was a child in Scorda.

It took her a quick moment to remember where she was. Then everything came flooding back—and with it came the same angry frustration she had felt last night. She tried to push that feeling from her as she pushed back the bedclothes, but it was not so easily removed. She would have to ride out this internal storm and try not to be drowned by its fury. It might even serve to push her farther down the direction she needed to go.

Resigned, if not happy, she dressed, and entered the main room of the little house. She had no *Sight* to guide her today as she got herself oriented, then found the cooking area and the food Father Renan had brought last night while she slept. Leaving out enough to feed herself and Cloud-Dancer, she used the rest to replenish the provisions in her bag, hoping Father Renan would not mind. Then, after fueling her body for the upcoming trek into the unknown, she again shouldered her bag, took up her walking stick, and, with Cloud-Dancer by her side, left her safe, if temporary, haven.

Father Renan was not in the rectory when she knocked, so Lysandra headed for the church. She entered through the back door of the sacristy through which they had exited last night. The thick stone walls of the church once more blocked the outside noises of the city, and, as the door closed behind her, Lysandra was again enveloped in the silence she had found when she entered this building the evening before.

Lysandra felt the anger drain and a new strength come from being in this quiet place. She still did not understand why this task should have fallen to her, nor did she feel qualified to accomplish it. But she realized that understanding might well be less important than acceptance after all.

Entering from the sacristy into the sanctuary of the altar, Lysandra tried to sense Father Renan's presence. Though she thought he must be here, she received no more impression of his nearness now than she had last night, and again she realized that he was the only person who had ever been so totally shielded to her.

She put out her hand for Cloud-Dancer, and when he put his head beneath her fingers, she again borrowed his vision to look around the little church. Father Renan sat in the same back pew Lysandra had occupied last night. He was deep in contemplation or prayer, his eyes closed and his face lit with a look of peaceful listening. Lysandra did not want to disturb him at such a moment.

She did not have to say anything, however, for he immediately looked up as she approached and gave her a smile. She saw that he had changed his cassock for warm traveling clothes and stout shoes, and that on the pew next to him rested a bag of provisions similar to hers.

"Ah, there you are," he said. Standing, he slung the bag over one shoulder. "Are you ready to go, then?"

"Ready?" she replied. "I am, certainly—but you? You have this church and its people to care for."

Father Renan shook his head. "I have sent a letter to

the office of the Archbishop explaining that I have been called away on urgent business. Another priest will be sent in my absence. I believe we all have a task ahead, if Aghamore is to be saved. Mine, like Cloud-Dancer's, is to walk by your side. You cannot read the scroll, but I can. I will read it and try to interpret its meaning. I will also try, to the best of my ability, to give you what help and strength I can."

Lysandra felt herself humbled and moved by his generosity. In this instant, there seemed a chance they might succeed after all.

"Thank you," she said softly. "So, where are we to go now?"

"North," Father Renan replied. "North lies all hope of the future for this land—and may God in His mercy direct our feet."

"Amen," Lysandra whispered, meaning the word with all her heart.

Chapter Eleven

The College of Bishops had been convened and, as Elon had expected, nothing was being accomplished. Everyone had plenty to say; Elon often thought that some of his brother bishops had only gone into the Church because they were in love with the sound of their own voices and it gave them authority to use them—too often and too loudly.

Elon, himself, had stayed silent and listened. So far there had been much discussion about the last few Kings and the problems with the House of Baoghil in general. Now, finally, the talk was turning to the future of Aghamore. As he had known would happen, each of the bishops was beginning to put forth the Baron of his province as the only right choice for the next High King.

Elon was exceedingly glad when, finally, the meeting was adjourned for Evening Prayer and then for the night. Pleading a headache, he turned down two invitations to dine. All he wanted was some hours free of the pomposity that now filled his days—and would until the bishops came to some consensus.

Once he returned to his house in Ballinrigh, he went straight to his wardrobe chamber where Thomas was waiting to help him divest. Thomas was, perhaps, the only individual to whom Elon could speak his mind freely. Time had proved that Thomas knew how to guard his tongue.

"You should have heard them today, Thomas," Elon said, as his manservant helped him undo the long row of buttons that closed the front of his purple cassock. "They sat around making as much noise as a bunch of hens in a barnyard—and accomplishing about as much, too. Who *cares* if the House of Caethal gave us 'Good King Stephan' sixteen reigns ago? We need to look to the *next* King, not the past ones."

Thomas said nothing as he eased the cassock from Elon's shoulders, put it aside to be aired and pressed, and held out the bishop's dressing gown. Elon shrugged it on and knotted the belt around his lean waist.

"And you should hear of the candidates we're offered,"

he continued. "To listen to the bishops talk, you'd have to believe that every one of the Barons is more pious than the last. Each one of them has promised great things for the Church—*if* we support his right to be King. I say, if they are so very devout, why don't they make these offerings or build these shrines regardless of the succession?"

Elon turned to see Thomas smiling knowingly. The sight drained away some of Elon's frustration with the day, and he began to see some of the humor Thomas obviously did.

"Yes, I know," he said. "I want *my* Baron on the throne, too. But at least Giraldus doesn't pretend a piety he does not feel—and we'd get a strong warrior besides. He'd make an adequate King on his own, and with myself and Lady Aurya to back him, he'll make a *great* one."

"Do you think you can get the other bishops to support him?" Thomas asked as he hung up Elon's mozzetta and brought down the box to put away the bishop's biretta.

Elon shook his head. "Not yet . . . but in time. I thought I'd let them argue for a while and keep Giraldus's name out of it. When it becomes clear that they will reach no other agreement—then I'll speak out. Perhaps, then, they'll be ready to hear what I have to say . . . or enough of them will, anyway."

"And if they're not?"

Elon turned and looked Thomas in the eyes. "As I said, Thomas, Giraldus is a strong warrior. *He* will be King— and *I* will be Archbishop. If I cannot reason my brother bishops into their support, there are . . . other means."

Elon could see that Thomas understood exactly what he meant. In the quarter of a century they had been together, many things had come to be understood between them. Just as Thomas alone, of all Elon's servants or other acquaintances, knew the bishop's active interest in the occult, Elon knew the secrets of Thomas's past.

Quiet, capable, subservient Thomas was the son of an outlaw and had ridden in his father's band for several years; he had robbed, raped—and murdered—along with them. Then, at twenty-three, Thomas had left that life, changed his name, and set out on his own to find an honest means of living. Through a series of other jobs and chance encounters, he had finally come to Elon's attention.

The newly appointed Bishop-ordinary of Kilgarriff engaged Thomas as a body servant and dresser. But it was not long before Elon realized there was more to his new hireling than had first appeared. Something in the way he kept himself apart sparked Elon's curiosity until, finally, he called upon several of the private contacts he already held throughout the provinces to discover the secrets hidden within Thomas's habit of silence.

Now only Elon knew Thomas's real name. He also knew that his parents were still alive and just what the law would do if these secrets were ever revealed. This knowledge had ensured Thomas's trustworthiness in the beginning of his service with Elon. Now, twenty-five years later, they were unnecessary.

Over the years, Thomas had come to share his interest in the occult and it, too, had created a bond between them. They were not friends exactly—Elon did not have anyone to whom he would grant that title, which suited him well. But they were more than employer and servant. They were partners of a sort, unequal but partners.

"Is there a fire in my private study?" he asked.

"Yes, Your Grace," Thomas replied. "I thought you might want one tonight."

"Precognitive powers, Thomas—or just a lucky guess?"

"Is there really much difference, Your Grace, if the ends are the same?"

Elon gave a sardonic bark of a laugh. "Perhaps not. Very well, Thomas, that's where I'll be. You can bring my supper and some wine there—but see to it yourself. No one is to disturb me. Use whatever excuse you need, but make certain that order is carried out."

Thomas gave Elon a slight bow. "As you wish, Your Grace."

Once Thomas had left, Elon headed for the private room next to his bedchamber. Like the room at his Residence in Ummera, the entrance to this room was hidden from casual eyes. Only he and Thomas had a key . . . and only he and Thomas knew of its contents.

Elon unlocked the door and went in. A fire burned steadily upon the hearth and the well-trimmed lamps were lit but turned down low, ready for him to adjust as suited his purpose. A bottle of claret had been decanted and set upon the oak sideboard near the fire.

This was the first visit he had made to this room since his arrival in Ballinrigh. He did not know how Thomas had guessed he would do so tonight; he had not known himself until the carriage ride back from the cathedral. The question he had posed to Thomas about precognition had been a jest, but for a moment Elon was not certain where jest ended and truth began.

On the table next to the chair burned one of the lamps, situated for ease of reading. Under it was the very book Elon had planned to study tonight. Once again, Thomas had anticipated him—and again Elon wondered how Thomas could have known. *How long has he been doing this and I've not noticed?* Elon wondered.

There was a soft knock on the door, and Thomas entered carrying a tray with the bishop's dinner—which he placed on the sideboard just where Elon would have told him.

"Come over here, Thomas," Elon said, "and have a seat. I want to talk to you."

"As you wish, Your Grace," came the always-subservient reply.

Elon waited until Thomas was seated comfortably. He waited, watching his manservant more carefully than usual, noting the signs of age that had touched Thomas's hair and face. Then he rose and went to the sideboard. He filled another goblet with wine and handed it to Thomas.

At first Thomas was hesitant. "Go on, take it," Elon pressed. "For a little while, let's put status aside and talk together. We've certainly known each other long enough for that."

Once Thomas had accepted the goblet, Elon went back to his chair. As he sat, he picked up his own goblet and sipped from it, watching Thomas above the rim. The servant sat ramrod straight, obviously ill at ease with this sudden change of venue.

"Relax, Thomas," Elon said. "I mean you no ill will."

"I know that, Your Grace."

"And for now, here in private, call me by my name," Elon continued. "We've been together for a quarter of a century—longer than I've known anyone steadily, even my own parents. For the sake of those years, let us forgo formality for a time."

Thomas nodded silently, as if unsure how to answer. Elon sighed but accepted it, hoping relaxation would come.

"You were what, twenty-four, when you came into my service?" Elon asked. "So you're . . . forty-eight, forty-nine now?"

"Forty-nine next week, Your—Elon."

"Forty-nine—a good age. Still strong enough to enjoy

life but without the follies that mark one's youth. You're of the laity, Thomas—did you never think to marry?"

"Never. I think that to marry, to be a husband, one needs to feel completely loyal to one's wife. I knew that my loyalty would always be divided."

Elon could see Thomas slowly beginning to relax. That would be necessary for what Elon hoped to accomplish tonight. He decided to keep up the casual conversation for a while yet.

"But you do not try to live by the rule of celibacy imposed on the clergy?" the bishop continued.

"Well . . . no," Thomas answered slowly. "No, I don't. I am a man, after all." His mouth quirked quickly toward a smile and back. "There are a couple of women in Ummera whom I . . . visit."

"A *couple*," Elon said, smiling himself. "Very good, Thomas. Who are they—anyone I know?"

"No one within the household, if that's what you mean. I would never . . . One is a serving maid down at The Fox and Eagle, and the other is a well-landed widow who lives across town. They don't expect more than I can give them—and neither do I."

"Just a bit of . . . warmth and companionship, shall we say?"

"Just so," Thomas agreed. "'Tis a sensible arrangement that suits all of us. They've no desire to give up their freedom, and neither do I."

Elon allowed himself a smile as he took a long sip of his wine. Thomas's posture had relaxed as he sat back in his chair. It was time to ask a few different questions.

But gently, gently, Elon told himself. He got up and went to the sideboard to retrieve the decanter of claret. Then he refilled both his own wineglass and Thomas's.

"I think, Thomas, I've come to take you for granted

over the years," he said as he sat back down. "An easy thing to do after so long together. But I can't help thinking how often you have things exactly as I want them before I tell you—almost before *I* know. Such anticipation is a great talent . . . and it could be a sign of an even greater gift."

"What gift?" Thomas asked. Elon did not miss the touch of wariness that sprang into his eyes.

"I mentioned precognition before. Do you know what that is?"

Thomas shook his head.

"Well, I suppose it can seem like just a guess," Elon began, trying to keep the explanation simple for now. He did not want to destroy the relaxed atmosphere. "But it's the *right* guess and the *right* time, more often than not. I think you have that ability. With a little training, it can be developed to serve more useful purposes than opening my study or laying out my clothes."

"What sort of training?" Thomas asked. His wariness had diminished, slowly being replaced by curiosity.

"Oh, nothing too difficult—and certainly not dangerous. Just some mental exercises to build what is already there, such as a soldier exercises to build his muscles or his skill with arms."

This explanation seemed to satisfy Thomas; Elon was gratified to see the last of the wariness fade and a burgeoning look of eagerness replace it.

"Tell me, Thomas—I know you've some interest in the . . . things I study here. Do you ever read these books on your own? It's all right—tell me the truth."

"Well," Thomas spoke hesitantly, "sometimes, when I'm opening the room and waiting for the fire to set, I look through one or two. Most of them are in foreign tongues, and those I can't read at all. But the ones I can—well, you told me I might, years ago."

"And I meant it." Elon got up and crossed the room to the chest where some of the books he had brought with him were stored. He knelt and lifted the lid, then carefully rummaged through them until he found the slim volume he wanted. It was a very old book from the land of Cilicia, handwritten and bound by leather that was tied together by a tarnished silver cord. Loose pages had been tucked into the back, where Elon himself had added a translation.

He brought the book back to the table. "I have here a book I want you to study. Every day. We will be here in Ballinrigh for—who knows how long. While I am gone each day, you are to find time to come in here and read . . . of course being careful that none of the other servants sees you."

"I understand," Thomas replied, his eyes focused greedily on the book.

Elon handed it over to him. Carefully, Thomas undid the cord and opened the volume. Then his expression changed as he saw the foreign writing.

"I . . . I can't read this," he said.

"No, I didn't expect you to," Elon replied. "It is the pages in the back you are to study. Those I translated, and those you *can* read."

Eagerly, yet still being careful of the aged pages, Thomas turned to the translation. One glance and his face lit up with anticipation. Elon was glad to see it. A plan was forming in his mind, one in which Thomas might well play a key part.

"I think it best if the book does not leave this room," Elon said. "We would not want the wrong eyes to see it.

But put it aside for now, Thomas. There is something else I would like to try."

He noticed how the servant's fingers lingered on the ancient volume. But he put it aside as Elon had requested.

"Now, Thomas, this is just one of those exercises that I mentioned. Nothing to be concerned about."

Elon took a candlestick from the mantel and lit the candle it held. Then, after turning down both of the lamps in the room, he put the candle on the table by his chair and moved it to be in front of Thomas.

"There," he said. "Now, Thomas, I want you to listen to the sound of my voice while you look at the candle flame." As he spoke, he came around Thomas's chair and placed his hands on the younger man's shoulders.

"Just relax," he continued. "Let your mind be free, empty, open. Feel the warmth of the fire, the comfort of the chair, the silence of the room. There is nothing but the sound of my voice and the candle flame. Watch the flame. There is only the flame and my voice. Let your body feel as if it is floating, warm and safe. Comfortable. Relax . . . relax . . . relax . . ."

Elon heard Thomas's breathing change. At the same moment, the man's shoulders went limp beneath his hands, and Elon felt a little burst of triumph. Ever since he was a young man, he had known his true sources of power were his intelligence and his voice, and he had learned to use them both to his advantage. But only once before had he used his skills as he was now with Thomas: on the woman who had been Aurya's mother. Even she had not responded so quickly or as completely as Thomas.

"Thomas, do you hear me?" he asked softly.

"Yes, Your Grace," came the reply. Elon smiled; even in this entranced state, Thomas thought of him by his title.

Perhaps that was the reason he responded so well; he was preconditioned to obedience.

"Thomas, are you watching the flame?"

"Yes, Your Grace."

"Good. Now, still relaxed, open your thoughts to whatever impressions might come. Tell me what you see in the flame."

There was silence for a moment. Elon kept his hands on Thomas's shoulders, but now he closed his own eyes and tried opening his own perceptions to see if he could share whatever vision Thomas might gain.

The silence deepened as the seconds ticked by. Elon refused to give up; even if nothing happened today, this was only a first attempt. Thomas was so receptive, Elon knew he could become far more valuable than just a manservant.

"I see," Thomas said hesitantly, "something . . . but it's not clear."

"It's all right, Thomas," Elon said, using his most soothing voice. "Relax . . . don't strain. Just watch the candle and let it come."

Inside his own mind, Elon could also see the beginnings of a vision, transmitted through his contact with Thomas. But it was too clouded to reveal more than indistinct blotches of shadow and light moving somewhere, somewhen.

Elon went on waiting, but the vision would not clear. Finally, it faded and disappeared. He was far from discouraged, however. This proved that Thomas had untapped potential—potential he could use in the quest for power ahead.

"Relax, Thomas," he said again as he lifted his hands from the man's shoulders. He came around and resumed his seat, thinking.

"Listen to my voice, Thomas," he continued. "When I tell you, you will awaken and you will remember what we accomplished here tonight. It will not frighten or upset you. Instead, you will be eager to train your mind for future use and greater control. Do you understand?"

"Yes, Your Grace."

"Very well, then—Thomas, wake up now."

The unfocused stare in the man's eyes changed. He blinked once, twice, then looked at Elon with a slow smile spreading across his usually reserved features.

"Did I really do that?" he asked. "Did I really see something in the flame?"

"Yes, Thomas—today you took a first step. But as I said, you now need to train your mind so that the images become clear. Soon you will not need my aid to reach that receptive state. But I think we have done enough for one day. Tomorrow, while I am gone, you will come here and begin your studies. For tonight, consider yourself off duty."

"Thank you, Your Grace," Thomas said as he stood and gave Elon a little bow, "and may I say, I enjoyed our conversation."

"As did I, Thomas—as did I."

After Thomas left, Elon blew out the candle and turned up the lamps again. Then he brought his supper from the sideboard to the little table. The way to the Archbishop's triple-crowned mitre suddenly seemed all the clearer.

With a true smile, Elon attacked his evening meal.

Chapter Twelve

With Father Renan now in the lead, Lysandra and Cloud-Dancer headed north out of Ballinrigh. Renan had first thought to head for Yembo in Lininch. But something—some personal intuition or divine guidance—told him that destination was too straightforward a solution to Tambryn's words. Oblique references to *the forgotten*, *the hidden*, and *those who dwell in the heart of the land* made him think there was another path to follow.

When he had first read those words, he thought they might refer to all the people of the kingdom whose voices were never heard at court; the farmers and shepherds, the hunters, merchants, crofters, craftsmen, and all the others who went about their business living quiet, simple lives. These were the "common folk" whose generations knotted the kingdom together, and who suffered most in the game of politics played by those who had vowed to undertake their care. Yet, as the miles went by, Renan began to believe that Tambryn meant something else entirely.

He possessed copies of all thirteen of Tambryn's scrolls. They were precious to him, reminders of both good and evil, and the only things from his previous life that he had kept when he entered the Church. Although some priests first join an Order, feeling the call to the priesthood only after life as a Religious, Renan had never felt compelled to become a monk, and therefore personal possessions were not banned to him. Still, the scrolls being what they were in the sight of the Church, they were the one thing he owned that he kept carefully out of sight.

Having a small parish in a poor area of the city allowed him to continue studying the scrolls without fear of discovery. Most of his parishioners could barely read, and none, he was certain, understood the ancient language in which Tambryn had written. Nor was the Archbishop likely to appear at his rectory door; like every other parish in the cathedral city, when the people had episcopal needs they went to the cathedral, *to* the Archbishop, not the other way around.

But though he had read all thirteen of Tambryn's scrolls it was this final one that time and again compelled him to unlock its secrets. It was almost as if a voice whispered constantly in his ear, demanding that each night, when all of his other duties were done, he turn again to the scroll. In these last seven months, since King Anri died, the whisper had oft times felt like a shout.

Yet there had been so much he did not understand—until Lysandra appeared. As they had talked, piece after piece had fallen into place. And as understanding had dawned, a new compulsion filled him, telling him not only that here indeed was Prophecy's Hand, but that he must go with her and help her as she undertook the fulfillment of Tambryn's visions.

But how? For that he still did not have the answers. Yes, he could read the scroll for her, as he had said, and help ease the journey as best he was able—but the same small voice that had directed him to study Tambryn's words now told him there was something more for him to do. He hoped he would have the strength for whatever lay ahead, and yet he feared it, too; he feared he might be called to break the one vow he had made in his life before the Church, the vow he held more dearly than his life.

But did he hold it more dearly than hers? More dearly than this kingdom's? How many lives were worth his vow?

They kept off the main roads and away from the heavy traffic, traveling by back routes as much as possible. By the third day they reached the more rural areas of Urlar. Here, many of the roads were little more than cart tracks, and buildings became dots viewed from a distance amid large tracts of farmland where trees had been cleared.

By the fifth day, they had reached the foothills where the mountains curved west like a hand cupped around Urlar. To the east, these mountains created the border between Urlar and Lininch; to the north, the direction they were now headed, the mountains extended part of the way along the Urlar and Rathreagh border as well.

There were well-traveled passes leading through the mountains, and, until he knew better, Renan was heading in their direction. But he did so reluctantly, still feeling they would do best to avoid being seen.

The more time he spent traveling with her, the more fascinating Renan found Lysandra. At their first meeting, during their long talk after Evensong, Lysandra had told him all about her blindness and its cause, about the inner *Sight* that helped her function as a healer, and about the wondrous gift of being able to share Cloud-Dancer's vision. But hearing of them was different than witnessing the abilities in action.

It is often as if she sees better than I do, he found himself thinking on more than one occasion. *I can only see a thing's form—she can see its Truth. She has the expe-*

rience of beholding how this world is "beautifully and wonderfully made." I envy her that joy.

Renan also admired Lysandra's tenacity. Walking all day was proving to Renan that he had spent far too much time in the city and in his church. He no longer had the muscular vitality of his youth.

Lysandra, on the other hand, trudged along as if covering twenty miles in a day was nothing out of the ordinary. With her bag slung over her shoulder, her walking stick in one hand and the other usually resting on Cloud-Dancer's head, she walked as if fatigue was something unknown to her.

Well, it's known to me, Renan thought as he adjusted the weight of his pack, silently apologizing to his body for all the exercise he had not given it over the years.

It was time to call a halt—and not just for the sake of his aching muscles. Renan felt the need to consult the scroll again. Now that they were entering the foothills, he could not shake the feeling that there was something near, something for which they should be watching. Unfortunately, he had no idea what that something might be.

As they finally neared the large stone outcropping Renan had been using for a reference, he called the day's halt.

"What do you think of this for our campsite?" he asked Lysandra while he gratefully eased the burden from his shoulders.

She walked around the area, using her touch to tell her what her eyes could not. Then she nodded. "It's a good choice," she told him. "The stone will keep us out of the wind, and it will reflect back some of the heat from our fire—once we find some dry wood, that is."

Renan left Lysandra to build a ring of stones for the fire and pile up layers of fir needles and bracken for their beds while he went to find the wood they would need. It was a task easier started than accomplished, however. Although the weather was warming, it had been a wet winter and an equally damp early spring.

Renan did manage to find an armload of burnable wood, enough to get their meal cooked and give them a bit of comfort through the night. But when he returned to camp he found that Lysandra had not moved. She stood looking up at the top of the little stony ridge, as if transfixed by something she alone could see.

"We need to go up there," she said when Renan neared. She raised her hand and pointed. "Up there, to the top."

"Why?" Renan asked. "I know I'm not as trained in the wilds as your life has made you, but I'm fairly certain this is a better place to camp."

Lysandra continued to stand as one transfixed. Her hand did not lower; her sightless eyes did not turn away.

This is not about the camp, Renan thought as he looked around for the best path upward. They would have to make the climb in a series of switchbacks, and even then it would be steep. But it was better than trying to scale the stone's face—something he doubted he could have done ten years ago and certainly could not now. And Cloud-Dancer was a wolf, not a mountain goat. As for Lysandra, he was beginning to think she could do almost anything.

He lifted his pack and once more slung it onto his shoulders, grunting a little as the weight settled onto his tired, protesting muscles. "This way, then," he said. "We go back to go forward, eh?"

Renan kept his voice light. So far, all the smiles she had given had been timid, unsure, as if they were something she was just rediscovering . . . and he had not heard her laugh at all.

Just how deep do the wounds from her past go? he found himself wondering. He hoped that a way for her true healing could be found—perhaps even by this journey. He did not know exactly what lay in store for them along the way, but his faith told him that everything happens for a reason. He would trust that; just as he believed Lysandra was Prophecy's Hand, he believed everything she had endured had prepared her for this destiny. Perhaps, given time, she would come to believe it, too, and the belief would bring her comfort.

Lysandra said nothing on the upward trek. There was a sense of expectation about her that Renan did not want to disturb. She moved as if in a daze, unaware of her actions. Renan watched, but surreptitiously, afraid that too open a stare might make her self-conscious and she would lose the sense of whatever was guiding her.

They finally reached the top of the outcropping, a shelf of stone. Where it pushed out from the hillside stood three large, straight stones. Suddenly, another line from the scroll dropped into place for Renan. Could these be the Three Sisters looking West Tambryn's words had described? He drew forth the words from memory and whispered them to himself.

"Three Sisters looking West, sentinels between two worlds. Prophecy's Hand shall point the way; a companion is the key to that which is forgotten."

Lysandra had indeed pointed the way, but what was the key and what had been forgotten? What were the two worlds of which Tambryn spoke?

Renan walked over to examine the tall stones. The first of them revealed nothing more remarkable than moss and lichens. He moved on to the next one, standing in the center. This stone stood out a little more from the hill, far enough that by dropping his pack, he could squeeze behind it. Dirt and woodland debris had piled up over the years, and Renan began using his feet to kick the way clear.

The pile of leaves and dead branches did not move easily. Renan had to kneel and use his hands to break the knot time had woven. Little by little, he cleared the debris, revealing a small opening in the face of the hillside. It was only about three feet tall and maybe as wide—but it was big enough for a person to crawl through if he tried.

First he needed a torch. He came quickly out from behind the stone and began to gather up some of the deadwood he had just cleared, concentrating on long, thin branches that he hoped would burn well. Once he had a good handful, he began to rummage in his pack for something to tear into strips to bind the branches together and to keep the wood from burning down too quickly.

"What is it?" Lysandra asked, stepping close to him. "What did you find?"

"I'm not sure yet," Renan told her. "It might be nothing more than a small cave. I'm going to find out."

"How can I help?"

"I'm trying to make a torch. Do you have anything that might help?"

"Yes," Lysandra replied, swinging her bundle off her shoulder. From it she produced a roll of cloth cut for bandages and a small vial.

"Here," she said. "The vial is an antiseptic I brew myself. It's quite flammable. You won't need much to keep your torch burning."

Renan accepted the offering gratefully. "What other wonders do you have in there?" he asked as he wound some of the cloth around the top of his torch.

"Medicines," Lysandra replied. "Herbs that I've grown

or gathered, a few little pots of salves, some ground roots and the like . . . just what I thought I might need on such a journey. I thought I was bringing too much—now I'm glad I did."

Renan had always wanted to know more about the healing properties of plants; he had little opportunity to learn, living as he did in the kingdom's largest city. But the torch was now ready to be lit. *There will be other times,* he told himself, *other evenings, other campfires and conversations. I'll ask her more then.*

From his pocket Renan withdrew the little box of matches he carried. Matches were relatively new to Aghamore. They had been brought by a trader about ten years ago, but they had swept through the country with the speed of their own blaze and were now easily accessible. Renan, like most people, carried them wrapped in oilcloth to keep them dry. The second the tiny flame touched the torch it ignited the spirits he had drizzled on the cloth, producing a fine steady light.

"Wonderful," he said to Lysandra. Then he headed again toward the back of the stone.

This time, Lysandra and Cloud-Dancer accompanied him. She held the light while Renan cleared away the last of the debris from the front of the little opening. There was not enough room between the standing stone and the face of the hillside to lie flat and squirm through the entrance, as Renan would have preferred. Instead he knelt; his knees were so hardened by his life as a priest that he hardly noticed the bits of coarse dirt and little twigs and stones beneath them.

Lysandra handed him the torch. Renan pushed that through the opening first, followed by his head and one shoulder. It was a bit of a tight fit, but before he squeezed the rest of his body through, he wanted to see what awaited him on the other side.

Directly before him was a ledge, perhaps four feet wide by ten feet long. It ended in a series of wide and gently sloping switchbacks that led into a huge cavern below. The presence of what was so obviously a trail puzzled him; he could think of nothing in nature that would have produced such a wide and regular pattern—and nothing about the entrance had suggested it was hand hewn.

Perhaps this is an abandoned mine, he thought as he squeezed the rest of his body through the opening.

Now he stood and held the torch high. The sight that greeted his eyes astonished him with its beauty. Veins of crystal ran through the walls, reflecting the flickering light of his torch. Some sort of glistening element also covered the stone itself, amplifying the brightness of the torch so that the cavern looked as bright as day. It would have been easy to stand and stare, lost in wonder. But time was pressing, and Lysandra was awaiting his word.

Renan turned and called back to her. "It's safe," he said. "I'll come back out to help you through."

"No need," Lysandra called back.

A moment later she pushed their packs through. Renan quickly moved them out of the way. Cloud-Dancer came next, then Lysandra herself eased through the gap in the stone.

He hastened toward her to help her stand, but she waved him away. Looking at her face, now smudged and dirty—no doubt like his own—he could tell that the *Sight* was still with her. Her eyes continued to stare in the unfocused manner of the blind, but there was a watchfulness to her expression that showed in the twitch of her eyebrows and the tightening of her lips.

And there was something more, something Renan tried

to define and failed. The only word he could think that came close was *Otherness*—and he wondered if mystics wore the same expression when divine visions were upon them.

"What is this place?" Lysandra asked as she stood.

"I don't know," Renan replied. "This ledge, the trail leading down, must have been artificially made. I'd guess we've just crawled in through the airhole of an abandoned mine."

"Why would a place like this be abandoned?" Lysandra asked. "It's so beautiful."

And beautiful it was. Veins of crystal—some clear, some colored—shimmered and sparked as if a fire had been lit within their heart. The natural angles and facets threw the light outward in all directions, making it dance to creation's still whispered song.

The effect was breathtaking. But, finally, Renan tore his eyes away and reached for his pack. With his movement, Lysandra did the same, and soon they started down the stone ramp. It was only when they reached the cavern floor, however, that Renan realized the full magnitude of the place. The tall spires on which the glowing phosphorous clung were easily five times the height of a man— and they reached less than halfway to the ceiling. It was like walking through a land of giants as he and Lysandra followed what felt like a natural path between the spires.

"*'Many, O Lord, are the wondrous works which thou hast done'*," he breathed in reverence of the hand that had placed such things within the earth—and that had granted him the privilege of seeing them.

As they walked through the cavern, Renan leading the way with the torch, he slowly realized that the air was a comfortable temperature, quite unlike any of the caves he had explored as a boy. Soon he began to notice the bright veins of what could only be gold streaking the cavern walls. Seeing these, his mind echoed Lysandra's earlier question—why would such a place be abandoned?

"*That which is forgotten,*" the prophecy had said, and that certainly described this place. Nowhere could Renan remember hearing tales of its existence, not even among old legends or fairy stories told to children. Nor, he decided, would he tell anyone. Greedy hearts and hands would soon reduce this beauty to rubble if the world ever heard of the wonders he was seeing.

But wonder was giving way to hunger and fatigue. They had hiked many miles today before finding the cavern, and more walking underground. It was time for food and a night's slumber.

Upon finding a wide, flat place between the stalagmites, Renan once more shrugged his pack from his shoulders. He wished they could have a fire, but there was no wood. Which meant that when the torch guttered out, there would be nothing more to replace it.

"At least the air is warm," he said to Lysandra when she stopped beside him and also dropped her bundle to the ground. "And we've food and water enough for a while. I hope—"

"We will," Lysandra said. Her voice held no hint of doubt. "If we're in the right place and if this journey means everything you say, then we will find the way out. We must—"

"Have faith?" Renan said with a smile. "I suppose I should have been the one to say that first. Oh well—sometimes the spirit is as weak as the flesh. At least mine is. Now, let's make what camp we can, then eat and get some sleep. Maybe tomorrow we'll find . . . whatever we're supposed to find here."

Renan leaned the torch against a stone and turned toward his pack to bring out a canteen of water. The torch stayed propped for a moment—then fell to the side, as if pushed by an unseen hand. It sputtered and went out before Renan could turn again and grab it.

But the cave did not plunge into darkness, as he expected. Instead, the luminous substance covering the walls, which Renan had assumed was merely reflecting the light of the torch, continued to glow on its own. It cast a light bright enough to reveal their surroundings, yet the light itself was softer than torchlight, easier on the eyes and mind.

Renan heard Lysandra gasp, and he turned. The look of wonder on her face could only mean that her miraculous gift of *Sight* was with her once more, and she was also witnessing the strange beauty of this place. Renan picked up the extinguished torch and put it with his pack. He would carry it with them in case they reached a place where this luminance did not exist.

"Where do you think this place goes?" Lysandra asked. "Does the scroll say anything about it?"

Her questions brought Renan's thoughts back to the many unknown problems that might still be ahead of them. "I don't know," he answered. "I thought I understood the scroll's words—but now I'm not so sure. I would never have found those stones—*The Three Sisters*—if you had not pointed us upward. How did you know?"

He handed Lysandra the canteen, which she gladly accepted. While she drank, he found a comfortable place to sit, his back resting against a stone while he pulled some food out of his pack for their dinner.

Lysandra did not reply at first. She half turned away, looking poised for flight or condemnation.

"You'll think I'm mad if I tell you," she said.

"No, Lysandra," he said quietly, seriously. "No, I won't."

"I . . . I *saw* someone . . . up on the rock . . . gesturing for us to follow." Her words came haltingly, as if pulled from her.

Renan felt there was something more, something she was not saying. But from what he had already learned of her life, he realized how difficult it must be for her to let down her defenses. So he would not push; whatever she shared with him must be by her choice.

"Then I'm grateful your *Sight* was functioning just then," he said, "or we'd still be outside in the cold night air. Who knows how far we would have walked and never realized we were on the wrong path."

Renan could see Lysandra relax as she heard the acceptance in his words. She looked so unsure of herself, so like a little girl that he wanted to take her hands and tell her not to worry, that he knew she would not lie and that he would always believe her.

But she was not a little girl, he reminded himself—and he was a priest who must be careful that such gestures were not misunderstood.

"Come, sit and have some supper," he said to her instead. "I think there's enough light in here to read well enough, and after supper I'll check the scroll again. Maybe it will give us some clue about what might be ahead."

I don't remember any such thing, he thought silently. *But I could have read it and not understood. Whatever this place is, I hope we can pass through it quickly. We have food, but after three days we'll have no more water. Beautiful as this place is, I don't want it to be our tomb.*

Chapter Thirteen

"I is an accursed time of year to be traveling through mountain passes," Giraldus grumbled. "I don't care *what* waits on the other side."

Aurya said nothing. Giraldus had been grumbling all day and she was tired of trying to placate him. She, too, could wish they were making this trip in . . . oh, July would be nice. Then nature would have cleared the roadway; the meadows would be bright with alpine flowers and alive with the bees and hummingbirds come to drink the sweet nectar.

But the Spring-Fest in Yembo took place every year on May 1st—two days hence. The road through this pass, being one of the lowest and most wide, was kept tolerably free of snow in winter with plows pulled by teams of great Shire horses. They should be over the crest before nightfall and into Yembo by the following evening, the night before the festival.

Aurya had not told Giraldus of her failure with the spirit of Tambryn, nor her vision of them riding with armed escort through the streets of Ballinrigh. For the latter, she still had no true interpretation; as for the former, Tambryn's dismissal of her Summoning still rankled. Although she hated to admit it, even to herself, the ease with which he had defied her frightened her a little.

While Giraldus mumbled and complained about the weather, the condition of the roads, the lack of entourage, and anything else that struck his fancy today, Aurya brooded over her failure. Time and time again she reviewed the spell, but she could think of nothing she had done wrong. Tambryn's spirit had appeared as called; how had he been able to shatter it at will? Tales called him a monk, a mystic and prophet, even a heretic—but never a sorcerer. How much more about him did she not know?

The question was unanswerable, at least for now, yet Aurya's mind worried over it like a hungry dog with a bone. If that spell had not worked on Tambryn, perhaps she could Summon someone else from his time in history. But whom? Ah, that was a question more worthy of her attention than her failure in the past.

Huddled down beneath her cloak, she let her thoughts drift to the snow-muffled clop of the horses' hooves. Somewhere in history had to be the answer and the aid she needed.

Perhaps, she thought, *when we reach Yembo, the Three Sisters will know. The scroll says they will reveal "the forgotten."*

Aurya still did not know who—or what—the Three Sisters were, but she was confident she would recognize them. And their insight would be the key to the final stage of this journey. Then, armed with the knowledge she gained, she and Giraldus would turn north to find the child whom the scroll called the Font of Wisdom.

Elon had said the Font of Wisdom must be destroyed. But what, she thought now, if they did *not* have to kill it? A child could be easily controlled. If she trained the child to suit her purpose, to use its gifts in pursuit of *her* goals—would not that in a way be destroying it? It would not then be the Font of Wisdom as Tambryn described, but someone else entirely. And they could always kill it later, if the need arose.

Aurya had never felt any particular maternal stirrings, but now she found that the thought of having a young mind to mentor and train pleased her. They would not be seeking this child if it were a being without powers—although Tambryn was particularly oblique on just what those powers were.

This child, Aurya thought, *must have a wealth of potential waiting to be tapped. And I will be the force that taps and trains it.* She wanted to laugh out loud. She wished Tambryn's spirit were here now so she could tell him that he had dismissed her too lightly. Using *her powers*, she would make certain that his words and warnings were rendered meaningless. Now, in the *"rising of the Ninth House"* would be the *power* of the Third.

Aurya smiled to think of all that she could teach the child. It would not have to grope and stumble to find its direction in life, as she had before she met old Kizzie. This child would have a purpose and know it from the beginning—a purpose set and directed by *her*: to put Giraldus on the throne as High King of Aghamore.

"How can you smile?" Giraldus growled, snapping Aurya's thoughts back to the present. She had not noticed how the wind had picked up. But as she turned her face toward her lover, tiny beads of frozen snow slapped into her face like tiny needles, stinging her eyes and chapping her cheeks.

"I can smile because I see a great future," she told him.

"All your fine words and fancy predictions will be no good to frozen corpses," Giraldus replied angrily, "which is what we'll be if a storm catches us. Look up, Aurya—

the sky is dark, and the air is shouting a warning. Do you have magic enough to turn the winds aside or cause the snow to miss us?"

Aurya laughed out loud at his scowl. "The only magic we need is beneath us," she said.

She dug her heels into her horse's ribs. It shot forward, the snow giving purchase to its hooves. Aurya laughed, throwing the sound like a challenge into the wind and back at her companion.

"Come, Giraldus," she shouted, turning her head to look back over her shoulder at him. "What we cannot turn, we can outrun."

As she watched Giraldus, still scowling, put his heels to his horse's side. His stallion, trained to war, soon caught up to Aurya's gelding and side by side they raced to beat the weather.

Lysandra was not finding it as easy as Renan obviously did to fall asleep on the hard stone floor of the cavern—even if the temperature was comfortably warm. She missed the fresh moving air of the outdoors, and the sounds of the night creatures whose activities were her sweetest lullaby.

Although she had her cloak to cover her and her bundle for a pillow—and, of course, Cloud-Dancer sleeping by her side—she found no comfort in this place. Something here was keeping her awake, alert, and waiting.

She listened to the darkness, filled only with the sounds of her sleeping companions and with her own thoughts. Even these seemed designed to keep her from relaxation. Every doubt and question about this journey combined with the aches and stiffness brought on by long days on the road. She was still no hardened traveler—and all she wanted, especially during these long, dark, sleepless hours, was to turn around and go home.

Lysandra usually had a reliable internal clock, but tonight—if it was indeed night—she had no idea how much time had passed or how long it might be before her companions awakened. Turning over yet again and still feeling uneasy and uncomfortable, she was about to sit up and reach for a drink of water when she heard a sound that made her stop. She held her breath, waiting.

Yes, there it was again, so soft not even Cloud-Dancer stirred. But as she listened, Lysandra grew certain . . . it was the sound of a foot moving across stone.

Quietly, she put a hand on Cloud-Dancer and felt him awaken to her touch. Using her fingers, she signaled him to stay and to be silent. Then, moving as quietly as she could and staying low to the ground, she slithered over to Renan's sleeping body.

He was not a heavy sleeper and came awake with a start when Lysandra gently shook his shoulder. Before he could sit up or say anything, she put her fingers across his mouth and leaned close to whisper in his ear.

"I heard footsteps . . . coming closer. Don't move, but be ready."

She felt his single nod. Then, softly and silently as possible, she returned to her own sleeping place and resumed her recumbent position. She put out her hand and found Cloud-Dancer's head. Then, familiar contact made, she used his eyes to look around the cavern. Although her hearing still confirmed that . . . something . . . was moving their way, even Cloud-Dancer's vision revealed nothing.

Listening closely, scarcely breathing, she was now certain there was more than one set of footsteps. Five, no six, she was sure of—but there could easily be more; stone muffled sound. She tensed her body, ready to spring to her feet.

There, she thought she saw something, a moving shadow within shadow. There again . . . and there . . . she did not doubt it now.

Get ready, she told herself. *Ready . . . now.*

As the . . . beings . . . slipped silently out of the deep shadows, Lysandra leapt up. Cloud-Dancer came with her, staying in contact so their shared vision was not broken. Renan, too, was on his feet.

For a single moment, she felt too stunned to move as, through Cloud-Dancer's eyes, she saw what was approaching. They walked upright like humans, though the tallest was an inch or two shorter than she. They wore no clothes except folded and tied loincloths, but their small, compactly muscular bodies were covered with hair. Their faces looked as if beards and eyebrows had grown to meet each other, leaving only eyes and noses clear. Their noses were small, with wide and flattened, barely noticeable nostrils.

But their eyes were remarkable. They were large, twice the size of any human's, round and as light as Cloud-Dancer's. They had huge, black pupils that could open to let in light humans could not see and that were already contracting as they stepped into the cavern whose only illumination was the soft glow emanating from the stones.

Lysandra saw all of this in an instant—and she saw the weapons these creatures carried. Cloud-Dancer recognized that here was danger; Lysandra's mind gave the danger names: picks and axes, sharpened iron stakes and broad serrated blades with shapes somewhere between a sword and a shovel.

"Cloud-Dancer, hide," she ordered sharply. She would

not risk his injury—and his uncaptured presence might eventually provide their means of escape.

As he jumped to obey and their contact broke, Lysandra's world went once more into darkness. She still had her walking stick in her hand; she lifted it and swung with more hope than direction—then felt the shock run up her arm as it made contact. She kept swinging until her arms became as leaden as her spirit, but with no more lucky blows.

Any vestige of hope died as strong hands gripped her arms from behind. Fingers pressed sharply into her flesh, making her wince and cry out. Her walking stick was torn from her grip.

Lysandra did not struggle. The strength of the hands holding her told her that such an action was more than futile—it could result in herself or Renan being injured. Instead, she grew very still. She sent her attention inward, feeling each breath, each heartbeat, trying to find that place where her *Sight* dwelt and call it forth.

Nothing happened. *Oh, please,* she prayed with the faith of the desperate as the hands began forcing her to walk. Her footfalls dragged, but she was no match for the strength of her captors. They pushed and pulled her until her only choice was to move or fall and be carried.

Lysandra's only defense was to emotionally detach herself from what was happening. Her body still moved under the forced guidance of the unseen gripping hands, stumbling now and then over stones or bits of uneven ground. But her mind, her awareness, her concentration continued to look inward, striving to call her *Sight* to aid her as it had so often in the past. She tried with all her strength to find a way to control that which usually came or went only of its own accord.

She heard Renan beside her, struggling against his capture. His occasional grunts of pain told her that his efforts were no more successful than hers.

Though it was not easy, Lysandra forced thoughts of him aside to concentrate on the single purpose of regaining her *Sight*. She felt the sweat pool on her forehead, under her arms, and run down the middle of her back, as if her strain was physical. Though it was her mind and not her body that strove and struggled, her already-meager reserves of energy were quickly being exhausted.

There . . . she thought she sensed the first small glimmer. Was it only a desperate hope, or was it true? Yes . . . there again . . . this time more bright, more detailed. Lysandra wanted to shout an hurrah but she did not allow herself to show either elation or relief.

Suddenly, her *Sight* opened up the world before her— just as she and Renan were pulled into a cavern that dwarfed anyplace they had seen thus far. All around this huge arena ran ledges, row upon row, circling upward toward the ceiling in rings too regular to be natural. And filling these ledges were more of these . . . creatures. Hundreds, perhaps thousands—a community, a civilization, underneath the kingdom of Aghamore.

In the center of the cavern, a delegation was assembled and waiting. These were obviously the Elders of the tribe; the hair covering their bodies was streaked and mottled with gray. Lysandra counted thirteen, male and female. Twelve of them were dressed in similar fashion, with long cloaks about their shoulders that closed at the necks with great golden clasps, each one in a slightly different design.

Standing in the center was the eldest and obviously most revered among them. The hair covering his body was pure white. Around his neck he wore a great chain of braided gold-and-silver ropes; it was nearly as big around as Lysandra's wrist. Suspended from the chain was a diamond the size and shape of a duck's egg, encircled by precious stones of different colors. Emeralds and rubies, sapphires and amethysts, garnets, peridots, bright opals, and yellow topaz all sparked vivid fire around the shimmering diamond heart. He leaned on a staff the size of Lysandra's walking stick, but his was wound and crisscrossed with braids of gold and silver, like the thick necklace he was wearing.

The beings who encircled this great meeting place began to slap their feet upon the stone, uttering strange chirping sounds at the sight of Lysandra and Renan. The eldest leader now raised his staff above his head; all became suddenly silent in a way Lysandra found eerie and ominous.

The entire Council of Elders came toward them and encircled them. Lysandra had a chance now to look at their faces more clearly. She *saw* the bright intelligence that coupled with suspicion in their eyes.

While the tribal leaders stood their ground in the entrapping circle around Lysandra and Renan, the eldest one walked around them three times, looking them over from head to toe.

"Ye are Up-worlders," he said finally, "and be not welcome in our realm."

His voice had an odd burr to it, with rolled r's and slurred ess's—but Lysandra was relieved to know there existed the hope of communication. Where there was communication, there might also be understanding.

"We have not come to do you harm or take anything from you," Renan said, obviously sharing Lysandra's hope. "We are only seeking passage. We did not know you or this place existed."

"Lies," the old one shouted, bringing his staff down

sharply upon the stone floor. "Always Up-worlders speak lies. Always come they to dig and to destroy."

Again, the cavern erupted in the strange chirping cries of the onlookers.

"We do not lie," Renan shouted to be heard above the din. "We want *nothing* from your world. Show us the way out, and we will leave."

"Enough of thy lies," the old one said, again raising his staff for silence. "Up-worlders may *not* come unto the Realm of the Cryf—nor may they leave here to carry forth tales of our Realm unto others. *That* be our Law. To break this law is to forfeit thy life. Take them unto the Black Waters."

Where is Cloud-Dancer? Lysandra wondered as their captors started to close in again. She hoped her dearest companion would be able to escape and find his way back home to the Great Forest. She had no such hope for herself and Renan.

Suddenly she felt the wolf's nearness, felt the touch of his mind and his sight in a way she never had before. *Run,* she sent the thought to him, hoping he could sense or hear her as she was now sensing him. *Run . . . run and find the way out . . . run and be free . . . run.*

Cloud-Dancer did not hear or would not obey. Lysandra could feel him coming closer. His presence was stronger, the link between them so fixed that it was as if Lysandra now looked through two sets of eyes—her *Sight* and his vision.

Then, as the first set of hands closed upon her arms, Cloud-Dancer came running, leaping, snarling, from out of the passage and into the arena. He charged at her captors. He bit and snapped, growled and snarled, teeth bared and hackles raised. He twisted and leapt, darted and moved like a crazy thing as he evaded the hands and weapons aimed at him.

"Stop," the old one suddenly shouted. At once, their captors loosed their grip and stepped back. Once they did, Cloud-Dancer calmed. He came to Lysandra, leaning against her in his familiar way of guard and affection.

Lysandra quickly dropped to her knees. She ran her hands over Cloud-Dancer's coat, using her fingers and her *Sight* to check the places where blood stained his beautiful fur. Only two were wounds and neither was serious; already the bleeding had slowed to an ooze. The other blood came from injuries he had inflicted to protect Lysandra.

She would offer to care for those wounds, too, if the—Cryf, had the old one said?—would allow it. Perhaps such an act would prove to them that she and Renan truly wished them no harm. But first she put her arms around Cloud-Dancer's neck and hugged him, glad and grateful that he had disobeyed her and was here.

The old one came toward her. "Lysandra," Renan said softly to get her attention.

She looked up and saw the Eldest regarding her solemnly. With her *Sight* she could see past his intent expression, into the feeling behind it. *He's worried*, she realized, *worried and frightened—and about more than just two strangers among them. Cloud-Dancer's appearance means something to him.*

Lysandra stood. She kept one hand on Cloud-Dancer's head to maintain the contact of both command and comfort as she faced the old man. He quickly reached out his splay-fingered hand toward her face. Then, when he saw that the action did not cause her to blink or flinch, as a sighted person's instinct would have demanded, he gently touched his fingertips, then his palm, to her forehead.

He stood that way, eyes closed, for the space of several heartbeats. Then he lowered his hand and nodded.

"Ye are the ones," he said. He lifted his staff above his head and slowly turned, so that his eyes took in all the Cryf who looked on in silence. "Time hath reached fullness," he announced. "They have come."

Chapter Fourteen

The storm blew past them to drop its snow on the higher peaks to the north; Giraldus and Aurya spent one more night on the road. When they awakened, the world around them was still lightening with the dawn. They wasted no time around a campfire, but ate a quick breakfast of cold rabbit left from last night's dinner and some of the travel-bread baked by Giraldus's kitchens in Kilgarriff. Then they were once more on their way. Aurya again took the lead, racing her gelding into the wind.

Giraldus was content to ride slightly behind and watch her. As always, her beauty took his breath away; her black hair streamed behind like long ribbons of captured night and her long cloak billowed, its silver threads flashing, giving Aurya the look of something fey, something not quite mortal.

It was late into the afternoon when they noticed far-off smoke rising toward the lowering clouds. The sight made Giraldus eager to race forward, for chimney smoke might well mean shelter for the night.

With the snake and curves of the road, it took them nearly an hour to reach their goal. They found it was a large inn, already crowded with other travelers on their way to the Spring-Fest in Yembo. As soon as they entered, they felt the jovial holiday spirit that pervaded the place. That mood seemed to suit Aurya's, and after taking their belongings to their room, she insisted that they join their fellow travelers in the celebration of nearing their journey's end.

Her mercurial nature, as always, caught Giraldus off guard. He would have wagered that the long hours riding against an icy wind would have sent Aurya into either foul temper or in search of a fire and a hot bath.

Instead, he thought, as he watched her saunter up to the bar to fetch them each back a mug of the hot mulled wine that was the inn's specialty, *just look at her. I swear the ice has raised a fire in* her. *Maybe I should take her into the mountains more often.*

Aurya did look lit from within. Her eyes were shining like dark blue jewels, and she seemed a creature formed out of passion's promise. Every male eye in the room turned toward her when she moved; every ear listened when she laughed.

Giraldus was glad to see the brooding that had marred her last few days was gone—though knowing Aurya as he did, he knew it was only a matter of time before her mood changed again. *She is like a whirlwind*, he thought, *always making me feel tilted, struggling to keep my balance. Will I ever understand her?*

Perhaps not—and perhaps he did not truly want to, either, his heart admitted as Aurya came back to their table.

She placed a steaming mug of spiced wine before Giraldus and, sitting across from him, took a long sip of her own. The deep red of the wine darkened the color of her lips, making Giraldus want to cover them with his own and taste the spices on her breath.

"Let's take our wine and go back to our room," he said softly. "We can have a meal sent up and have it there in comfort."

Aurya, however, misunderstood his intent—or so it seemed to Giraldus. He did not want to think otherwise, or that she was so eager to deny him as she shook her head.

"No," she said, "not yet. I think we should stay here—listen to what the people are saying. When you are High King, you'll need to know the minds of your people and you'll not be able to go out so easily among them. This is an opportunity, Giraldus. Learn to seize them when they come along."

At this moment, Giraldus did not care about the people or the throne. He only wanted *her*. And he knew she saw the hunger in his eyes, for again she laughed.

"Later," she said, her voice full of promise. "It will be worth the wait."

Reluctantly, Giraldus accepted that he would have to be satisfied with that. He drained his mug of wine and stood. "If we're going to join the festivities," he said, "then let's add to them."

He cast a quick glance around the room, estimating the number of people, then reached for the pouch of coins he kept securely tied to his belt beneath his leather vest. He drew out two silver sovereigns and headed toward the bar.

"Innkeep," he said with a loud voice, "a round of your fine wine here for everyone. Let us celebrate our good fortune in finding this place of warm beds, hot food and drink, and good company. 'Tis a fine place to pass the cold hours of the night."

Around the room, a cheer went up. Giraldus smiled broadly, feeding upon the approval of the crowd. As fast as the innkeeper poured mugs of his steaming spiced wine, Giraldus grabbed them and started delivering them to tables—and soon he had other willing hands to help him.

Across the room, someone started an old familiar drinking song. More voices picked up the tune, and still more. Giraldus was in the middle of it all—swinging his mug in time to the music and happily adding his rich, deep voice to the tune.

The first song died and a second was taken up. Giraldus was glad to see the fey light remain on Aurya's face as she, too, joined in the song. He relaxed a little and sang with gusto, roaming through the room. People made places for him to sit, but he shook his head good-naturedly and continued his circuit.

In time, he noticed that not everyone was singing or drinking. At a corner table, far from the center of the festivities, four men sat hunched over their barely touched mugs. Their posture made it clear that they wished no intrusion upon their privacy and most of the people, caught up with their own pleasures, were happy to oblige them.

Giraldus accepted a seat at the table nearest them. Now that the singing was holding the room's attention, the men were not bothering to whisper. Listening carefully, Giraldus could overhear them well enough.

"Hueil's army is two thousand strong already and growing greater each day," one voice said. Giraldus did not dare turn to see who had spoken, but he recognized the name of the Baron of Rathreagh, and that was enough.

"But why should my master join him?" a new voice said, a voice with an arrhythmic rise and fall that told Giraldus this speaker was not from Aghamore. "What is to be gained in this for *us*?"

The first speaker laughed. "You mean besides the gold that he has been paid already? How does the hand of Hueil's daughter, Margharite, sound to sweeten the bargain? As Hueil's only child, she is also his only heir. When he is King, she—and her husband—will have the province of Rathreagh to rule . . . and the throne of Aghamore to inherit. Tell your master this as well—when *my* master sits upon the High Throne in Ballinrigh with the crown firmly upon his head, he will not forget those who have helped put him there. Once those who stand against him have been punished, then those who have been his friends shall gain their rewards."

"Done," said the foreign man. "The great Wirral of Corbenica, my master, can be ready to sail within the month."

"No," again the first voice spoke. "The timing of this must be exact. Baron Hueil is not the only one in Aghamore who seeks to occupy the throne. Your ships must reach the harbor of Owenasse on the night after the summer solstice."

Giraldus sat a moment longer, finishing his wine and putting up a show of jolly conversation. But his mind was whirling with what he had just heard. Hueil, Baron of Rathreagh, the northernmost province of Aghamore, was conspiring with the Corbenicans, their ancient and mortal enemies.

This changed *everything*. Giraldus knew he now had a supportable reason to amass an army and march on Ballinrigh. He could draw upon every province for men and resources . . . and who else would they crown as High King but the Baron who had just led them in saving the kingdom?

Giraldus had to force himself not to rush back to Aurya and tell her what he had just overheard. But he knew he must not; if the men had any suspicion that their plan was no longer secret, it might force them to move before he had time to prepare, or give up the venture altogether. Knowing their timetable gave him an advantage he intended to put to full use.

Under the loudly proclaimed pretense of refilling his mug, he left the table, blessing Aurya's insistence that they join the festivities with every step he took. He stopped at the bar, refilled his mug and another one for Aurya, and went to their table. Someone pulled out a fiddle and struck up a lively tune. Feet began to pound and hands to clap in time; chairs and tables were shoved back to make room for dancing.

Perfect, Giraldus thought as he grabbed Aurya's hands to pull her out onto the floor. He let his balance appear just a little impaired, like a man on the verge of a touch too much wine but full of the frolic of good humor. His performance was perfect; for the first moment they began to dance, even Aurya believed it.

But he was, in fact, quite sober. All effect of the wine had been banished by the hot surge of energy that had rushed through him when he realized what he was overhearing.

"Look in the corner," he whispered into Aurya's ear as they danced, turning her so that her view would not be obvious. "Do you see the four men sitting there?"

He felt her tiny nod.

"After this dance we must go to our room. I have news . . . *important* news."

Again he felt the single small nod against his cheek. He said nothing more as he twirled and jigged them through the remainder of the dance. When it was over, he made a great show of wine-induced passion though, in fact, these desires had now taken second place to the new reason he had to get Aurya alone.

She caught his lead, as he had known she would. A few minutes later, after they had once again downed the contents of their cups, it was many a knowing laugh that followed them from the room.

They kept up their act as they went to the third floor. It was only with the door firmly closed behind them that Giraldus dropped his inebriated farce. Then he caught Aurya up into his arms and twirled her around.

"All right, Giraldus," she said with a laugh when he at last put her down, "tell me now. Just what has happened?"

"Do you remember the men I pointed out?" he began. "They've just given us the throne, and they don't know it."

The interest on Aurya's face sharpened as Giraldus began to tell her what he had overheard.

"But now we don't *need* this . . . this . . . Font of Wisdom—or whatever it is we're after," Giraldus said impatiently. The news he had brought her had turned from triumph into anger.

"Don't be a fool, Giraldus," Aurya snapped in return. "Now the need is all the greater."

"But going to this festival—and going north after this . . . wisdom-child . . . just wastes time when I need to be back in Kilgarriff, strengthening my army and getting the word out to rally the others to our new cause."

"Think, Giraldus." Aurya's tone had an infuriating edge now, as if she thought she was instructing a child—or at least a childish mind. "If you can raise the kingdom, so can any one of the other Barons . . . and if they have the

Church's backing, it would turn their efforts—theirs, not ours—into a *holy cause*. Elon hasn't had time to win the Church's support for us yet. We *must* give him the time he needs . . . and we must have control of the Font of Wisdom to guide us through the threat of war and to back our claim when it is won. It's all right there in the scroll. 'The rise of the Third House—' "

"Damn your scroll," Giraldus shouted. "It's just the ancient rantings of some half-mad monk. Even his own kind turned their backs on him. I've no time for such nonsense now."

"You *are* a fool," Aurya said back, her voice low and cold, steely hard. "You don't deserve to be High King. But *I* deserve to be Queen. If not with you, then with someone else."

She turned her back on him. Giraldus suddenly felt as if a spear had pierced him. He did not miss the real threat in her voice. Grabbing her arm, he swung her around to face him, fingers digging into the softness of her flesh in a grip that made her wince in pain. He did not care; it could not compare with the pain her words had just caused him.

"No one else," he said through clenched teeth. "No one."

He crushed his mouth onto hers, feeling the smoothness and the heat of her lips. He felt her body start to yield, and his hands went from her arms to around her waist, pulling her body more tightly against his own.

In his renewed eagerness to possess her physically, he completely missed the look of triumph on her face.

Aurya's single threat of finding another partner enflamed Giraldus; their passion lasted through the night. Aurya knew that any thought he might have entertained of abandoning their journey was gone—at least for now. If it arose again later on . . . well, she would deal with it then.

She *knew* Giraldus, strengths and weaknesses, as he would never know her, and that made him hers, body and soul, and the perfect tool for her purpose.

They slept late into the morning and ate breakfast at a leisurely pace, preferring to leave the inn on their own rather than in a group with their fellow travelers. The Festival at Yembo did not start until the following day; their only need to rush now was to be certain of finding a room.

As she had tried to explain to Giraldus last night, the conversation he overheard strengthened her certainty that they were on the right path. It also reinforced the necessity of finding the Font of Wisdom. In the cool light of morning, she found that she still relished the idea of controlling the child once it was found, of molding it into what she wanted—and into what Giraldus needed. But she also accepted that if the child could not be controlled, it must be killed.

Could she do it? she asked herself. She knew the task would fall to her; Giraldus would never have the stomach to kill a child, not face-to-face. Certainly, children were inadvertently killed during war and Giraldus's soldier's mind accepted that as a sorrowful but undeniable fact of battle.

This, however, would be different—in his mind if not in Aurya's. To her, this *was* war . . . and the prize was supreme power. Those who were not her allies were her enemies, regardless of personal connections, social status, gender—or age.

But can I do it? she asked herself again, as she and Giraldus left the inn. Her mind, her will to succeed said yes; of her heart, she was not so sure. She, however, had an advantage Giraldus lacked.

She could kill from a distance.

It was no easy thing to kill this way. It required every bit of the same courage a warrior takes, like his sword, into battle. The dark power she would have to conjure was just as dangerous. One false step, one missaid word or second of faltered intent and the spell could turn back to destroy the destroyer.

Yet, with sudden and complete clarity, Aurya knew she would do it if she must.

Chapter Fifteen

They have come." The voice of the eldest Cryf seemed to echo through the great chamber. Then Lysandra realized this was not an echo; the other Cryf, the hundreds upon hundreds of them filling the ledges that were the walls of the cavern, had picked up the words.

Lysandra was confused by the swift change in attitude. One moment, she and Renan were facing death for entering this place, this *realm*, of creatures they did not know existed—and now, in a sudden turnabout, they were being treated like long-awaited heroes.

But before she could demand an explanation, from the

distance came a sound like rolling thunder. It came as sensations as well as sound; Lysandra could feel the sharp vibration through the soles of her feet. All around, the Cryf gave a collective gasp of shock and fear.

Then there were running feet and a voice shouting in that strange chirping language Lysandra did not understand.

"What is it?" she demanded of the old one as he started to turn away again. "What has happened?"

"A wall hath fallen," he said sharply. "Many be trapped. Yet, as the Divine is merciful, there may yet be some who live."

"We will help," Renan said quickly.

"Ye be Up-worlders," the old one said with disdain. "What can ye do? Ye know not the ways of the Cryf."

"I have strong arms and hands," Renan replied. "I may not know the ways of the Cryf, as you say, but I know how to work hard, and I know what it is to suffer. I will help you so that the Cryf do not suffer any loss another pair of hands might have saved."

"Ye be Up-worlders," the old one said again. "Why should ye care if the Cryf suffer?"

"Because I am a healer," Lysandra said, now joining the conversation, "and because he is one who serves the Creator God. All life is precious to us, whether Upworlder, Cryf . . . or animal," she added, running her hand over Cloud-Dancer's head.

The old one said nothing for a few seconds. Then, again, he nodded, as if her words meant more than she had said.

"Come," he said finally to Renan. "Thou shalt work beside the Cryf. And thee," he said to Lysandra, "I shall work with thee. Many Cryf may yet be saved this day, if the Divine giveth power unto thy hands."

"Our belongings," Lysandra said. "They are still back where we were sleeping, where your people first found us. We must have them. My medicines, the things I need to heal, are in them."

"They shall be brought," the old one said. He called out, and one of the younger Cryf immediately came to answer. The Cryf Elder quickly conferred with him, issuing orders in the same chirping language Lysandra had heard them use twice before. The young Cryf dashed away. The old one led Renan and Lysandra up a ramp off the huge cavern's floor, to one of the other council leaders.

After a few swift sentences in the Cryf tongue, he turned to the priest. "This one shall take thee unto the digging," he told Renan. "His words in thy tongue are few, but thou shalt obey his orders. Dost thou understand and agree?"

Renan nodded, then followed his new guide down one of the passages from which Lysandra could hear other voices calling. She waited to hear what the Cryf leader would say to her.

"Art thou truly a healer," he asked, "though thine eyes be dark?"

"I am," Lysandra replied.

"Then I shall work beside thee—and if thy words or touch be true, I will know."

Know what? Lysandra wondered, though she did not question him. It was enough that for the moment she had his trust. She only prayed that the *Sight* would not leave her and that she would be able to help all those who might need her.

It would take some time before the first of the injured would be brought out. The runner returned with Lysandra's things and while they waited, the old one helped her set up a hospital area. After laying out her meager supplies, Lysandra shook her head, wishing fervently that she had access to her garden and medicine cupboard at home. She did not know what might be needed during the hours ahead, but she was certain she did not have enough of anything.

The old one, who had watched silently as she arranged her pouches of herbs, the three small pots of salve, and the two rolls of cloth strips in the order she liked, saw her sad look and finally spoke.

"There is worry upon thy face," he said. "Dost thou fear thou canst not heal the Cryf?"

"I fear there will be too many injured, and I will not have enough to help all who are in need," she replied. "Do the Cryf have medicines I might add to my own?"

"We do. Come, I shall show thee."

Cloud-Dancer stayed close by her side, for he would not leave her again. They walked only a short distance, around a bend to where the underground opened up again. This new cavern held a pool that sent great ribbons of steam swirling upward. She could smell the minerals in the water. It would be a great source of healing, she realized, and a comfort to those with painful joints and tired muscles.

Next to the pool was a great cave. It was there that the Elder led her, and it was like walking into a healer's fond dream.

The inside of the cave was bright. Here, the strangely luminous stones had been gathered and piled. Some of the piles reached nearly to the ceiling, concentrating the illumination. In other places, stones had been placed inside lanterns of crystal that caught and further amplified the light.

Plants grew in lush abundance, their roots filling troughs of water instead of soil. Mushrooms and other fungi, healing molds and lichens also grew, these carefully shielded from the brightness. The scent of growing things made the air fresh with the aroma of life.

On long stone shelves were pots of unguents and creams, stoppered vials of tinctures and tonics, oils and infusions. Neatly stacked to one side were long poles—some straight and flat, others hollowed out to carefully cup a broken bone. Bandages of every size and width were rolled and placed near coils of rope that ranged from the thickness of her wrist down to the fineness of silk thread.

"How did all these things get here?" Lysandra asked, amazed by it all.

"In times far past," the old one began, "when thy kind did not yet cover the land, the Cryf were free to go Upworld. There was then many an open way betwixt our Realms, and the Cryf had only to wait until the Great Brightness had passed beyond the far shore. Then, in the time of the Soft Light, would our Healers or Hunters ascend unto the Up-world and bring back all that our Realm could not provide. But as the numbers of thy kind grew and spread like grasping fingers across the land, it became not safe for the Cryf to be seen. Up-worlders name the Cryf as monsters. Thy kind did capture and kill the Cryf whenever they were seen.

"It was then the men of the Up-world came unto the Realm of the Cryf. We welcomed them, for we did hope to show them our ways that they would know the Cryf were not monsters. Our Elders did hope for friendship betwixt our kinds. We were wrong. The men of Up-world saw the beauty of our Realm and greed did join the enmity in their hearts. They killed the Cryf who had welcomed them and did begin to tear our Realm apart.

"But the Cryf know many places, places deep within

the heart of our Mother the Earth, that no Up-worlder may find—then or now. Our Guide did wait until the Mind of the Divine opened unto him to show him what the Cryf must do. Soon the visions came unto our Guide and to the Elders of the twelve. The Divine, who loveth the Cryf, showed unto us how to hide the shining stones—for Up-worlders can not see as we do. Many fell into the deep pits that they themselves had dug and perished there. We mourned them not, though they, too, be the children of the Divine, as are all living things.

"Others ascended back Up-world so they might bring their brightness back with them. But again the Divine did guide us. It was then the Cryf sealed all but two doors betwixt thy world and the Realm of the Cryf. Those that remained open we did hide behind stone. By the Wisdom of the Divine was this done, and only the Guide of the Cryf knoweth where those last doors remain.

"The Mind of the Divine then revealed unto us how we may grow what we need and never again be forced to enter unto the Up-world. There be many such places as this in the Realm of the Cryf," he said, waving his hand to include the whole cave. "This one be for our Healers. Others grow the food we eat or the plants to make our clothing. We go not Up-world—and our law be that no Up-worlder may come unto the realm of the Cryf."

"Where are your Healers now?" Lysandra asked. "Didn't they hear the cave-in?"

"They heard," the elder replied calmly. "They shall be ready if thou canst not help the Cryf, as thou hast said. But I send word that thou alone shalt act as Healer in this. Then shall we know if the Hand of the Divine be truly upon thee."

Lysandra drew a deep breath. She was being asked to undertake—alone—the healing of those whose survival might completely depend on what she did in the next few hours. She turned back to the stone shelves and the medicines stored there, trying to hide her uncertainties from the far-too-observant gaze of the Elder.

"Gather what thou needst," the old one said. "We must return and ready ourselves. The ones who now dig may well have reached the trapped ones. Thy healer's touch will be needed."

Once more drawing a deep breath, Lysandra began quickly sorting through the vials and pots before her. Her fingers trembled, and she could taste the bitterness of fear.

Oh, please, she prayed—to her *Sight* or to the Source from whence it came—*please don't fail. If not for my sake, then for the sake of the injured. Stay with me so I can help them.*

Chapter Sixteen

Even though the Festival did not officially start until the next day, the streets of Yembo were a riot of happy noise and color. Banners, woven or stitched with bright springtime flowers, hung from balconies and upper-story windows. Window boxes were filled with artificial bouquets, flowers of impossible hues fashioned of silks and satins. Building doors, window boxes, and shutters had all been freshly painted in brilliant jewel tones, shining in the sunlight.

The Enfawr River ran through the center of the town, the main and most famous street, with buildings built up on either side. Down these streets, vendors had set their stalls, all covered with bright canopies. Many had tied long streamers to the tent poles that fluttered with every breath of breeze.

The streets were already crowded. Like the buildings and stalls, the people were dressed up in bright colors so that they looked like flowers moving in the wind. Once the Spring-Fest began, these streets would be closed to all but foot traffic.

For now, Aurya and Giraldus were still on horseback. As they picked their way through the crowd, Aurya looked around, seeking some clue that might lead her to the Three Sisters. Were they people or landmarks, something native to Yembo or something brought here for the Festival? If the latter, would she find it on the first day or the last?

Nothing caught her eye, but Yembo was a big place, and they were still far from the site where the children's choir would sing. Aurya was not discouraged; she would not allow herself to be. Under her breath, she repeated the words of the scroll, making sure they remained ever-present in her thoughts.

Finally, they entered the part of town given over to inns and public houses. The crowds were thinner here. Stable hands scurried through inn yards, dashing on errands to care for their charges. Giraldus called to several of them, trying to learn which inns were already filled. They were finally directed to the seventh inn on the long row, The Dancing Dolphin.

The wooden placard that hung over the door showed a great sea creature, a kind Aurya had never seen, balancing on its tail and surrounded by ocean waves. It was a comical creature with a long-nosed snout and a mouth that looked open in a grin. If such a creature truly existed, she thought, it was not in the waters around Aghamore.

Aurya found herself grinning back at the charmingly carved face. She took it to be a good omen that they should be housed in a place where the known and the unknown were blended. She was suddenly certain that tomorrow, when at dawn the children sang before the city's Water-Gates, she would find the Three Sisters.

Satisfied with the comfort, the good food, and good cheer that filled the Inn of the Dancing Dolphin—that, in fact, filled all the town of Yembo—Aurya slept well and deeply. She did not awaken until the hour before dawn, when the innkeeper came around to knock on the doors of all the guest rooms. Almost everyone planned to attend the opening of the Festival, when the children gathered to sing to the brightening day.

Aurya awoke at the first knock, and she, in turn, awakened Giraldus. He opened his eyes as readily as she had. He seemed just as eager to reach the Water-Gates and find a place in the surrounding parks where the crowd did not impede their view of the event.

"There's a breakfast waiting downstairs," Giraldus told her as he added some wood to the fire he had just built to chase the predawn chill from the room. "And I've a good appetite this morning."

Aurya smiled. She was hungry, too—but not for food. Her appetite was for knowledge and for the power awaiting her discovery at the park. Seeing her smile, Giraldus rose from his knees and came to her. He slipped his arms around her waist.

"You're in a good mood," he said, nuzzling her neck softly.

"I'm eager for the day," she replied. "We'll find what we're looking for . . . I'm sure of it."

"Humph—we'd better," Giraldus said, a bit more gruffly. "We've wasted enough time with this scroll nonsense. I still say we'd do better with a dozen armed men at our backs."

They had already had this argument—several times— and Aurya did not want to have it again this morning. She still had not convinced Giraldus, but he was here, and that was enough for now. When he sat on the throne of Aghamore and saw that it was her powers that had put him there . . . *then* he would believe.

With that belief could come her destiny. She would then see that Aghamore became the kingdom it had once been, a *great* kingdom where the old gods and the old ways were still mighty. Then Aurya would no longer be an outcast among society . . . she would be *First* among all the rest.

Then she remembered Elon's words about her need to publicly embrace the Church and marry Giraldus in accordance with its precepts. She shook her head. *After I have the child,* she thought, *and know what powers it conveys and controls,* then *I'll consider Elon's advice. If what I hope is true, I won't have to worry about the Church or marriage. I'll be a Priestess-Queen, Servant of the Great Goddess, as Queens once were and are meant to be.*

Yes, *that* was a worthy goal, one toward which she could willingly work. It would not be easy to banish the Church from Aghamore. For the last several centuries it had been slowly building its influence and power until now its insidious tendrils had wormed their way into every aspect of Aghamore's society. The hearts of the people would need to be changed and redirected in their devotion.

But the old gods and their ways had been part of this land since before time was measured and counted. Those gods and their powers would rule in Aghamore again— even if it took Aurya her lifetime to see it made so.

After dressing and eating quickly, they left the inn to join the others heading down to the Water-Gates and the opening of the festivities. Torches wavered in the predawn air, giving a dancing glow to the crowd following the same path walked every year at this time. Aurya strolled along with them, her hand on Giraldus's arm and filled with a sense of inner ease. It all felt so *right* to her this morning; no shadow of doubt was present to darken her thoughts.

The Water-Gates were awash with lights. Huge torches had been lit at each end and in the middle of the high, arched bridge, and lanterns were hung across the face so that the wonderful carvings could be seen.

Here were carved flowers and trees, and the wildlife that had lived along the banks of the river. It was Yembo of the past, honored and celebrated by the Yembo of the present. At the very center, three swans were carved in flight, their long graceful necks extended and their wings caught forever in mid-beat.

The Three Sisters, Aurya thought with a sudden burst of excitement that raced through her body as if lightning had struck from within. *Wait,* she told herself. *Their beaks are pointing north, the direction you already know you must go—and the prophecy said the Three Sisters would be looking west . . . but they are on the west face of the bridge . . .* Her thoughts were beginning to chase themselves in unprofitable circles. *Wait,* she finally told herself, *wait and see what the dawn reveals.*

Long ago she had trained herself to outward calm despite whatever she might be feeling. She called upon that training now. *The ways of magic are sometimes subtle,* she reminded herself; she must not miss them because she had no more self-control than the lowest initiate.

Far in the east there was the merest change of light. At that same instant, from either side of the bridge, rose the pure, soft sound of children's voices. Walking four abreast, they came. Their song became louder, clearer, as with each footstep the two groups neared each other.

Their voices rang like tapped crystal, trilled like a summer brook flowing over stones. Off in the east, the light grew in shades of violet and roseate gold. The crowd, so full of festive noise just a scant moment before, was now stilled in hushed appreciation.

Aurya, too, was silent, waiting for the revelation she was certain would come. Off in the distance, the sky continued to grow brighter by the second. The violet gave way to the soft blue of a clear springtime day, and the rose-washed gold turned tawny, then bright as the sun at last lifted above the horizon.

With her eyes fixed upon the swans, Aurya stared, strained, to see even the smallest nuance of change. She saw . . .

. . . nothing.

The children concluded their first song, an ancient hymn of haunting melody sung in praise of Creation, to the appreciative applause of their audience. They began a second tune, this one sprightly and full of musical movement. It was a familiar folk tune about blackbirds and thrushes, sheep and fishes, all looking for their mates in the beauty of spring. Soon, everyone but Aurya was clapping in time. Many in the crowd began singing along—including Giraldus. *He* was having a wonderful day.

Aurya wanted to scream at everyone to be quiet and let her think. That, of course, she could not do. Instead, she felt a sudden and undeniable urge to get away. She turned from Giraldus's side without a word and headed north—away from the people, from the noise and distractions, and in the direction the swans were pointing.

Pushing through the crowd proved difficult. She felt like a fish swimming upstream, the current dragging her the wrong way. Gone were the elation and certainty she had known upon awakening. All she had left was her determination.

It had carried her this far in her life—it would carry her the rest of the way she intended to go. *She* would never fail or disappoint herself.

The children had begun a third song by the time Aurya reached the edge of the crowd. She began to search the north end of the meadow, looking for anything that might fit the clues given in the scroll.

Still she found nothing. Everything here was clipped and pristine, well cared for; nothing was *hidden* or *forgotten.* She pushed aside bushes and peered into shadowed places, as the children continued singing their festal greeting to the sun.

Aurya was so intent on her search that she did not notice when the children ceased to sing. She ignored the thinning crowds as she began her second search of the park's perimeter.

"What are you doing?" Giraldus asked, suddenly at her side. His good humor had turned to impatience when he discovered she was gone, and now his voice was hard.

"It has to be here, somewhere," she answered him. "The swans' necks were pointing to this direction."

"And on the other side they no doubt pointed the other way."

"The other side—the sun's side. But that's east, not west," Aurya said, speaking to herself and ignoring his question. "We have to go to the other side. Come on."

She started to hurry away, but Giraldus grabbed her arm. "What are you babbling about, woman?" he said. "I'm not going anywhere until you tell me what you're doing."

Aurya swung around to face him, her impatience now matching his own. "Didn't you see the three swans carved on the bridge?" she asked him.

"Of course I saw them," Giraldus replied. "Nice bit of work."

"Don't you understand, Giraldus? There were *three* of them. *Three*. The *Three Sisters*, just like the scroll said. They're what we came here to find, remember? They're supposed to reveal the next steps we're to follow."

"You know, Aurya, I've had enough of this scroll nonsense. Even though you say you know we need to end up in the *north*, in Rathreagh, we're here—in Yembo, in Lininch. *East* not *north*. I've done everything you have asked of me, everything you and your scroll said to do. But this is enough. We'll cross the bridge and we'll search the other side. But if we find nothing, that's it. After that, we start doing things *my* way."

Giraldus kept a hold of her arm as he began to march across the field toward the bridge. Aurya could tell that he was angry . . . and she was fast becoming angry, too. She knew what he meant by doing things *his* way. He meant to summon his army and storm the capital, to take the throne and the crown by force.

And she knew it would not work . . . but could she trust her sense of certainty anymore?

Then Aurya remembered her vision on the night she had performed the Summoning of Tambryn's spirit, the vision of herself and Giraldus riding into Ballinrigh with an army at their back. If that had been a warning, she would heed it now; she was *not* going to give up on this journey and the reward it promised.

It was then she made a decision that had been whispering in the back of her thoughts for a long time. She would make Giraldus the King in spite of himself.

A Spell of Obedience will change your mind, she thought as she and Giraldus neared the bridge. *Tonight, when you're sleeping—I'll set it then. The moon is still full and the power of night at its greatest strength. By tomorrow when you awaken, you'll have no choice but to obey me.*

That decision made, Aurya stopped walking. Her action made Giraldus swing around to face her. She put on her most pleasant smile as she gently disengaged his fingers from her arm. There were other people on the bridge, and she was not about to be dragged across like a recalcitrant child.

Instead, still smiling, she stepped closer to Giraldus and slipped her arm through his. Her sudden change brought such a look of confusion to his face that it made her want to laugh aloud. He still, after all these years together, did not understand her—would *never* understand her.

And that was how she wanted it to stay.

They found no more from searching the southern side of the river. As Giraldus had threatened, he now proclaimed this journey at an end. Tomorrow he would send a message to his men, then they would turn back and meet his army en route to Ballinrigh.

Aurya smiled and agreed, knowing that nothing he was

saying would ever happen. She let Giraldus see her disappointment; she acted agreeable and submissive, as if her failure to find the next signs of the scroll had taken all the will from her.

While she played through this latest round in the eternal male/female contest, letting Giraldus *think* he had won, she was busy reviewing the spell she would cast once the moon was high.

She did not waste her strength on a Sleeping Spell. Instead, she slipped a powder into his wine and kept him drinking. Once it finally took effect, she had to help him to the bed, where he fell into a stupor before she even had the chance to remove his boots. Now she was certain he would not awaken while she performed the ritual that would bind his will to hers.

Aurya removed Giraldus's clothing, then changed her own into a simple shift of palest silver, the color of the moonlight. Once that was done, from out of her bags she brought a blue-crystal wand, about twelve inches long. It had a groove hollowed into one of its facets, which she would make use of tonight.

This, and a candle, she put on the table. Then she found Giraldus's dagger and brought it with her as she sat before the fire to prepare herself.

Many times during their years together Aurya had been tempted to use this spell. Until now, she had always resisted. A Spell of Obedience, like spells for love, always seemed to her of a self-defeating nature. To force someone's compliance, like forcing their affection through magic, rendered the emotion meaningless.

But too much was at stake here. *After it's over*, she promised Giraldus's sleeping form, *after you are High King, I'll remove the spell. If I'm careful, you'll never know it was there. Or if you do, you'll have reason to thank me for it.*

The moon was finally high enough to shine through the window, beaming silvered light into the room. Aurya moved the table into the center of that light, then extinguished the lamps and lit the candle. She was ready to begin.

Standing in the moonlight, she lifted her arms up and out, reaching toward the ancient and eternal symbol of the Goddess—the Goddess whom old Kizzie had served and on whose power Aurya would call this night. It was an old spell, passed from teacher to student through countless years of women. Aurya would cast it as she had learned it from Kizzie.

"Great Goddess, Mother of All," she began. "Giver of Life, Bringer of Death; I call upon Your power. Aba, Macha, Morrigan—triple aspect of the One, hear my call and give me aid."

Aurya picked up the dagger, passed it three times through the flame as she repeated the sacred names. Then she quickly brought the heated blade down across the thumb of her left hand. The blood welled. She dripped one red drop onto the flame as the symbolic blood offering to the Goddess. Then she took up the crystal wand.

This, too, she passed through the flame three times. Then she gathered her own blood onto the crystal and with it drew a pentagram on the table. When that was finished, she held the wand within the candle and let the flame burn the remaining blood away.

Now it was time for Giraldus's blood, and this was why she had drugged him so heavily. Using his own dagger, she cut a lock of his hair and shaved three cuttings from his fingernails. These, she took back to the table. Then, finally, she also cut the ball of his thumb and collected the fast-welling blood into the groove of the crystal wand.

Aurya quickly wrapped his thumb in a strip of cloth before any of the blood could stain the bedclothes. Then she returned to the table, bringing the blood-filled crystal with her.

Into the center of the pentagram she placed Giraldus's hair and fingernails. The hair, from his head, represented the obedience of his mind that after tonight she would command; his fingernails were the sign and symbols of his actions. With his blood and hers mingled, she would bind him to her will with cords of magic stronger than any ropes.

She took the hairs and dipped them in the blood. Then she dragged those along the lines of the symbol she had used her own blood to create.

"Thy mind to my mind," she chanted. "Thy mind to my calling. Thy mind at my command. By this blood I bind thee in obedience."

Aurya dropped the hairs, one by one, onto the candle flame, where they singed and burned in the incense of sacrifice. She then picked up the fingernails and repeated the process.

"Thy will to my will," she said this time. "Thy actions be at my calling. Thy will at my command. By this blood I bind thee to obedience."

Logic said that the fingernails would not burn so easily as the hair, but as the first one was dropped onto the flame it flared up as if the fire was hungry for the offering. It consumed the fingernails as if they were of no more substance than a spider's web.

Now Aurya reached for the wand and the blood it contained. This she poured into the center of the pentagram.

"Thy blood to my blood; thy life to my life. By the

blood of life, I bind thee at my command. My will shall be thy will; my desires shall be thy desires. My hopes shall be thy hopes and my goals shall be thy goals until the time that either I, or death, shall release thee. By this blood I bind thee; only blood can set thee free."

Once more, Aurya picked up the wand. The blue crystal shimmered in the light of the flames and the moon. This wand was ancient; the magic set into it centuries ago by a mage more powerful than any the world now knew. Aurya had spent years searching for it or one of its eleven sisters, all cut from the same blue Mother-stone. When at last she found it, it had taken all her powers—and all her purse—to persuade the owner to part with it.

She passed the wand three times through the candle, then dipped it into Giraldus's blood. By magic, the stone began to drink. It pulled all of Giraldus's blood into its heart; his blood, his *life*, was now captured and in her keeping.

Aurya now traced the wand backward over the pentagram she had drawn with her own blood. That, too, the crystal absorbed. Their blood was now mingled, her blood laid over his just as her will would now overshadow Giraldus's own.

One final time, she held the wand inside the flame. Again, the candle flared, burning off any lingering traces of blood.

"Mind and body, life and spirit, these I claim by the power of fire, stone, and blood. Three to hold thee; three to bind thee; by the three powers shalt thou be mine forever more."

Aurya drove the tip of the wand down into the center of the candle. For an instant, just before the pressure extinguished the light, the crystal pulled the flame deep into its heart. Fire was now inside the stone, trapped with the blood by the power of the spell.

Giraldus's obedience was hers.

The ritual was nearly complete. Once more, Aurya raised her arms toward the moon, now high in the west.

"Great Goddess, Mother of All," she cried in a voice fervent with emotion but still soft enough not to wake the other people at the inn. "As I have and do honor Thee, I beseech Thee to lend Thy power to my spell. What I have bound here on Earth, let it be so bound in Thy universal home. By mortal and Immortal command, by human and Divine decree."

Bathed in the moonlight, Aurya stood with arms outstretched, waiting to feel the Goddess's presence. Slowly, deep within, far past body or mind, she felt a warming. The sensation swiftly grew until she felt as if the blood within her veins had turned to flame. It engulfed her, overwhelmed her. For one instant, Aurya felt herself suspended somewhere beyond reality, outside of life and death.

Then, between one breath and the next, she found herself back where and as she was before, arms outstretched to the Mother-Goddess, feeling only her own heartbeat, the cold of the floor beneath her feet.

Slowly, she lowered her arms and let a tiny smile form upon her lips. Her body ached with the exhaustion only those who traffic in magic can understand. But it was a weariness Aurya welcomed.

It would take all her strength to restore the room to its previous appearance. But even her exhaustion could not dim her triumph. Giraldus's heart and body she had owned for years; now the rest of him was hers as well.

And tomorrow they would ride toward Rathreagh.

Chapter Seventeen

The Elders stood, silent as a row of apothecary jars, watching every move Lysandra made as she cared for the injured. The Healers did little to help. They would hold a patient while she set a bone or run back to the cave to replenish any supplies she had used up—but nothing more. They had been given their orders; unless Lysandra proved incompetent, she alone was to care for the victims of the cave-in. By her actions, they said, would her heart be known, and by that, she and Renan would be judged.

Lysandra worked as she never had before. Not all of her patients had been injured in the cave-in. Several of the rescuers also needed treatment—for cuts and scrapes, bloodied fingers, sprained wrists or ankles, and an occasional pulled muscle. But such minor injuries were quickly treated as excavation of the cave-in continued.

It was Lysandra's *Sight* that allowed her to keep working without rest or relief. Her empathy made her share what her patients were feeling, and she could not turn away from the injured until all their pain had been eased.

Exhaustion soon flooded her. It wound through her body like a living thing, eating up her reserves of strength that were already depleted by lack of sleep and a long, captive march. But she still pushed herself on, until the last trapped Cryf had been brought out.

Finally, with her mind numb and her arms feeling like bars of lead, there were no more patients to treat. She rose to go over to the Elders, hoping that she and Renan had now earned their trust. But this one action was past her strength and as she stood, the blood drained from her head and dizziness swept through her. She put out a hand to find Cloud-Dancer, to ground and steady herself. Her fingers barely touched him before she fell.

Lysandra did not feel the arms that caught her. Renan, back from his work with the rescue parties, had seen Lysandra sway as her face turned ashen white. He pushed past the Cryf and reached her barely in time to break her fall.

Surprised by how light she was, Renan found himself staring down at her, unconscious in his arms. He could not help but notice how wisps of her richly golden hair had come loose from its braid to curl, damp with perspiration, around her face. He saw, too, the creamy beauty of her skin and the way her thick dark lashes looked like half-moons of sable resting above the satin of her cheeks.

Renan closed his eyes. He could not allow himself to see Lysandra—or any woman—this way. He had relinquished that privilege when he had taken his vows as a priest. He had given up everything he was before. He would never again take the chance that . . .

No. He pushed the memories away, ran from them the way he knew Lysandra fled from hers. He understood how and why she ran—and it did not change what he believed of her.

To live as she did in spite of her blindness, and to have undertaken this journey, was a testament to her indomitable courage. She did not see it; when she had told him of her life—past and present, of the reason for her blindness and the wondrous gift of her *Sight* that allowed her to have a purpose—he had also heard what she did not say. There was a part of her heart that viewed the peace of her life in the forest with guilt, believing that she was only running away from anything, past or present, that might cause her more pain.

But he knew better. She had not been running *away;* she had been running *toward* herself. Like the prophets of old who sojourned in the desert, needing to learn to be alone before they could hear the Voice of the Creator, she had to travel through solitude to come to that place where her gifts were free to manifest.

He also believed that she had more gifts than she had yet to suppose and more power than she realized. She was truly the most amazing person he had ever known.

Cloud-Dancer whined once as Renan gently laid Lysandra on the ground and stayed kneeling beside her. The wolf immediately lay on the other side of her, his head upon her shoulder, his nose gently nudging her cheek in an effort to wake her.

Her eyes slowly fluttered open. Renan was again struck by her beauty. Even reddened from exhaustion, the rich forget-me-not blue was something he found exquisite.

Once more, he made himself look away. Then he waited until the lump that had suddenly filled his chest subsided. Only when he was certain he could look at her with the eyes of a priest did he turn back to her.

Renan took her hand—no, he would not notice how small and fragile her hand felt in his or the way her fingers curled around his own. She started to sit up, but he put his other hand gently on her shoulder.

"No, Lysandra," he said. "Rest. You've done enough."

"Ye have both done enough, and more."

Renan looked up quickly. The leader of the Elders had come to stand beside him. His expression was no longer wary or judgmental.

"Ye are, indeed, the ones for whom the Cryf have waited," he continued. "Though ye be Up-worlders, ye need no longer fear our Law. All three of ye"—he included Cloud-Dancer with a glance—"are welcome here."

Renan stood, a hundred questions on his lips. But the old one held up a hand for silence. Then he waved a signal to the others behind him and immediately four of the younger Cryf appeared, carrying one of the stretchers that had been used to transport the wounded. Despite her protests, they lifted Lysandra onto it.

"Thou and the Healer shall be taken unto a soft place that ye may rest in comfort," he told Renan. "All that your bodies need of food and drink shall be brought unto ye, that ye may also be refreshed. Only then, when strength hath returned, shall we talk."

Renan nodded. "We are glad that the Cryf now believe the truth of our words—and our hearts—that they have nothing to fear from us. I am called Father Renan and the healer's name is Lysandra. I must know, if we are to rest with easy minds—will the Cryf show us the way safely through their realm?"

The old one seemed to consider Renan's words for a moment, and the priest wondered what more they must do to win his trust.

"The Cryf do not share their names easily," the old one said at last. Then he drew himself up, standing as straight as his advanced years allowed. "I am Eiddig," he said. "Guide of the Cryf. Into my keeping have been given the Holy Words. With the Voice of the Divine, I guide the

Cryf through the time that is and by the Will of the Divine, I guard all that be still with us from the First Times.

"Of these must we speak when the Healer hath slept and eaten. There be words ye must hear—and words the Cryf must hear of ye."

Renan glanced at Lysandra, now deeply asleep upon the stretcher. The pallor of exhaustion still tinged her skin. *All right,* he thought, *for now. But I need answers soon.*

At a signal from Eiddig, the stretcher-bearers lifted Lysandra. Cloud-Dancer paced on one side, staying as close as he could, and Renan walked on the other. He found himself longing to reach down and take her hand once again, to hold it as they followed Eiddig.

The underground passages, though marked here and there by piles of the glowing stones that seemed to be the only source of light for the Cryf, were too dark for Renan's comfort. He wished for a torch in his hand. But the Cryf navigated the many turns without a falter until at last they entered yet another cavern.

Here, the walls were studded with openings too regular to be natural caves. Renan saw hundreds of Cryf, mostly women and children, some in laughing groups, some sitting or going in and out of the caves that must be their homes.

It's like a city, Renan thought in amazement, *a city and a people that no one above—Up-world—knows exists. These truly are "the forgotten."*

He and Lysandra were taken into one of the caves level with the cavern floor. It was a large chamber, brighter than the passages through which they had just traveled. Crystal lanterns that magnified the glowing stone were set into little niches throughout the cave. Everything within the room was made of stone, different kinds and colors carved into shapes that were both useful and beautiful. In spite of the material used, the overall effect was not harsh . . . it was unexpectedly harmonious.

Lysandra was carried to the back of the cave. Here, two sleeping platforms had been carved to extend out from the wall. They were covered with a material that made them look like little nests. Renan stepped quickly in front of the stretcher-bearers, to examine the beds before Lysandra was placed on one.

The stone had been slightly hollowed. Each platform was padded with some type of moss, but not one Renan had ever seen. It was soft and spongy, and when touched it gave off a warm, slightly spicy scent that was comforting. On top of the moss lay a thick layer of a material Renan could not name. It was obviously spun, but it was softer than newly washed and carded lamb's wool.

What was it? he wondered. Did the Cryf have animals here, of a kind just as forgotten as the Cryf themselves? What other discoveries were waiting to be made?

Renan turned around. Although he did not distrust the Cryf, they still had not answered any of his questions, and until he knew more about them, he would care for Lysandra himself. He lifted her gently from the stretcher and settled her onto the center of the bed. Without waking, she shifted, nestled, and sighed with contentment. Cloud-Dancer jumped onto the bed, picking his way gingerly across the unfamiliar material until he could take his usual place beside her.

The other sleeping platform was only a few feet away. Renan knew that he would sleep well and deeply . . . *after* the Cryf had left them. He turned back to find Eiddig looking at Lysandra with a strange expression in his large eyes that seemed something between the paternal and the reverent.

"Thou shalt not be disturbed while thou rest," the old

one said, not taking his eyes off Lysandra. "If thou hast need, thou hast but to call. One of the Cryf shall be near to hear thee."

Finally, Eiddig looked up. He held the priest's eyes firmly with his own. "Sleep thou well, Father Renan," he said. "The Cryf and the future wait upon thine awakening."

The old one turned, followed by the stretcher-bearers. Renan pondered his final words as he watched them go. He had no doubt that the Cryf were The Forgotten of whom Tambryn had written—but what could the Cryf, living here in this realm of stone and solitude, know of the Scrolls of Tambryn or the state of the kingdom?

Renan shook his head; it was an unanswerable question—for now. With one more glance at Lysandra, he crawled onto the waiting bed, settled himself onto its softness, and gave himself over to sleep.

When he awakened, the first thing he saw was Cloud-Dancer's muzzle only inches away. The wolf's chin was resting on Renan's sleep platform, and he was staring at the priest as if willing him to awaken. The sight of the wild-tame, unblinking blue eyes startled Renan into fast awareness.

He raised his head, drawing back a bit from Cloud-Dancer's scrutiny. "Lysandra?" he said softly, not wanting to awaken her if she still slept.

"Where are we?" she asked. Her voice was stronger than before she slept, but it had an odd tone to it he did not quite recognize.

"We're in one of the Cryf homes—or sleeping chambers, anyway," he told her.

"Describe it to me. I cannot *See*, Renan—or even share Cloud-Dancer's vision."

Now Renan heard the fear, bravely covered, in her voice. He tried to think of something to comfort her.

"You are tired, Lysandra," he said, "perhaps more tired than you realize. Give yourself a chance to rest and regain some strength. You're a healer for everyone else, try thinking like a healer for yourself. I'm sure everything will be all right soon enough."

When she did not answer, Renan wondered if everything he had said came across as empty platitudes. It sounded so to his own ears, even though he meant every word.

"You're right, of course," Lysandra said suddenly, sitting up. "Rest is all I need, and then it will all come right again. Silly of me to make such a fuss. I'm sorry."

Once more, Renan thought how remarkable and how strong she was. He still heard a hint of fear in her voice, but Lysandra was choosing to deny that fear any power over her. Renan would honor that choice . . . and he would do so with admiration.

He, too, sat up, glancing around their quarters. "I see they've brought us some food," he said. "I'll get it. You stay quiet a while longer."

"No," Lysandra said, "I've been in bed long enough. I need to find out what this place is like. Do you know what happened to my walking stick?"

"It's here—I brought it. Let me get it for you."

Lysandra let Renan do that much for her, but after he helped her from the sleeping shelf, describing as he did its size and height from the floor, she insisted on walking.

She used her stick and her hands to navigate to the front of the cave, where a table and benches made of creamy white and silver-veined marble were situated. She paused each time her fingers touched something new. After she had felt it for herself, she had Renan describe it, as if verifying the knowledge gained through her fingertips.

Reaching the table, Renan looked over the platters of food. He started to tell Lysandra what they were—or at least what he recognized—but again she stopped him. In this, too, she wanted to find her own way.

There were three large platters and a bowl, all beautifully carved from a pale green stone that was almost translucent. Tiny flecks of color deep within the green sparked each time the dishes were moved. The containers granted an almost ethereal beauty to the plain fare they contained.

One platter held rounds of bread, another strips of meat, or perhaps dried fish, Renan thought. The bowl contained a thick liquid; it was dark green and very fragrant. The final platter was piled high with what Renan guessed to be fruits, though he recognized few of them.

There were also smaller platters, plates for personal use. These appeared to be made of thin slices of white stone.

He watched Lysandra's fingers lightly touch the different fruits. She paused over some of them, examining by feel their unfamiliarity. She then took some of the bread and the dried meat. Calling Cloud-Dancer, she fed him what was in her hands.

Once he was fed, she turned her attention to the bowl. Finding the large spoon that rested in it, she ladled some onto her plate and lifted that closer to her nose.

"Rosemary," she said aloud, "watercress, sorrel, chasteberry, parsnip, and . . . I'm not sure what else yet. It should be very nutritious."

There were no small spoons. Lysandra immediately used some bread to mop up the liquid and, seeing her, Renan followed suit. The bread was soft, slightly sweetened, with a crunchy outer crust. The liquid was savory at first, then released a spicy bite. The dried meat was fish, as he had guessed, but it, too, was unlike any he had tasted before. It was wafer thin and flaky, and had a slightly salty flavor that somehow seemed to complete the other tastes that lingered in his mouth.

Renan knew himself to be a poor cook, and his inadequacies had made him usually indifferent toward food as long as it satisfied most of his hunger. But it was impossible to be indifferent toward *this* meal. He crumbled some of the dried fish into the liquid on his plate, scooped up a mouthful with the wonderful bread—and the resulting bite made him smile as he chewed.

He looked over at Lysandra, expecting to see her enjoyment of the meal as obvious as his own. He found a little frown on her face instead.

"What's wrong?" he asked. "Don't you like it?"

"Oh, no, it's wonderful," she said. "It's just that there are so many flavors here, I can't identify them all."

Renan laughed. "I don't need to know what's in it to enjoy it," he said. "Maybe there's an advantage to being neither a cook nor a gardener."

Lysandra did not share in his laughter. "There's more to this food then the way it tastes," she said. "I don't know exactly what, but in the same way I can *see* an illness or an injury, with this food I can *taste* the health and the strength it gives. How old do you think the Elder, Eiddig, is?"

Her question, asked so suddenly and seemingly out of context, surprised Renan. "I don't know," he replied, his voice slightly hesitant. "Seventy, maybe seventy-five."

Lysandra shook her head. "I don't think so. My *Sight* showed me that he was *old*. How old, I don't know—but it's far older than seventy-five. Well over a century, I would guess."

Now Renan was truly startled. "Your *Sight* could be wrong," he said.

"It could be," Lysandra agreed, "but it never has been before, and I've learned to trust it. There's so much about the Cryf we don't know. Even if they do live here, in this place no one has ever heard about, these people are part of Aghamore, too."

"Perhaps that's why the scroll directed us here," Renan said softly, as much to himself as to her. "We're here to find a way to bridge the differences and the fears that keep us separate."

As he spoke, Eiddig entered. "Hast thou found the food to thy liking?" he asked.

"Yes, indeed," Renan replied, coming to his feet. "The food is wonderful. Thank you."

"And thee, Healer?" Eiddig continued. "Hast thou recovered thy strength?"

"Some," Lysandra answered. "Enough."

"Good," the old one said. "Then ye both must come with me. And thy beast. He, too, hath a part in what now awaits. It is time."

Aurya did not *order* Giraldus, but using a few well-placed suggestions given with coaxing smiles, she let him think he had changed his own mind about marching on Ballinrigh. Instead of sending for his army, he sent word to a few specially chosen men to meet them as they continued north into Rathreagh.

Whatever she was supposed to find or do in Yembo had eluded Aurya, but she was determined to continue following the scroll. The child was still the key to everything—and Aurya would get the child no matter whom she had to use or what she had to do along the way.

Giraldus would be furious when he discovered that he, too, had been an unwitting victim of her magic. It would not be the magic that infuriated him; her powers were a tool he did not hesitate to use when he could profit by them. His anger would be that she used magic *on* him rather than *for* him.

But, as they rode away from Yembo, Aurya had every confidence in her ability to appease his anger—and with no more magic than every woman possessed.

They were the only ones riding away from Yembo; the Festival would continue for a week. But Aurya was becoming anxious to get back to Kilgarriff, where she was recognized—and obeyed. She'd had enough of places she did not know and people she could not control.

Soon, she told herself as she lifted her head in the bright May sunlight. She glanced at Giraldus riding beside her, their horses keeping time in an easy lope. A surge of confidence filled her like an internal breath from the warming day.

Do you see, Kizzie? she thought to the spirit of her former teacher. *Do you see how well I use all that you taught me? I am everything you once said I could be— and more. And do you see, Mother? As I vowed when I left you, I am* nothing *like you. I am ashamed of* nothing, *afraid of* nothing. *I* will *have it all.*

Chapter Eighteen

Lysandra held Renan's hand as they were led from the cave where they had rested. Without her *Sight*, or even the ability to share Cloud-Dancer's vision, she walked in true blindness, trying to ignore the fear that whispered in each breath.

Renan kept up a softly spoken stream of descriptions. It helped; she did not feel the darkness quite so heavily while he talked. Cloud-Dancer, too, was beside her. As always she was comforted by his closeness.

Despite his age, Eiddig set a quick pace, going as easily through these tunnels of stone as if he walked down a long corridor of a house. He did not take them back to the Great Cavern. Instead, Lysandra could hear the sound of running water. Soon, she began to feel the finest of sprays upon her cheeks, and the rock of the passageway became slick with moisture.

Then the passageway opened onto another cavern. Renan began to describe the sight to Lysandra. "This is truly amazing, Lysandra," he whispered to her. "I could never have imagined such a sight. It's not as big as the cavern where we were first taken, not even half as big, but there's no ceiling. When I look up I see only darkness—as if it goes on forever. But the most amazing thing is the water . . . it falls straight down, out of the darkness, straight from the world above into a pool that is deep and shines like green crystal. Then the pool flows out from here—a river cutting through the stone.

"And the stone itself," he continued, awe ringing in his voice. "Lysandra, I don't know if my words can begin to convey the beauty here. The ledge on which we're standing seems to be a slab of white crystal, somehow opaque and translucent at the same time. The walls have veins of gold and silver, pockets of crystals, both clear and colored—and oh, the colors in the stone itself. Luminous whites and deepest, shining black too dark for the eye to penetrate . . . greens, some almost as pale as a pearl and others as deep as a forest . . . blues that the sky and the ocean would envy . . . reds, purples and . . . oh, I wish you could see it. No garden above ever had colors more rich or beautiful than these."

"Perhaps, sometime I shall *see* it," Lysandra said, hoping her voice contained the confidence she did not feel. Her mind's eye tried to form a picture from his words— but even her imagination remained in darkness.

Eiddig had waited silently while Renan described their surroundings. Now he turned toward them.

"Before ye is the heart of the Realm of the Cryf," he said. "This is the birthplace of the Great River, which is the life's blood of our world. Though the water falleth from the Up-world, no hand of your kind hath touched nor tainted it. Above this place in your world, stand the frozen peaks where no man walks. But the great Hand of the Divine hath opened the frozen places and turned the water aside, that it might come unto the Cryf and we could live. We honor both the Great River and the Hand that hath sent it unto us."

Eiddig turned and bowed deeply toward the falling

water. "Come," he said to them. "We go now unto the Holy Place, where the words ye must hear have been safely kept from age unto age."

The old one started walking across the crystal ledge, following the circle of the pool formed by the waterfall. Renan put his arm around Lysandra's waist and his cross-hand held hers firmly.

"The water has made the footing slick," he told her. "I won't let you fall."

His arm fell right, comforting and comfortable. The warmth of his body against her side made Lysandra want to lean into him—not to walk, but just to stand here being held. The feeling frightened her; she had not felt it since the last time Ultan had held her—ten years ago. She had never thought—or wanted—to experience it again.

And Renan . . . *Father* Renan, she reminded herself . . . was a priest. He would not, he *could* not, be feeling the same way.

You're just tired, she told herself as they started to walk. *These feelings aren't real. They're just born out of the situation and because you feel helpless again. They'll go away when the* Sight *returns.*

Spray doused her face as they neared the waterfall. The sound of falling water became too loud for her to hear anything else . . . except her own thoughts, and those she would not allow.

Finally, their clothing becoming soaked from the thickening spray, they followed Eiddig *behind* the waterfall. There, another cave welcomed them. It was filled with warmth, and Lysandra was glad to get out of the chilling shower.

Renan began to describe their new path. The ceiling here was scarcely a handbreadth above his head, and the entryway was both long and narrow. The stones, providing illumination, were laid out as a single row on either side. The whole effect sounded claustrophobic, and Lysandra was grateful for once that she could not see it.

Finally, the long entrance opened into a larger room. It was from there the heat emanated. Hot air rose from fissures in the rock, filling the place with a welcome warmth.

"The other Elders are here," Renan whispered to her. "They're all seated at the back. I don't think they look pleased."

Lysandra gave a little nod to let him know that she heard, but she concentrated on trying to feel the emotions of the Elders. But, like her *Sight*, that, too, was denied her. For all that her inner senses were telling her, she could have been standing alone.

In this cave, where the walls were closer and the air warmer, she noticed for the first time the scent given off by the Cryf. It was not unpleasant but it was distinctive— warm and earthy. It was also sweet, reminding Lysandra of her garden in the sunshine.

The Cryf are truly a people of the earth, she thought suddenly. *Much more so than the farmers or woodsmen who claim the title. They are so much a part of this realm that even the scent of their bodies proclaims their unity.*

Eiddig motioned them toward a rock shelf that extended, bench high, from the wall on their left. Once they were settled, Eiddig turned to the other Elders.

"Full eighty cycles of the Great River have I been Leader and Guide unto our people," he said to them. "Eighty times hath the River swelled and eighty times fallen. With the rebirth of each cycle, eighty times have I returned unto this Holy Place to read again the Words, that my heart would be purified and my eyes opened, prepared for the day when the Words would be fulfilled.

"I, Eiddig-Sant, Keeper of the Holy Words, Leader and Guide of the Cryf—whose name meaneth Strong—say that the time foretold unto us by the Mind of the Divine, given unto the great Dewi-Sant, first of us who carried the Staff, is now come. If any here believeth not with me, speak thy doubt aloud."

Eiddig waited; so did Lysandra. She was fairly certain she understood the oddly styled speech of the Elder. The scrolls and prophecies of Tambryn had their counterpart here with the Cryf, and Lysandra felt somehow certain that these Holy Words were far more ancient than Tambryn's.

One of the Cryf Elders finally stood. "I be Jarim," he said formally, "Elder of the Fourth Clan. I question not the Will of the Divine nor the great wisdom of Eiddig-Sant. Thou hast Guided the Cryf well. I say only that before the Holy Words be spoken unto the ears of Up-worlders, thy heart must be certain. Past deceit hath taught the Cryf that the hearts of Up-worlders be not true. Once the Holy Words be spoken, they can not be hidden again. If these Up-worlders be not true, the tears of the Cryf shall fill the Great River."

There was a soft murmur of agreement among the Elders. Then Eiddig spoke again.

"For his wisdom was Jarim named Elder of the Fourth Clan, and with wisdom doth he now speak. Yet I tell thee, since first these Up-worlders did come among us, long hours have I spent in this Holy Place, reading again the Words and seeking the Mind of the Divine upon this question. I say that these be indeed The Ones. All that was shown unto Dewi-Sant hath come to pass. They be as he said they would be."

Eiddig brought his staff down hard upon the stone floor.

The sudden *crack* that ricocheted around the cave walls was less unsettling, however, than the words that followed.

"'. . . *And so shall the Up-world be in turmoil,*" Eiddig said, his voice taking on the singsong cadence of recitation. "*Darkness shall threaten all and only the Hidden One who holdeth the Core of Wisdom within can keep the darkness from destroying both the Up-world and the Realm of the Strong.*

"'*At this time shall three travelers find the shadowed door and enter where no Up-worlder may find their way. But they are as no other Up-worlders, for their hearts contain not the stain of greed, and they come unto the Cryf to heal not to destroy.*

"'*By these signs shalt thou know them. One traveler shall be a Servant of the Divine. This one walks the Path of Light and carrieth that which gives guidance unto their journey. The second traveler seeth with eyes of blindness and heareth the unspoken word. This one doth own the Hands of Healing and is one with the gifts of the earth. The third of this company walketh not on two feet, but on four, a beast whose fur is like unto veins of silver that runneth through white crystal and whose eyes shine like unto blue agates. This one hath chosen a heart of loyalty and turneth from the wild and fierce ways.*

"'*These travelers shall take the sorrows of the Cryf as their own. Their hands shall be quick to help in trouble, and their hearts shall be filled with understanding . . .*'"

Eiddig stopped his recitation of the Holy Words. Immediately, one of the Elders stood. It was a female this time.

"I be Berla," she said, "Elder of the Seventh Clan. I say that once more the vision of Eiddig-Sant hath been clear for he hath seen and known these Up-worlders as the Travelers foretold by Dewi-Sant. I say, let what remaineth of the Holy Words be spoken unto our ears and unto the ears of these Up-Worlders so that the Cryf may show that we serve the Will of the Divine in this, as in all things."

"So say I," came another voice and then another. Lysandra counted twelve all told; the Elders were in agreement.

"Sixteen times did the Divine reveal unto the great Dewi-Sant what was to be. It is of the Thirteenth Showing we speak now," Eiddig said.

Like the Thirteenth Scroll, Lysandra thought. *Does the number mean something? Something I don't understand?*

She heard Eiddig's footsteps coming closer. He stopped in front of Renan, and she wondered if the priest was aware that his hand tightened on her own, or if he even realized that he still held her hand though she no longer needed his guidance. It felt so right, so comfortable for their hands to be joined, that she had stopped noticing until just now.

"Thou art truly a Servant of the Divine," Eiddig said, somewhere between a question and a statement.

"I am a priest," Renan answered, "a Guide for my people."

"For thee was Dewi-Sant given these words. Listen well, for thou knowest that the Divine giveth only the Truth, but the Truth be ofttimes difficult to hear."

"I will listen," Renan assured him, "and I will hear."

"Well dost thou speak and with wisdom—as must a Guide."

Lysandra heard the little note of surprise in Eiddig's voice as he said this. She wondered if Renan was aware that his status among the Cryf had just been elevated. *That could help us,* she thought.

"To thee, then, be these Words spoken," Eiddig continued. "'*Thou art the Eyes of Guidance, for thou hast journeyed long upon the Path of Light. But past secrets follow thee and can not remain hidden. The Light shineth on all. All that was, is, and the Holy Hand hath not given in vain. To wound can be to heal; to strengthen can destroy.'"*

Lysandra heard Renan's sharp intake of breath. What past secrets could the priest be hiding? She realized again how little she knew about the man with whom she was traveling. Yet their paths seemed locked together, at least for now, and she did not doubt that it was right.

Eiddig now turned to her. "To thee, Healer, do the Holy Words also speak," he said. *"'Thou art the Hand of Prophecy, for thou hast walked a path of tears and knowest both the good and the evil that liveth in human hearts. Though thy tears be now unshed, they keep thee from receiving all the Hand of the Divine waiteth to give. A heart filled with fear and anger hath room for little else. Thy true self lies hidden in the darkness of thy choosing. Choose instead Light, that another may also See.'"*

These words cut like a sword into Lysandra's soul. Although she recognized their truth, they also filled her with new questions. What more was she supposed to receive? The gifts she now possessed had already turned her life upside down and taken her far from the peaceful life she craved.

But was it peace—or was it hiding? What Light was she, a blind woman, to choose, and how could she make *anyone* see, who could not see herself?

"Of thy third companion," Eiddig continued, barely pausing in his recitation, "are these words given, but to thee, Healer, not to thy beast. *'Here, in the Heart of Truth, be the treasure which thou must guard, for such hearts be not given in vain and they come as teachers as well as friends. Learn, and much thou seekest will be revealed . . . and not unto thee alone . . .'"*

Eiddig was not finished. He now turned to the Elders. "To the Cryf doth Dewi-Sant now say '. . . *The Strong have been Guardians throughout the ages and Guardians ye shall remain. Unto ye must the Travelers come, if they be true, and unto ye they return. They shall bring the One in whom the Core of Wisdom awaiteth release. Fear not to lend your aid, for the Wisdom cometh not for the Up-world alone. Wisdom is given of the Divine and is given that all may walk again together in peace. The arms of the Strong must carry Wisdom unto your midst, and the ears of the Strong shall hear the first Words that arise from Wisdom's Core. Ye shall hear and know that they be Truth.*

"'But if in your fear, born of past sorrows, you have turned from the Words of the Divine, then shall fear and sorrow forever be your Way. Your hidden doors shall be opened, your hallowed places destroyed, your men shall know of death and your women bondage and tears. What awaiteth ye, awaiteth all. Now is the time of Choosing.'"

Finally, Eiddig's voice grew silent. Lysandra was aware of the sound of her heart pounding in her chest. Then she became aware of something else. The world before her looked again like gray fog lifting in the early morn; her *Sight* was returning.

Lysandra wanted to shout with the joy of the moment, to get up and dance around the room. She did neither. Instead, she gave Renan's hand a little squeeze. When he turned his head toward her, she *saw* the movement—not clearly, still as through a fog, but she *saw*.

From the entry to the cave, there came a noise. All, including Lysandra, turned toward it. Each second lessened the fog clouding Lysandra's *Sight* and when a young male Cryf entered the cave, she could *see* him.

The newcomer knelt before Eiddig, and the Elder put a hand upon his bowed and waiting head. *A prayer? A blessing?* Lysandra wondered. Then the elder Cryf reached down and by the elbow, raised the younger one to his side.

Lysandra's *Sight* was continuing to clear; details were coming into focus. This Cryf looked barely into adulthood. His posture was straighter than any of the Elders'; the hair that covered his body was finer, shinier, and less dense, and his face was more visible and unlined. He seemed to radiate youth, health, and strength.

"Here be Talog," Eiddig announced, "son of the Twelfth Clan. In him, the Voice of the Divine is strong. Although he hath seen but twenty cycles, already he traineth in the Way of the Guide. I, Eiddig, say now that the Cryf remain true. Never hath any of our kind forsaken the Ways of the Divine nor hath our heart closed unto the warnings of the Holy Words. I, therefore, say that Talog must now join these Travelers, to be the Arms of the Strong that carrieth Wisdom's Core back unto our Realm."

"So say the Twelfth Clan," came a voice from among the Elders.

"So say the Third Clan."

"So say the Fifth Clan."

Soon all of the voices clamored their agreement with Eiddig's words.

Renan leaned close to Lysandra. "I don't think they're going to ask us," he whispered. "But I've no objection. Do you?"

Lysandra shook her head. "You keep saying the scroll brought us here for a reason," she whispered back. "This must be it."

As if to give lie to Renan's words, Eiddig brought the young Cryf to stand before Renan and Lysandra.

"Ye are the Travelers whom the Cryf have long awaited, and our Choosing has been made. But from ye must come the final words. Thou art the Eyes of Guidance who findeth the pathways through the darkness of unknowing; thou art the Hand of Prophecy that holdeth the power to release Wisdom's Core; thou art the Heart of Loyalty and Truth whose ways contain a lesson for us all. Do ye accept Talog as your companion, to guide ye through the Realm of the Cryf and the hidden places that await, and to give the strength of the Cryf unto your moments of need?"

Renan spoke first. Being familiar with the old tongue and the language of prophecy, he used some of Eiddig's stylized manner of speech.

"I, whom thou hast named Eyes of Guidance, accept Talog as one of our number. From this time forth we shall be four, as are the four directions to the earth from which all things arise. Now we are complete."

After he had finished, he nudged Lysandra gently. She, too, tried to fit her words to the tone now established.

"I, whom thou hast called the Hand of Prophecy," she began, the words coming far more hesitantly to her lips than to Renan's, "accept Talog as one of our number. He will be our companion and our brother. Together we shall walk through both darkness and light."

She could think of nothing more to say. Instead, she lifted her hand from Cloud-Dancer's head to see the wolf's reaction to Talog. If Cloud-Dancer would not accept him, then no words mattered.

Cloud-Dancer crept forward. Lysandra kept a close watch, using the full powers of her restored *Sight* to notice any warning signals and quickly call the wolf back if necessary. Cloud-Dancer, however, seemed more curious than threatening. He reached Talog and began to sniff, walking around the young Cryf three times.

Then, suddenly, the wolf stood on his hind feet and placed his paws on Talog's shoulders, tongue hanging out one side in a relaxed canine grin. Cloud-Dancer had given his approval.

Lysandra laughed, and the sound dissolved the tension that had filled the cave ever since their arrival. Everyone grinned at Cloud-Dancer's antics as he licked the young Cryf's face before returning to sit beside Lysandra.

"So be it," said Eiddig, his voice lighter than it had ever sounded to Lysandra. "Talog shall go Up-world with the Travelers . . . and may the Hand of the Divine guide and protect ye all. All that the Cryf possess that might give ye aid shall now be prepared. Rest and gather your strength, trusting that all shall be done that may be done."

Lysandra, her hand once more resting on Cloud-Dancer's head, gave a sigh of relief. Her *Sight* had returned and they would soon be on their way again. That meant this was all one step closer to being over—and she and Cloud-Dancer were that much closer to going home.

Chapter Nineteen

Elon was becoming tired of unproductive meetings—and *very* tired of the company of his brother bishops. Day after day, he listened while the others argued, each extolling the virtues of his Baron and explaining why he should have the Church's support as the next High King. Every Baron in Aghamore, it seemed, was godly and devout, mindful of his people's welfare before his own, a leader of men, gentle at home . . .

And no doubt beloved of animals and small children, Elon thought with sarcasm as he listened yet again to Awnan of Dromkeen drone on about Baron Curran.

Elon had still said nothing about Giraldus. The other bishops, aware of Lady Aurya's open hostility toward the Church, seemed to expect that the Baron of Kilgarriff was not a choice for the throne—or at least not for the Church's support in obtaining it.

The Archbishop, however, had accepted Elon's tale of Aurya's changing attitude. As their confessor, only Elon could know how much of this "conversion" could be told, and every once in a while Elon found the old man's eyes upon him, silently questioning why he did not speak up. But Elon had been hoping to receive some word from Giraldus and Aurya before he went any further with their plan.

Glancing around the room, Elon saw his boredom mirrored in most of the other faces. A few wore the set expression of minds determined to see their own way served. As things stood, the College of Bishops had reached an impasse. Without some new element introduced, they would talk in circles indefinitely.

It's time, Elon thought. *They're ready to listen.*

He glanced over and waited until he caught the Archbishop's eye. Once he was certain of the old man's attention, he gave a little nod. Then, without waiting for Awnan to finish, he stood. Immediately, the room quieted. Awnan stopped mid-sentence, which caused Elon to suppress a sardonic smile. At least he had succeeded in quieting the loquacious bishop of Dromkeen; that alone should win him some support, he thought as he saw the surprised expressions all around him.

"We recognize Elon, our brother from Kilgarriff," the Archbishop said, using the royal pronoun as befitted a Prince of the Church. "You have been too long silent, Elon. Speak now and without hesitation, for we are all brothers here, united in service of Our Lord, His Church, and of this land—though at the moment, we seem to be united in little else," the Archbishop added with a gentle, fatherly smile.

Elon gave a slight bow to his superior. "Your Eminence," he began, "my brothers—we have all listened to each other for many long days. I must say that we in Aghamore are certainly blessed to have so many worthy leaders to care for the welfare of the people. But what we do not have is a *King*.

"It is a heavy burden to know that the one to whom we give our support may indeed become the one to wear the crown. We, whose lives are dedicated to the welfare of souls, must now look to the worldly welfare of this land and people. To do so, we must call upon every bit of wisdom we possess and our prayers provide.

"This, of course, you all know—but I ask you to truly think again what it means. *Worldly* welfare of a kingdom is not necessarily won or maintained by the same virtues as *spiritual* welfare. The one who wears the crown must be able to both pray *and* fight. He must be able to keep his soul at peace with Our Lord *and* keep his kingdom in peace from its enemies.

"All of you, my brothers, have spoken on behalf of the Barons of your sees—and rightly so. But as I have listened, I have asked myself each time whether this is the man who possesses both the virtue and the strength this kingdom needs. The late King Anri left Aghamore much weakened, and the threat from our old enemies cannot be overlooked. Of virtue, I have heard much; of *strength*, I have heard far too little. Therefore, I must now speak the name few of you thought to hear at this gathering. I say that Giraldus of Kilgarriff is the only Baron who possesses the strength and the worldly understanding necessary to rule this kingdom into peace and prosperity again."

Immediately there was the eruption of voices Elon expected. He let it continue, waiting for someone to have the courage to stand and give voice to the objections most of them were feeling.

Finally, Gairiad of Sylaun stood. "We all know that Elon believes he speaks of the good of Aghamore," he began, looking around the room but carefully avoiding Elon's eyes. "But I must ask our brother how we can be expected to give our support to a Baron whose enmity toward this Church and whose open ungodliness is known across the kingdom? Only two centuries ago, there were still places in this land where heathen practices existed and those who followed the True Faith were persecuted. Are we willing to turn this land and its people, who look to us to guard and protect their *souls*, back into the hands of one such as Giraldus of Kilgarriff—or more importantly, to his godless concubine Lady Aurya, who practices the devil's own tool of magic? Surely, our brother cannot mean this."

Thank you, Gairiad, Elon thought as murmurs of agreement rose around him.

"I do *not* mean that we should give the crown to the ungodly or Aghamore into the hands of the heathen," Elon affirmed. "I say instead, that we must *prevent* such a thing by having a strong ruler upon the throne.

"As you all know, Aghamore is a haven of the True Faith, surrounded by enemies who still worship false gods. Without a King who gives the land strength again, we become a target for invasion. Do I need to remind this assembly of the terrible wars in our past, particularly with the people of Corbenica, who still give blood sacrifice to their gods? Do we want this for Aghamore? No, I say. For this reason, I again state that Giraldus of Kilgarriff *must* be our choice for King."

Still, the shocked and angry whispers ran through the room. Elon watched Dwyer of Camlough begin shifting his quite considerable bulk, as if gathering strength to stand. Before he could convince his overtaxed legs to bear his weight, Elon held up his hand for silence. He had one more surprise to offer before he sat down again.

"As Bishop of Kilgarriff, I, more than any of you, am aware of the past hostility of the Baron and his lady. But, to answer more fully the concerns our brother Gairiad so rightly put forth, I will tell you this. Not long before this council was convened, I was called to the home of Baron

Giraldus to meet with him—and especially with the Lady Aurya. Although, as their confessor, there is much I cannot say of that meeting, even to you my brother bishops, I can tell you that they are now on a pilgrimage of contrition and reparation. When they return, Lady Aurya has asked to be baptized into the Faith and their union will be legitimated by the Sacrament of Holy Matrimony."

"Are we to believe that after so many years, the Lady Aurya has renounced her evil practices of magic?" Dwyer of Camlough's disbelief was obvious.

"I, myself, heard her confession," Elon responded, "and I tell you that her repentance is real. Do you think, Dwyer, that I and all the faithful in Kilgarriff have not prayed throughout the years for just such a thing? Do you no longer believe that prayers are answered or that miracles can occur?"

There, Elon thought, *that should silence them—at least for now.*

As Elon resumed his seat, the Archbishop thumped his crozier three times on the floor. Immediately, the room grew still, and all eyes turned to the old man.

"I seems that our brother Elon has brought us news that we must all carefully and prayerfully consider. For myself, I congratulate him, and give thanks to Our Lord, that by Elon's prayers and example he has tamed the ungodly and led the Lady Aurya to Grace. The Church may now thrive in Kilgarriff greater than ever before. I admonish all of you to take heed of this example and follow it, so that all the ungodly within this kingdom may be brought unto the converting and healing Grace of Holy Mother Church.

"Let us adjourn now and go into the chapel for our Evening Prayer. Tomorrow, we shall not meet. Tomorrow shall be a day of retreat, of prayer and contemplation.

Perhaps then, when we gather again on the following day, the decision we must soon make will have become clear."

The Archbishop rose to lead the way into the private chapel adjoining this conference room. He motioned to Elon.

"Come, my son, and give me your arm to lean upon. My old bones have grown weary from these long days."

Elon hid his smile of triumph as he hastened to the Archbishop's side. The meaning of this act was not lost on Elon—or on the others in the room. Without saying a word, the Archbishop was letting it be known that he was ready to support Elon . . . *and* Giraldus.

"Tell me, my son," the old man said softly. "Why did you not mention the reason for this pilgrimage undertaken by the Baron and his lady?"

"As I said, Your Eminence, I was their confessor. This pilgrimage is part of the penance that came out of that long meeting and confession. I prayed for many days before reaching the decision to mention it here . . . and I would not have done so were I not certain the future of Aghamore depended on sharing this knowledge."

The Archbishop nodded. "A difficult decision," he said, "but wisely made. If Baron Giraldus's and Lady Aurya's repentance is as sincere as you believe, then I think we will soon come to an accord in this matter. Yes, it was well done, Elon," he assured him, "well done, indeed."

If you only knew how *well done,* Elon thought, congratulating himself on a well-played bit of fantasy. The tale about a pilgrimage not only struck a chord within the hearts of traditionalists such as the Archbishop, but was a brilliant way to explain why Giraldus and Aurya were not in Kilgarriff during this time when the future of the whole kingdom was so unsettled.

Now, if only I would hear from them, his thoughts continued. *Though no one else need know, I should be kept informed of their progress. The others will want to know when they will return. If they're gone too long, they'll lose everything I've won today.*

But for today, the cause was won. Elon contented himself with that as he entered the chapel and helped the Archbishop into the Cathedra, the tall, thronelike chair reserved for the Primus of the Church. Then, before Elon could turn away to leave the sanctuary within the altar rail, the Archbishop stopped him. The old man motioned to the nearby lectern on which stood the large missal, opened and waiting.

"I am weary, my son," the Archbishop said softly— but not too softly, allowing himself to be overheard. "I would deem it an act of charity if you would take my place and lead us in the Office tonight, so that I may rest while we pray."

"It would be my joy to do so," Elon replied.

He knelt to receive the old man's blessing, carefully appearing the soul of piety. Then, standing, he kept his expression controlled and humble, making certain the others thought him surprised—even overwhelmed—by the honor. His heart jumped and pounded with glee as he approached the lectern, but before beginning, he glanced out over the assembled bishops.

The marked favor of the Archbishop had not been lost upon them. Bresal, Bishop of Rathreagh, looked thunderous; he had disliked Elon as far back as seminary days. Tavic of Farnagh looked surprised. The rest wore expressions of resigned acceptance, signaling their recognition that the Archbishop had done more than give his support to Giraldus. He had just publicly picked his preferred successor.

Elon kept his face a model of proper humility as he

slowly lifted his hands in the ancient attitude of supplication.

"Let my prayers be set forth as incense," he intoned the opening line of the Office, chanting in his preferred mode, one as familiar to the others as it was to him.

"And the lifting up of my hands be evening sacrifice," came the response in the rich tones of well-practiced male voices.

Elon continued, confidently leading the others through the chanted prayers. He let his elation slowly bloom across his face in a careful timing that let the others think he was responding to the ecstasy of prayer. In truth, as he mindlessly, automatically, conducted the ritual that had long ago ceased to have any meaning for him, he could already feel the weight of the triple-crowned mitre upon his head.

Chapter Twenty

Lysandra and Cloud-Dancer, Renan and now Talog, prepared to leave the Realm of the Cryf. They would travel as far as possible on the Great River, in boats provided by the Cryf. Their provisions had been restocked and, much to Lysandra's delight and relief, so had her herbs and medicines.

The Cryf had been lavish with their gift of supplies. Eiddig, speaking for the Healers, also promised Lysandra that after she and the others returned, she would have both seeds and live cuttings of several plants to take back to her own garden.

Now the Council of Elders, along with many of the other Cryf, were gathered to see the travelers off. One group of a dozen or so were clustered around Talog, embracing him by turns. With the resurgence of her *Sight*, Lysandra's empathic abilities were also renewed, and she could feel the fear with which Talog's family was sending him forth. She wanted to give them words of comfort, assurances that their loved one would be all right, but she could not. She knew no better than they what might await.

Renan was talking with Eiddig. He had the scroll rolled out and propped open with rocks while the two of them squatted and drew in the sand. *Like little boys playing a secret game,* Lysandra thought, hoping that the old one and his Holy Words had insights that would clarify the journey ahead.

Lysandra sat upon a rock by the water's edge, Cloud-Dancer by her side. With her *Sight* she was examining the boats and the river, trying to build up her courage. She had never been in a boat before, had not been swimming since she was a child, and though she had told no one, the idea of traveling by water terrified her.

She did not realize Renan and Eiddig had concluded their discussion until suddenly the priest was beside her. He was smiling confidently.

"The boats will take several days off our journey," he told her, "and make the going easier. The help of the Cryf is truly God-sent."

"You know where we're going, then?"

"I think so," Renan answered. "Not the name of the town, but the area and what to look for. You remember how Eiddig said he'd been Guide of the Cryf for eighty years? Well, he was sixty before he took that office and he's been studying those Holy Words since he began his training at the age of twenty. He knows them by heart. I thought I understood the Scroll of Tambryn fairly well, but he's helped me see many little things that I was missing. I wish we could stay longer."

His voice was so enthusiastic, Lysandra could not help herself. "Can't we?" she asked. "If the boats are going to shorten our journey by so much—"

"No," Renan said, shaking his head. "One thing both writings make clear is the need for haste. The Words of Dewi-Sant speak continually of the 'beasts of darkness' biting our heels. Eiddig believes this means that others are following us, trying to find the same child we seek. If these others, these 'beasts of darkness,' find the child first, then according to Tambryn, the 'light that dawns in Aghamore will be put out and our eyes shall see no light again.'"

Lysandra made no reply; what could she say to that? If they failed, the Aghamore she knew would die. Compared to that, riding in a boat did not seem so horrific after all.

She stood, straightened her shoulders, and took a deep breath. "Well," she said, "we'd best go then. 'Sooner started, sooner finished,' my mother used to say."

"And I agree," Renan replied. "I'll go tell Eiddig we're ready."

The Cryf Guide was now with the others saying good-bye to Talog. When Renan approached them, Lysandra felt the burst of new fear race through the group. One of them, a slightly older female, suddenly threw her arms around Talog, as if not wanting to let him go.

That's his mother, Lysandra realized, feeling the unmistakable fear of losing a child.

She suddenly felt a sense of loss for her own mother, something she had not experienced in too many years gone by. *What would she have done?* Lysandra wondered. *Would she have cried and not wanted to let me go, fearful of the unknown?*

Then Lysandra shook her head. No, that would not have been her mother's way. Her mother, in whom courage and duty ran as surely as this river, would have sent her daughter off proudly, her eyes dry and her head held high—and saved her tears for private.

And I will do my mother's memory proud, Lysandra thought, lifting her chin. *Like her, I'll try to keep my fears to myself and give only strength and encouragement to my companions . . . and I have Cloud-Dancer to help me, something my mother never had.*

Eiddig, Talog, and the other Cryf came with Renan back to where Lysandra and Cloud-Dancer waited. While they crowded around, Talog knelt to receive the Guide's blessing. The old one placed his hand upon the younger Cryf's forehead.

"Talog, son of the Twelfth Clan," he said, "thy shoulders be made strong to bear the burden now placed upon thee, for thou carriest the future of the Cryf with thee. The Divine, who hath created thee, shall be with thee and grant clarity unto thine eyes, wisdom unto thy mind, strength unto thy body, and courage unto thy heart."

When Eiddig finished, Talog rose and went to his boat, stepping into it with confident ease. Lysandra noticed that he did not look again at his family, but kept his eyes fixed on the river path they were to follow. Of his emotions, she could feel nothing.

Eiddig now turned to Renan. The priest did not kneel, but met the Cryf's stare as an equal—both Servants of the Divine. Lysandra could feel Eiddig's approval.

Still, he put his hand upon Renan's forehead in the gesture Lysandra had seen him use in many situations. It was a sign of blessing, but Lysandra had the feeling there was more involved than that, something the Cryf Guide was sensing through that simple touch.

"The Divine be ever with thee," Eiddig said, "and guide thee, who art the Guide of this journey."

"And the Divine keep ye safe until we return," Renan imparted his blessing in return, "and prepare your hearts to aid the one whom we now seek."

Renan, too, went to the boats and stepped into the second one with the same confidence Talog had shown. Lysandra would ride with Talog, the most experienced on the water. Renan, who knew boats from his youth, would follow with Cloud-Dancer.

Eiddig now came over to Lysandra and put one hand upon her shoulder in a gesture of comfort. His other hand he placed on her forehead. He stood for a moment saying nothing, but Lysandra could feel the encouragement flowing from him and the strength he wished to share with her.

"The Divine be with thee, Healer," he said. "On thee hath been placed the heaviest burden of all, for Prophecy's Hand alone can unlock the Wisdom that must be a salvation unto this land. But the Divine chooseth not unwisely. Thou hast been given all thou needest. It dwelleth within thee. Trust unto the Gifts of the Divine and so shall thy heart find its surety and strength."

Lysandra bowed her head, silently praying Eiddig's

words were true. Then she *saw* the Cryf lay a hand on Cloud-Dancer's head and heard him softly say a blessing for the wolf as well.

It was now their turn to get into the boats, but even with her *Sight* Lysandra felt none of the confidence the others had displayed. With a word, she sent Cloud-Dancer into Renan's boat, and at her order to stay, the wolf settled down peacefully.

Lysandra now turned toward the boat that was to carry her. Although she had promised herself to hide her fears, she knew the intensity of this one must show on her face. But Eiddig was there to guide her, and Talog turned to take her other hand. As she touched the younger Cryf, she was suddenly flooded with all the emotions he was keeping so firmly locked away.

He, too, was afraid—afraid of her and Renan as Upworlders, afraid of leaving the safety of this underground Realm and his people, afraid of all the unknowns that awaited him and afraid he would never return. All of these fears were overlaid with his deep sense of duty and his unwavering belief in the protection and Will of the Divine.

But he's not afraid of this boat or of the water, Lysandra thought. Taking a deep breath, she let herself be guided to her seat.

Once she was settled, Talog used his paddle to push the boat out into the river's current. As the boats began to move away, Eiddig raised his staff high above his head.

"Remember that the Divine goeth with ye," he called after them, "and hath already chosen your way. Though troubles lie before ye, fear not. Ye are companions by the Hand of the Divine. Walk ye in faith and ye shall return to us. We shall await your return in that same faith . . ."

The current was swift and they were being carried

quickly away. Eiddig's voice faded, and soon they were traveling in silence. Not even the river made a noise as it carried them through the stone-walled wonder that was the Realm of the Cryf.

The silence was so complete Lysandra could not tell if they had been on the river for one hour or three, if they had traveled five miles or fifty. Her *Sight* became an intermittent thing, coming or going on its own whim. In the moments of its absence, with not even Cloud-Dancer's presence to comfort her, Lysandra felt the silence like a physical weight on her chest, pushing her down and making it difficult to breathe. In those moments, she had to fight against the panic that threatened to overwhelm her. She wanted to shout at the others to talk to her, tell her anything just so she would know she was not alone.

During the times when her *Sight* returned, Lysandra lost her fear in the breathtaking beauty of the river's course. It wound through rock worn to shapes her mind could not have constructed, where the different strata of stone painted the walls with stripes of wonder. Veins of gold and silver, clusters of crystals and colored gems caught the light of the luminous stones that were everywhere in this strange and amazing Realm. She understood why the Cryf spoke of the Divine so often and intimately; they lived in a Realm no human hand could have created.

Through all this time and distance, her companion made no effort at conversation. Lysandra was not certain how to break his silence, but gathering up her courage, she knew she had to try and find *something* they could say to one another.

"If we're going to travel together," she said at last, "we should get to know each other—don't you think? Eiddig said we would need to trust and—" she let her voice trail off.

The young Cryf turned and looked at her over his shoulder. "I am Talog," he said, turning back around.

"That much I know," Lysandra replied, not ready to give up. "I also know that you are twenty years—twenty cycles—old and that you are training to be the next Guide to your people."

Talog lifted one shoulder in a stoic shrug. "What more needest thou know?"

Lysandra was quiet for a moment, thinking. She would have to try another tack.

"Why would Eiddig choose you to come with us?" she asked. "Or did you volunteer?"

Again Talog threw her a glance over his shoulder. "What be that word—volunteer?" he said it slowly, as if feeling it in his mouth.

"It means you asked to come with us—yourself, instead of Eiddig telling you to."

"I did not—volunteer—to leave my home," Talog said, still speaking slowly. "Eiddig did not tell me. The Divine chooseth and so I go."

He doesn't know our language well, Lysandra realized, listening to the hesitant way he put the words together.

"Talog," she said, "how is it that you and Eiddig speak our language when the Cryf have a language of their own?"

"All the Cryf know the tongue of the Holy Words," he replied.

Had she finally found the way to reach through his barriers? Lysandra wondered. "I would like to learn the language of the Cryf. Will you teach me?" she asked.

Talog gave a single nod. "I shall teach," he said. "Thou choosest."

Choose? she thought. *Choose what—the words?*

"All right," she said. "Cryf, the name of your people—it means *Strong* in our language, right?"

Again came the single nod. "We are The Strong," he said, pride ringing in his voice. "Strong be we in body and strong in service unto the Divine."

"You are training to be a Guide of the Cryf. What is that word, Guide?"

"*Arweinydd.*"

"*Arweinydd,*" Lysandra repeated, trying to match his pronunciation but failing her attempt to roll her "r" or to produce the same lilt that ran through the word.

"What is the Cryf word for healer?" she asked next.

"*Meddyg,*" Talog said. "Thou art *Meddyg.*"

Over the next hour they traded words. Most of them were simple, like *cwch* for boat and *dwr* for water. Lysandra learned that Cloud-Dancer's name in the language of the Cryf was *Cwmwl-Dannsio* when translated exactly, though Talog explained that the Cryf would say *Dannsio gan Cwmwl*—Dancer of Clouds.

Her pronunciations were far from perfect, but Talog never laughed. He occasionally corrected her gently, and it was a pleasant way to pass the time.

Renan will enjoy this when we make camp, she thought. *Perhaps by the time we return we'll be able to talk with the Cryf in their language—at least a little. Maybe then more of them will learn that not all Up-worlders are the same or need to be feared.*

They did not make it out of the Realm of the Cryf that first day, but made camp along the river when their bodies told them it was time to rest. For the first several hours, Lysandra found that her balance was precarious; walking or sitting, she still felt as if the boat were beneath her and she was yet being rocked by the gentle motion of the river. It was disconcerting enough to make it difficult to sleep—but her fatigue finally won.

When she awoke in the morning, the sensation was gone and solid land felt solid again. The Cryf had provided them with plenty of travel-food, so breakfast was quickly consumed. The one thing Lysandra missed was a fire over which she could make some of the herbal tea with which she was used to starting her mornings. But the Great River provided cold, clean water for both drinking and washing, and Lysandra started her day feeling refreshed if not fully satisfied.

"How much farther before we leave the underground?" Lysandra asked Talog, as they once again settled into their boat.

Talog gave the single, one-shouldered shrug that Lysandra recognized as his general response whenever he did not know an answer or understand a question. Sometimes, it was difficult to judge which one he meant.

Lysandra saw that she would have to be content with that answer; Talog knew no more than they how long it would take to reach the outside. *The outside.* That thought made her smile. As beautiful as were the tunnels and caves that comprised the Realm of the Cryf, she missed the fresh air and the sounds of the birds; she missed the smell of the soil and the feel of the sun. She missed her own *realm*, the Up-world, where she belonged.

It did not take long to get both boats cast off. Lysandra and Talog resumed their pastime of yesterday, exchanging words and sentences in each other's language. But sometimes it was comfortable just to sit in silence. The fear with which she had begun this journey was gone. Today, as she became increasingly used to the gentle motion of the boat, she found it lulling—rather like being rocked to sleep. It was easy to close her eyes and let her thoughts drift.

As she sat, eyes closed, during one of these times of companionable quiet, a strange noise began to touch the very edges of her awareness. It was both familiar and yet unlike any she had ever heard. Recognition nagged at her.

"Talog," she said finally, "do you hear that sound? Do you know what it is?"

"*Plantgan yrAwyr*," he said. "Where the Great River entereth the Up-world, the *Plantgan yrAwyr*, Children of the Air, make their homes where the two worlds do meet. They give their song unto the air which is their home. The Holy Words say the *Plantgan yrAwyr* were fashioned from the joy of the Divine, and they give their songs in thanksgiving for Life."

"Plantgan yrAwyr," Lysandra tried. As she spoke the words, recognition dawned. Children of the air . . . singing their song . . .

They were birds.

"Birds," she said aloud to Talog, "we call them birds. And there must be hundreds of them to make this much noise."

Excited now, she swung partway around. "Do you hear them?" she called to the boat behind her.

"Yes," Renan called back. She heard the sound of his paddle in the water. His boat was beside hers when he spoke again.

"Do either of you know what the sound is?" he asked.

"Birds," Lysandra replied confidently. "At this time of year, it's probably mostly the nestlings singing, calling for food from their parents. Talog calls them the *Plantgan yrAwyr*, the Children of the Air. Isn't that a lovely name?"

"... 'The hollow places where the children sing,'" Renan quoted Tambryn's words.

"Yes," Lysandra agreed. "We found it. What do we do next?"

"I'm not sure," Renan replied. "Talog—do you know what's ahead?"

The Cryf shook his head. "It is Up-world," he said.

Although the twists of the river made it impossible to see very far ahead, the echoing sound was growing ever louder. Soon they needed to shout in order to hear each other. With a gesture, Lysandra gave up trying and sat back, grateful that her *Sight* had chosen to return this morning.

The river course turned again and she *saw* the brightness pouring in from the distance. It was the light of the Up-world, the light of the sun and for Lysandra, it was a light she welcomed; it was the light of home. *But what about Talog?* she suddenly wondered. *How will he fare in this new brightness?*

Just then she felt a blast of fear and pain coming from him, too powerful to be hidden or controlled. "Talog," she said, automatically reaching out for him.

He could not hear over the growing din of the birds and he jumped, startled, at her touch. He looked at her over his shoulder. His already-large eyes were now huge with his fear and, above them, his brow was furrowed against the pain that the growing brightness was causing him. Lysandra could feel how badly he wanted to close his eyes, to bury his head in his arms. She wished she had enough experience with boats to take over so he could turn away.

The river was carrying them along in its current, but it was Talog's guidance that kept them where they should be in the flow, guided them around obstacles and rocks, and made certain that their passage was as safe as it was swift. Lysandra could do nothing more than admire the strength of purpose and character that kept Talog at his task.

There was one thing she could do. She had only ever tried this with an animal, never with a human—or a Cryf. And the last time she had failed, she thought, remembering the sick ewe. She was not certain she could reach past the presence of so many thoughts, past the emotions and fears—and now pain—that were part of a sentient mind. To do so, to absorb the pain into herself, meant she had to be able to keep her own mind clear so that she could remain receptive.

But for Talog, she was willing to try.

During the time she had spent in the Realm, the Cryf's nearness had never overwhelmed her; their emotions, when she felt them at all, had usually come in soft waves. Not so with Talog's feelings now. They were sharp and pounding. If Lysandra could receive them so intensely, she could hardly imagine what they must be like for the Cryf.

Closing her eyes to concentrate, Lysandra willed her own mind to silence. Then, taking a deep breath to ready herself, she again reached out. This time her touch was firm and practiced, the touch of a healer upon a patient. She opened her mind to him and made herself a cup into which his pain and fear could pour.

But what came into Lysandra's mind did not pour like water into a cup . . . it flooded like a dam let loose. Although the language of the images and perceptions was unknown to her, the emotions were familiar—far too familiar.

In the last two days, everything in Talog's safe and happy life had changed completely—and to his mind, not for the better. He would do the duty Eiddig and his own belief in the Divine laid upon him, but his thoughts were filled with loss and fear.

How well Lysandra knew those emotions. Her life had once ended in a day; all she had known, loved, believed, and held to, had been stripped from her, too.

And, as Lysandra's new life had come with blind darkness, Talog's rode on the blinding glare of the sun.

But the only pain her blindness had caused was internal. The sunlight hurt Talog's eyes in a very real way; Lysandra felt the pain of knives stabbing into his eyeballs, blazing a fire in his brain.

As Talog struggled to keep his eyes open enough to guide the boat, Lysandra fought her instinct to retreat from his pain. Her will finally won. Little by little, Talog's physical sensations followed the route into her that his emotional turmoil had opened.

Slowly, his distress became less debilitating; behind him, Lysandra was near to weeping with the pain she now carried for him. She barely noticed as the boats passed through the last great cavern of the underground, where tall columns of stone, hollowed out eons ago by moisture collecting and dripping into them, housed hundreds upon hundreds of nests, all filled with hatchlings calling to their parent birds.

The air was alive with sound and movement. Bright wings beat the air with glossy feathers shining in the sunlight. They were like living jewels, shimmering in shades of crimson and yellow, brilliant blue and onyx black. The sound of their flight was like the heartbeat of the air.

Lysandra's *Sight* revealed it all, but her mind did not care. She cared about nothing until at last she heard Renan call to Talog to head for the bank. A long moment later, she felt the soft bump of landing, but she did not break contact with Talog until he moved away from her hand.

As the pain began to fade, she *saw* that Renan had directed them to a place where trees grew to the water's edge, giving thick shade to protect Talog's eyes. Relief flooded Lysandra as she knew it had the young Cryf.

Weak from her efforts, she let herself be helped onto dry land. Then she lay still upon the ground and waited for her strength to return. Cloud-Dancer came immediately to her side. He lay beside her, resting his head on her shoulder and softly nosing her cheek to make certain she was all right.

Though it took great effort to move, she managed to lift her arm and drape it around him. His nearness, his warmth and his strength were like a balm. Cloud-Dancer gave her all of the comfort that she hoped she had given Talog.

After a few minutes Lysandra felt she could sit up again. When she did, she found that some of their provisions had been unloaded and camp made. Renan was dressing Talog in some of his own clothes. His extra pants and tunic would cover the Cryf's hair-laden body and make him look less strange to a casual glance. But most important of all was the knee-length cape now tied around Talog's shoulders. Its hood could be pulled up to give shade and protection to the Cryf's sensitive eyes.

Her head was throbbing with residual pain; she could only imagine what Talog was feeling, even with the hood. As her companions noticed her movement, she used her *Sight* to study their expressions. Her sensitivity was in such a heightened state that their emotions reached her across the distance.

From Renan, she felt admiration—which touched her, as did his concern for her safety, though she did not feel worthy of such esteem. She did no more than any healer would have done; she tried to ease the pain of a person in need. Melded with his concern for her she felt the fears he tried to keep hidden about the success of their mission. And there was something else, something Renan kept carefully locked away.

From Talog she felt how much of his fear—at least of herself and Renan—had been banished. What remained was slowly being calmed by Renan's kindness, just as his physical pain was relieved by the green shadows of the trees. His determination had grown and was no longer based solely on a sense of duty. He now wanted to be one of the company, to help herself and Renan and repay them for the ways they were helping him.

Lysandra managed a weak smile. "I think," she said, "that we had best do our traveling at night. The sun, it seems, has become an enemy. Our path must now be walked in darkness."

Chapter Twenty-one

Lysandra and Talog, Renan and Cloud-Dancer traveled four nights on the Great River that formed the border between the provinces of Rathreagh and Tievebrack. Dressed in Renan's clothing, the hood of the cape pulled over his head, Talog drew no attention from the few people they passed. With the warming weather, it was not unusual to see fishermen trying their luck with the spring runs.

If they were seen at all during the brief gray times just after dawn or just before sunset, they elicited little more than a pleasant wave or slightly shouted greeting. Still, Talog was nervous. He had accepted Renan and Lysandra, but he believed all others might kill him if they knew that he was Cryf. So far, nothing his companions could say had convinced him otherwise.

Now it was time to leave the river, and Renan was worried about how Talog would react. For this reason, he had put off saying anything when they had drawn their boats to shore to sleep through the brightness of the day. But now that the sun was setting, he could delay no longer.

Their map of the river was recent, for the Great River, Eiddig said, began within the Realm of the Cryf and was "given unto them by the Hand of the Divine." Therefore, under the cover of night, some were still brave enough to travel it. The Great River was holy to the Cryf, and every change the seasons brought had been carefully and faithfully charted to show every twist and turn of the watercourse, every inlet or rocky outcropping along the bank.

That alone would have made it a fine map, as worthy a work as that of any cartographer Renan had ever seen. But there was more. The Cryf map indicated every change in depth and current, each area of danger to be avoided— even where the fish gathered, fed, or spawned.

If their mapmakers are willing to brave leaving the realm for the sake of this information, Renan thought, *there must be something I can say to Talog that will ease his mind for the overland journey ahead.*

The evening fire to cook their meal was already burning, warm and welcome in the lowering dusk. Lysandra had, as usual, brewed them a tea. Each day, the infusion changed as she chose which herbs to use by the properties she thought would best meet the travelers' needs. Renan's favorite one so far had been the licorice root and mint, and now he thought of each new cup as a pleasant discovery waiting to be made.

Grabbing the oilskin pouch that contained the Scroll of Tambryn and the maps that were guiding them, Renan came around the fire to sit beside Talog. Lysandra began pouring the newest tea into three wooden mugs. She moved with such confidence, that Renan was certain her *Sight* was active again. As always, he was struck with nothing less than awe at this gift, and the many others that made up this complex and fascinating woman.

Renan would not let himself dwell on that thought, although his heart did not want to think of anything else. That way lay danger. Becoming a priest had been more than just his spiritual salvation—it had saved his sanity and probably his life. Despite how his heart whispered that in Lysandra he had met the one woman he could love beyond the bounds of time, there was too much at stake now to risk . . . not only for himself, or for her, but for all of Aghamore.

Without looking at her face, her gentle expression that never failed to move him, Renan accepted the mug she held out to him. He murmured a quick thanks, pretending to be fully engrossed in the pouch of maps. The aroma of the tea reminded Renan of a spring meadow; it smelled to him like growing plants and sunshine. It was a bright clean aroma that made Renan smile even before he took a sip.

"Lemon balm and betony," Lysandra informed him before he could ask, "with a touch of mint and honey to blend and bring out the flavors."

Wondering why she had chosen that particular combination, Renan reached inside the pouch and withdrew two of the Cryf maps. The first was the map of the river. The second was of Rathreagh; again, the finest, most exact map he had ever seen. He rarely bothered to consult the map of Aghamore with which they had begun this journey. It could not compare with the maps of Cryf origin.

He started with the map of the river, folding it back to show the stretch they had covered last night. Then he turned to Talog.

"If I'm reading the map Eiddig-Sant gave me correctly," he said, "I think we're here. Do you agree?

The young Cryf looked at the map for a moment, then looked out, studying the river. When he looked back at the map, he moved Renan's finger minutely.

"Here," he said.

With a little nod, Renan then brought out the map of Rathreagh. This took a little longer to find just the right place, but after a moment he again asked Talog if he had found the right place. He wanted the young Cryf to say it was time to leave the river.

Perhaps he thought, *if Talog is the first to say it, if he's guiding us, he won't find the idea so frightening.* It was not much of a plan, but he could think of no better way to help ease Talog into the first night's journey overland. The river was still a connection with the Realm of the Cryf, though a tenuous one at this distance. By leaving the river behind, Talog would truly be traveling "Upworld."

Once Talog had confirmed their location on this new map, Renan unfolded it further still and smoothed it across his knees. He wished, briefly, that he had a lantern or a torch, or even some of the Cryf's glowing stones to add some light to the thickening twilight. But Talog could see much better in this semidarkness than he could—and it gave Renan a reason to need the young Cryf's help.

"I should have checked this before the sun set completely," he said, using his best excuse, "but I slept too long. Will you help me check tonight's course, Talog?"

The Cryf, never one for unnecessary words, gave a sharp nod. Now, Renan knew, he must choose his words carefully.

"Eiddig-Sant showed me where he believes the Holy Words of the Cryf—and the words of our ancient Guide, Tambryn—are leading us. He has marked the map, but I can't see it. Can you?"

Talog had been studying the map. Renan held very still, hoping his ploy would work. To stay on the river any farther would take them *away* from their direction; Renan hoped Talog would see this clearly and make the choice of the way they should go.

The Cryf put a finger on the map, studying it. Then, finally, he looked at Renan.

"Eiddig-Sant hath marked this place," he said of where his finger rested. "Our path now leaves the Great River, which giveth Life unto the Cryf. We go now where our travels shall know no peace." He stood. "I shall empty the boats."

Renan thought he detected a slight waver in Talog's voice, but rather than embarrass the young Cryf Renan said nothing. He gave Talog a small nod and turned his attention to folding the map. Then he rose to help Talog— and perhaps offer some words of encouragement.

But Lysandra stopped him. "Don't," she said softly. "He needs to be alone. He knew this day was coming, and he needs a few minutes to make peace with it. He will—he's stronger and braver than he thinks."

"How do you know all this?" Renan asked.

"Because we are all stronger and braver than we think, if the need is great enough," she said. "It is life's demand of us—and its gift to us. Without it, few of us would survive past childhood."

She's right, Renan acknowledged silently. Life was full of unseen moments and possible dangers, threats from within and without, that each person's heart was continually called upon to face and conquer. To be *alive* was the bravest act of all—everything else was just circumstance.

"Tell me about today's tea," he said, settling back down and turning the subject to something pleasant while they waited for Talog. "What was it you gave us?"

"Lemon balm and betony," she said, smiling, "with mint and honey. Both lemon balm and betony calm anxiety. Betony also strengthens the heart and promotes courage. Lemon balm clears the head and encourages insight while banishing fear and tension from both the mind and body. The mint helps regulate breathing and digestion—and it tastes good, as does the honey. It's a highly beneficial combination."

"How did you know we'd need it today?" Renan asked.

"This morning when we put in to shore, you were nervous about something. I could hear it in your voice and in the way you moved. I decided then that if you were affected by whatever was coming, the rest of us would need calming, too. Although, I have to admit that while riding in a boat is not as terrifying as I anticipated at first, I'll enjoy having solid land beneath me. I think Cloud-Dancer will, too. Won't you, boy?" she said as she ran a hand down his fur.

The animal looked up at her with adoring eyes. Renan wished, briefly, that he had the freedom to do the same. Then he pushed the thought away, burying his feelings again before they became too strong.

Lysandra, done petting Cloud-Dancer, was busy again. "Talog has had his time now," she said. "Will you bring him back to the fire? It's time we all had something to eat before we start walking."

Food consumed and provisions unloaded, Renan and Talog hid the boats deep within a nearby thicket, hoping they would not be found before they could return and claim them. Their supplies were redistributed into three packs, with the lightest one given to Lysandra. As they began the final long stage of their journey to find the one whom prophecy named the Font of Wisdom, Lysandra could feel the young Cryf's fear—and the lessening of his tension as hour by hour passed without encountering another soul.

Rathreagh was a wild and desolate place, not at all like the forest in which Lysandra was used to walking. Had it not been that both the scroll and the Holy Words insisted the Font of Wisdom "resideth within the Ninth House, yet unto a place where men's eyes gaze not," this province would have been the last place Lysandra would have chosen to go. Here, the poor, rocky soil and the stunted, gnarled trees frequently gave way to sudden and treacherous bogs. The hard stones were tiring to walk across, making Lysandra's legs ache as they had not during all her long trek to Ballinrigh. She found herself actually missing the gentle rocking of the boats and wished, like Talog, that they were still safe upon the river.

She kept a tight hold on Cloud-Dancer for she feared he might go dashing after a rabbit or some other creature and get trapped in one of the bogs. She borrowed his vision often, until that, too, became tiring. Most of the time she walked with neither vision nor *Sight*, guided by her wolf or by her human companions. While she walked, however, she tried to remember the clues Renan had read her from the scrolls. It was an exercise to keep her mind off her discomfort as much as to find new insight about their destination.

Without the maps of the Cryf marking their path, Lysandra doubted any of them would have made it through the first night's travels without disaster. *Surely all of Rathreagh can't be like this*, she thought, as they circled yet another unsafe area. When at last they stopped to rest and eat, Lysandra posed that question to Renan.

"There are bogs all through this region," he said, consulting his maps, "and this isn't the only one we'll have to cross. The scroll did give a warning when it said *'beware the earth of the Ninth House that beareth not footsteps'* and that only *'in the memory of the forgotten will safe passage be found.'* Of course," Renan added with a little half smile, "like so many of Tambryn's words, the warning only makes sense now that we're here. The good news is that we're almost through. Another . . . three miles I think, and we'll be on the other side."

"And the bad news?" Lysandra asked, knowing that there usually was some. But Renan said nothing . . . and his lack of answer told her that ahead was something he did not want to reveal.

A town, Lysandra thought. *Maybe several—and that means people. Up-worlders.*

She understood Renan's silence. It was better to wait and see if they could skirt the town than to upset Talog. Lysandra held out little hope that they could cross an entire province, even by night, without some contact with other people. But she refused to borrow trouble.

No need, she thought, as rest and mealtime ended. She stood and shouldered her pack. *If trouble is coming, it will find us easily enough.*

They safely crossed the first of the boglands that night, but Renan knew from the map that there were others coming that would not be so easy. On the other side of the bog, the land grew soft and fertile and the traveling became easier. The trees grew straighter, and while they were not thick enough to be called a forest, they would provide welcome cover.

Rathreagh was the largest of all the provinces and, except for the bogs, it looked to hold few obstacles to travel. There were no high mountains or unfordable rivers to stop them; towns were well spaced, rather isolated, and connected by a well-developed road system that carefully avoided the boglands.

It would make their travels easier if they could stay to the roadways, but there would be no way to avoid the towns and all the questions that might well arise were they seen. Had he been traveling alone, Renan could have gone anywhere without arousing suspicion—a priest could be traveling for any number of reasons, from a personal retreat to carrying a message from the Primus, visiting friends or taking on a new parish. But a priest traveling with a woman—and a wolf—was sure to be remembered, even if Talog could manage to avoid notice. Maintaining their pace, Renan was fairly certain that in another three or four days they could reach the northernmost tip of the province that he believed was their destination.

But what if he was wrong? This question remained ever present in Renan's mind as they searched for a place to take their day's rest. Eiddig had seemed very certain that the Holy Words of Dewi-Sant agreed with the Scroll of Tambryn and that both pointed to the little fishing village of Caerryck, built where a little crook of land curved out to meet the sea.

But Renan still feared failure—and at some point during this journey, the bigger question of the future of Aghamore had become less important to him than not being a failure in Lysandra's eyes. That meant the one they were seeking *had* to be in Caerryck—and that Renan must get them all there and back in safety.

They finally found a dense thicket, a natural shelter. Although he was as tired as the others, Renan could not sleep. Turning over on his pallet, trying again to find a comfortable position, he finally sighed and accepted that no amount of tossing or turning was going to help. He had too much on his mind.

He sat up and looked at the prone figures next to him. Talog had the hood of his cape once more pulled up over his head. His deep, untroubled sleep was a testament to the trust the young Cryf had placed in Renan—and while he valued the gift, it made him feel all the more afraid of failure.

Lysandra lay on the other side of Talog. She slept curled on her side, one hand tucked under her cheek. Renan found himself filled with such tenderness as he looked at her, and such a need to be certain she was always safe, always protected, that it shook him down to his bones.

Cloud-Dancer, curled against Lysandra's back, raised his head to look at Renan. Beast though he might be and only one step away from the wild, Renan knew that at that moment he and Cloud-Dancer shared an instant of perfect understanding. Then the wolf closed his eyes, the same blue as Lysandra's, and lowered his head back to watchful sleep. By his simple, silent action, he had let Renan know that not even slumber would keep him from protecting his human companion.

Renan decided to give up on sleep. He would scout the land in daylight, thinking that it might make this night's travels easier if he knew what lay ahead. Moving slowly and carefully, he eased himself off his bedroll and crawled from the thicket, not standing until he was well away from the sheltering undergrowth.

Once out in the relative open, he finally stood and stretched. It felt good to be awake and active during the daylight again, to hear the sounds of the birds, the way the woods moved in the daytime breeze that was so different from the sound of night . . .

To hear voices, men's voices . . .

Renan dropped down into a crouch, praying he had not already been seen as he quickly moved behind a tree. He stood very still, trying to catch what the voices said. Though there was an occasional bark of laughter, the voices sounded rough—and not like the shouts of farmers going about their day's business. They held an edge that sent a shiver up Renan's back. But at least they were not coming closer. Silently, he sent a prayer of gratitude for the thickness of the trees and undergrowth here—and for his good ears that had heard the voices quickly.

He was in a quandary. Should he stay where he was until the men went away? Their voices did not sound as if they were on the move. Should he wake the others so that they could find another place to hide, even if it was daylight and Talog would have to brave the pain the brightness might cause him? Or should he try to get closer, to find out who these men were and what they were doing?

Renan decided on this latter course. To awaken and

move his companions might put them in far greater danger than letting them sleep on unawares.

Renan crept toward the voices, keeping behind tree trunks and moving carefully enough not to break twigs or rustle bushes. He only needed to get close enough to hear what was being said, he decided. He was wearing one of his clerical shirts, and he was fairly certain that his collar would protect him. Even so, he did not want to draw attention.

Without buildings and city noises to block or disguise it, sound can carry quite a distance; the men were farther away than Renan had thought. He was glad, for the farther away he was from his companions the safer they would be.

Finally, Renan drew close enough to glimpse the men between the trees. There were several of them, maybe even a dozen. As he feared, these were not farmers.

The trunk behind which he was crouching belonged to a towering yew tree, and was big enough for Renan to feel quite safe. He leaned against the solid wood for support while he eavesdropped.

"'Ow long do we have to wait in this God-forsaken place?" one of the men barked, his voice making it plain that he had no patience, whatever the answer.

"We wait as long as it takes," another voice answered in tones that were both quieter and full of command.

"Then why here? There be a town not more than a couple of miles distant," said the first man. "It's not much of a town, true enough, but it's better than 'ere. I've a hunger for a meal I've not cooked m'self, if nothin' else."

"We was told to wait here, and here we wait."

"I say I be tired of waitin'." The first man's voice grew louder. "We all is. Giraldus is a soldier hisself. He'd not grudge us a bit of comfort to pass the hours. Right, lads?"

Renan listened to the murmur of agreement, startled by the mention of the Baron of Kilgarriff. He slowly eased his head far enough around the tree for one eye to look at the men. They were lounging in various attitudes of boredom around a bit of a campfire—all except one, who was pacing angrily.

Renan knew in an instant that the men were soldiers, though they wore neither uniform nor heraldic device. Both their own clothing and the trappings of their horses, tethered a few feet away, were carefully unremarkable and the black griffin of Kilgarriff was nowhere to be seen. Even so, the way they moved, the way all of them had long swords, not daggers or hunting knives, laid carefully within reach, even the order of command they obviously followed, said these were trained soldiers with a lifetime of service—and Renan did not want to think what they might be hunting.

"Giraldus might understand," the quieter man who was certainly their leader replied, "but *she* wouldn't. We was told to be waitin' on the edge of the woods outside the town of Diamor, and here we be waiting—unless ye be the one what wants to explain to *her* why we disobeyed."

The first man, for all his anger, did not reply. But Renan had seen and heard enough. The *she* of whom the soldiers spoke could only be the Lady Aurya.

But what were she and the Baron doing in Rathreagh? And with soldiers? He would have expected them in Kilgarriff, preparing to follow Giraldus in his bid for the throne.

Or perhaps they were; Renan's heart grew cold with this new thought. Aurya's use of magic, her adherence to the old ways and hatred for the Church, were well-known throughout the kingdom. If she was as well learned as her reputation proclaimed, Renan could only guess at the resources and contacts she might have outside of Aghamore. What if she, too, possessed copies of Tambryn's scrolls, and was searching for the Font of Wisdom? Were Aurya, Giraldus, and the soldiers the *"dogs of darkness"* whom both Tambryn and Dewi-Sant had warned would be *"biting their heels"*?

The scroll and the Holy Words had also both warned to *"beware the rise of the Third House"*; that meant Kilgarriff. But what could Lady Aurya want with the Font of Wisdom whose rise was supposed to *"vanquish the rise of the Third House"*—what, except destroy it?

Renan knew he had to get back to the others, wake them, and get them moving. Whether Aurya and Giraldus were an hour, a day or even a week behind them, they were too close. Yet Renan found himself paralyzed with unexpected fear.

Renan knew the dark side of magic—the magic Lady Aurya practiced. Running from it—even into the Church— was no protection, it seemed. It was here, hard on his heels, and even after all these years, even though his life was now dedicated to the service of Light, Darkness threatened to overtake him again.

He struggled with his fears, forcing them—and his memories—back into the hiding place. Now he knew why he had been unable to sleep; that long-disused part of himself, the part where magic lay in chosen somnolence these last twenty years, had felt and responded to Aurya's nearness and the magic she brought with her.

For a long moment, Renan felt both powerless and hopeless. But then, from somewhere, new life and strength began to fill him. It started down deep, in that still, small place where resides the core of personal truth.

Down in that place of deepest solitude, Renan found he was no longer alone. The Light was there . . . and in

that Light was hope . . . and hope looked at him with eyes
that were the rich blue color of forget-me-nots.

Chapter Twenty-two

Renan woke Lysandra first. Mindful of how the soldiers' voices had reached him, he kept his voice to
the barest whisper as he told her of what he had learned.
She agreed that there was no time to rest; they would
have to wake Talog and put some distance between themselves and Giraldus's men. They could only hope that Giraldus and Aurya were days rather than hours behind them.

It was a hope not a certainty. Until they had reached
their destination, found the child, and were safely away
again, they would have to eat on the move, rest only when
they could go no farther and only for the shortest time
possible . . . and pray that their strength did not fail them.

Although he did not know who the Lady Aurya was,
Talog accepted Renan's statement about the need for speed
and silence, uttering not a single complaint about the daylight. Renan was grateful and he wished that he had something more to offer the Cryf to protect his sensitive eyes.

It now became imperative to avoid any towns—not an
easy thing to do in such a marsh-and-bog-ridden place as
Rathreagh, where the towns were built wherever solid land

presented itself. However, Renan wanted no rumors of their passing to reach the ears of those who followed.

He consulted his map often. That Giraldus or Lady Aurya possessed a copy of the scroll made him fear that she also possessed some chart or map that showed her the lay of the bogs. Lacking that, Giraldus's party would be slowed by having to stay to the roads. Even Lady Aurya's magic could not change all of Rathreagh into solid ground, and horses could not run through bogs. That was Renan's one hope.

They marched for two hours before he called a halt. By now, he hoped, they had put enough distance between themselves and the soldiers to be able to wait out the rest of the daylight.

"Keep the fire as small as possible," he told Lysandra as she began piling sticks around the tinder she had collected, "and try to find wood that is very dry so that it doesn't smoke overmuch." Even as he spoke, he realized that Lysandra knew what she was doing better than he. But there was no sense taking any chances. If Giraldus and Aurya had arrived, and the company was on the move, Renan did not want to give them a signal toward which they might aim.

While Lysandra tended to the fire and a meal, Renan brought the maps over to Talog. He wanted the Cryf's eye to make certain he was not missing anything.

"We've reached the end of the woods, at least for a time," Renan told him. "But I think we're safe here until nightfall. The safest way I see is to go by the road for a time, here." He traced it on the map. "But the *fastest* is across another area of bogs. What do you think?"

Squinting in the shaded daylight, Talog also studied the map. "The ones who follow, take they the road?" he asked.

"Yes," Renan answered. "Their horses will keep them to the roads, but also means they can travel faster."

"Then we shall follow this path," Talog said. His finger began to trace a trail through the bogs. "Seest thou how it goes? In the first times, when Up-worlders were few, the Cryf also walked here. There will be signs to grant guidance unto our steps."

"Signs?" Renan said, new hope flaring. "You will recognize them?"

Talog gave his sharp single nod. "I shall guide," he said. "But the Great Light hideth the marks, for Cryf travel not in the time of the Great Light."

"Then it's back to traveling at night," Renan said. "But I think from now on, we'll do best to sleep in rounds, with one of us as guard."

Renan was watching Lysandra as he spoke. He had learned to read her body signals and knew that right now her *Sight* was active. He knew also that she was listening closely, even though her hands were busy elsewhere. As always, she brought them a cup of hot tea. This one was familiar, smelling slightly of apples.

"Chamomile," he said even before he took a sip. Lysandra smiled at him. At the sight Renan felt an instant of light-headedness, as if his heart was racing far too fast. She did not smile often enough, he decided, wanting to think of ways to make and keep her smiling forever.

There's little enough reason to smile here, he thought quickly. *Perhaps when all this is over . . .* But when all this was over, they would go their separate ways. He would not see her or know if she smiled.

The thought gave Renan a stabbing pain, making him feel as ill as just a moment before he had been elated. Once more he shied away from these thoughts and made himself return Lysandra's smile so she would not *see* or feel his private turmoil.

"You see," he said aloud, "I'm learning."

"Oh?" Lysandra's smile broadened, revealing a little dimple in one cheek that Renan had not seen before. "Then why did I choose this herb and not another?"

Renan swallowed around the lump that constricted his throat. "That," he said, "I do not know."

"But you should," Lysandra said. "Chamomile grows everywhere, an easily found and harvested herb that should be in every kitchen. There's so much that can be done with it, but best of all is this tea. It soothes and calms. I thought that if we're to try and sleep again, this might help."

"So it might," Renan agreed. *And we need every bit of help we can find,* he thought. *I wish sleep were the only problem we faced.*

At that moment, while Renan and the others once more settled to rest and the soldiers waited with bored anticipation, Aurya and Giraldus were stuck in a small town where Giraldus's stallion had thrown a shoe. Now the town's blacksmith must be found—and the farrier, if they were not one and the same—the smithy fired and a new shoe made while the horse's hoof was prepared.

But neither man was in town. They and several others, having no immediate work to hold them, had gone hunting. When they would return, no one knew; they had been gone two days already.

While Giraldus cursed and paced and drank too much of the local ale, Aurya studied the scroll. The three swans carved into the bridge at Yembo, the swans she was certain were the Three Sisters mentioned in Tambryn's words, had been pointing north. North they had come—but she had neither seen nor discovered anything to fulfill more of the scroll's words. There was nothing *hidden* that she had found, nothing *forgotten* that she had discovered.

What clue was she missing, she wondered, and what was supposed to come next on their journey? Would she even know it if she saw it? If she did not, would they still be able to find the child they sought?

No, she told herself as she unrolled the scroll onto the little table in the back corner of the local pub, *failure is one thing I will* not *accept.*

Giraldus was up at the bar talking with the innkeeper. His voice had grown more strident with the ale he had consumed. It easily filled the near-empty room and grated on Aurya's nerves.

She could order him to silence and he would obey— but what a waste of magic that would be, she thought. She tried to make herself ignore Giraldus's voice—but it continued to cut into her thoughts until the last thread of her patience snapped. Willpower was not enough; she would have to take more active measures. She closed her eyes and breathed deeply. Two . . . three . . . four times, each breath taking her more deeply within, down to that silent place where magic dwelt. Six . . . seven . . . eight breaths . . . she could feel the power within her start to throb in answer to her call. Ten . . . eleven . . . twelve.

There, power wielded and wielder met and merged. It was only a little need she called upon, but the power within her was like a living thing. The feeling of it, like sweet fire in her veins, made Aurya smile.

She brought the power upward with her, out of its resting place. She wrapped herself in it, willing that any observer would look unseeing past her. Most of all, it would muffle the sounds she did not wish to hear. She needed to be undisturbed—nor did she care to have any curious eyes light upon the scroll. With the spell in place, even Giraldus would not bother her.

Under her breath, Aurya began to chant the spell she needed.

> *"Light that is hidden now shine,*
> *Reveal the knowledge to most eyes blind.*
> *Folly bound and wisdom freed,*
> *Hide no truth away from me.*
> *Of Ancient words on parchment*
> *Penned by the seer's hand,*
> *Let me with Tambryn's eyes behold,*
> *To see and understand."*

Aurya rolled the scroll out farther, confident that she would now be granted a fresh understanding of its contents. She had thought her years of study would be enough and magic would not be needed to read the meanings of Tambryn's words. But she had not known that Tambryn wielded magic along with his prophetic gift. Her failed Spell of Binding had taught her otherwise. And if Tambryn had set a magic seal upon his words, she would use magic to unlock it.

Wrapped now in magic, Spell of Seeing cast, she went back to the prophecy of the Three Sisters, expecting sudden insight to flood her. Instead, the words became garbled in her mind. Sentences written in words she knew suddenly made no sense. It was as if some unseen hand was taking the words and rearranging them into incoherent nonsense.

Magic; she could nearly smell it wafting up from the ink, nearly see it outlining the letters in power. Well, she was not undone yet. If more power was needed, she had more—*much* more—to call upon. She would break whatever spell of protection Tambryn had laid upon and around his words.

Once more Aurya closed her eyes, calling up the magic within herself. It came, ready at her call. She spread her hands out, fingers extended, over the scroll and began again to chant.

> *"Magic bound by Seer's hand,*
> *I summon thee to my cause.*
> *Magic set on thee today*
> *Be stronger than the spell that was.*
> *Old magic broken, Seer's power*
> *Dimmed by death and time now gone.*
> *I claim the vision here revealed*
> *And to my spell it now belongs."*

Again, Aurya looked down at the scroll. The words upon it started to glow, as if the ink with which they had been written had been made of pure gold—been made of fire. The sight brought a look of triumph to Aurya's face.

Then, to her horror, the glow of the ink became true flame, burning the parchment before her eyes.

She slapped at the scroll, heedless of the heat that scorched her palms. At the same time she quickly muttered a Spell of Breaking, aimed not at Tambryn's magic but at her own.

She felt the power she had sought to use begin to fade, taking the flames with it. As they died, Aurya understood what spell had been set upon the scroll. Understood and knew there was no way around it.

Tambryn had set a Mirror Spell upon the scroll. Any magic she used in attempting to unlock its secrets would be reflected away and turned backward. A Spell of Seeing resulted only in the words being confused; the attempt to gain insight, illumination, only caused the meaning to be lost and burned away. Aurya, though angered that she had been so impugned, could not help but feel a grudging admiration at Tambryn's cleverness.

Well, she still had her knowledge and her wits. She unrolled the scroll once again to see how much damage had been done. It was more than she hoped but not as much as she feared. She would draw upon her well-trained memory to fill in what had been destroyed.

You haven't defeated me yet, Tambryn, she sent her thought out to his ancient spirit . . .

. . . and thought she heard the echo of his laughter in return.

It was Talog's turn on watch. Daylight was dwindling toward darkness; the Great Light that burned his eyes had moved until it was behind both trees and hills, bringing the Cryf a great feeling of relief. He hated this land of the Up-worlders more with every hour he spent in it. The open air made him feel exposed and vulnerable, and he had seen nothing to compare with the beauty of the Realm of the Cryf.

But Talog was warming toward his companions, especially Lysandra. He knew she had the Hand of the Divine upon her—even if ofttimes she did not.

It was part of his training as a Guide to be silent, to watch and wait and listen. Each person revealed themselves more than they knew. It was true for the Cryf, and Talog was learning that it held true for Up-worlders as well.

Many things about his companions still puzzled him, however, and he pondered them now while he was alone. Cloud-Dancer puzzled Talog; he had never before seen such a creature. Did all healers have such companions?

he wondered. Was that why Renan and Lysandra were not Joined—because she was a Healer? Little as he knew about Up-worlders, it was plain that they had the same feelings for each other that meant a male and female of the Cryf would go to the Guide to say the words of Joining.

But Renan and Lysandra each tried to hide their feelings from the other. It made no sense to Talog. The only thing he could guess was that it was forbidden for Healers to Join and that having a creature like Cloud-Dancer to protect her, proclaimed her Healer status to all.

Talog shook his head. The ways of these Up-worlders made no sense at all.

The Great Light had sunk even lower and the soft darkness had begun. It was time to awaken the others. Talog had heard nothing during his turn at watch except the calls of the Children of the Air and the scurry of small creatures searching for food. He would have let Renan and Lysandra sleep on until the brightness of the Great Light was completely gone—but Renan had been insistent that they not sleep overlong.

Talog wondered about these *soldiers* of whom Renan spoke. It was not a word he and Lysandra had shared during their language lessons. Perhaps they were like the Up-worlders who had long ago invaded the Realm of the Cryf, filled with hearts of greed and destruction.

If so, then Renan is right to fear them, Talog thought. *He said Up-worlders are not like that, but he fears them, too. I do not know if I want to find this One-Who-Is-Wisdom, who will unite our two worlds. The Cryf do not need the Up-worlders.*

But, perhaps, the Up-worlders need the Cryf, he decided. *We walk always with the Divine, and our hearts do not lie. Eiddig-Sant has said it is right for us to be again united, as in the first times. Eiddig-Sant is Guide and hears the Voice of the Divine. His words are always Truth.*

Talog stood and turned to awaken the others, knowing he would obey the directions of Eiddig. He would help Renan and Lysandra find the one for whom they searched. He would help them even to the point of sacrificing his own life for their safety, for that was his duty. But in his deepest heart and for the first time in his life, he had doubted the wisdom of the Holy Words—and that doubt shook him to the very core of whom he had always thought he was.

Chapter Twenty-three

The College of Bishops had just voted again by secret ballot. The count had come up five to four. Elon needed only one more vote to make the six he needed to affirm Giraldus as the Church's choice for the throne.

One more vote, Elon thought as he looked around the room, studying the faces of his brother bishops. *But whom? Which ones do I need to woo and win—and how much longer will this take?*

Most of their faces remained impassive, telling him nothing. The Archbishop's support he knew he had, and he was fairly certain of Farnagh, Dromkeen, and Lininch. They would vote for whomever the Archbishop favored. And, of course, he voted for Kilgarriff. That was five— who still voted against him?

He looked at them individually. Bresal of Rathreagh was ever his enemy and would vote against him no matter the cause. Elon dismissed him completely. But what of the others? he wondered.

That left the bishops of Sylaun, Tievebrack, and Camlough. Elon dismissed Dwyer of Camlough as he had Bresal of Rathreagh. But Sylaun and Tievebrack might still be won over. One of them *must* be won over; Elon would allow himself no failure. And it must be done quickly. All must be ready when Aurya and Giraldus returned.

What did he know of Sylaun and Tievebrack that he could use against them? Mago was young for a bishop, barely past forty, appointed to his See of Tievebrack shortly before King Anri's death. He was still filled with the ideals that a few more years of politics would dim. Gairiad of Sylaun, by contrast, was not much younger than the Archbishop. Elon would not be surprised to hear of his retirement soon.

But both were still human. Both had failings and passions just as other men did. Elon intended to find out what they were and use that knowledge any way he must.

I'll ask Thomas, he thought. *Servants love to talk about their masters. What he doesn't know yet, he can find out far more easily than I.*

Thomas had already proved himself to be a worthy and willing instrument—now he would become the perfect weapon wielded in a master's hand.

*   *   *

Lysandra missed her home and her garden. She missed the peaceful rhythm of her everyday existence as it had been. But most of all, she missed her bed.

She was tired of sleeping on the hard ground. Here in Rathreagh, where stone was barely covered by a layer of poor soil, finding any comfort while she tried to sleep was proving to be impossible.

Nor were there enough hours of sleep. The necessity of keeping on the move, never knowing how close Giraldus might be, meant that they made camp later, broke camp earlier, and had fewer stops in between. Even though the boats of the Cryf had shortened their journey by several days, each evening when she rose again from sleep that was too brief and far too unrefreshing, the road ahead felt intolerably long.

They had taken a rest while Talog scoured the path ahead for the ancient Cryf signs left to mark safe passage. He had shown some to Lysandra and Renan. In the light of day, they could not be seen. Even at night, they seemed to her like nothing more than small reflective particles of the rock shining in the moonlight.

But Talog recognized them and could read the message they conveyed. Without his help Lysandra knew that she and Renan would have been quickly lost. Each day she became more grateful the young Cryf was with them.

I must tell Talog, she thought in the abstract way of the weary. *I don't think he realizes how important he is to us or how much we need him.*

Talog's part in this journey was obvious and likewise Renan's, who possessed and understood both the Scroll of Tambryn and the maps that guided them. *But why am I here?* Lysandra wondered, as she had numerous times before. *Renan and Talog could make this journey faster without me. What is it I'm supposed to do?*

Self-doubt was something Lysandra had learned to face; to be blind *and* full of doubt would have paralyzed her, even in the secluded life she lived. But ever since the beginning of the journey—called forth by a power she did not understand, to go to a place she did not know—doubts assailed her at every turn. Now, more weary than she would have believed possible, a kingdom away from everything that was home to her and with no end to this journey yet in sight, doubts grew insidious tendrils though her mind, almost overwhelming her before she realized their existence.

It was as if the darkness of her eyes now dropped a veil over her heart. For all Renan's talk of her being Prophecy's Hand, she had done very little—certainly nothing more than, as a healer, she might have done anytime, anywhere. She wanted to curl up beside the rock on which she sat and not move until Renan and Talog completed the rest of the journey and found her on the way back.

It was Cloud-Dancer who got her moving again. When the others, having consulted the maps, stood and were ready to go, Cloud-Dancer began nudging Lysandra, butting her gently with his nose and head as a female might a recalcitrant pup.

Lysandra did not stand. She merely ran a hand absently through his fur, continuing to stare sightlessly at nothing. She felt as if iron weights had been tied to her arms and legs. But Cloud-Dancer would not accept her stillness. He became more and more insistent, nudging her harder and, when that did not work, taking the cloth of her sleeve into his teeth and pulling.

Annoyance finally cut through the fog that had enveloped Lysandra, and she realized what she had been doing. Already once in her life she had dwelt in that place of unremembered blackness. She had vowed never to make it her home again.

She stood, shaking her head to clear it, to deny power to the gloom that threatened to hold her captive. But her inner voice still whispered, telling her to sit down again, sit and do nothing, that the others did not need her and could do just as well without her . . .

Once more, Cloud-Dancer took the cloth of her sleeve between his teeth. This time he growled as he tugged. When that did not bring the response he wanted, he sat down and released her sleeve. He tilted his head slightly, looking at her with puzzled eyes for one brief moment, then raised his head and sent out a long howl.

Lysandra heard it as if from far away. But second by second it grew louder until, finally, it began to pierce its way into her consciousness. Then Renan and Talog were beside her, too. She could not see their faces, but the concern in their voices—especially in Renan's—she could not miss.

Once more she shook her head. Everything still felt and sounded muffled. She *wanted* to respond to the questions the others were asking her; she *wanted* to throw off their touch and stride forward, showing them and herself that she could emerge from this cocoon of bleakness that somehow held her fast.

Suddenly, Renan swept her up in his arms and they hurried away from the place where she had been sitting. As the distance grew, Lysandra felt her mind slowly, *finally,* clearing. Her thoughts became her own again.

It felt wonderful—warm and safe and comforting—to be held like this in Renan's arms, and she allowed herself the luxury of it for a few seconds longer. She could hear his heart beating, feel his chest rise and fall with his breath. She felt that she could stay this way indefinitely . . .

He's a priest, she reminded her heart, which kept refusing to remember it.

She stirred in his arms. "I'm all right now," she said aloud. "You . . . you can put me down. I can walk on my own again."

"Are you sure?" Renan asked, still holding her.

Lysandra heard the concern that rang through his voice, but she would not allow herself to read special meaning into it. *Being kind and concerned is part of what he is,* she reminded herself.

"Yes," she answered, "I'm sure. I'm all right now."

Renan put her down, setting her carefully on her feet and not truly letting go until he was certain she was steady.

"I'm sorry," she said. "I don't know what happened. I just suddenly couldn't think or move or . . ."

"That place," Talog said, startling her. She must still be fuzzy, she thought, to have neither heard his footsteps nor felt his nearness.

"What about the place?" Renan asked. She heard Talog's sharp exhale.

"It is truth, then, as Eiddig sayeth," the young Cryf replied, his voice both sad and amazed. "Up-worlders know not the power that dwells within the land."

"What power?" repeated Renan. "Talog, we don't understand."

"Come," Talog responded. "Let us go farther away. Then shall I teach ye what all Cryf know as Truth. Hath the Healer strength to walk?"

"Yes," Lysandra told him. "But my things, my medicines . . . I left them."

Worry turned Lysandra's voice sharp and discordant; again she felt Renan's comforting touch, light and gentle upon her shoulder.

"Talog has them," he said softly. "Don't worry, Lysandra. Let's do what Talog says and get away from here. Sunrise is not far off—we need to find a place to make camp for the day. Then we can hear whatever it is he says he must teach us. Are you certain you can walk now?"

"Yes," she told him again. "I'll keep up."

She put her hand out, and immediately Cloud-Dancer slid his head beneath her waiting fingers. She took a few seconds to caress him, running her hand across his head, ears, and neck, knowing—and letting him know—how lost she would be without him.

Then, as she heard the others begin to move again, Lysandra wound her fingers deeply into Cloud-Dancer's fur. She drew again upon their deep and mutual bond, on the love that kept him by her side, until their minds united and she could see through his eyes once more.

Together, they followed Talog and Renan across the desolate boglands.

Finally, Aurya thought, as Giraldus mounted his newly shod stallion. *Finally we can leave this little hole on the landscape and get moving again.*

Over the last day and a half her patience had been stretched, to its limit and past, while they waited for the blacksmith and farrier to return from their hunting trip. The only thing that had kept her from lashing out—at Giraldus, at this whole uncultured, uncomfortable, backwater village—was the time she spent studying the scroll.

She would not try a spell on it again; she had been lucky enough the first time that the scroll had not been completely destroyed, and she would not underestimate Tambryn's powers, or his intelligence, again. None of the tales she had heard ever mentioned magic, but Aurya now knew Tambryn had been a mage of great power. It took nothing less to set such a spell and have it maintain its cohesion through six centuries.

But though the Mirror Spell was protection against her magic, it had granted her a revelation that might well be the salvation of her quest. She had been taking the words of the scroll too literally. She had indeed found that which was *hidden*—when she found the spell upon the scroll. And she had found the *forgotten* by realizing the truth about Tambryn himself.

This new knowledge would have filled her with satisfaction had it not been for the dream that had disturbed her sleep last night. In it, she had seen two birds racing through the skies. One had been the black griffin of Giraldus's crest. The other had been a dove, a small bird by comparison, with bright white plumage and a body that was sleekly plump.

They were racing toward the same goal, a glowing spot upon the northern horizon. The griffin, much larger and more powerful, soon overtook the dove and closed its black talons around the snowy body. But even as the griffin brought its long hooked beak down to close upon its prey's neck, to sever its head and destroy it in one swift move, the dove drove its own sharply pointed beak into the griffin's heart. Then, from the dove's beak, bright flame erupted, shooting deep within the griffin's body and consuming it. In its death throes, the griffin released the dove to fly onward, free and unchallenged, to its goal.

Aurya had awakened from this dream two hours before dawn. Rising from beside the sleeping Giraldus, she wrapped a blanket around herself and went to sit before the remnants of the fire, in the cramped and dingy room they had rented the night before.

The dream could only have one meaning. Someone else possessed a copy of Tambryn's scroll and was also trying to find the child. But whom? To that question she had no answer; she knew of no Baron or House that used a white dove as its symbol.

Aurya stared into the embers, watching their red-orange glow slowly become covered and dimmed by ash, while she asked that same question over and over. It was not until the glow was almost gone that she moved.

She grabbed the poker and quickly stirred the dying fire to life, adding new wood. Her heartbeat counted the seconds until little tongues of flame began to appear, licking the undersides of the logs. Then, satisfied, Aurya sat back on her heels thinking, trying to decide the best way to deal with this unexpected threat.

Magic was the only answer, but she must move carefully—the scroll had taught her that. And, who but another mage would own the scrolls of someone like Tambryn, whose writings had been forbidden by the Church? To use magic against another who practiced in the arcane could be very dangerous—and to use too strong a spell would drain her, both of body and power, leaving her defenseless.

Finally, Aurya settled upon a spell that would only work if the one against whom it was cast carried any unresolved doubts. If he or she were moving with confidence, completely convinced of their course and action, the spell would dissolve into the ether. But, if such doubts existed, this spell would find them, cast a cloud of darkness and malaise that would keep its victim mired.

Once the fire was burning brightly, Aurya focused her eyes and mind upon the flames as she called forth her place of power and began to Cast . . .

Now, in the bright light of late morning, as she and Giraldus rode away from the little village of Fintra, she was certain she had made the right choice. She needed all of her strength today if they were to reach the town where Giraldus's soldiers were to be waiting.

Tonight, she thought as her horse settled into its smooth canter, *when I'll have time afterward to sleep and regain my strength, perhaps I'll try a Spell of Finding. That will show me just who this white dove is—and then I'll know how to stop him.* No one *will get to the child before I do . . . No one.*

Chapter Twenty-four

When Talog finally led the others out of the bogs, Renan released a silent sigh of relief. The sun was up, but thankfully it was a dark and cloudy day. Although the heavy overcast signaled a spring storm by nightfall, it also meant they could cover some extra distance before needing to stop.

Renan was still worried about Lysandra. She insisted she was fine now and that whatever strange humor had taken hold of her earlier had passed, but she still looked . . . "deflated" was the word that came to Renan's mind.

She looks as if a part of her has been drained away, he kept thinking every time he glanced at her. *But what part? Of purpose? Of self? How can I—we,* he reminded himself—*help her get it back?*

He was relieved when they finally found a safe place to settle for the day. This time it was a cave, one of many etched into a tall stony ridge on the north border of the boglands. The cave they chose required a small amount of climbing to reach, but it was safer than one close to the ground, where anything might enter while they slept.

Renan and Talog helped first Cloud-Dancer and then Lysandra clamber up to the cave. Then Renan signaled Talog to follow them.

"I'll find some wood for a fire," he said softly, aware of how sound might carry.

Foraging in solitude gave Renan a chance to sort through some of his feelings. They were in an uproar. Just a short time ago, he had thought all of his major life-decisions were made, his future in place. But now, it seemed that each day something new happened to call them into question.

Lysandra was at the heart of most of his turmoil. His feelings for her grew with every day he spent in her company, until now his respect and admiration had deepened into something infinitely richer. They were also the very reasons he would never speak of his feelings to her.

He would never put Lysandra into the emotionally uncomfortable—or spiritually dangerous—position of being the unacknowledged "hearth-mate" of a priest who held his vows in little esteem. Renan knew that many of his brethren thought nothing of such a relationship, especially in the more isolated parishes. In a Church where younger sons and daughters were given into the Religious life at ages as young as five or six and for reasons of economics rather than true vocation, such abuses were inevitable—and frequently overlooked by the disciplinary hierarchy.

But Renan was not one of these. He had sought out this life of his own accord, with a willing heart and a belief that this was the vocation he was meant to follow. Now, whatever his feelings elsewhere, he must honor the dictates and responsibilities of that decision.

The greatest danger to his vows was not Lysandra; it was Lady Aurya. She threatened not his vocation, but something that went even deeper. It was the vow that had sent him into the Church and that defined who he was and what he wanted to be.

Before all this was over, he feared it would be something he would be forced to break.

But he was not the only one to whom Lady Aurya posed a danger. Lysandra's recent behavior, so completely out of character, could only be of Aurya's design. He could not say how she knew of their presence, or what spell she used against Lysandra, but the more he thought about it, the more certain he became that it was her handiwork.

He was also increasingly convinced that she and her companions were on the same quest to find the Font of Wisdom. This made it all the more imperative that his party be the first to find the child. Aurya's purposes could bode no good for either the child or the kingdom. Whatever plans she might have once she could claim whatever powers the Font of Wisdom might hold, they no doubt began with putting Baron Giraldus on the throne of Aghamore.

Renan admitted that, alone, Giraldus might make a passable, perhaps even a good King. But Aurya was by his side and partner in every aspect of his life. It was well-known that in the ruling of Kilgarriff, Aurya's whims were Giraldus's laws. What that promised for Aghamore's future was not something Renan wished to see.

As great a threat as that might be, the more immediate danger lay in Aurya's knowledge of Renan and the others. Her weapon was magic—and he feared that only more magic could turn it aside.

Filled with this dread, his heart now as heavy as his laden arms, Renan headed back toward the cave where the others waited. He did not yet know how much he would tell them—he would wait to hear what Talog had to say—but he did know they must do all in their power to keep the child they sought away from Aurya. If they failed, then just as both the scroll and the Holy Words of the Cryf had forewarned, a future of darkness awaited the people of Aghamore.

It was not until the fire was going and their food had been cooked that Renan again asked Talog about the danger he had mentioned in the bog. The young Cryf's face grew grave as he set aside his cup of chamomile tea.

"We face now a troubled path," he began, "and not only such danger as can be found upon thy maps. I ask thy forgiveness that I saw not the warning marks left by the ancient ones. Had I seen with clearer eyes, never would we have rested in that place. It be a place of greatest evil."

Although Talog's use and understanding of their language had greatly improved, he still used the archaic form of many words, and Renan was not certain Talog meant *evil*. How could a place be evil? Dangerous, yes—but evil?

"I don't understand," he said. "People can be evil, certainly, or they can do evil *deeds*—but how can you say a place is evil? Are you sure of the word?"

Now Talog looked as confused as Renan. "Do not Up-worlders have holy places? Have ye no places wherein the Spirit of the Divine may be felt?"

Renan considered carefully. Certainly there were churches and even great cathedrals—but were they holy *places* or were they places *made* holy by the people and the practices they contained? Yet throughout history, all religions had mentioned places where the Divine, by what-ever name, was said to abide. Mount Sinai for the ancient Hebrews or Delphi where the Oracle of the Greeks and Romans prophesied, to name just two.

"Yes," he said at last to answer Talog's question. "Yes, we do."

"Why then dost thou not believe some places may be evil?" Talog asked.

Renan had to acknowledge it was a fair question. "I don't know," he replied honestly.

"The Cryf know," Talog stated, "for the Divine hath made us to know. The land speaketh always unto us, and those of wisest hearts have learned to listen. Always do the Cryf feel of the land both the good and the evil therein.

"At the time of the beginning, all was good, all was holy. In perfection all was made and in perfection did abide and the First Ones of all living things did live in peace unto one another, for peace is the Gift of the Divine Who giveth all Life. Even the First Ones of the Cryf and the Up-worlders did know peace together and fear did not yet grow in any hearts.

"But peace did not satisfy every heart and thus greed was born into the world. Though it saddened the Divine to behold it, it was left to be, for the Gift of Life had been freely given. Greed be a thing of greatest danger, for it cometh never alone. With greed cometh jealousy, envy, selfishness, and these give birth unto anger, hatred, and fear. Thus was the peace of the first times destroyed.

"Then did the First Ones of the Cryf cry out unto the Divine, pleading to be set free from the world wherein greed abideth. Then did the Divine lead the Cryf unto the Realm and did place us as guards upon the peace that abideth there."

Renan realized, fascinated, that Talog was telling him the Cryf story of Creation. *How much is he not saying?* he wondered, certain that Talog was telling it in a much-abbreviated form. Was he doing so because of his listener's lack of knowledge in the history of the Cryf, as one would tell a child, or because of his own limited, though increasing, vocabulary?

"Are there Cryf in other lands?" he asked Talog. "Are there other Realms?"

The young Cryf shook his head. "The Divine did gather the Cryf from every land to enter unto the Realm. These did become the twelve Clans of the Cryf who now live together. We came, led by the Hand of the Divine, unto this place thou callest Ag-ha-more." He pronounced it slowly, each syllable separately formed to make certain he said it correctly.

"But why here?" Renan asked.

"Thou truly knowest not?" Talog asked in return, his voice both sad and surprised.

Renan shook his head. *When all of this is over,* he promised himself, *I'm going to return to the Realm and ask Eiddig to tell me all the stories. If they're not already written down, they should be.*

"Onto this place thou callest Ag-ha-more," Talog continued, "was the Hand of the Divine laid and power given. There be but few places in this world where such power abideth. It dwelleth within the land, the water, the air, the plants, and all that doth live.

"In the first times, when the Voice of the Divine was heard by all, the power that dwelleth in this land was freely felt and freely used. When the greed was born unto thy kind and many turned away from the Path of the Divine, then did some use the power of this land unto their own evil deeds. Then were born such places as we did encounter. Deed upon evil deed did gather the darkness unto these places, and the darkness twisteth the Gift of the Divine, marring the beauty that was first created and meant to dwell there.

"The Divine speaketh not to those who will not hear nor taketh the heart withheld. Thus did the Voice of the Divine cease to be heard, save by the few, and the power within this land was soon forgotten, for what hath been forgotten may not in evil be used.

"But the Cryf remember, for unto us was it given to remember, and always we guard the Truth. The Divine Hand is laid upon the Realm of the Cryf. No power may enter unto the Realm nor touch upon the Cryf. This hath the Divine given unto us. Thus Darkness may not enter unto our hearts and we remain ever true unto the Will of the Divine."

Power, Renan thought, wondering at Talog's use of the word. *What kind of power is in the land, the air . . . does he mean* magic? *There is magic in everything here, but it cannot touch the Cryf? If that is true, Talog may have just saved . . . everything.*

Renan smiled and leaned forward as he began to question the young Cryf, wanting to know everything Talog could tell him.

* * *

Another day lost, Aurya thought with frustration. It had taken all day to ride from Fintra to outside Diamor, where Giraldus's men were waiting. Now it was too dark to travel, and the time they were losing made Aurya fume with annoyance.

She begrudged every second lost not looking for the child. A part of her whispered to use the spell and force Giraldus to order his men to break camp and head north with her at once. But there were no fresh mounts waiting along the road for them. These horses, which they had ridden across the kingdom and halfway back, had to be treated with care.

At least there's fire and food, she thought as she and Giraldus entered the soldiers' camp. In truth, she was glad of both, and glad to see that the soldiers had erected tents—including the large one bearing Giraldus's arms with which he usually traveled. Although it would proclaim Giraldus's identity to any who saw it, it would also provide shelter and far more comfort.

The weather had been cool and damp all day, and two hours earlier it had begun to drizzle. The soft but constant rain had saturated Aurya's cloak and begun to seep through her clothes. It was not unseasonable weather for the northern part of the kingdom, but it was uncomfortable.

As they entered the camp, the soldiers scrambled to their feet, two of them rushing to take the horses. Their leader, Sergeant Maelik, did not rush. He swaggered a bit, as if confident of his master's approval.

Which he had. He and Giraldus greeted each other as the old friends and comrades-in-arms that they were. They had known each other since childhood, had been often partnered when training as young men, whether with sword or bow or staff, or lance and quintain. Side by side they had also fought in such campaigns as a kingdom most often at peace had to offer—which was not enough for either of them.

When she and Giraldus had first become lovers, Aurya had felt a little jealous of the special bond the years had forged between them. But now, after nearly a decade, she regarded Maelik with a sense of familiar ease, even trust.

"God's Blood—it's good to see you, Maelik," Giraldus said as he all but vaulted from his stallion's back and strode forward to grasp the sergeant by the shoulders. "What a time we had getting here, I tell you."

"Aye?" Maelik replied, gripping Giraldus's shoulders just as warmly in the rough male substitute for an embrace. "My men and I've been 'ere for two days, waitin'."

"My stallion threw a shoe in some God-forsaken hole," Giraldus explained as he went to help Aurya from her saddle. "It might not have been so bad if the local ale had tasted better. Like warm horse piss it was—and the food was little better."

"Well, we've ale with us," Maelik said, "and wine for m'lady. Young Rhys here would na' let us leave without 'em. 'E said you and Lady Aurya 'ad been traveling long enough and would want a taste of your own. 'E's who insisted we bring your tent, too. We put it up as soon as this blasted rain began. There even be a bit of a fire on the brazier so's it'd be warm and the damp'd be gone."

"Well, bless you for that," Aurya said as she, now dismounted, nodded a greeting to the sergeant. "But just how many others know where we are?"

"No 'un knows exactly, m'lady," Maelik answered. "I didna even tell my men until we was well under way. I only told young Rhys we was ordered to ride out and meet you so's 'e could order up our supplies from the kitchens. Me orders was to tell no one, and obey them I did."

"Of course you did," Giraldus boomed. "I had no doubt otherwise. Now, where's that ale—and food? We've been astride too many hours, and it's only my outside that's wet. My throat's as parched as an August day."

Aurya let Giraldus and Maelik lead the way to the fire, staying quiet and watchful while Giraldus greeted the soldiers. He called each one by name, using the big, blustery voice he only used around his men.

And the men responded, as they always did to his presence, with a mixture of obedient deference and camaraderie. Here, Aurya knew, was where Giraldus felt most at ease—in the field with his soldiers rather than in a court or conference room. Although he was competent enough when he put his mind to it, the truth was that Giraldus was also quickly bored, and he was only too happy to turn what he considered the tedious matters of government over to Aurya. And in these, she excelled—making them again a perfect match for each other.

And when Giraldus is King, Aurya thought as she accepted the wine that was brought to her and settled back to watch the interplay between the Baron and his men, *he can go off and play soldier all he wants. Perhaps he can invade a neighbor or two and expand the kingdom. That should keep him busy and away from the throne for a while—as long as he names me Regent in his absence.*

"No, m'lord," Maelik was now telling Giraldus. "We've seen no one. Not even the villagers have come out this way. O' course, there's naught but bogs if you go much away from 'ere."

Good, Aurya thought. *Then we're still ahead of The Others, whomever they are. This is the only road here, and no one would be foolish enough to travel through*

*boglands. Or, if they were, then no doubt the bogs have
taken care of them for me.*

Aurya allowed herself a small, triumphant smile behind the rim of her wine cup. To these soldiers, as to the
people of Kilgarriff—*and soon all of Aghamore*, she
thought—she was ever implacable. *Enigmatic . . . mysterious . . . inscrutable . . . as unmovable and impenetrable
as stone*—Aurya did not care which of these or the many
other descriptions of herself she had overheard throughout the years, people cared to use. They all meant the
same thing to her. They all meant that she had succeeded
in her efforts to be unreadable, if she chose . . . which
most often she did. It was only with Giraldus, and sometimes with Bishop Elon, that she would let her guard
down—and never often enough for either of them to think
they knew her completely.

Giraldus's easy, outgoing manner might work well
enough with his men—or with the people in a tavern or
at a faire—but it would not aid them when he was High
King. *He might wear the crown*, Aurya thought, *but I will
rule.*

She watched the way the soldiers grew a trifle uneasy
beneath her stare. She saw the way even her slightest
movement sent them hurrying to appease her needs. They
brought her food and more wine without being asked,
fetched her a dry cloak and built up the fire for her comfort, all while Giraldus gulped his ale, joked and chatted
but was left mostly to fend for his own needs. It was a
feeling she liked.

In those moments Aurya acknowledged a decision her
heart had been whispering for several days. She would
never fully remove the Spell of Obedience from Giraldus.
Oh, she would use it carefully, delicately and skillfully,
but she would never remove it.

And Elon? she asked herself. *When Giraldus names him Archbishop, shall I do the same to him?*

Yes, her heart whispered gleefully. Then both thrones of Aghamore, secular and sacred, would be hers to control.

"Tell me, Sergeant Maelik," she said, setting her now empty platter aside. It was instantly removed by the soldier sitting nearest her, toward whom she barely spared a glance. "Do you know Rathreagh at all?"

"Nay, m'lady," he replied. "But young Rhys 'ere, 'e does. That be why 'e's 'ere."

The sergeant motioned toward a soldier sitting not too far to Aurya's left. When she turned to look at him, he immediately blushed, turning the pale skin beneath a myriad of freckles, ruddy—and reflecting the fiery color of his hair.

"You know Rathreagh?" she asked again.

"Aye, my . . . m'lady," he stammered nervously in a voice that was not too long from cracking. "Me grandda's from this province, and we'd visit 'im when we was young."

"We're going north, Rhys," Aurya continued, "far north, to the tip of land that curves out into the sea. Do you know what towns are out there?"

"Aye, m'lady. Me grandda's family was all fishermen, far back afore any could remember. The best fishermen in all of Aghamore come from that part o' Rathreagh—though there's not much there what you'd call a town."

Aurya waved away the last statement as unimportant. "Can you get us there by the shortest and fastest route?" she asked. "Our map shows the roads, at least the larger ones. But I'm sure the locals have other ways they take, ways only they know."

"I 'aven't been 'ere in a few years, m'lady," Rhys began

slowly, "but aye—I believe I remember. I can take you by such ways as you mean—and cut a full day or more from the journey."

Aurya gave the lad one of her rare smiles and watched the look of wonder and delight spread across his face. Once more a ruddy flush rose up from his neck to his cheeks.

"Thank you, Rhys," she said, amused. "That is just what I wanted to hear. I will trust you, then, to lead us."

Rhys's blush deepened and he lowered his eyes. Aurya nearly laughed. She knew she had just made another conquest, and this one needed no more magic than a smile.

Chapter Twenty-five

For days now, Elon had spent his evenings courting the favor of Mago of Tievebrack and Gairiad of Sylaun, the two bishops whose votes would assure Giraldus the Church's backing in his bid for the throne of Aghamore. Unfortunately, he knew that Bresal of Rathreagh and his cohort, Dwyer of Camlough, were working just as hard to keep Giraldus off the throne. And they had far less prejudice to overcome; it is always easier to convince someone that his original opinion is right than to try and make him change it.

Elon's one consolation was that the College of Bishops was no nearer giving their support to any other Baron. Perhaps even less near, since he had surprised them all with the story of Aurya's "conversion."

So far, Thomas had been unable to uncover anything useful about either Mago or Gairiad. Gairiad had entered the Religious life at the age of ten, a youngest son promised to the Church at birth, in accordance with tradition. But in Gairiad the vocation seemed to be genuine. He had been ordained a priest at twenty, served as curate, then priest, going happily wherever he was assigned, finally returning to serve as Abbot to his Community before being elected Bishop-Ordinary of Camlough. His life appeared to be just as colorless and uninteresting as Elon found the man to be.

As for Mago of Tievebrack, his idealism not only bored Elon, it showed just how little Mago knew of the real world and the people in it. But it was this very idealism Elon was now preying upon. It gave him a better chance of success with Mago than Gairiad's colorless perfection.

Elon and Mago were seated before a small fire in the study of Elon's house in Ballinrigh. This was not his private study; this room was on the main floor and displayed all the expected trappings of a Prelate of the Church.

The decorations were tasteful, if a little bland for Elon's personal preference, and the chairs were comfortable. The highlight of the room's contents was a beautiful illuminated manuscript of the Gospels, kept under glass so that the colors of the ink would not fade. Elon had opened it to the third chapter of St. John and the story of the redemption of Nicodemus. Mago had been drawn to the book as soon as they entered the room, as Elon had known he would be, and the connection between the verses and their current situation had not been lost on the young bishop.

Although the calendar said spring was well advanced, the nights could still be chill and the fire was welcome. As they sat in the comfortable, high-backed chairs, sipping a mellow red wine, it was an easy thing to guide the conversation in the direction he wanted it to take.

He found that getting Mago to talk about redemption was as difficult as getting a kitten to drink cream. The young bishop, it seemed, had a passion for the subject. All Elon had to do was nod agreeably, occasionally ask a question or make a comment, and Mago did the rest. He seemed close to convincing himself that Aurya had not only ceased to be a liability to the Church, but had become an asset.

"St. Paul, of course, is the quintessential example of what I'm saying," the young bishop continued. He was now leaning forward in his chair, speaking as enthusiastically as if *he* were trying to persuade *Elon*. "Paul, when he was still called Saul of Tarsus, was the greatest enemy of the Church—he said so himself. He even held the cloaks of those who stoned St. Stephen, giving his support and approval to that terrible act. Yet look at who he became—*Saint* Paul, perhaps the greatest saint of the early Church. Why? Because of *redemption*."

Elon bit the inside of his cheek to keep the amusement from his face; Mago was drawing a correlation between Aurya and St. Paul.

"I think, perhaps, you are being overgenerous," he said solemnly.

"Why?" Mago asked, his enthusiasm mounting. "If Lady Aurya's conversion is as genuine as you believe, then who can say what might be ahead for her. Do not limit God, Elon. His ways are mysterious and they are also mighty—and He can do unimaginable things in the lives of the redeemed."

"I do not believe Lady Aurya aspires to *sainthood*, Mago."

"Did any of the saints set out to be so? Did they as children think, 'when I grow up I shall be a saint'? No— it was not their hands that so fashioned them. It was the Hands of God. Oh, this will be an exciting time for you, as Lady Aurya's spiritual advisor, to see what great things happen in her life."

"It could be an exciting time for all of Aghamore," Elon said, "if Lady Aurya were Queen. Think of what an example her redemption would set for the kingdom."

As Elon watched, Mago grew instantly wary. His eyes narrowed and lost the brightness that had shone in them this last hour.

"Yes, perhaps," was all he said as he sat back in his chair and took a sip of wine.

I thought I had him, Elon thought as he, too, brought his wineglass to his lips. *What am I still missing?*

Tactics demanded he change the subject. "How much longer do you think Colm will continue as Archbishop?" he asked, turning to a common speculation. "I know he longs to return to the monastic life when he retires. I've heard him say so."

"As have we all," Mago answered, his body relaxing now that they were back to a safe subject. "Do you ever long for the same, Elon, away from all the duties and responsibilities that come with the mitre?"

No, Elon's thoughts screamed, but he kept his face impassive. "The monastic life has its appeal," he said aloud. "Are you finding your new duties as bishop difficult?"

"Not difficult, just tiring," Mago replied. "I'm not sure I'll ever get used to them all."

"Oh, you will," Elon said. "Tell me what tires you, and perhaps I can help. I've carried the crozier for many years now."

Elon let Mago again take over the conversation, only half-listening to what the younger man was saying. Elon was trying to hear the message *behind* the words. Somewhere within them must be the secret that would bring about the support Elon needed. Now he only had to find it.

The more Talog told them, the more Renan became convinced that the Realm of the Cryf—and the Cryf themselves—were impervious to magic. This surprising knowledge did much to set Renan's mind at rest. If he and Lysandra were somehow stopped by Aurya's magic, Talog would still be able to get the child away. He could take the child to Eiddig; the old one would know what to do.

For the first time since he had overheard Giraldus's soldiers, Renan was able to sleep through the day and travel the next night with a clearer mind. But though that one worry was relieved, Renan was growing more uneasy about Lysandra every day. She still protested that she was fine, but ever since that sudden lethargy of body and spirit had overtaken her, it was as if the light within her had been extinguished. She moved like she was half-asleep and, even as Renan watched, it seemed as if she was continually striving, unsuccessfully, to throw off the dream-filled fog of slumber.

Lysandra spoke, but only when spoken to, and often her sentences drifted off before completion, as if the effort tired her too much. She smiled, but there was a new sadness in the expression that turned it wistful. She kept her hand always on Cloud-Dancer now, or if he needed to leave her side, however briefly, her entire body grew tense awaiting his return. By keeping a careful eye on her movements, for she made no complaint nor uttered a word about it, Renan knew that her *Sight* had not come to her in over two days.

He did not know whether all of this was a result of some evil humor exuded by a certain place in the land, as Talog insisted, or if Lady Aurya had cast a net of dark magic that had somehow caught Lysandra in its tangles, as he had come to believe. Perhaps the truth was a combination of both. Renan only hoped they could find some way to help Lysandra before it scarred her spirit permanently.

They had finally cleared the last of the bogs and were now heading to the far north. Tambryn's words had guided them right so far; now the scroll was sending them to *"the place wherein the Ninth House doth begin and end."* Renan believed—hoped, prayed—that the seer meant the little crest of land that the maps showed curled out like a tongue lapping up the waters of the sea. Depending upon which way one traveled, that tiny lay of land either began or ended the province.

They were about to set out on what Renan hoped would be their last night of traveling. He had the Cryf map of Rathreagh open before him and was studying it by the dying light of their cooking fire. Across the fire, Lysandra's shoulders were slumped, as if life had become an unbearable burden. Her eyes stared sightlessly ahead. Her arms were locked around Cloud-Dancer's neck as if he were her one anchor to safety.

She looks *blind now, as she never did before,* Renan thought. *Her blindness before was just something that had* happened, *not the thing she* was. His heart ached with his inability to help her.

Sitting next to Renan, Talog was also looking at the

Cryf map. Although Renan had more experience with maps, having traveled and read a great deal in his youth, he valued Talog's input. The young Cryf could correlate the ancient signs he had found along their journey with the symbols on the map and give them a more exact location and forward route than Renan on his own.

"We are here," Talog finally said, using a finger to mark their place. It was just slightly closer to their destination than Renan had guessed.

"Will we reach this northern tip by sunrise?" Renan asked, hoping his estimation had been correct. There were marks on this map that were self-evident and others whose meanings he did not understand until he reached the spot and saw the area for himself.

Talog, however, was confident. He nodded, but then his face grew as grave as Renan's and he glanced at Lysandra.

"If," the Cryf said, "our movements be swift." His voice lowered. "But great evil hath touched the Healer and holdeth her still. Its pull at her doth slow her feet as well as her mind. At such pace, I know not if we can cross the land before the Great Light riseth again."

Lysandra knew Renan and Talog were talking about her. She could feel their concern and wanted to respond to it. But she could not. Nothing seemed able to penetrate this thick fog that held her—at least not for more than a few minutes at a time.

For those few minutes she would think clearly, feeling the spark of the person she had always been. But those moments occurred less and less frequently. Most of the time, Lysandra was a stranger to herself, going through the familiar motions of life but without any connection to the reasons.

Cloud-Dancer alone was real to her, and she clung to him knowing that without his nearness, his solidity, she would be adrift. If that happened, if she truly lost herself within this . . . whatever it was that held her . . . Lysandra feared she might never find her own mind and soul again.

As for Renan and Talog, each hour they were becoming less real to her. Even when she looked at them using Cloud-Dancer's vision, they were vague and out of focus, like shadowy figures glimpsed at twilight. She followed them because she did not know what else to do and because Cloud-Dancer took her in that direction. She ate and drank when food and drink were given to her; she slept when Cloud-Dancer curled up next to her and then arose unrefreshed to begin the cycle again.

Now, sitting by the last light of the cooking fire, her arms around Cloud-Dancer's neck, she experienced a moment of lucidity. In a way, it frightened her because she did not know how long it had been since her last one or how long the clarity would last this time.

"Renan," she said softly. Immediately, the priest who was now her friend looked up from the map. He handed it to Talog and came over to her side.

"I'm here," he said, placing a gentle hand on her arm.

"Renan, I don't know if I can go on," she said. "Something has happened to me, something I don't understand. But it's getting worse. I can't stop it, and my strength is almost gone."

"Hold on just a little while longer, Lysandra," Renan said. "Just one more day. We're almost there . . . don't give up yet."

"I'm slowing you down—I know that. Leave me here and go find the child. I'll be waiting when you return."

"*No*," Renan said sharply, surprising Lysandra with the force of the word. "No," he said again, lowering his voice.

"We're not leaving you—or anyone. We stay together. We *need* you, Lysandra, to find the child. You're Prophecy's Hand, remember? It will take all of us to do what we need to do."

"But how can I help you find the child when I can barely find myself anymore?"

"We're staying together," Renan said emphatically. "I'm not certain what's happening to you either, Lysandra, but we'll find out. And we'll find a way to stop it— I promise you that. But we have to be together to do it."

Lysandra knew there was no arguing with him. He was right; they should stay together. But she was also right— she was slowing them down at a time when speed was important.

"Don't worry, Lysandra," Renan said, the hand on her arm giving a small and reassuring squeeze. "Talog and I will help you. We'll carry you, if the need comes. It will be all right."

Lysandra nodded though her heart remained unconvinced. But it was ceasing to matter anyway. Again.

Renan watched Lysandra's features become slack, and he knew that they were once more losing her to whatever place her awareness went. There was no way to hold her here. But at least they had had those few moments. He could only hope that something of what he had just said would stay with her, some inner core would know she was not alone.

Renan longed to take her in his arms and cradle her as he would a child frightened by nightmares. He wanted to hold her until he had banished all of her fears, to keep her safe and never let her go. Instead he gave her arm another gentle squeeze, letting his fingers linger briefly against the softness of her skin. Then he reached over and ran a hand across Cloud-Dancer's head.

"We'll both take care of her, won't we, boy?" he said softly. It was the first time he had actually touched the wolf, but Cloud-Dancer appeared not to mind. The two of them shared a common bond in their concern and affection for Lysandra.

Renan found Talog watching him. The Cryf wore a knowing expression for one so young.

"Your love for the Healer grows," he said. "Soon even her blindness will see it, if it doth not already."

"I am understandably concerned for her well-being," Renan replied, carefully keeping his voice even.

But Talog shook his head. "No," he said. "There is more betwixt thee and the Healer. Before the place of darkness did take away her mind, she also felt love awakening within her. Yet, she hath feared to love for too long, and fear hath made the eyes of her heart more blind than the eyes of her body.

"But I be not blind," Talog continued. "Betwixt thee and the Healer groweth the bond that cometh from the Heart of the Divine. Why dost thou deny this greatest of gifts?"

Renan shook his head. He needed to make Talog believe he had mistaken friendship for love, so that the young Cryf would not reveal his feelings to Lysandra.

"You do not understand," Renan settled next to Talog and began to again fold up the map. "Among my people there are many kinds of love—as there must be among the Cryf. There is the love of a man and woman who wish to unite their lives. This is a great and special love, that is true. But there is also the love of a parent for a child or a child for a parent. There is the love between brothers and sisters. There are loves and bonds such as

Lysandra and Cloud-Dancer share and there is the love felt toward God, the Divine as you call Him. All these are different, and all are gifts to be treasured.

"And there is also the love that develops between friends. This grows and changes over time, as they come to know each other better. This is what exists between myself and the healer. We are friends."

Talog just stared at Renan, as if waiting for him to say more. His silence seemed to dare Renan to embrace the epiphany of self-realization the Cryf believed to be waiting. But it was a challenge Renan could not accept, and he looked away from Talog's too-honest, deep-seeing eyes.

"It is time we break camp," he said abruptly. He stood and began kicking dirt across the remnants of their fire.

"To hide from one truth is to hide from all truth," the young Cryf said at last. "How canst thou be a Guide unto thy people if thou wilt not see Truth?"

Because some truths are too painful to look at, Renan thought, though he gave Talog no answer. *Or, though they are known, they can never be given voice.*

And Renan did know. He knew that, despite his words to Talog, he was completely and irrevocably in love with Lysandra—just as he knew that the collar he wore and all it represented must forever keep him from acting upon it.

Renan finished packing the supplies. He and Talog had divided Lysandra's belongings between them, and Renan now shouldered his slightly heavier pack, wondering if they would soon be carrying Lysandra as well. He went and gently helped her to stand. She gave him no resistance, but little help, as he turned her toward the direction they would be walking and put her hand on Cloud-Dancer's head, watching her fingers automatically wind themselves deeply into his fur.

Renan could not bring himself to leave Lysandra's side.

He could never tell her the truth of his feelings, but he could be with her. Walk beside her and help her, be ready to carry her if he must—this much, at least, he could do.

He motioned for Talog to take the lead. His eyes once more locked briefly with those of the Cryf. Talog's expression declared plainly, that for all of Renan's protestations and explanations, the young Cryf believed not a word.

Oh, Talog, Renan thought in answer to that look, *life is too complicated for such black-and-white answers, as time will teach you. Each action, each decision—each moment—is filled with infinite shades of gray. All we can do is try not to hurt those around us or lose our way amid the shadowlands of this life—and hope for greater illumination in the life to come.*

Chapter Twenty-six

Despite Rhys's childhood familiarity with the area, Aurya's party stayed to the roads. Rhys did take them by turns Aurya would never have known, shaving little bits of time from their journey with each new side road or unmarked horse trail. Even the main routes were difficult going, rocky and uneven, and the horses tired more quickly than Aurya liked. With each stop to rest and water them, a little more of her patience ebbed away.

By nightfall they were deep in the interior of the province; what she had thought would be a four-day journey was, by the grace of Rhys's directions, only going to take three—or possibly even two. Yet that was still not as fast as she would have liked. She felt the threat of failure keenly, as her dream about the beak of the white dove piercing the breast of the griffin refused to fade.

She knew the dream to be prophetic and often felt as if the golden beak had driven itself deeply into her own flesh. But horses—and men—had their limitations, and not even Aurya's powers could alter the laws of Creation. She could, by magic, force them to continue to the point of exhaustion, even death. Doing that, however, would foul her own plan, for even if she did find the child before The Others, she would have neither transportation nor arms and protections to allow her to make use of her prize.

So, instead, Aurya used her magic to try and inhibit the success of her rivals. Her Spell of Finding, cast in the night while Giraldus slept, had been unsuccessful, but not because her magic failed. It had been turned aside by a power she did not recognize. It had not felt like magic meeting magic . . . but what else could it have been?

Still, her failure confirmed to her that The Others were out there, that the prophetic nature of her dream had been real. And it told her that they did not travel unprotected. She would have to be very careful, subtle in her use of the arcane. The Finding she had used had been direct and had been blocked, but the other spell that night had come from a book of Sumerian magic, translated into Greek and then to Latin a thousand years before Aurya ever learned of it—and it had been ancient then.

This Spell of Darkness had not been repelled; Aurya was hopeful, even certain of that. It had found fertile soil and was even now spreading its poisonous tendrils through her rival's mind. Each night when the moon was high, Aurya rose from her bed and used the darkness to strengthen the spell's power.

This night was no different. She left Giraldus snoring beneath his blankets as she wrapped her cloak around herself and left such warmth as their tent offered for the cool openness of the night air. As usual, a watch had been set, and when Aurya stepped out, the guard immediately turned toward her.

Aurya saw that it was Rhys, and she smiled as the young man hurried toward her.

"M'lady," he said softly as he neared, mindful of the others sleeping nearby. "Is there some'ut wrong?"

"No, Rhys," she said sweetly. "I merely wanted some fresh air. I see they have you on late watch tonight."

"Aye—I drew the long straw, and rotten luck it was, too. I'd a mind for a good night's sleep."

"As do we all," Aurya replied, but her thoughts were not on her words. They were on Rhys and how she might benefit by his presence.

He's just the type to make an excellent subject, she thought, *young, strong—and not overly bright.* And, like most young men his age, Rhys was easily besotted—which meant he was easily used . . . in the right hands.

Aurya went over to one of the many large stones that dotted the landscape like some giant's game of marbles left half-played. She chose one big enough for two people to sit side by side and sat down, pulling her cloak more tightly around herself to block out the chill. Then she motioned to Rhys.

"I can't sleep," she told the young man. "Come sit and talk with me. You'll still be able to keep watch from here."

After one brief hesitation, Rhys complied. Aurya smiled her sweetest at him; even the moonlight could not hide the blush that once again darkened his fair, befreckled skin.

Rhys sat down so gingerly beside her that Aurya nearly laughed. Instead, she lowered her head to hide her smile, then looked up at Rhys through her lashes. She knew how the soft moonlight flattered her, how it made her skin look luminous, her hair like a cascade of silk, turned her lips and eyes into mysteries waiting to be explored.

She began to speak in a low, soft voice, a voice both hypnotic and enticing. Rhys had no will to resist it. It took only a very short time before she saw his eyes glaze over and she knew he was hers to command, body and soul.

"Rhys," she said again once she was certain he was ready, "my words are all you hear. Do you understand me?"

The young man nodded.

"Good. Rhys, you are doing well. Now relax, there is nothing to fear. No harm will come to you or to anyone here. You are doing your duty by obeying me. Do you understand? Obeying me is your first duty."

Again the young man nodded.

Now Aurya did smile; this was even easier than she expected. She stood and moved around behind him, putting her hands on Rhys's shoulders.

"Do not be afraid, Rhys," she said again. "Open your mind to me. Your thoughts are like water, flowing unhindered and swiftly away. Do not try to stop them. Let them flow until your mind is clear."

There was nothing hidden in Rhys's mind. His thoughts

were only what she had easily read on his face: how beautiful he thought her and how bemused he was by her nearness and her interest in him, however small and passing it was; how much he liked being a soldier—and how much he hated night watch; how excited he was to have been chosen for this mission; how proud he felt to be the one guiding them through Rathreagh . . .

Deeper thoughts, thoughts of home and family, memories of his parents, grandparents, siblings, all passed by even more swiftly and with less detail. Soon, Rhys's mind was like the clear water Aurya had suggested to him. Now he was ready.

She moved her hands from his shoulders to his temples. Like a succubus, she began to drain the strength of his youth into herself. Tonight she would add to the ancient spell she had been using these past nights and plant within it her own seeds of destruction.

She began, keeping her voice low enough not to be heard by the rest of the camp.

"Magic black as moonless night, power strong as earth and sea;
Find the one by distance hidden, whose purpose makes my enemy.
Around this one I weave this Binding, a web where fears and doubts are caught
A darkened soul my magic sends thee, the death of all thy hope hast brought.
Mist and shadow insubstantial, ghosts of vision, thoughts unheard;
Doubts, confusion, now become real; from silence speak the halting word.
Feet make heavy, muscles weaken, eyes be blinded, mouth make mute;

Reason, logic, will, and purpose, darkness swallow,
    stain and root.
Into the void now I send thee; blackness deepen,
    hold thee fast
With chains of magic none can sever, be thou bound
    unto the last."

Aurya lifted her hands from Rhys's temples. His head, no longer supported by her touch, slumped slightly forward. She smiled as she came around to sit once more beside him. The energy of his youth and his eagerness to please her had added a new strength to her spell. She felt wonderfully certain that the wings of the white dove had now been clipped.

Softly, she placed a hand on Rhys's arm. "At my word you will awaken," she told him, "and remember only that we sat here for a few minutes while I asked you questions of your childhood in Rathreagh. When your watch is ended, you will sleep peacefully. Though you remember none of this, you will remain ready to aid me at my word. Do you understand, Rhys?"

The young man's head gently nodded. "Very good, Rhys," Aurya said. "Now—awaken."

Rhys came instantly awake, and Aurya yawned to cover the brief interval between his passivity and his awareness. He remained oblivious that there had been an interval at all.

"Thank you for your company, Rhys," she said, once more speaking sweetly to him. "I think I can sleep again now. And I hope your watch is soon ended so that you have time for some rest. We are all relying on your guidance."

"I'll be fine, m'lady," Rhys assured her, "and I'll get you to Caerryck, never fear."

"I'm sure you will." Aurya gave the young man one last smile, then headed back to her tent, glowing with her renewed certainty of success.

Renan knew that their greatest enemy now was Time. Hour by hour, the lethargy that had laid hold of Lysandra was growing stronger. He did not know what reaching their destination and finding the child would do to help her, but something told him it was her only chance of recovery. Lysandra was Prophecy's Hand, and so he had to believe hope was ahead.

It was still two hours before sunrise when at last they came in sight of the northernmost village in Rathreagh, Caerryck. The town, like the countryside around it, had a wild, fey look. The wind blowing in from the sea had dwarfed and twisted what trees there were into shapes that would have seemed at home in a madman's dream. Even the stones here were oddly formed, as if some giant's child playing in the mud had left the clouts squeezed between its fingers to dry in the sun.

Nor was there silence, not even in the hours before dawn. Here, where the northern tip of Rathreagh curled like a beckoning finger to the sea, the sea answered. Waves crashed and wind howled, thick with salt spray and heavy with the aromas of sand and water, kelp and sea grass, and all manner of aquatic life.

The people of Caerryck, who took their living from the sea, moved to its rhythms and tides. Already, the town was awake. Fires of peat and driftwood sent their aromatic smoke rising from the chimneys. Lights flickered in the windows of the oddly shaped houses built of driftwood and stone, and occasionally voices could be heard calling to one another over the sound of the surf.

For the last half mile, Renan and Talog had all but carried Lysandra to keep her moving. Now they eased her down into a little hollow that was protected on three sides by a jumble of wind-shaped rocks. She immediately curled onto her side, lapsing further into her withdrawn state. When Cloud-Dancer lay down next to her, Renan was glad to see that Lysandra still possessed enough awareness to reach out for him.

Talog, too, crawled inside the little hollow. He looked out at Renan, his huge eyes glowing with the reflected light of the moon.

"I shall watch the Healer," he said solemnly, "and await thy return. The Divine be thy Guide and lead thee swiftly unto the child. We shall be safe here, but tarry not. I fear the Healer's strength be nearly gone."

"I'll be back as soon as I can," Renan assured him. "Try to get her to eat if you can—and you, too. I fear we will all need our strength before this is over."

Renan crawled back out of the hollow. He would go alone into Caerryck, knowing that his collar would protect him and that he would arouse far less unwanted attention on his own. He wanted to find either an inn where he could rent them safe lodging until they found the child, or a church whose guesthouse they might use. Again, his collar would be an asset.

Renan had read through the scroll and Talog had recited those parts of the Holy Words that Eiddig had made him memorize, in an attempt to find some hint of how they were to find the child once they reached Caerryck— but without success. Both the writings of Tambryn and the Holy Words of the Cryf were silent on the subject. It filled Renan with extreme uneasiness as he walked toward the town.

He drew a few curious glances from people who were out on the streets, but their faces were friendly enough as they hurried to reach their boats before they missed the tide. The main street of the town faced the shore, following its uneven line and giving a meandering definition to the town's layout that was quite unlike the rigid blocks of Ballinrigh.

Just then a church bell rang, calling the town to Lauds, the first canonical Office of the day. The familiar sound coming through the slowly fading darkness was more than welcome; it made Renan's heart almost shout with joy and relief. He immediately turned in what he hoped was the right direction.

The little church was built entirely of stone. Renan entered it and breathed in the mingled aromas of beeswax and incense, not realizing how much he had missed them until this moment. Here, they combined with the tang of salt and sea, but even that could not mask the fragrance that had been part of his life for so long. It was a coming-home.

The old priest, standing inside the sanctuary of the altar rail, was going through the motions as familiar to Renan as breathing—lighting candles, turning the lectionary to the readings of the day, smoothing minute wrinkles from the fair linen upon the altar . . . His thinning gray hair seemed like the glowing nimbus of a saint to Renan as he dipped his fingers into the holy water font and crossed himself. Then he quietly slid into a pew and knelt as the few worshipers began to come through the door.

The priest turned to greet his tiny congregation, his eyes widening slightly with surprise as they lit upon Renan. The congregation, including himself, numbered only six in all, and Renan smiled. The "Faithful Remnant," he thought, familiar with celebrating the daily Offices in a church far more empty than full. It gave him a feeling of immediate kinship with this parish priest. No one who served in a large parish could understand the disappointments—and the rich rewards—of ministering to a congregation such as this one or Renan's own.

Renan enjoyed the morning Office. The priest, for all his age, proved to be a loud, joyful celebrant who entered into the prayers with exuberance and greeted his tiny congregation with a hearty welcome. When the service concluded and the people left with the quick footsteps that would take them into the demands of their day, the priest came toward Renan with his hand extended in greeting.

Renan was happy to shake the hand of this brother-priest, whose eyes were as warm as his hand. His words during the short homily had shown that here was a man with an encouraging spirit and a joyful heart. After the long days and nights of travel and his current worries, Renan felt his heart growing lighter just being in this man's company.

"I am Father Peadar," the priest said, eyes twinkling in a face as lined as old leather. His voice at close quarters did not soften. "Welcome to the Parish of Saint Peter the Fisherman, and to Caerryck, Father—?"

"Renan," he supplied, a bit more loudly than was his usual wont, wondering whether Father Peadar's volume came from being hard of hearing or from a lifetime of shouting over the sound of wind and surf.

"Father Renan, welcome," Peadar said again. "Are you here on retreat or visitin' family—or has the bishop finally granted Mother Bedina's request and sent a priest to take up residence? I know the Sisters at Saint Gabriel's will be very relieved. I do what I can, but—"

"No," Renan stopped Father Peadar, who seemed not only content to hear his own voice but happy to supply all the conversation. "I'm not from the bishop. I'm sorry."

"Well, the bishop's most likely too busy with settlin'

the succession, God grant him wisdom, to mind the needs of a small convent like ours. Still, Mother Bedina's a formidable woman who doesn't like to be overlooked. If you're not bound for the convent, have ye time to stop for a bit of breakfast w' me? I get aweary o' eatin' alone."

Renan could not imagine that this man's joyful spirit grew weary of much of anything, and he happily accepted. In a town this size, where everyone was well-known and secrets could not survive, Father Peadar would be the best source of information he could find.

The rectory of Saint Peter the Fisherman reflected the occupation of its congregation and was little like the neatly appointed quarters that were Renan's own. Fishing nets were draped across the walls in a way Renan supposed was meant to be decorative. The furniture was crafted of driftwood, giving such mundane articles as chairs a wild and primitive look. More driftwood, oddly shaped and colored stones mixed with round glass floats, and assorted shells of all sizes and shapes scattered across most of the flat surfaces in the room and the floor had a dusting of sand that crunched beneath Renan's feet. All in all, it looked—and smelled—far more like the home of a fisherman than of a priest.

Father Peadar laughed as they entered, giving explanation without apology for the mess and the decor. "The children like to bring me things," he said, waving his hand toward the odd clutter. "I haven't the heart to tell them I already have countless 'pretty shells' and such. The wee ones give with such pure hearts, I'll not take the joy from them.

"Now, sit ye down, Father Renan, and I'll put the kettle on the fire. Soon there'll be a good, strong cuppa to drink while our food cooks."

Three hours later, remnants of their meal lay ignored upon the table, and they were just finishing their fourth pot of tea.

Renan had found that for all his jovial demeanor, Father Peadar was an extraordinary listener. However, Renan insisted that Father Peadar don the purple stole of the confessional. Now, everything that passed between them was sealed under the protection of one of the most sacred laws of the Church and secular as well as sacred authorities recognized its inviolate rule.

Father Peadar's knowledge of ancient writings—including the Scrolls of Tambryn—surprised Renan. It had taken little convincing to enlist his aid.

"So you see," Renan concluded, "now that we're here, I don't know what else to do. Do I wander the streets questioning each child until I find the right one? That seems nothing more than a great waste of time we don't have. And there's Lysandra's condition—"

"Aye," Peadar said, "the blind healer. Do ye think ye can get her here, to the church?"

Renan nodded. "Though not without attracting some attention."

"Aye," Peadar said again. "And that ye'll not be needin'. But folks in Caerryck rise early—and sleep early. If ye come an hour after the Vespers' bell, the town'll be dark and most folks fast sleepin'. I just might have somethin' for ye then."

Renan rose and held out a hand to Father Peadar. "I'm not sure how to thank you," he said. "Just talking with you has been a blessing."

"Thank me later," Peadar said, "after ye return and we see if what I'm thinkin' be right. Now, if ye take this door instead of goin' through the church, ye can cut around back o' the town."

Renan heard Peadar's soft *"Benedicite"* as he turned away. Grateful for the blessing, he slipped out the back door of the rectory and onto an empty back street.

With most of the men out fishing, the women of Caerryck were too busy with the chores of home and family to pay much mind to a priest of unremarkable form or attire. Still, Renan tried to be inconspicuous as he again traveled the winding streets of the little fishing village. Then, being fairly certain no one was watching, he headed out across the countryside.

When he reached the stone-covered hollow, he was surprised to find Talog not only awake, but watching for him anxiously. "What is it?" he said as he eased himself down into their hiding place.

"The Healer," Talog answered. "Her sleep be not natural. She waketh not for food nor drink. Nor doth her companion's cry waken her. I fear she may be now lost unto us. Or if not now, soon."

Lysandra lay unmoving and still curled as he had left her. Her chest was rising and falling with her breath, but her lips and cheeks were far too pale.

"Only Prophecy's Hand can set free the Font of Wisdom," the words of Tambryn's scroll echoed in Renan's mind.

If she is lost, then so are we all, his thoughts came in a tumble. *Lysandra—hold on. Don't leave us. We need you; Aghamore needs you.*

I need you . . .

Chapter Twenty-seven

"Y ou look very pleased with yourself, m'dear," Giraldus said as he handed Aurya onto her mount.

"I am—and why not?" Aurya returned. "Everything is proceeding well . . . better than well."

"I was just commenting," Giraldus said. "A mood like this one, so early in the day, usually heralds good things."

As Giraldus turned toward his own horse, Aurya settled herself more comfortably into the saddle for the long hours of riding ahead. And she smiled a very private little smile. She was pleased . . . with herself and all she had done to ensure their success.

She had spoken in passing to Rhys this morning, asking him how long it would be before they reached Caerryck. The young man assured her they would be there either late that night or, if she preferred not to ride past dark, by early morning. While he talked, Aurya had watched him closely for any residual effects from the previous night. Aside from a little fatigue that showed around his eyes, something easily dismissed as the result of having late watch, he gave no sign.

She assured Rhys that she did not mind riding in the dark as long as he was certain of the way.

"Oh, yes, m'lady," he told her confidently, proud of

the role she had given him to play. "I'd never forget that road. It was the joy of m' childhood each time we traveled it. I know every foot of it."

Tonight, Aurya thought. She could barely contain her excitement as she waited for the signal to move out. She wanted to dig her heels into her gelding's side and gallop forward, gallop all the remaining miles to the north. But while she might show such a wild side to Giraldus, now that they were in the company of his soldiers she would retain her implacable façade. Nothing that they would see or hear would give any indication that she was other than completely calm—and in complete control.

Giraldus, however, was neither controlled nor illusory in his feelings. He brought his well-trained stallion sidestepping nearer to her until he could easily place one of his hands over her own where they rested on the pommel.

"By this time next month we'll awaken in the *royal* bedchamber," he said, his voice caressing her. "You're a wonder, Aurya, and soon all of Aghamore will be at your feet."

"And yours," she answered him confidently.

He leaned over and gave her a hearty kiss, not caring that the eyes of his men were upon them. Then, with a broad grin, he gave the signal to move out.

Aurya set the pace, using her knees to signal her gelding into the canter that would both eat up the miles and ease some of her impatience. She spared a thought then for Elon, hoping that the bishop was experiencing his own measure of success.

It won't be long now, her thoughts went out to him. *Have them ready for us in Ballinrigh, and you'll wear the triple mitre you so covet at the same time I wear the crown.*

* * *

Elon's success, however, was by no means assured. Mago of Tievebrack, for all his idealism, remained oddly wary. He had not as yet been willing to change his vote in favor of Giraldus. Nor had Gairiad of Sylaun. The old man blew hot and cold, sometimes seeming convinced by Elon's persuasions, then in the same day changing his mind again.

The morning meeting had just been convened, and a new vote was about to be taken to start the day. Elon glanced at his primary opponents, Bresal of Rathreagh and Dwyer of Camlough, then dismissed them again as immovable. Mago refused to meet his eyes, telling Elon silently that he remained unchanged; Gairiad was talking with Awnan of Dromkeen, a contemporary and lifelong friend. From the way the two of them were laughing, Elon was fairly certain their talk had nothing to do with the succession.

The Archbishop banged his crozier three times upon the floor, signaling for silence. Each bishop had eight white balls and eight black balls in front of him. Soon a closed container would start making the rounds as each of the Barons was named. At the end of each round, the balls would be counted by the Archbishop, who voted last. It was a long—and boring—procedure.

"Once more, my brothers, we are met over the question of the succession," the Archbishop began. He did not bother to stand, and his voice showed that he was growing even more weary of these endless days than were the rest of them.

"Let us put aside our differences and personal feelings," he continued, "and work together for the good of Aghamore's people, who look to us for guidance as well as the care of their souls. We have been too long at this question. If we do not reach accord soon, I fear that civil war will tear this kingdom apart. It is the people who will suffer—and we, my brothers, will bear the fault. I pray that you will think of this as we now vote."

The Archbishop picked up the ceramic jar with the single hole in its lid. "Baron Phelan of Tievebrack," he announced as he passed the container to his left.

They would now go in order through each of the Houses, though all of them knew that most of the votes were moot. Only one vote truly mattered—the Third House, Giraldus of Kilgarriff. Elon picked up his first black ball and waited.

The first vote concluded with no unexpected surprises and the second—seven black balls and one white, voted for loyalty. Now it was the Third House, and Elon watched each bishop as he voted. Bresal and Dwyer voted defiantly, not trying to hide the black balls they dropped. Mago again refused to look at Elon; he, too, then, had blackballed Giraldus.

Elon held his breath as the jar reached Gairiad. The old man, still talking with Awnan seated next to him, did not bother to look at his hand. He merely picked up the first ball his fingers contacted and dropped it in the jar.

The jar finished its round and reached the Archbishop. The old man removed the lid and began bringing out the balls. White . . . white . . . black . . . white . . . black . . . black . . . white . . . white . . . Elon took a deep breath. *White.* He had done it. He now had the two-thirds majority Giraldus needed.

The Archbishop looked at him and gave a small smile. Then the old man stood and brought his crozier down three times.

"We need go no further," he announced. "All that is needed has now been declared. Giraldus, Baron of Kilgarriff, the Third House of Aghamore shall, by the Grace of God, have the support and prayers of the Church to become the next High King of this land. Let us now go together into the cathedral to celebrate a Mass of Thanksgiving for the guidance the Holy Spirit has given us. A proclamation shall be prepared and this Sunday shall be read throughout the kingdom, for the joy and peace of mind of the people."

"No," Bresal of Rathreagh shouted, coming to his feet. "I'll not support putting a witch upon the throne—and make no mistake all of you, it will be his witch we have ruling us if Giraldus wears the crown. *Thou shalt not suffer a witch to live.*' I'll not hand her the kingdom."

"Bresal," the Archbishop said sternly, "I call you to the vow of obedience you took at your ordination."

"Obedience be damned," Bresal said, his voice hard and final, "for damned is what this kingdom shall be if Giraldus is made King."

He turned and stormed from the room, Dwyer of Camlough following as quickly as his immense size would allow. In the shocked silence, Elon stood. The Archbishop nodded once, giving Elon the floor.

"My brothers," he said loudly, drawing their attention over the murmurs. "We must not let our brother of Rathreagh's ill-advised action overshadow the great thing we have accomplished here today. I know he is doing what he believes to be right, and a month ago I would have gone with him. But each of us knows the power of redemption and the change that God can cause in a life. I have seen this change in Baron Giraldus—and especially in Lady Aurya. The Holy Spirit has borne witness to that change by moving your hearts to support Baron Giraldus as the next High King. We must pray that our brothers of Rathreagh and Camlough will be also led by the Spirit to return to their vow of obedience, for the good of the Church, this kingdom, and their own souls."

Elon sat down again, bowing his head in an attitude of humility and concern. But his thoughts were not on the bishops—not on those who had left or those still assembled. They were on Giraldus and Aurya, from whom he still had heard nothing.

I've done my part, he thought. *Now just be sure you do yours.*

All through the long day Renan remained awake, guarding the safety of their hidden camp. He did not awaken Talog to take his turn at watch, but let the Cryf enjoy his unbroken and well-deserved rest. Renan was not certain, by contrast, if Lysandra's state could be called slumber— or if it was, as he feared, something different and far more dangerous. She did not adjust her position on the hard ground; only the rise and fall of her chest showed she still breathed—and that was becoming more and more shallow.

But if this was magic, why was he not affected? And, if it was not magic, then what else could it be? They had all consumed the same food and drink, slept in the same places.

As daylight turned to dusk, deepening the darkness in the stone-covered hollow, he gently shook Talog awake. He had thought about starting a small fire and trying to brew some of the strengthening tea with which Lysandra had started their days, but he found he had not the heart. Somehow it seemed wrong, like giving up on her, to take over this act she had chosen as a personal duty.

Instead, he and Talog breakfasted on some of the travel-bread and preserved fish given them by the Cryf, washed down with plain water. Renan shared their food with

Cloud-Dancer so that the wolf did not have to hunt—not that he showed any inclination to leave Lysandra's side.

Finally, Renan heard the bell for Vespers. The long sleepless day of waiting made the sound all the sweeter and more welcome. Only an hour now, he told himself, an hour that, at the end, could mean life or death for Aghamore. But what was more important to Renan—it could mean life again for Lysandra.

Lysandra slept now without dreams, for even dreams demanded a state of awareness she no longer possessed. Somehow she had kept moving throughout the night, but when at last they reached the outskirts of Caerryck and she had lain down to rest, she had fallen into a place where not even dreams existed. She did not have a body or a mind . . . perhaps, even, for those hours she did not have a soul.

Lysandra did not stir as the long hours passed. She knew nothing of light or darkness, morning or evening. She did not feel Renan and Talog carefully maneuver her out of the hollow in which they had made their camp or Renan's arms as he carried her into Caerryck.

But something stirred in Lysandra as they entered the little parish church of Saint Peter the Fisherman, and she began the long upward struggle back toward the light.

Father Peadar was watching, and he quickly motioned them into the church as Renan and the others neared. Then he locked and barred the door behind them.

"Best take no chances," he said, turning around to lead the way from the ill-lit narthex into the nave. Here, oil lamps burned in niches built into the walls, giving a golden illumination to the room that filled it with a charm it lacked in the harsher light of day.

Renan went to the front of the church and, without waiting for Peadar's permission, took Lysandra inside the sanctuary of the altar and gently laid her there, pausing for one brief moment to stare down into her face. He hoped for some sign of resuscitation; he was not certain what else to do except pray that Divine Mercy would accomplish what he could not.

When he turned around, he found Father Peadar slowly circling Talog, a smile of wonder creasing his already-lined and aged face as his eyes kept going from the Cryf to Cloud-Dancer and back again.

"By all the saints, 'tis a wonder—that's the truth of it," he said with enthusiasm. "A tame wolf and a whole 'nother type of being whose people live underground, ye said. What be ye called, m'lad?"

Talog shot a bewildered, slightly pleading glance at Renan. "His name is Talog," Renan reminded Father Peadar, "and his people are the Cryf. You'll have to speak a bit more . . . simply." Renan chose the word with a smile; he had almost said *normally.* "Talog's vocabulary in our language is still growing."

"Aye, to be sure. I didna think o' that. I'm sorry, m'lad," he said to Talog, curbing his excitement a bit.

Talog still looked confused. "What be 'mlad'?" he asked. "I am Cryf."

Father Peadar let out a bark of a laugh that caused Talog to step back. Cloud-Dancer rose, his posture showing he was ready to spring into defense of Lysandra—or Talog and Renan—if this stranger showed the slightest sign of threat.

While Peadar clamped a contrite hand over his mouth, Renan touched Cloud-Dancer's head, as he had seen Lysandra do so often, signaling the wolf that all was well.

"M'lad is another way of saying 'young man,'" Renan

explained to Talog. He kept his voice soft to reassure the Cryf.

"Aye," Father Peadar said, lowering his voice to a gruff whisper. "Young man be my meanin', and I've never seen yer like. I'd ask ye more about yerself and yer people, but I know yer time be short. Mayhap someday we'll meet again and ye can tell me then."

Renan cleared his throat. The night was getting away from them and the danger coming closer. He lightly touched Talog's arm before the young Cryf could reply.

"We don't have much time," he said to Father Peadar. "You said you might be able to help us find the child—"

"Do ye swear by Our Lord and his Blessed Mother, and by yer vows as a priest, that what ye've come here for be not evil?" Father Peadar said sternly. "Swear that, or I'll no' help ye further."

Renan turned to the altar. He picked up the large crucifix and brought it to his lips.

"I do so swear, by the broken body of Our Lord and by all the angels and company of heaven," he said. "Now, Peadar, please. There *is* evil following us and could be here anytime."

"Aye, then," Father Peadar said. "That be a vow no priest would take lightly, and I believe ye. I'll help ye."

The weathered little priest went to the door just off the sanctuary that led into the sacristy and opened it. "Come along, child," he said softly, speaking to someone on the other side. "These be the people I brought ye here to meet."

Renan braced himself. Without realizing he was doing it, he held his breath as he waited for a child—*the* child, if Father Peadar was correct.

But the person who walked out of the sacristy was not

a child. It was a young woman; she came with her head bowed, wearing the habit and short white veil of a Benedictine novice.

For a few seconds, Renan was too stunned to say anything. "Peadar," he said, finding his voice again but unable to keep the disappointment from it. "I think you misunderstand. The scroll said a *child*, not a grown woman."

"Did it?" Father Peadar asked, "or did it say 'an innocent'? Did it speak of one with a pure heart, one who had not yet learned the ways o' the world? I've always known there was something about her, and when ye told me yer tale, I knew immediately who ye were here to find."

Father Peadar was right, Renan thought, remembering those very words from the passages of the scroll that spoke of the Font of Wisdom. But how did he know the words so exactly? Before he could ask, Peadar pushed the novice a bit forward.

"This be Father Renan, child," he said, his voice gentle and encouraging—but the young woman made no response.

Renan took a step toward her. "What's your name?" he asked, keeping his own voice low.

"I am Selia," she replied, still not lifting her head.

The girl's hesitation to speak was obvious, as was her reluctance to be here. Though lacking Lysandra's empathic abilities, Renan still felt these emotions as surely as if they had been his own. *She wants no part of us or of this world,* he thought with absolute certainty, recognizing in Selia emotions were ones he had felt once, long ago.

* * *

While Talog and Renan were staring at the newcomer, they were not watching Lysandra. They did not notice the fingers of her left hand slowly twitch open and closed. They did not see the little movement of her head or hear the sigh that escaped her.

But Cloud-Dancer did. After Renan's touch of assurance, the wolf's attention had returned to Lysandra. He saw her movement, sensed the beginning of her inward battle and, as always, went to her side to lend his aid.

There was not much he could do against this enemy, but he could be near her. Lying close by her side, he gently nosed his way beneath Lysandra's fingers. At last her hand lay in its usual place on top of his head.

Ignoring all others in the room, Cloud-Dancer settled down to wait.

Inside Lysandra a silent battle had begun to rage, pitting Light against the thick, pervasive darkness that held her. She did not know from where the spark of Light had come—but it was there. Growing stronger, giving her a single thought of hope toward which her mind and soul could aim.

Again, as if by their own power and not any will of hers, her fingers twitched. But this time she felt something beneath them. *Cloud-Dancer.* His name flowed into her thoughts like a welcome scent upon a breeze. Cloud-Dancer was here; he was with her. Always.

But where was she? She did not know. She knew only that for this brief instant she felt a breath of Life enter her. For as long as she could, she would aim toward the Light and not give up.

Once more, she moved her fingers. This time it was at her command and though the movement was small, it was a triumph. She moved them again and again, slowly down into Cloud-Dancer's fur.

Though the darkness still claimed her, the Light—that single, beautiful, crystalline spark—had not left her. Lysandra wanted now what the darkness had stolen from her.

Lysandra wanted to live again.

Chapter Twenty-eight

Some of the roads Rhys remembered from his childhood looked as if they had not been cleared in that long. The sun had set, and they were still five miles from Caerryck. The horses were tired, and so were the men. So, in truth, was Aurya. It was easy to let herself be persuaded to stop and make camp for the night. Tomorrow, by midday at the latest, they would reach the little fishing village that was their goal.

Aurya gratefully lowered herself to the ground, then took a few halting steps to stretch the stiffness from her knees and inner thighs. Even a gait as smooth as her gelding's became wearying after too many hours.

Five miles, she thought, *and we'll arrive tomorrow, rested and stronger than ever.* She allowed herself a smile of triumph, one she did not care if the soldiers saw.

The first hour of darkness passed with firelight and camp chores. By the passing of the second hour, food was eaten and cleared, animals tended, and the camp was quieting with welcome slumber.

The moon once again cast its Goddess-light upon the world below; Aurya decided that now was the moment to set her spell one last time. By tomorrow night, when the child was in her possession and they were on their way back to Kilgarriff, the protection of the soldiers would be all that was needed.

Tonight, however, she would take no chances.

It was not Rhys who stood watch this time, but Sergeant Maelik. Had she cared to take the time, Aurya had no doubt that she could bring Maelik as much under her control as Rhys—or Giraldus. But Maelik had a stronger mind and sense of self than his junior counterpart, and the lure of returning to her bed was too strong for Aurya to want to take the long moments that would be necessary to subdue Maelik's will.

As it was, when he noticed her emerge from her tent, she waved away his attention. He gave her a knowing grin and a nod, erroneously assuming he understood the reason for her venture into the night air. He turned away to give her privacy.

Aurya took herself off a little way from the camp, where she could not be overheard. Then, slipping behind a tall stone, she stood with her face turned upward in the moonlight and dropped her blanket, letting the silver Goddess-light bathe her as she lifted her arms in an attitude of supplication.

For a long moment she stood there, caressed by the silver moonlight, remembering all the times she had stood this way beside old Kizzie, giving worship to the Queen of the Night, Great Mother of All. What would Kizzie

think of her now, she wondered briefly, of the power she
wielded and the power she was soon to claim? Would she
say she had always known Aurya was destined for such
great things? Or would she warn her erstwhile student to
be careful where and how she used her power—that power
ill-used offends the Goddess and what has been given can
also be taken away?

Aurya shook her head against the thought. What was
hers was hers and *nothing* would take it from her. Old
Kizzie might have lived her life by such restrictions, but
Aurya would not. She closed her eyes, ready to speak the
words of her spell.

She felt the power build within her, welcome as a
lover's touch. Speaking softly, she recited the words she
had said into the moonlight these last few nights, building on them as she had each time, to deepen the magic
they contained.

But, though she stood in the Goddess's light, though
the words—and their intent—were correct, though the
power in her swelled and rose as strongly as ever . . . nothing happened.

Nothing.

There was no flaring release as magic was given form
and function. There was none of the now familiar feeling
of her spirit soaring on the wings of power, coupled to
that universal flame that gave birth and sustained magic's
life.

Nothing.

Aurya's heart was suddenly racing, pounding, making
the blood ring in her ears and her breath catch in her
throat. Her magic had not been merely turned aside, it
had been stopped entirely.

She fell to her knees in fear and confusion; such a
thing had never happened to her before, and she was not

certain what it meant. She felt a burst of fear as she thought again of Kizzie.

No, her mind screamed. She had not lost her magic; the *power* had been there. Her magic had been stopped *by* magic. And that meant only one thing—

They had to ride on to Caerryck. Now.

Aurya turned and ran back to camp. At the sound, Sergeant Maelik came rushing toward her.

She wasted no time to explain. "Raise the camp," she ordered as she pushed past him and into her tent.

She shook Giraldus until he came awake with a start. "What . . . what is it?" he asked with groggy concern, his voice rough with sleep.

"Get up," Aurya ordered as she threw his clothes at him, then reached for her own. She began to pull them on with hurried, shaking fingers.

Glancing over, she saw that Giraldus still had not moved. "Aurya—what's going on?" he demanded. "We're not under attack—and you can't tell me we are or Maelik'd sound the alarm. Why can't you leave a man to sleep?"

"We are under attack, you fool—"

"By who? What army?" Giraldus countered. His voice was rising, growing as angry as hers.

Aurya let out a bark of a laugh. "Army . . . an army you, your men, could fight. This attack is by magic and against magic—*my* magic. Now get dressed. There's no more time to waste."

Giraldus threw his clothes across the room at her. "Magic—I'm sick of the very word. If your magic is under attack, then *you* fight it. Make a spell or kill a bird—or do whatever it is you need to do. Just leave me and my men alone. In the morning we'll ride into that village— on horses, not magic—and get the child you insist we need—again, not by magic—then *finally* go home, to Kilgarriff where we belong. *Then* we can march on Ballinrigh. No *magic*, Aurya. It's an army—*my* army—that will get us the throne. And an army needs *sleep*."

Aurya had become more and more angry as Giraldus talked. Now she had listened enough. She would *show* him magic. She had invoked the Spell of Obedience only once since casting it. She had used it carefully, letting him think that continuing on their quest for the child had been his own decision, to humor her.

Now, she cared only that he obey her before the child was lost to them. Under her breath she began to chant, once more calling up her powers. She began slowly, softly . . . letting her voice rise in volume as the magic mounted and flowed from her into her victim. Into Giraldus.

> *"Power come and power claim,*
> *In voice of storm, of wind, of rain;*
> *Power strong and power fast,*
> *Within my voice find home at last.*
> *Turn stubborn mind and stubborn heart*
> *Willing now to do his part;*
> *To hear my voice is to obey*
> *And from obedience never sway."*

Aurya turned and pointed at Giraldus. "Get up," she ordered, "and get dressed. Now."

Immediately, the angry defiance left Giraldus's eyes. But his awareness remained. Had Aurya wished it, she could have subdued that, too—as she had with young Rhys. But she was angry enough with Giraldus not to care and too hurried to take the time.

Let him know, she thought. *Let him realize and re-*

member that I am in command. I'll take no more argument from him than he would from his lowliest soldier. His army—ha! I'll show him just how little his army counts . . . for anything.

Behind Giraldus's new look of compliance, Aurya saw his anger, and a touch of fear. She did not care. He was her minion . . . her *soldier* . . . now.

"Order your men to break camp and prepare to ride," she told him as he finished dressing. "And tell them to hurry. We're going to Caerryck now . . . before the hour is out."

Giraldus turned and left the tent, hurrying to do her bidding. She heard him outside barking orders, followed by the sounds of running feet and rustling gear as the men hurried to comply.

Aurya smiled. Her smile turned to laughter. She knew with certainty now that her powers were not failing. Her control over Giraldus was as strong as ever—and, yes, she liked the feeling.

Later, when the child was theirs and they were headed back to Kilgarriff, she would let this invocation of her spell die away. She would not remove the spell; tonight had proved how useful it was. But she would let Giraldus *think* it was removed . . . until the next time.

Outside the tent, Giraldus was talking with Sergeant Maelik. That he would be angry—terribly angry—she did not doubt. For a single, brief moment, the mundane female part of her felt a whisper of fear. But it was a feeling quickly subdued. She was no ordinary woman to fear a man's wrath. She would fear no one and nothing. She was Aurya—soon to be *Queen* Aurya, she thought as she, too, left the tent. She would deal with Giraldus's anger . . . by magic, if necessary. Soon he would learn that he could be her partner or her slave. But either way, *she* would win—she and the magic he disparaged.

"Excuse me, m'lady." Rhys was suddenly standing next to her. "Your horse be saddled and we'll be ready to ride in a few more minutes. I'm to ask if there be anything else you require."

"No, thank you, Rhys." Aurya favored the young man with one of her rare smiles. His ready deference softened her mood, as did his obvious enthrallment.

His habitual blush glowed dully in the light of the torches. Yes, she thought, he would be a good tool for the future. When they returned to Kilgarriff, she would have him assigned to her personal guards.

Each minute that passed felt like an hour, and Aurya's impatience grew again. She had never liked to be kept waiting, and at that moment, with so much at stake, she wanted to scream her frustration at the night. But even she could see that the men were moving as quickly as human limitation allowed.

She tapped her fingers on the pommel of her saddle, counting the seconds as the men folded the tent and packed its furnishings. Finally, she could stand no more. She swung herself back off her horse, slid to the ground, and stormed across the half-denuded campsite to find Giraldus.

He was still talking with Sergeant Maelik. "What are you doing?" she demanded. "Why aren't you in there helping? Don't you understand—we have no time to spare."

"Beggin' your pardon, m'lady," Maelik said. Though his tone and words were respectful enough, his eyes told her plainly how foolish he thought this nighttime rush. "Me boys know what they're about, and we'd just slow 'em down. If we be in the great hurry Your Ladyship says, then we'd best all stay out of their way."

There was no missing that Maelik's words were meant to put Aurya in her place—which to Maelik's mind, she was certain, did not include ordering him or his men around. She did not miss the amused light that gleamed, however briefly, in Giraldus's eyes.

That was all Aurya would stand. She once more turned her voice into a weapon of command.

"Go," she ordered them. "Get the men moving faster. There's to be no more time wasted by you or anyone. Go!"

As Giraldus moved to obey, Maelik had no choice but to follow him. Aurya saw the sergeant's surprise that Giraldus would let himself be ordered about by a woman. She also did not miss the look of hatred Maelik threw her way.

So, he fancies himself my enemy now, does he? she thought. *Well, he doesn't know what an enemy is—yet. But he will and soon.*

After this was over, she would get Maelik away from Giraldus. She would think of some mission on which to send him—and make certain an accident awaited him on the way. He would be buried with great honor, as befitting a soldier who died in direct service of the King— but Aurya would have no enemies in her own camp.

Nor, when she was done, would there be any—alive— anywhere in Aghamore. Once she had the child . . . she smiled . . . she would be unstoppable.

The activity around her increased to a fever pitch while she thought of Aghamore—the *new* Aghamore under her rule. Someday, and soon, the entire kingdom would be re- built, reborn, into *her* vision of what it should be.

And that vision began here, now, with the obedience she commanded.

She smiled as the noise began to fade away. Rhys approached, leading her horse.

"M'lady," he said, breathlessly, "Lord Giraldus is waiting for you."

Aurya nodded, then mounted and wheeled her horse to the side of a soldier carrying one of the torches that would light their ride. She was not going to be held back by someone else's pace. On this ride, she intended to *lead* the way.

Without ceremony, she took the torch from out his hand and lifted it high. "To Caerryck," she shouted.

Then she dug her heels into her horse's sides and it sprang forward, swiftly moving into the gallop she craved. Torch held aloft, she sped down the road, racing to meet the destiny she had come to claim and would not be denied.

Chapter Twenty-nine

They did not hear Cloud-Dancer's first soft whine. But his second, third, his fourth—each growing louder—finally interrupted the hesitant interview between Renan and the young novice who named herself Selia.

Renan's eyes flew to Lysandra. He saw her fingers digging their way into Cloud-Dancer's fur as if trying to hold on to the life she was in danger of losing. The wolf's blue eyes looked up and met Renan's own.

And Renan *knew*.

He did not care now about Selia; he did not care about the scroll, about their mission or their goal or who Selia might or might not be. He cared only that Lysandra needed him. Dropping to his knees beside her, Renan took her hand into his own and began calling Lysandra's name, urging her to come back—to life, to this place . . . *to him*.

A few seconds later, Talog was also there. He, too, began to call to Lysandra, speaking to her in the strangely melodic language of the Cryf. Renan absently recognized a few of the words—but it did not matter what Talog was saying. Renan could feel how the young Cryf, too, was doing all he could for Lysandra's sake.

But it was not enough. Though the fingers of her hand moved, though Cloud-Dancer's whine and actions all seemed to promise Lysandra was still there, buried inside her inert form but wanting to be freed—nothing more happened. Renan wanted to scream, to rage with his frustration that he could do no more; he wanted to weep at his own helplessness to save the woman he loved.

Then, suddenly, Selia was there. Without a word, she knelt beside him and took the hand Renan had been holding. Then, still saying nothing, she bowed her head and closed her eyes.

Everyone in the room became silent. Like Renan, all they could do now was wait.

Inside Lysandra, the war for her life continued. She heard Cloud-Dancer's whine; loud and glorious, it was the beautiful sound of his love for her. It became her one channel of strength and she tightened the grip of her fingers in his fur.

Then came another sound, sweet and welcome, too. Renan's voice was calling her, speaking her name over and over. His touch on her hand was like fire and ice; burning and then soothing the burn, freezing and then warming away the cold.

His voice, his touch, also empowered her to fight. She demanded back the possession of her body, her life—her soul.

Finally, she heard Talog's voice added to Renan's. Though she did not understand all of his words, she heard him call her Healer, *Meddig,* and speak the name of the Divine, *Diwinydd Creawdwr.* But it did not matter what else he said or that she did not understand him, for she heard him with her heart rather than her ears. He put a hand upon her arm, lending his strength to her battle.

Soundlessly, Lysandra's soul screamed into the blackness, demanding her right to *Be.* Motionlessly, she clawed and kicked, gouged and fought the suffocating pressure that was telling her to give up. It whispered into her with thoughts more felt than heard, that she had nothing waiting, *was* nothing; told her to let go of the struggle, to let herself float where she was free of pain and need and sorrow.

Then, suddenly, Renan's voice and touch were gone. All was silence again.

Into the silence, into the Darkness, came a presence. It was unknown to Lysandra, and yet . . .

. . . It called to her from the spark of Light in the distance; it beckoned to her, giving her new strength to fight again.

Lysandra felt the Darkness lift a little. The Light strengthened. It came, pouring hope into her weariness.

And with that hope, Lysandra recognized the Light for what it was.

It was Truth.

Truth called to her, and Lysandra listened. It told her the time of Darkness was at an end—*if* she would refuse it power.

How? her mind cried.

And Truth answered. It came not in words or in pictures; it came as nothing her mind perceived. It came as the breath of Spirit into spirit. With that breath, the Darkness began to swirl like fog disturbed.

As the Winds of Truth blew through her, Lysandra knew she was done giving power to the Darkness, done listening to its voice speaking to her heart, her soul, of all the pains she sometimes suffered—of loneliness and self-doubt, of the empty hours and sorrow-filled memories. In Truth, she knew that these were offset by many more moments of joy and peace. Life *was* worth living—and she *was* worthy of its gift.

That surety was lifting the Darkness . . . a little. As she let go of her fear—of living, of loving and of hoping for love—she felt the power that held her captive begin to lose its form. Whatever had been its source, she now knew that her own heart had given it a place to flourish.

Again the Truth blew, reminding Lysandra that she was not alone, never alone. How could she have forgotten that? She had Cloud-Dancer's unswerving companionship and loyalty. The Heart of Loyalty and Truth, Eiddig had called him, and she saw with awakening insight that this, too, was part of the Light embracing her.

And there were Talog and Renan—friends, companions, and . . .

Renan, her heart whispered. What was he to her, really? Was she ready to know? Could she face the answer?

With that question, with the doubts it brought, the Darkness thickened again. This time, however Lysandra realized what was happening. Suddenly, she knew how to combat it. The question came, the doubts whispered . . . and she accepted them, letting them pass through her. The answers did not matter. She accepted this moment, *in faith*, that all was as it should be. She accepted the past, *in faith*, that even its pains had a purpose. She accepted the future, *in faith*, that the path ahead, though sometimes difficult, would be a journey well worth taking.

She accepted *faith* again.

It came not with childhood teachings or other people's names and dogmas. This faith, in whose simplicity lay strength, embraced all that had been, was, and would be; all that was named and unnamed, seen and unseen.

At that moment, the swift Winds of Truth blew open the doors and windows of her soul. Her doubts became like chaff that lay upon the threshing floor, lifted upon that wind and carried away. As the doubts blew free, the blackness lifted and the Light grew.

Into the Light came a presence. This was the one who carried Truth within her and gave Truth to all she touched. This was the one of Wisdom they had traveled so far to find.

Their minds touched—and for Lysandra it was as if lights exploded in her brain. They came in brilliance, full of sound and color; they came in stillness, full of silence and shadow. Her mind was awhirl with all the possibilities that had been hinted at but were never true . . . until this moment.

What these new powers meant, Lysandra did not yet know. But now, again, she had a future in which to find out. She had Life and Hope—and *Truth*. That was the greatest gift she felt awakened, filling her—for without Truth at their heart, no other gifts, no other powers had meaning. Without Truth, there was only Darkness.

Slowly, Lysandra became aware of herself again. She felt the breath in her lungs; she felt the weight of her body and the hardness of the floor on which she lay. She felt again the warm softness of Cloud-Dancer's head beneath her fingers, and her other hand . . .

She felt her hand being released as the one who was Wisdom, and who had helped Lysandra find the Light of Truth amid the Darkness, backed away.

Lysandra tried to open her eyes. At first it felt as if her eyelids were made of lead. Then, once more, she heard Renan call her name. She felt his touch upon her forehead, gently stroking her hair as he called her to come back to them. Again, Talog spoke to her.

Talog, Renan, Cloud-Dancer—they blended and became one within the Truth that now filled her and had called her forth. Against such a union, where faith and caring, where unselfishness and Truth, abide, no magic can prevail. The last vestiges evaporated, and Lysandra was free.

She opened her eyes. She tried to sit, but her body still felt weak. For the moment, that single moment, she did not care; it was her own again and she rejoiced in the simple and yet divinely complex reality of *being*.

Lysandra reached out and felt the faces—first Talog's and then Renan's—of her dear companions. She found a tear on Renan's cheek. Of joy? Of relief? The reason did not matter. It was a gift and she treasured it.

"Where . . . where are we?" she asked. Her voice was barely a whisper, and she realized how dry and raw her throat felt.

"We're in Caerryck," Renan told her. He brought something to her lips. It was a cup and she sipped from it greedily, feeling the cool water wash the dryness away, letting the sweetness of plain, clean water rinse the taste and feeling of Darkness from her body. Never before had she realized the true blessedness of water.

"Caerryck," she said, her voice stronger this time and her memory beginning to return. "Oh, Renan, where is the child? I know it—I know *she* is here."

"We were wrong," Renan said. "It's not a child."

"Then who?" Lysandra folded her legs under her and tried to stand—but her knees buckled and would not hold her. With each new second, more memory, more purpose returned to her. She wanted to stand and take up her part in what they had come here to do.

Gone was the apathy with which she had begun and made most of this journey. No longer was she driven merely by the desire to complete an unwelcome task so that she could return to her solitary life. For the first time she truly understood that each day, each moment, not lived in caring and in Truth, was a little death, a choice of Darkness when all could be Light.

And she was done with Darkness.

"Slow down, Lysandra," Renan told her. "Whatever you've just been through has barely passed. You've got to be careful. We . . . we can't lose you again."

She heard the little catch in his voice. With new understanding, she knew what had given it birth—just as that same part of her knew that these feelings, hers and his, would be treasured and never spoken. She gave him a weak but gentle smile as she touched his cheek again, in a silent gesture of the friendship they *could* share.

Then she tried again to stand. Talog reached down and gave his strength to her—as he had throughout this journey—with a hand beneath her arm. In a new appreciation, she also touched his cheek. Up through her fingers she felt the Life that filled him, that filled all the Cryf. It was *Life* that was the Truth of their connection with their Realm and at the heart of their union with the Divine.

These new perceptions were coming so fast upon each other, Lysandra had to stop for a moment and catch her breath. But she did not want to stop; she wanted to find the one whose touch upon her mind had awakened such new thoughts and all the new possibilities within she felt she had still to discover.

Standing on her own, somewhat unsteady feet, she held out her hand in its familiar way. Cloud-Dancer immediately took his place beside her. His body, solid and strong, gave her balance as she leaned against him, and with her touch, the bond that was between them bloomed anew. With it came an ever-deepening sense of gratitude for being alive . . . something Lysandra had not let herself feel for far, far too long.

Through their bond and shared vision, Lysandra looked around. She saw the little church in which they stood, saw Renan and Talog watching her with expressions that mingled delight and worry. Then she saw the stranger, a priest, looking at her with obvious astonishment. He took a step toward her.

"By all that's holy, from the look of ye when Father Renan carried ye in, I thought ye were all but dead. What are ye, girl, that even death can not harm ye?"

Father Peadar crossed himself as he spoke. Though his cheeks had gone white when she stood, his eyes were now fierce.

"I am a healer," Lysandra replied, as if that explained everything. This priest's fears or superstitions were not her concern; he was not the one she still needed to find.

With Cloud-Dancer's vision she looked farther around. There was a young woman withdrawn into the shadows. She stood within her head down, as if by looking away she could disappear.

With the discernment that now filled her, Lysandra knew this was the one she sought. She moved her hand on Cloud-Dancer's head in the silent, familiar signal to walk. The girl slowly raised her head and met Lysandra's eyes.

Suddenly, her *Sight* flared into existence. Yet it was different, too. She could *see* with it—truly *See*, in more than just outlines and shadows, or colors and depth. She *saw* feelings and auras; she *saw* intentions of truth or falsehood; she *saw* the past in wisps of shadow that followed and shaped each person's present.

And, if she concentrated but a little, she *saw* the future paths waiting to be taken.

Startled, almost overwhelmed, Lysandra dropped her hand from Cloud-Dancer's head. Then the explosion of information settled into her more familiar pattern of *Sight.* Familiar and yet different—for what Lysandra *saw* of the young woman before her was youth upon her face and the timeless knowledge that shone from her eyes.

This was the one.

And with the new powers of her *Sight,* Lysandra also *saw* the path ahead. She knew in an instant that it was not only herself this girl was meant to save—it was Aghamore. The Truth of it shone all around her, crowning her and proclaiming that here was the true sovereign; here alone was the one who could expel the Darkness threatening the kingdom.

"Who are you?" Lysandra asked. She watched the young woman draw a deep breath, and she *saw* the resignation within that breath.

"I am Selia," she said, telling Lysandra what the others already knew.

But Lysandra knew what the others did not; she could feel that Selia's inner battles were far from over.

"How old are you, Selia?" Lysandra asked softly.

"Seventeen," came the answer.

The blood left Lysandra's face and she gasped. Seventeen . . . she knew what it meant to have all that one expected, the life one had thought to live, ripped away, destroyed . . .

At *seventeen* . . .

And this time *she* must be the destroyer.

Above all, Lysandra could feel Selia's desire to run away—not just from her, from this place, but from who she was and who she was meant to be. Again, Lysandra recognized herself in Selia's pain.

As much as she hated the role now forced upon her, what she had just come through had taught her how very close the Darkness was—for all of them. She had battled her own demons and won . . . this time, and not without help. But next time?

This young woman, who had the power to touch Lysandra's mind and heart, to awaken the power of Truth within her, had demons of her own life to bear. It had taken Lysandra ten years to learn to rejoin the world. Selia did not have that luxury. There were too many innocent and unwitting people who would suffer the Darkness if either of them, she or Selia, could not find the courage to act— *now.*

As Lysandra continued to meet Selia's eyes, the presence of new powers built again. Force upon force, power upon power, they filled her until, overwhelmed, she could not comprehend all that was happening. Then again, the onslaught stopped as suddenly as it had begun, but when it was over, Lysandra knew herself to be irreparably changed.

Sight became insight and suddenly Lysandra understood. She reached out and took Selia's hand. As she did, their minds touched again and they both knew with the perfect clarity only Truth can give, that there *was* a connection between them. It was more than the circumstances of life or fate that had brought them both there. They were Wisdom and Prophecy, each part of the other's future, each instrumental in the other's full awakening.

As Prophecy must have Wisdom, so Wisdom must have Truth. There was more, much more, stirring, awaiting discovery within Lysandra, but it would be revealed as time and need dictated. It was not her own needs she must face; it was Selia's. Lysandra knew that just as Selia had brought Truth to her, awakening its presence forever in her soul, now she must use that gift in return.

This time it was Lysandra who reached out and touched Selia's mind, showing the young woman the path and the Truth she was meant to follow. But Selia did not want to see. She pulled herself free from Lysandra's touch and backed away. The young woman's pain encircled her like a cloak, covering her true self, the person she could be— *must* be—as surely as the novitiate veil covered her shorn hair.

But, just as a few wisps of dark hair escaped their confines, to curl softly across Selia's forehead, so Lysandra caught glimpses of Selia's true self shining through the covering of her sorrow.

The girl backed up another step, away from the revelation Lysandra had given her. "I don't want this," she said. "I never have. I don't want any of this."

"I know," Lysandra replied calmly. She could feel the anxious anticipation in the others' silence.

"You know?" Selia responded harshly to Lysandra's words. "What could you possibly know? I'm not here because of you—any of you. I'm here because Father Peadar asked it. He's the only one who was ever . . . kind . . ." Her voice trailed off.

She looked at Lysandra with eyes that blazed her pain. But Lysandra *did* know. She knew all of it—Selia's past, her pain, the feeling of abandonment and years of silent loneliness. But there was another future waiting, and Lysandra *saw* that it was all there for Selia if only she could find the courage to walk the path ahead.

Lysandra understood because she had lived that other life. Now she had found her future; she had to help Selia find hers as well. For Aghamore's sake, yes . . . but most of all, for Selia's own.

"I know," Lysandra said again.

Selia shook her head. "You don't know," she said. "You can't. What Father Peadar, you—all of you—call Wisdom, my parents didn't. They threw me away, abandoned me to die because what you call Wisdom, they called demons. And I would have died if Father Peadar hadn't found me. He saved me, body and spirit. He and the Church gave me the only true home I've ever known."

And now you're being asked to leave it, Lysandra thought. Again, she knew what Selia felt. Lysandra's parents had not abandoned her—but she had lost them to death, lost all she had known and loved, and the pain was just as real.

But no birth comes without pain; no new life is born without labor.

"I know," she said one more time.

Selia turned to Father Peadar, burying her face in his shoulder. Her own shoulders shook with her silent sobs.

But Lysandra followed her. She reached out and

touched Selia, gently turning her from Father Peadar's shoulder into her own. She let Selia cry there for a moment, cradling her maternally as her own mother had long ago held Lysandra through her tears.

"I don't want this," Selia's words were muffled. "I don't want to be what I am, know what I know. I just want—"

"Everything," Lysandra said softly, remembering her own heart at seventeen. "Selia," she said softly but firmly, "look at me. See who I am—see who *you* are."

Hesitantly, the younger woman brought her eyes up. Calling to use some of the new gifts in her possession, Lysandra now touched Selia's mind with a question the girl could not ignore.

Which of us is truly blind, Lysandra's thoughts asked. *The one who cannot see—or the one who will not?*

I have seen too much, Selia's thoughts answered her. *Life is only pain and sorrow, suffering and loneliness. I don't want to look ... I don't want to see anymore. At least if I take the veil, my loneliness can stand for something.*

Lysandra's thoughts reached out to touch and comfort Selia as her own mother had comforted her, remembering the fragility of a seventeen-year-old's heart.

Oh, Selia, Lysandra's thoughts told her, *there is more— much, much more. You have seen only one side of life. The fear and the pain it brought blinded you to everything else. Don't be afraid to look now. Don't be afraid to truly see. You hold Wisdom within you, and it has given you the power to walk in Truth. Look at it now and see that on the other side of the Darkness, the Light shines brightly.*

Lysandra opened her mind to Selia, then guided her to that place of prescience Lysandra now called her own.

This was the place from which Prophecy came, where hope was given birth, where the future danced to the music of possibility.

Lysandra held nothing back. She shared her past with Selia in all its doubts and darknesses, in all its joys and triumphs. Then she showed the girl all she was now. Together, they saw the promise of the gifts it would take Lysandra a lifetime to fully understand.

Then the Hand of Prophecy opened and Lysandra showed Selia the truth of who she was and all she could become—if she had the courage. A kingdom waited for Selia; a kingdom and a people who needed her. The way would be fraught with difficulties, valleys and mountain peaks, as all life was. But it was the journey that mattered. Her choice now would decide whether she made that journey in the Darkness or in the Light.

Selia bowed her head. "I will come with you," she said.

Through the silent tension of these last minutes, no one had noticed Cloud-Dancer. Now, suddenly, the wolf gave a long howl. Lysandra closed her eyes and sent her *Sight* out into the town and beyond.

Then she looked at Renan. "Giraldus," was all she said. It was enough.

"Where are they?"

"They've entered the town. Some are riding guard upon the roads—others are headed this way."

"Aye, then," Father Peadar spoke for the first time since he brought Selia out. "I've just the thing. Renan, and you—Talog, is it?—give me a hand here. We must move the altar a bit."

As the others rushed to help the old priest, Lysandra took Selia's hand into her own. She felt the girl trembling, yet little of the fear came from who was now approaching.

"It's all right, Selia," she told her. "It's all right to be afraid—and it's all right to trust in spite of the fear. Trust the Wisdom that is within you and it will show you what is worthy and honorable."

"This way," Renan called to Lysandra. "Hurry."

Hand in hand, the two women hurried to where the altar had been pushed aside to reveal a long staircase descending into the darkness. Father Peadar retrieved one of the oil lanterns from a wall niche and handed it to Renan.

"This was built to hold the bones of the first priests of this parish," he said. "But it was later enlarged with a tunnel that leads out past the town, to where a cloister was once planned. It was never built, and most people have forgotten the tunnel exists. Go quickly now, and with God's help."

"How will you be able to move the altar back?" Renan asked.

"There's a lever at the foot of the stairs. Pull it and the lock of the altar will be released. It will swing back on its own. Hurry now."

Selia stopped and knelt before Father Peadar to receive the old man's blessing. Lysandra waited while the priest laid a hand on the young woman's head and softly spoke a prayer, then raised her up and kissed her cheek.

"Go with God, my child," he said, "and do not forget to trust Him. It is He who made ye—and He always knows what he's doin'."

"Thank you," Selia said, "for everything." She threw her arms around the old man's neck and embraced him. Then she turned and hurried toward Renan.

Lysandra softly kissed the old priest's weathered cheek. "We would have failed without your help," she said. "We were looking for a child and would never have found Selia."

"We're all children," he replied, giving her one of his merry grins.

Calling Cloud-Dancer to her side, she followed Selia down the stairs.

Talog waited below, lantern in hand. As Lysandra and Cloud-Dancer descended the stone stairwell, she heard Renan and Father Peadar saying their farewells.

"One thing," she heard Renan say. "How did you quote the scroll so exactly? I know I didn't read it to you."

But Father Peadar made no answer that Lysandra could hear, and a few seconds later Renan was on the steps behind her.

"God go with ye," she heard Father Peadar call softly after them. "Trust Him and He shall be the lamp unto yer feet. Remember, when ye walk in that Light, the path becomes clear."

They reached the bottom of the stairs and Renan found the lever. He pulled; it would not move.

"They're getting closer," Lysandra said tensely, and no one needed to ask whom she meant. "But they're confused. It's slowing them down. Most of the houses in the village are dark, and they don't know where to search."

Talog added his strength to Renan's. It took several more seconds but, finally, together they were able to shift the lever. Overhead, there was the groan of stone upon stone as the lock was released and the altar swung back into place.

"I will lead," Talog said. He handed the lantern back to Renan, disdaining its use.

As they all followed him, Lysandra *saw* the symmetry of their union. All of their gifts had been necessary to find Selia and get her away.

She also *saw* that the danger was far from over and that all of their gifts would be still necessary before this flight was finished.

Chapter Thirty

Aurya and Giraldus rode down the silent streets of Caerryck, with Sergeant Maelik and two of his men. The other soldiers had been set as guards on all the roads that led from town. Each of them carried a torch and had been ordered to keep careful watch. Aurya had made it plain that it was *her* anger they would face if they let anyone slip past.

The silence of the sleeping village was broken only by the sounds of their horses' hooves and the constant crashing of the sea. It was eerie, this darkness and this silence. Aurya knew that neither Giraldus nor his men were happy about being ordered from their beds to ride into this town in the dark. But she did not care. Her hair flowing loose, her eyes wide and her senses of body and of magic extended, she rode like a mad goddess out of some half-forgotten myth.

You cannot hide, her thoughts sent along their magic current, searching for the one she was here to claim. *I will find you—you shall be mine.* Yet, as certain as she was that Caerryck was the town of the scroll and that the child was here, she received no impression from those searching tendrils of magic to tell her where in this town to go.

Riding beside her, Giraldus still had said nothing. But his silence was a function of her Spell of Obedience and she could feel his fury pounding as relentlessly as the sea. Aurya tried to ignore it. *He'll understand soon,* she promised herself, throwing a glance at him over her shoulder. *The child is the key to the future—our future. He'll see that as soon as we discover where it is hiding.*

Only the moon gave illumination to the darkened streets. The riders slowed their horses to a walk. The stone-cobbled streets were hard on the horses' hooves and could be treacherous at a gallop. Nor were the streets straight enough to be traveled easily in the dark. Following the line of the shore, they meandered and curved, dipped and twisted. Aurya muttered a half-silent curse that she had ordered no additional torches made.

Still they followed Aurya's lead, though she knew no better than they where they were heading. Then, suddenly, something stirred, touched her magic, and was gone again. It was faint, like a whiff of fragrance carried on a breeze, but to Aurya it was as unmistakable as the scent of a rose.

She pulled her horse up short and looked around. The stirring came again. It sent a shiver down to her core; *power* was close. She closed her eyes to better focus, trying to capture the feeling and follow it through the labyrinth of this unknowing darkness.

But even as her magic tried to hold it, it disappeared again. It was like wrapping her fingers around smoke—the more she tried to tighten around it, the more it slipped away. It had told her, however, what she needed to know. She turned her horse east, away from the shore and the village's main road, down an alley and into the back part of town.

They walked their horses even more slowly here, where not even the light of the moon reached between the houses. A baby cried in the distance, breaking the silence with its sudden wail. The sound made Aurya start. She had to rein in, close her eyes again to find that fragile, elusive sensation that was her only guide.

Her senses were extended to their fullest. She could feel the energy draining from her and wished there were time to tap Rhys or one of the others as a source of strength. But time was what they did not have. Her body would make her pay for this night, she knew and accepted—but later, after the prize was won.

There—she had it once again; she could *feel* the place they needed to be. Aurya touched her heels to her gelding's side. A minute passed . . . two . . . three; finally, through the darkness shone the softly colored light of lamps through stained glass and Aurya knew the church ahead was their destination.

They rode into the little churchyard. Aurya dismounted quickly and rushed toward the door, the others a step or two behind. From within the church, all was quiet. If not for the light from the windows, the church would have seemed as shut down as the rest of Caerryck.

Aurya *knew* it was not. The elusive scent of power wrapped around Aurya's extended senses like the billowing smoke from a thurible at High Mass. Magic upon magic, it touched and surrounded her until at last she understood. The child, the Font of Wisdom, was a catalyst to power such as she had only dreamed of possessing.

She put her hand to the latches of the double doors and pulled. Nothing. Neither door would budge. She stood aside and let Giraldus try, but his strength, too, could not open them.

"The child is in there," she said aloud, her voice sounding odd in the pervasive silence.

With a curt nod, Giraldus withdrew his sword and banged with the hilt upon one door. The sharp crack of each strike echoed dully down the silent streets.

At the same time, Aurya sent her magic to the locks. She wrapped her awareness around them, hoping to find a way to shift the parts open. But the locks were not what held the door; she could feel the solid beam barring the entrance, and no magic of hers would shift such a thing.

"You"—she pointed at one of the soldiers—"go try the back way. You and you"—she pointed at Maelik and the remaining escort—"go around and try the windows. We'll break them, if there's no other way to get inside. I'll not be stopped now."

The soldiers all moved to obey. Giraldus began to force his sword through the crack between the doors.

"Don't bother," she told him. "The bar's too heavy for one sword to lift."

Just as Giraldus was about to pound again upon the wood, a scraping sound came through the door. The bar was being slowly slid out of its place. Aurya felt as if something had slowed time and motion as the sound continued, prolonging the moment of entrance. Finally, the doors began a tiny outward motion. Aurya had no more patience. She grabbed a handle and pulled, yanking the door from the hold of the old priest who stood outlined in the light streaming from within.

Aurya spared the priest barely a glance as she strode past him into the church. The *empty* church. As Giraldus shouted to his men, Aurya once more tried to pick up the traces of the child. But with the opening of the door, it was as if everything she had been sensing had flown out in a single gust, to quickly dissipate in the open air. She whirled on the priest, who had followed her with aged, shuffling steps.

"Where is the child?" Aurya demanded.

"What child do you seek, daughter?" the priest asked placidly. "The only child here is Our Lord in the arms of His Blessed Mother."

The priest waved toward a crude painting of the Madonna and Child that adorned one wall. Aurya barely spared it a glance. Eyes blazing, she stepped closer to the priest, surprised that he neither flinched nor drew back from her.

"Do not try to lie to me, priest." She spat the word. "I *know* the child is here. You cannot hide anything from *me*."

The old priest laughed—actually *laughed* at her. Aurya felt her anger double, grow to dangerous proportions.

"I have nothing to hide, daughter," he said. "Search if you will—I am alone, except for the Presence that is always here."

At a nod from her, Giraldus and his men began to search. Aurya stood watching the priest for any signs of nervousness, any sudden twitch or shifting of his eyes that might betray the child's location. But he remained placid as a sheep. His pale, rheumy eyes did not leave her face and the little, almost dim-witted half smile never wavered from his expression.

It was maddening for Aurya. "If you have nothing to hide, why was the door barred—and why are you here when the rest of the town is home and asleep?" she demanded.

"I often stay late," the priest replied pleasantly. "I enjoy saying the final Office here instead of alone in my rectory. I barred the door to protect the sacred vessels. There have been rumors of armed men abroad." He stared pointedly at the sword in Giraldus's hand.

"Your rectory, where is it?" Aurya was unwilling to give up.

"It is behind the church. Come, daughter, I will show you. You may search there, too, if you wish. Again I say, I have nothing to hide from you."

At those words, Aurya knew there was no point to continue. The child was gone; the white dove of her dream had flown away in triumph after all.

But not for long, she thought. *I will find you yet.*

"Come," she called to Giraldus and the others. "There's nothing here anymore. I don't yet know how they got away or what part you played in this, priest," she said, turning back to the old man. "But be assured, I will find the child—and I will *destroy* any who get in the way."

Aurya headed for the door. Once away from the town, she would do a true Spell of Finding . . . and she did not care how many of the men she had to drain to do so.

Talog led the others down the long dark tunnel with a swiftness that would have been impossible without him. Although Lysandra's *Sight* was still strong and not dependent upon any external vision, although Renan held a lantern that kept himself and Selia from stumbling, it was the Cryf who was able to see obstacles long before the others and guide them quickly past.

That this route had not been used in many years was obvious by its state of disrepair. They had to scuttle around rocks and crawl over places where walls had partially collapsed or pieces of ceiling beam had given way. But their passage was never blocked completely, and somehow they managed to keep going.

"Giraldus has reached the church," Lysandra told them at one point, though how long they had been underground or how far they had traveled, she could not say. In such a place as this, time and distance felt obscured. But her words sparked them to even greater effort; each of them knew they had to get Selia safely away.

Part of Lysandra wished they could travel this tunnel all the way back to the Realm of the Cryf, for as long as they were underground they could escape detection. But another part of her, the greater part, longed for the feel of open air. She had to fight not to give in to the occasional wave of claustrophobic panic that swept through her, whispering of collapsing tunnels and cut off air.

Finally, the floor began to slant upward in a long, gentle slope that was easily climbed. As they ascended, Lysandra felt herself breathe more easily. *We're going to make it*, she promised herself. Still, it seemed an impossibly long time before, *finally*, Lysandra felt the soft kiss of fresh air upon her cheek. The others felt it, too, for Renan whispered the call for a brief rest before they left the safety of the tunnel.

They all dropped gratefully to the floor, giving their muscles a chance to recover. Renan squatted next to Lysandra for a moment.

"Where are they?" he asked her softly. "Can you *see*?"

This ability, this *Far-Seeing*, was still too new to Lysandra for her to use easily. In time, perhaps, that would come—but for now it took concentration. She closed her eyes as she endeavored to turn her *Sight* backward along the route they had just traveled.

"They're still at the church," she told Renan after a moment. "They're searching it. Father Peadar is talking to Lady Aurya. She's very angry that he is not telling her what she wants to hear. I think they'll leave the church very soon. We don't have much time. How long do you think it will take us to reach the boats again?"

"That depends on how many hours a day we can travel," he said. "If Talog can stand more light so we can keep going longer, we should be there in two days instead of the three it took us to get here. Are you strong enough for that after—"

He did not have to say the rest. She knew what he meant; he meant after the magic pursuing them had almost destroyed her.

"I'm fine," she told him. "The Darkness is gone. I don't believe it will be a danger again."

What she did not need to say was that many other dangers were waiting to take its place. Renan's touch on her arm said he understood.

He rose and went back to Selia's side. The girl needed more reassurance than any of them and Lysandra was glad Renan was here to give it.

There was joy ahead for Selia—if they survived this journey and the many trials that still stood between her and the throne. When that joy came, it would be carried on the wings of trust and friendship, and it would forever replace the dull ache with which Selia had lived for so long.

Lysandra could hear Talog's breathing where he sat by the entrance to the tunnel, surveying the landscape outside. Feeling her way along the wall, she crawled over to him.

"What do you see?" she asked him softly, grateful again for his eyes, formed to see in the realm of the Cryf.

"We be two miles, mayhap three from the town," Talog told her. "But, the way before us crosseth open ground— and if we find not shelter before the rising of the Great Light, we shall be revealed unto our enemy's eyes."

"How far to the bogs?" Lysandra asked.

Talog shook his head slowly. "I know not."

"The maps—Renan's maps—will they show where we are?"

"Again, I know not," Talog admitted. "The maps reveal the land, but not this passage. The map of the Cryf showeth what the Hand of the Divine hath devised, not the hands of the Up-worlders." Talog took a deep breath. "But for thee, Healer, and for She-Who-Is-Wisdom, I shall try."

Talog joined Renan, and Lysandra heard the rustle as the priest unfolded the map of Rathreagh. The two conferred over their possible location. After a moment, Selia's voice joined them.

Good, Lysandra thought. *She's getting involved. The shell she has built around herself is beginning to crack. Youth heals so quickly.*

And Selia has grown up here, Lysandra's thoughts continued. *Perhaps she will know something that can help us, something Renan and Talog can't see on the map.*

Talog returned. "Healer," he said. "She-Who-Is-Wisdom hath said the first of the boglands lie but a night's travel east and south. If we go swiftly and rest not, we shall be there in safety before the coming of the Great Light."

"And then?" Lysandra asked. "How long into the day can you travel, Talog?"

"I am Cryf," he answered solemnly, "whom the Divine named *Strong.* I shall go as long as is needed. She-Who-Is-Wisdom must reach the Realm of the Cryf. Eiddig awaiteth our return. He knoweth the Holy Words. He shall know what must be done."

I hope you're right, Lysandra thought but did not say. *Someone had better know.*

Lysandra stood. One of them had to signal the end of their rest—it might as well be her. Once more she sent her *Sight* back along they way they had just traversed.

"They are leaving the church," she said just loudly enough for all to hear. "They have to find their way out of town and gather their men, but they will not be long behind us."

"I shall lead," Talog said again. Lysandra nodded, and winding her fingers deeply into Cloud-Dancer's fur, she prayed that in this darkness would lie their salvation.

The same prayer was in all their hearts as, one by one, they emerged from the tunnel. Then, with only the moonlight and Talog's wondrous eyesight to guide them, they set out at as quick a pace as they could manage, hoping to cross the open land before the dawn.

Chapter Thirty-one

Aurya and the others picked their way back through the town with the same frustrating slowness that they had entered. But the cobbled streets were becoming more treacherous with each moment. The wind had shifted and now blew straight in from the sea, picking up the spray of high tide and beginning to deposit a light, slick layer of moisture over the stones.

Inwardly, Aurya screamed; outwardly, she gritted her teeth and forced herself to keep her horse to a safe pace, reminding herself that a fall and a destroyed animal would mean a delay that could put any hope of overtaking her quarry far out of reach.

Finally, the narrow, winding streets gave way to hardpack and the horses' hooves could once again gain purchase. But even now she would not let her control slip. She could not just *follow* her enemies, hoping they were soon found—but a Spell of Finding took both time and energy.

Outside of town, she reined her horse to a stop and called to Sergeant Maelik. "Gather your men who are guarding the roads," she ordered. "Baron Giraldus and I will await you at the next open field. And do not delay, Maelik—is that clear?"

Aurya's voice grew hard as she said this. She was gratified to see the understanding flash in Maelik's eyes; it held a spark of fear, assuring her he would obey, even without the use of magic. For all his swagger, Maelik was a superstitious man, and men of his type were more easily controlled than they appeared to those who did not know the truth of human nature.

As Maelik motioned to his men, Aurya turned to Giraldus. She reached out and laid a hand gently on his cheek.

"I know you're angry," she said, her voice more gentle this time. "But shortly you will see that I've only done what was needed—for both of us."

The light of anger in Giraldus's eyes faded a little with her touch. Not completely, but enough to let her know that when the time and circumstances were correct, she would be able to persuade him into forgiveness.

She gave him the smile that he alone ever saw. "We're

close," she said, "so very close to having all we've ever dreamed of together."

Aurya clicked her tongue and gave her horse a little nudge. The gelding sprang forward as if it, too, was tired of the sedate pace necessitated by the cobbles. She did not need to look back to know Giraldus followed; the Spell of Obedience was too well set for him to have a choice—and Aurya *liked* this control far too much to give it up.

As soon as he was able, Aurya knew Giraldus would demand the spell's removal, and her explanation. She had to be ready for that moment. Giraldus loved her—but he was also someone whose temper rivaled her own, while his *control* did not. She could, of course, *magic* away his anger . . . but she preferred to *persuade* it away, using that magic all women possessed but too few used adequately. As she rode, she prepared herself with the arguments she would give Giraldus for the spell's necessity and yes, she would make a great show of removing it.

She would also reset it as soon as he was once more asleep.

A half hour outside of town, Aurya found a clearing to suit her purposes. Rathreagh was not a province of forests, like Camlough, where meadows had to be discovered among the trees and farms cut out and claimed from the woodlands. It was a province of bogs and stones.

But here, in this clearing south of Caerryck, the stones had been removed. The place, though not large, lay uncluttered and level in the moonlight, as if waiting for Aurya to come along and make use of it. She rode into the center of the area and dismounted, giving her reins to Giraldus. While he saw to the horses, she walked the perimeter of the clearing. It was a circle, nearly perfect, of ancient design and made by human hands. This had been a place of power; Aurya could feel lingering traces of it still, as if the earth itself had absorbed some of the magic once performed here.

Who, she wondered, had cleared this circle, and what had been its purpose? What magic was powerful enough to have left its imprint still discernible? Here and there around the perimeter, she found little piles of stones. There was no doubt they had been put there deliberately, but they told her nothing of the hands that had so placed them.

She returned to where Giraldus was standing. "Maelik and the men should be here soon," she said, "and then I can begin. But I need a fire—there, in the center."

"Why?" Giraldus said harshly, forcing the words out through gritted teeth. "Why do you need them—and the fire?"

Aurya was surprised to hear Giraldus question her. She could feel that her spell still held him and that he spoke at all was a testament to his strength of will and his concern for his men. With every word, speaking became easier for Giraldus. His voice became more clear, more *normal*, and Aurya could plainly hear the anger and the accusation it contained.

"What are you planning?" he demanded. "You charge us into that town like the devil's burning your tail and now, instead of chasing your prey, you have us stop and build a fire. Tell me in plain words what you're planning. They are my men, and I'll not see them harmed."

Aurya was annoyed by his questions. But for the sake of their years together and the future to come, she answered him.

"Yes, we have to chase *our* prey," she said, "but look around, Giraldus . . . which way did they go and how many are they? What road did they take and what is their destination? Where along the way can we catch them? What

I'm about to do will tell us all that—that and more. Now, do as I have ordered and make the fire. I must be ready when the men arrive."

Her last words were spoken as a command, and though Giraldus did not like it, he obeyed. It took him several long minutes to collect enough wood from the fallen branches of the sparse and twisted bushes that dotted the landscape to make enough of a fire for Aurya's needs. He was just setting it when Aurya finally heard the sounds of the soldiers' horses.

Once they arrived, she sent them to gather any remaining wood they could find and set it beside the fire. It was neither as big a flame nor as large a stack of wood as she wanted, but it would serve—it would have to.

Finally ready, she ordered the men to form a circle around her. Then she faced the flames, using them as her focus as she called forth her powers. Soon, she felt the magical fire burning, filling her with heat as surely as that coming from the flames before her. She began to chant.

> "Elements of night and darkness, into this waiting
>   vessel flow;
> Power given, Power taken, Power rule, and Power
>   know."

Her magic, already astir, flared with a sudden rush that sent Aurya's senses reeling. Rarely had she felt such a burst of power.

The men waited nervously in the circle she had directed them to make. Now she turned from the flames to face them. She began to walk withershins around the circle, chanting her spell. She found the fear and fascination on their faces invigorating as three times she made the circle, weaving a thread of magic behind her.

She stopped at the head of the circle, the north where Giraldus stood. She stepped closer and closer, finally forcing him to take three steps back. When he was in position, she touched his forehead with her fingertips.

"Element of Fire, I name thee," she said. "Power of Fire, I claim thee. Fire, in might, stand guard this night."

As her fingertips left his forehead, Giraldus's body stiffened slightly. The first sentry was in place. Giraldus, as anchor of the spell she was now casting, would feel the connection of powers meet in him most strongly of anyone here, save herself. Aurya wanted him to feel it, to know something of what she felt each time she called her magic forth.

Still walking withershins, Aurya stepped back into the circle and went a few more paces, to the soldier whose back was to the west. Here, too, she stepped forward, forcing him three paces back. She repeated the words of the spell, naming him Water.

South was Earth and east was Air; the guards were set at the four corners of the ancient magical elements. Aurya once more made three circuits around, this time outside the main body of men; three circuits walked *between* the elemental sentries and those whose energy she would soon be harvesting.

Finally, Aurya stepped back into the center by the fire and raised her arms, up and out, palms turned toward the night. In a louder voice, she completed her spell:

"Fire, Water, Earth, and Air
Summoned by my power here;
Here to watch and here to guard,
Here to protect—this circle Ward.
Close this circle with ancient might,
My magic and my will alone

May pierce the strength of Ward and watching
Until I break thy web of stone."

To the others within the circle, it felt as if they suddenly stood beneath a clear canopy. Only Aurya could actually *see* the charge of power all around them. To her, the stars overhead dimmed, the outer landscape blurred, and the sounds of the night were muted to silence.

She glanced at Giraldus. His eyes were wide with surprise as he felt the arcane forces meeting in his body. Aurya knew this spell could not continue for long, not if she wanted to ride on tonight. If held too long, even such a basic casting as a Warding Circle could drain those through whom the magic flowed.

Aurya would not need much time. All of the men were woven into a single current of power. She was ready to harness that energy, gather it into herself to mold and shape and cast it outward again. What returned would tell her all she needed.

Aurya knelt. She shrugged off her cloak to let herself be bathed more fully in the heat rising from the fire and in the Goddess-light of the moon. She looked deeply into the heart of the flames:

"All are one within this place,
This circle now by magic shielded;
In one combined and woven strong,
One in power, shaped and wielded.
Into me now I do command,
For magic's sake, the life force flows
Until my words shall send it forth;
My will commands where power goes."

Aurya felt the spell working. At this moment she was a creature of magic, her tether to her mortal life was anchored only by ambition and the greed for what this life could still give her.

> *"On wings of Will, my magic flies*
> *To find the ones now from me running,*
> *And see more clear than eagle's eyes*
> *My enemies' acts of stealth and cunning.*
> *Reveal my prey and let me see*
> *Within these flames, this province wide;*
> *One path to find, one path to follow—*
> *Let none from me have power to hide."*

Aurya waited, glowing from the heat within and without. In the dream of several nights ago, she had been the black griffin of Kilgarriff. She used that image to send her Spell of Finding flying on magic wing, colored and shining as onyx, searching for the white dove that was its prey. But this time *she* would be the destroyer, not the destroyed.

The flames flared as a picture began to form. It was hazy, hard to discern—as if some magic she did not know was blocking it. Had she been alone, she might have been defeated. Now she drew even more greedily on Giraldus and his men. She channeled the power outward on her will and through her eyes, to force the revelation she desired from the unwilling night.

There, she had it; she wanted to shout her victory, but she dared not break her focus. She saw the little band of travelers she thought of only as The Others. In the flames she saw the outline of two women, one accompanied by a large dog; she saw a man—a priest, his clothing proclaimed. And there was someone else—some*thing*—else, but its identity her magic refused to penetrate. Whatever it was, had a power to shield itself such as she had never before encountered.

But where is the child? The thought contained a touch of panic she refused to acknowledge. *Perhaps it is the child who is shielded.*

That had to be it. If these were not the ones she sought, her magic would have passed over them, as it had all the other inhabitants of Rathreagh.

She saw where they were heading—through the bogs to the river. *Fools,* she thought with a renewed sense of triumph. Who did the child have for protection—a priest, two women, and a dog . . . and now those *protectors* were leading the child straight where it should not go. The bogs were dangerous enough by day, but trying to traverse them by night was an act as foolhardy as it was desperate.

Aurya smiled, for she and the others had only to ride to the far side, between the bogs and the river, and catch this weak band as they emerged. Perhaps the bogs would even decrease their number before she caught them.

But before she broke the circle, Aurya would do one more Casting, this time directly against her enemies.

"Hearts of haste and footsteps running,
Falter on the path ahead;
Muscles fail and focus wander
Each step make feel like feet of lead.
Slow and slower become thy travels,
Each breath exhaled thy strength doth spend;
Cease thy passage, end thy running,
And thus our separation mend."

Aurya's smile grew for she could feel that this spell was well cast. It would find those toward whom it was directed, further ensuring that her company would be able to overtake them. Before the next night was through, the child would be in her control.

Now she must break the circle and see how much time would be demanded in recovery before they could ride on. She stood and began retracing her steps, going deosil this time.

As she released each man, he fell to the ground, unable to move. Aurya was bewildered; her spells had not lasted long enough for such a reaction. Each man should have been tired, but after an hour or so of rest been fine.

The men of the inner circle were now all released, and lay upon the ground like boneless heaps. With a sudden touch of fear, Aurya began releasing the four who stood as the Guard of the Elements.

They, too, collapsed as her touch upon their foreheads freed them from the power that had held them captive. Finally, she reached Giraldus, the anchor of the Wards. Though he stood still straight and tall, it was not of his own power. His eyes were rolled partway up into his head and there were flecks of foam at the corners of his mouth.

Quickly Aurya touched his forehead, murmuring the words of release. She caught him as he started to fall and lowered him gently to the ground.

What went wrong here? Her thoughts raced. *What have I done?*

She went to examine the other men. Some of them were barely breathing. It was as if the life force within them had been sapped by something other than herself.

This place, she thought with a recognition of danger that had come too late. *What is this place? Who made it?*

Aurya built up the fire again, then began examining the perimeter of the circle. Once again the little stacks of stones drew her attention. Kneeling, she saw that the stones bore marks she had not seen earlier. But nothing she recognized, and they told her nothing.

Then, suddenly, she felt weak, dizzy. She tried to stand and found she could not.

Out, she thought, her mind feeling as fuzzy and disconnected as did her body now. *I must get out. . . .*

She could barely make herself move. It was by sheer force of will that she dragged herself past the stack of stones she had been examining. Then the weakness became too much, and she sank to the ground.

Her breath came in gulps at first. Slowly, breath by breath, her head cleared. She sat up and stared back at the circle. Whatever it was, it was dangerous—perhaps the most dangerous thing Aurya had ever encountered. Somehow, she had to get Giraldus and the men out before the circle claimed all of their life force.

Aurya felt stronger with each passing second. Finally, she felt ready to brave the circle again. She took a deep breath, steeling herself, and headed for Giraldus.

It took her three tries, three times of entering the circle again and dragging him for as long as she dared, only to have to leave him while she staggered back out and away until her strength returned.

Giraldus breathed easier once he was also out in the open, but he did not revive. Aurya was going to have to do this on her own. Any thought of ambushing The Others was abandoned in favor of keeping her own party alive.

But as she entered the circle a fourth time, to grab the ankles of the next man and begin pulling him to safety, Aurya vowed to discover the nature of this place. Once she was Queen, she would find its creators and make them pay. Above all, she vowed to see this circle destroyed—by her own hand and by her own magic. If there were more such places in Aghamore, she would destroy them as well.

Chapter Thirty-two

Lysandra and the others walked all through the night and into the day. Stops were brief and never long enough. Conversation became a thing of the past as all their concentration became focused on putting one foot in front of the other long after their bodies were crying out for sleep.

Finally, pursued or not, they could go no farther. They had made good progress and were well into the boglands; if they could maintain this pace, they were certain to reach the boats near dawn the next day. But without rest, they would go nowhere.

The stones of Rathreagh served them well, and they found a place to camp where one huge monolith had fallen and lay at an angle on top of another. It provided them with the shade Talog needed, and underneath the stone roof, the ground was firm and dry.

Once camp was made, Lysandra sent her *Sight* back along the path they had just traveled. This ability was becoming stronger each time she used it.

"What do you see?" Renan asked her softly.

Lysandra shook her head. "Nothing," she said. "But I don't know if they're not there—or if I just can't *see* them. My *Sight* has never worked like this before," she added softly, for his ears alone. "It's changed. Everything has changed since Selia's mind touched mine. I don't understand it all yet, but I think that part of what she does, part of what she *is*, is to awaken what lies dormant in others."

Renan laid a hand upon her arm in a gentle gesture of friendship and comfort. "Well, I'm going to believe your *Sight* and say we dare chance a small cooking fire. I think a hot meal and some of your tea would do wonders for us all."

Lysandra gave him a small smile. "Then if you'll hand me my medicine pouch, I'll find the right herbs."

Renan did so, and then moved off to start the fire. As Lysandra sorted through her dried herbs for the chamomile, lemon balm, and mint she had decided to use now, as well as for the betony, rosehips, and licorice root she would brew when they awakened, she thought about Renan's touch. Although it had been light and passing, she could still feel the warmth of it on her arm.

Lysandra nearly smiled, but then she stopped herself. She would not cause Renan either the pain or the embarrassment of letting him know that she was aware of his feelings—and that she shared them.

Had Renan's soul been as lonely as hers, she wondered, his heart as empty? She did not know, but she doubted it. He was a priest, a man whose vocation filled those empty places—didn't it? Again, she realized how much about Renan she did not know.

She gave her head a small, private shake. Perhaps the answers did not matter. What they could share—openly and proudly—was the friendship this journey had given them. It was what mattered, and it was enough.

And yet, deep in her secret heart, where self-deception cannot survive, Lysandra knew that love lived in her again.

It was full daylight before Giraldus and his men began to stir. They moved groggily, painfully. Even Aurya, though the effects on her had been minimal by comparison, felt as if she had drunk far too much wine.

"What happened?" Giraldus demanded in a voice that Aurya thought would make her head shatter.

"I don't know," she told him, "and I won't know until we get away from this place so I can think clearly. Whatever that circle is, it's going to destroy us if we don't get far away from here . . . now."

Aurya could see that Giraldus was in too much misery to be angry—but she knew that anger would come, and soon. Although she had spent some of the long night working out what she would tell him, she was in no condition right then to handle any kind of confrontation.

And she had far more on her mind than Giraldus's anger. The Others were getting away. If she did not act soon, everything would be lost. She had let her concern for the men—for Giraldus—delay her last night. She would not do so again.

Aurya now doubted that the spell she had cast last night had weakened her intended victims. She had begun to think it had not left the circle, but had been amplified and fed back into her companions. The more strength she drew from them to send her magic *out*, the more it had looped back so that they were both drained by her need for their energy and bombarded by the spell she was casting.

The presence of so many others within the circle had protected her, standing at the center. Yet, if her spell had gone on a moment longer, she would not have had the strength to save any of them, including herself. As it was, they only had to deal with their hangovers. At least the horses were still tethered and packed, and they could ride again almost immediately.

Aurya called Rhys over to her. "We have to get to the other side of the boglands," she told him, "between the bogs and the river—and we must get there quickly. Do you know the fastest route?"

Rhys said nothing for a long moment. Aurya could see that he was considering, but her temper was shortened by the pounding in her head and she wanted to scream at him to answer.

"Aye, I think so—maybe," he said at last. "We never went to the river much when we was kids. I think I remember a way, but we'll need to take a different road than this 'un."

"Fine," Aurya replied, standing slowly so that the action did not make her head reel . . . much. "Then you will guide us again. Pass the word to mount up. It's time and past to get away from here."

Rhys was recovering with the resiliency of youth. He quickly turned to obey. Feeling as she did, it made Aurya tired to watch him.

As she began to walk toward her horse, Giraldus joined her. She could feel the anger radiating from him now as she had last night. But he said nothing until they reached their mounts. Then, as he put his hands on her waist to help her into the saddle, he held her still for a moment and looked down sternly into her face.

"We *will* talk," he said, "later, where we'll not be overheard, for I'll not argue in front of the men. But before this day is over, I will know all of what happened last night. And understand this, Aurya—I had better like the answers."

"I understand," she said.

As Giraldus walked toward his own mount, her thoughts continued the unspoken remainder of her reply. *I also understand what I will tell you . . . which might not be the same thing at all.*

The farther they traveled from the circle, the better everyone felt. The residual effects of whatever force the circle contained evaporated with distance. By noon, they were able to once again set a hard pace.

Aurya was again impressed by Rhys's usefulness. The young soldier quickly got them onto the right road, one he assured her would have them to the river by the next day. Giraldus remained silent as he rode beside Aurya—which did not bode well—but he put off their confrontation until camp was made for the night.

Finally, while the men were busy unloading horses and setting up tents, Giraldus grabbed Aurya's upper arm and unceremoniously led her away. Aurya's first reaction to the way his fingers dug into her flesh was anger, but when she saw how Giraldus was clenching and unclenching his jaw with each step, she realized there was a better way to play this.

When he decided they were far enough away for at least a semblance of privacy, he turned on her.

"Well, madam?" He waited, as if those words were all he needed to say.

He wants to be placated, Aurya thought, reading his face. *He wants me to tell him something—anything—so that he doesn't have to remain angry.*

"Giraldus," she began, "I don't know what that place was or what happened there. But *I* was the one who dragged you—all of you—to safety, even though each time I reentered the circle it nearly killed me."

She looked up at him, her face a mask of false feminine weakness and concern. "It was hard, too," she continued, putting all the fatigue she was feeling into her voice, letting him know how difficult her task had been. "But I didn't let myself stop—not until everyone was safe."

"Humph," Giraldus grunted. Although he was not quite satisfied with that answer, she could see that he was willing to let that go for the sake of peace between them. But then his face grew hard again as he got to the true source of his anger.

"And what spell did you place on *me,* madam, to make me obey your commands? *Me,* Aurya . . . you put your damned magic on *me.* How dare you."

"Giraldus," she said softly, coaxingly, moving closer to him, "I did it only for your protection. Truly," she lied. "I didn't know what or who we might encounter also looking for the child. We *still* don't know who it is. It almost certainly is a mage, a sorcerer, to have the scroll, but just how powerful . . . ? I used the spell—and it's only a *small* Spell of Obedience—because I was afraid the moment might come when it was the only way to save your life."

Aurya could see that Giraldus was softening. She stepped closer still, putting her hands flat on his chest and leaning into him so that with each breath he inhaled the scent of her body.

"I only wanted to protect you," she said, looking imploringly into his eyes. "I know the ways of magic and those who wield it. I didn't want to take the chance of losing you."

Giraldus's arms had automatically begun to close

around her. Then he realized what he was doing and stepped away.

"I'll not be toyed with, Aurya," he said, "or made to dance to your tune like a puppet on your strings."

Giraldus was trying to keep his voice stern, but much of its force was already fading. Aurya knew her plan—and her lies—were working. Much as she hated the "weak-and-dependent-woman" role, she would continue it a bit longer.

"Giraldus," she said sweetly, "I *know* how strong you are and how great a warrior and leader you are. I count on your protection every day of our lives together. But magic is a different battlefield, where a strong arm and a warrior's heart count for nothing. They can, in fact, be dangerous. It is *because* you are so strong and *because* I know that you would act to protect me—and your men, as the great Baron you are—that I cast this spell."

"Aurya, I—"

"Think, Giraldus," she pressed on. "If we were on a battlefield and you saw a danger to me that I did not, you would expect me to obey you, wouldn't you. Well, we are in a battle—and I might not have time to explain a danger. This little Spell of Obedience was only to protect you until we reached our goal. Trust me, Giraldus, just for a little while more."

She smiled up at him through her lashes, making her lie the sweetest of medicines to swallow. She watched the last vestiges of anger fade from Giraldus's eyes, as she had known it would. *This* was the true magic of woman-hood. Although the spell she had cast made things sim-pler when she had not time to flatter a male ego, most often all she—or any other woman—needed to control a man was her wits and her body. This was a truth as old as Eve.

Now that Giraldus's anger was assuaged, Aurya slipped her arms around his waist. "Tell me," she said brightly, "last night, before the circle became a danger, what did you feel when the magic first touched you?"

Giraldus was returning her embrace this time. He smiled at her question, a look of wonder—and of greed—igniting in his eyes.

"It . . . it was like nothing I've ever felt before," he said. "I felt as if the wind roared inside of me, as if lightning filled and flowed through my veins. Is that what it's like for you each time?"

"That and more," she told him. "Would you like to feel it again? Would you like to become my partner in magic, as you are in life and in bed?"

Giraldus tightened his grip around her, pressing her body into his. "Yes," he said. Then his mouth sought hers hungrily.

Aurya knew that—again—she had won, and more than she had hoped. She would make him her partner, but in ways he could not begin to imagine.

Their lips separated and Aurya met his smile with her own, one that seemed to promise all the ecstasies of heaven and Earth combined. Then she took a step back and slipped her arm through his.

"Let us go back to our tent, my love," she said, her tone suggesting more than her few words said. "The night is too short and we must ride again with the dawn. Let us go and seal our new partnership."

As the sun went down, Lysandra and the others were preparing to take to the trail again. By midmorning tomorrow, Talog said, they would be on the river. It would be a grueling pace and the Cryf would have to keep going hours into the sunlight, but they had no choice.

Selia had remained quiet all through last night's travels and the day's rest. She spoke only when spoken to and then only with the barest reply. But Lysandra could feel no sense of depression from her. If anything, Selia was becoming resigned to the new direction her life had taken, as if a part of her had always known she would someday be forced to abandon the quiet cloistered life she had thought to choose.

Lysandra hoped this acceptance would continue, for Selia's sake even more than for the sake of the kingdom. But experience had taught her that this might well be the calm that so often comes before a storm. If it was, then Lysandra intended to be near at hand to help the younger woman through whatever tempest—of mind, heart, or spirit—might still be coming. Lysandra could not change the sorrows that had already scarred Selia's short life, but she intended to be certain the younger woman knew that she would never be abandoned or cast off again.

Once again Talog led the way, finding safe passage through the bogs. For Selia's sake, Renan had kept the lantern they had used in the tunnel. It was shielded on three sides, giving off only as much light as necessary to show the area immediately ahead.

By dawn, they were almost out of the bogs. The stunted, twisted trees gave way to healthier growth as better soil gave firmer support to their roots. Finally, the company felt safe to rest long enough for Lysandra to brew them another dose of her strengthening tea.

As they sat, sipping from mugs filled with three of her strongest strengthening herbs—wood betony, licorice root, and rosehips, sweetened with honey for extra flavor and energy—Talog and Renan were once again at the maps.

"Three hours you think," Lysandra heard Renan say, "and we'll be back to the boats?"

"Three, mayhap four—but not longer," Talog agreed.

"Ah," Renan sighed with relief. "I think we're going to make it. Did you hear that, Lysandra—Selia? We're almost safe."

"We heard," Lysandra assured him, though she did not quite share his confidence. Something was nibbling at the edge of her consciousness, something she could not name but that added to the discomfort in her already-weary body.

She finished her tea and stood. The rest had been welcome, but to sit longer was to invite stiffening muscles. So, after once more raising their packs onto weary shoulders, she and the others started to walk.

There were no more stops; hour after long hour, there was just walking. Lysandra kept one hand on Cloud-Dancer and in the other gripped her walking stick. There were moments she felt as if her entire existence had been this journey, this silence, and these footsteps.

For the last hour, an odd, uncomfortable feeling had been prickling at Lysandra. It did not come from the walking; tiring as it was, by now it held nothing unfamiliar. Nor was this feeling a return of the Darkness that had so nearly destroyed her.

What she felt now was unknown to her, a whisper from that part of her newly enlivened by the melding of Wisdom and Truth, when her mind and Selia's had touched. But it was a feeling too new for Lysandra to interpret. Until experience taught her otherwise, all she could do was wait until knowledge came of its own.

Suddenly, understanding dawned. She *knew.* . . .

"Renan, we have to hurry," she said in a rush. "They're coming. They're behind us, but not far enough. Run . . . we have to run . . ."

Vague pictures were forming in Lysandra's mind. *Peo-*

ple . . . on horseback . . . The vision was clearing; Lysandra nearly stumbled as she lost the awareness of the ground beneath her with the power of the new *Sight* forming within her mind.

A woman leading . . . soldiers . . . black power radiating in waves . . . power of anger and greed and hunger . . . coming closer . . .

This new manifestation of her *Sight* had caught Lysandra completely unawares. Now its gift gave them their only chance to get Selia to safety.

"Run," she said sharply. "Now—and don't stop until we reach the boats."

Renan put his hand beneath her elbow to guide her. Ahead, she could hear Talog and Selia running; behind, she could feel the approaching danger as if the horses' breath were hot on her neck.

As she ran, Lysandra silently reproached herself for not having recognized the warning this new part of her *Sight* had been trying to impart. Next time—if there was a next time—she would give it closer heed.

For now, she hoped and prayed that Talog and Renan remembered correctly where they had hidden the boats. If not, there was no hope, and all the running in the world would not save them.

Chapter Thirty-three

The river was ahead—but their pursuers were too close behind. Renan no longer needed Lysandra to tell him of the danger. He, too, could feel it . . . and he knew what he had to do.

He had made his decision while they ran—for their lives, for Selia's life . . . for the life and future of Aghamore. There was no denying the touch he felt, questioning and malevolent, trying to find and stop them. It reawakened a core in himself he had long ago buried and vowed never to resurrect again.

But such vows meant nothing now. A greater good was served by its breaking than by the keeping of it.

Reaching the place where they had hidden the boats, Renan left the women panting while he went to help Talog. Together, they maneuvered the boats free of the concealing branches and brought them to the water's edge.

Talog got in the first one. "Selia," Renan called to her. "You're next in. Hurry."

Selia came without objection and was quickly settled. Renan called for Lysandra next, but she refused.

"No," she said. "I'm staying with you. We'll put Cloud-Dancer with them and send them off—but I'm staying to help you."

"Lysandra," Renan began, but she shook her head.

"There's no time to argue with me, Renan," she said. "I know what you're planning, and you need me. But Selia must get away—now."

She was right, there was no time . . . but how could Lysandra know what he was planning? He only knew that to stop their pursuers he must again embrace what he had forsworn; what he had most feared must now happen.

What will you be then? a trembling corner of his soul asked.

The only answer he could give it was the desperate need of the moment. As long as Selia got safely away, Aghamore's hope and future survived.

And Lysandra? The trembling now filled his heart. Her safety was far more precious to him than his own. Or Aghamore's. Alone, he would not care if his next act demanded the last breath of life and spirit to accomplish; once he broke his vow, he broke faith with his honor—and without honor, how could a man live on?

He was aware that seconds had passed while his internal debate raged. Renan wanted to pick Lysandra up and put her in the boat—but one look at her face told him that he could not make her stay there. Lysandra would be here, with him, and therefore he would choose life, even without honor. He would do what must be done, and then survive so that he could be certain she was protected.

"All right," he said. His questions now resolved, he turned to Talog. "Get Selia to Eiddig-Sant," he said. "We'll follow as soon as we can."

"But thee, and the Healer—" Talog began.

"Will be all right," Renan finished for him.

He turned to see Lysandra, just straightening from giving Cloud-Dancer a farewell hug, signal the wolf into the boat. As soon as the animal was settled in, Talog pushed away from the riverbank and began to paddle upstream, the strong muscles in his arms working hard against the current.

Renan watched them for a few more seconds, then turned again to Lysandra. "How did you know?" he asked her.

She gave a little shrug. "As soon as you made the decision I knew," she said, "and I knew what you've been hiding. Why didn't you tell me you were a mage before you were a priest?"

"No one knows," he said. "When I entered the Church, I vowed never to use magic again. But now I must break that vow in order to save the land, and the Church, I love."

"Let me help," Lysandra said. "Tell me what to do."

Her voice contained no judgment, no condemnation, nothing Renan had feared to hear, and he marveled as he knelt on the soft grass. He glanced around and found a stone, white and round, nearby. This he put in front of himself to use as a focus.

"Stand behind me," he told Lysandra, "and put your hands on my shoulders. It's been almost twenty years since I last tried anything like this. I hope I remember how—and that between us, we'll have enough strength for this to work."

"It will," she assured him confidently, and when she stepped behind him and placed her hands as he had directed, she tightened them briefly upon his shoulders in a gesture of encouragement. "It will work," she said again, softly and yet loudly enough for his heart to hear. "I know it will."

Renan looked down at the stone. He began to focus, to see it alone. There were many ways to call up the power men named *magic*. Some mages, male and female, used words of incantation to focus their intent. But magic required no voice to make it real and Renan had never been one to whom such spontaneous phrases came easily. As a priest, it would often take him days to prepare even the shortest of sermons.

Other mages used special types of breathing or chanting, and some preferred physical objects such as wands or crystals, water or fire, for focus. A student of the arcane always developed some specific combination of techniques that silenced the mind to outside distractions so that the forces of magic could be harnessed and made to flow on command.

Renan, whose powers had always been in Earthmagic—magic aligned with the forces of nature—this time was using a round and shiny white stone.

It seemed incongruous to pray at this time, but Renan did. He prayed for forgiveness at breaking his vow, and he prayed for help, for memory, for strength. Most of all, he prayed for success, at least long enough to slow their pursuers until Selia—and Lysandra—were safe.

He could feel Lysandra's hands warm on his shoulders. He could feel her strength and her trust in him. He prayed he would not let her down.

He stared at the stone. *Focus,* he told himself, trying to remember back to the days of his youth when all of this had seemed as natural to him as breathing. *Focus,* he told himself again, trying to quiet his mind and to reach that place where his magic might still be found. *Focus,* he told himself a third time, urging himself more deeply inward.

The world around him faded as, slowly, memory was reborn. He took a deep breath and followed it, seeing it fill not only his lungs, but feed the power that had lain dormant for so long, to breathe life again into that tiny flame.

Now there was only himself and the stone. No longer could he hear the river or feel the grass. Lysandra's presence was something he felt with his heart, no longer with his body. With his conscious mind, all he could see was the stone and all he could feel was the approach of danger.

With each breath, his awareness traveled deeper . . . deeper . . . until at last he touched it, and the sleeping beast that was his magic awoke. Now Renan was ready. He began his first spell in twenty years, hoping—praying— he still knew what to do.

Everything he needed was around him. He put aside his fear, born of buried shame and guilt; he silenced his doubts, born of two decades of shunning this part of himself. He concentrated only on what he wanted and *needed* to do. Later he would accept whatever the toll and recriminations that would come.

Deep within his mind, he drew a wall between himself and those who were fast approaching. From the land beneath him, he gathered the coolness left of the night just passed. From the air, he gathered the warming of the sun, now risen. From the river, he gathered moisture, the drops that were cloud and dew. Then he mixed them, formed them, and sent them forth, holding the image of his intent clearly in his mind.

Sharp and precise, he built the picture; layer upon layer, never wavering as his focus built and his power slowly, finally, began to blaze. Fog gathered at his knees and began to rise. It was not enough, not yet, to stop the creatures of Darkness who sought them. He poured more and more of himself into the fog, using his strength and then Lysandra's to bind the spell.

The fog thickened; it rolled in billows into the trees, building and building until no light or sight could penetrate it. Then he sent it back, toward the river road and their pursuers.

So long out of practice, Renan could feel that he was almost spent. With one last effort, he sent a Spell of Confusion into the fog, binding it there until it was part of every drop of moisture that formed this earthbound cloud. As long as the fog surrounded the horses and riders, they would lose all sense of direction and purpose.

Renan tore his eyes away from his focus before he passed the point of survival. The stone, that for these last moments had loomed large enough to fill his vision, shrank back to its normal size. Renan slumped to the ground. He had done all he could; he prayed it would be enough.

He might have waited too long, he realized then. Breathing was difficult and he could not find the strength to move, but it did not matter what happened to him as long as the others were safe. He sensed Lysandra kneeling at his side. She took his hand into her own. At her touch, new strength—*her* strength—flowed into him. He did not understand how she did it, but suddenly he could move again.

He would wonder about it later. Hand in hand, they rushed to the remaining boat.

Aurya led the way eagerly. They had left the road and were galloping through the trees. In her mind's eye, in her magic's vision, she could *almost* see the child she meant to have.

Fools, she thought to the child's would-be protectors, *with your backs to the river, you'll have nowhere to run. You'll not escape me this time.*

She could hear the river through the trees, see the mist that rose from it. She galloped on, into the mist . . .

. . . and mist became fog. Her horse whinnied and shied, nearly throwing her. The fog built, rolled, surrounded. All around her, the other horses were behaving the same as her gelding. Bewilderment spread across the faces of the men.

Aurya could taste the magic in the fog with every breath she took. Her thoughts began turning to shadows; her mind felt heavy, numb . . .

"*No*," she said aloud.

Aurya fought to keep her thoughts clear. She wanted to ride onward; she wanted to leave the men and gallop after her quarry . . . but her horse would not be controlled. It took all her strength to keep the gelding from bolting away from this strange, magic-saturated fog.

The shrill and frightened sounds of the horses built around her. The murky air filled with the equally frightened voices of the confused men trying to remember who they were and what they were doing while they struggled to keep atop their shying mounts.

Aurya pulled on her reins until her arms ached. Her knees and thighs burned with the effort of keeping her seat. She heard one man go down, and muttered a curse as his horse went galloping away. Her magic was giving her more protection than the others, but it was not enough. She kept feeling the tendrils of the fog trying to enter her brain, threatening to suffocate her thoughts, her will, her purpose . . . her magic.

Magic, that was the key; she knew that she should do . . . what? . . . the fog . . . she could not think . . . Slowly, struggling to find the words, she began to chant a halting, barely connected Spell of Protection over herself.

Word by word, second by long second, the mist was lifting from her mind; slowly, it was being driven off. Seconds turned to minutes . . . how many? . . . each one was a little war—of her will against the horse's, of her magic against the fog's.

Finally, her thoughts began to flow again into words of impunity and power. Now, at last, she could think well enough to form a counterspell that would free herself and her companions from the confusion that had trapped them.

As she spoke, each word became charged. Her power became heat, it became light, evaporating the fog with the speed of the summer sun. The horses began to quiet, the men to look around, trying to regain their sense of identity and place.

Aurya ended the flow of power. She felt drained, physically and magically. Having spent itself on this spell, her body desperately craved sleep. But Aurya would not, could not, give in yet.

Once more she reached down into the depths of her being. The bright flame that usually burned there was sputtering, like a lamp whose oil had been used up. Still, she could not rest. Whatever the physical source within her body that her magic had to take for fuel, whatever price she would later have to pay, did not matter. She would not stop until she had the child.

Aurya fed the flame of her power with fuel of herself and felt the magic respond with new strength, banishing her weariness and preparing her again to give chase. Later, she would pay for this false and arcane burst of energy, with a true weakness from which she would not easily or rapidly recover. She did not care. When the child was hers, she would have its power to return her strength.

Giraldus was approaching her. "That fog," he said, "was it—"

"Magic?" she finished for him. "Yes—they've a mage with them, whoever they are."

And this changes everything, she thought but did not say aloud. Giraldus and his men would be useless in a battle of magic—as this fog had proved.

Or maybe not, Aurya thought. Giraldus had said he wanted to feel the magic again, to become her partner in the arcane. If there was time before she met with this unknown sorcerer, perhaps she could establish a link between herself and Giraldus, so that his strength was at her call. It might give her the advantage she needed to prevail.

Aurya glanced around at the men. She saw the one who had lost his horse, but she would not wait until he found it again. Whether he rode pillion behind someone else or did not ride with them at all, she did not care.

"Let's go," she called, and once again led the chase.

She quickly pushed her horse into a gallop, bending her body low over its neck as it ran through the band of trees that grew between the river and the bogs. Her horse, eager to be away from the place that had terrorized it, needed little urging.

Even so, the pursuit was too slow. Aurya would gladly have sprouted wings and taken flight to find the white dove and lock her black talons around it.

Coming finally out of the trees, Aurya pulled back on the reins. Here, for a time at least, she had to go slowly enough to find their trail. But the mage had made that task easier by revealing himself. Magic would touch magic, leaving traces that she needed no elusively written scroll to follow.

She kept her horse to a walk while she searched the riverbank, every sense of magic extended. She knew, she could *feel*, that she was close. A small, white stone suddenly caught her eye. It shimmered with a brightness far beyond its natural appearance, pulsing with the magic it had so recently channeled.

I have you, Aurya thought as she quickly slid from her gelding's back and picked up the stone. He was clever, this mage, to have used so small a focus. Anyone else, less sensitive, less driven than Aurya would have easily ridden past it, losing the trail without knowing where or why.

Aurya closed her fingers around the stone. The magic thread between the focus and the mage was fraying, but it had not broken yet. It glistened like sunlit dew upon spider silk.

"They're on the river," she said aloud, opening her eyes to look at Giraldus. "That's where we must go."

Giraldus looked at her, dumbfounded. "Are you crazy, woman?" he said at last. "We have no boats. Do you expect the horses to gallop along on the currents? It's over, Aurya. I've humored you enough."

"No!" she shouted. "Send the horses home with some of the men. Their swords will make little difference in a battle of magic. It will not take long to tie a raft together— enough for ourselves and a few others. But I *will* go, Giraldus, even if I must swim the entire way. Now is not the time to turn coward—not when the child is almost in our grasp."

Giraldus looked as if someone had struck him, which was exactly what Aurya had done when she called him coward. Quickly dismounting, he strode up to her, his height and brawn dwarfing her body. But not her spirit. She met his eyes unflinchingly.

"Once more," he said through clenched teeth, "and then it is finished. If we do not catch them this time, it's done. Do you understand? It's done."

That said, Giraldus turned to his men and began issuing orders.

Lysandra paddled the boat as hard as she could, matching Renan stroke for stroke. It had taken three days to ride the current downstream. They had no such luxury now. Their only chance of safety was to reach the Realm of the Cryf.

Lysandra paddled till her arms ached and her shoulders burned, and kept on paddling.

They had caught up with Talog and Selia on one of the few stops that nature necessitated. Cloud-Dancer rejoined Lysandra, refusing to leave her side again. Then Talog led the boats to the other side of the river and closer in to shore, where the current was less strong and the paddling easier.

The two boats now stayed close together. All through the rest of the day they drove themselves, all of them working harder than Lysandra ever thought possible. She did not have the time or the energy to spend on trying to *see* their pursuers. Now that the first elation had worn off, the ability of *Far-Seeing* was too new for Lysandra to know what its effects or demands upon her might be.

They kept going into the night. Their only sleep came in little naps, one at a time while the others continued paddling. Their bodies were working too hard to feel the cold, as the night wore on hour after long hour.

Dawn came in a brilliant glory that was noticed by eyes and minds too tired to care, and by Lysandra not at all. She had stopped using her *Sight*, stopped thinking or doing anything that might distract her from the rhythmic motion of her arms.

Then, finally, two hours into the daylight, Lysandra heard the first faint sounds of hope. She snapped her head up, drew a deep breath and held it, heart pounding as she strained to hear more clearly.

There it was again: the unmistakable sound of hundreds of birds, carried outward on the morning breeze.

"Do you hear it?" The sudden burst of hope and excitement gave volume to her voice as she spoke for the first time in hours.

Renan and Selia did not, not yet—but Talog did. The young Cryf's joy rang in his voice as he agreed with her. He was almost home. Lysandra envied him the feeling; her cottage was still over half the kingdom and many dangers away.

The nearness of his home gave Talog new energy, and he paddled all the harder, making Lysandra and Renan struggle to keep up. But within minutes, the sound became loud enough for them all to hear—and what had been a desperate chore now became an act of anticipation.

Safety was ahead: safety within the secret Realm, where they could all rest, at least briefly, from the danger of this pursuit. Whatever was coming, they would not face it alone.

Each moment, every dip and pull of the paddle, brought them closer. Finally, they were floating again between the hollowed columns of antediluvian creation, into the beauty and wonder of the long first cavern that stood between the Up-world and the Realm of the Cryf.

But they would not travel the heart of the Realm afloat. Talog paddled his boat to the bank and motioned for Renan and Lysandra to do the same.

"Our travels shall be faster now by the pathways of my people," he said. "The ways of the Cryf go straight unto the heart of the Realm, where Eiddig awaits. Those who follow know not our paths."

Lysandra was overjoyed by the thought of dry land again. Selia said nothing. Lysandra could feel her fighting to control the fear that had filled her every moment since she left the convent. Every hour since then had taken her farther away, every action had been precipitated by dangers suddenly heaped upon her as she was forced back into the world she had eagerly thought to renounce.

While Talog and Renan unloaded the boats, Lysandra went over to Selia's side, wishing she had some words of comfort to offer. But she would not give her empty promises or say that all danger had passed and only a bright future lay ahead. Instead, she put her arm around the young woman's shoulders, offering in a gesture the warmth that might give Selia some of the encouragement her words could not.

Unexpectedly, at her touch, their minds and thoughts merged. The impact of it stunned Lysandra, but only for an instant. Selia, too, was taken aback—and yet they both immediately knew that their minds would always be open to each other. It could be no other way if Wisdom and Prophecy were to combine into that one Light that was *Truth.*

As the surprise faded, Lysandra felt again the emotional turmoil that raged within the younger woman. Selia was holding herself in the delicate balance between desire and duty. It was a mixture of feelings Lysandra understood well—and she knew how precarious the balance could be.

Do you truly trust them so much? the younger woman asked her finally—of Talog and Renan, of this place they were now entering . . . and of what waited ahead.

Yes, Lysandra told her. *That much and more. I do not know why each of us was called out of our chosen existence, to do what none of us ever wanted or expected to do. But I do know that without faith that there is a purpose, without the trust and hope that are part of faith, there exists only Darkness. It might not be felt today or tomorrow, but the Darkness is there. I have been to that Darkness, Selia. It is not the Darkness of the mind or the body. It is the emptiness of the soul and blindness of the spirit.*

Before Lysandra could say more, Renan called to her. He and Talog had carried the boats far enough into the passage not to be easily seen.

Lysandra briefly tightened her arm around Selia's shoulder. "Trust," she said softly before turning away, "and your fears will have no power. Remember that even the smallest beam of Light banishes the Darkness."

She was glad to find Renan had remembered her walking stick. After so many miles together, it was comforting to have it again in her hand and her other hand on Cloud-Dancer's head. Although her *Sight* was now something she could call upon at will, she used Cloud-Dancer's vision as they started down the long passageway ahead. Their bond was stronger than ever, and Lysandra was using this touch of mind upon mind to let the wolf know her continued gratitude for his companionship.

They had all had too little sleep and had worked far too many hours. Lysandra's arms felt like lead and her legs were as wobbling as a new fawn's. Only Talog seemed unaffected, too filled with the joy of being back in his beloved Realm. Lysandra did not begrudge him his excitement; she would feel the same way if her cottage waited at the end of this road.

They kept going, somehow. Step by step. Talog, who bounded ahead, had been back to check on their progress three times. But they had not seen him now in almost an hour. Lysandra did not know how much farther she could walk, even to save Selia—even for the unrealized hope and future of the kingdom.

Then she realized that the sound she had been hearing without it registering in her too-tired mind was the sound of running feet—Cryf feet. It was a unique sound, unlike the tap and clatter of the heavy, shod feet of her human companions. There were many of them coming; she tried to count but that, too, took too much effort.

The sound was nearer; then it was all around her. "Talog?" she said aloud.

"I am here, Healer," he replied. "All shall now be well. Eiddig-Sant hath called the Cryf to readiness. Thou mayst rest now."

Strong arms lifted Lysandra and laid her in a long sling filled with the soft nesting material that had been her bed once before. The sling was suspended on poles and carried by the runners. Lysandra relaxed back into this portable bliss and finally let her efforts cease into unconsciousness.

Chapter Thirty-four

Giraldus would send only two men with the horses, one of whom was young Rhys. The other eight he insisted on keeping with them. Aurya did not waste time arguing. She did not care about the numbers as long as they *hurried*.

Finally, two rafts were done and they were on the river, working in shifts at the long poles that gave them momentum against the current. It was far slower going than Aurya liked, but it was the only way to follow the fragile trail of magic that was their guide.

She kept expecting that trail to lead to the other bank of the river and continue on land, but as long as it continued along the water, so would they. All through the rest of the day, through the night, and into the next day—she would not let them stop for fear the thread of magic would lose its cohesion.

It was nearing noon the following day when Aurya first heard the birds. The sound carried over the water like no birdsong she had ever heard before. As they continued their passage upstream, the sound got louder and louder. There had to be *hundreds* of many varieties, all singing their calls together.

Birdsong became cacophony as, at last, the river rounded a bend and she saw the huge cavern, like a great maw opening in the side of the mountain.

"You can't mean us to go in there," Giraldus demanded. "I've heard many a tale of people going into these caverns and caves—and never coming out again. It's too dangerous, Aurya."

"Yes," she said. "We're going in there. *They* went in there—and it's not as dangerous to us as losing the child. Are you to be turned away by the fear of old tales told to frighten children? If that's true, perhaps you shouldn't be King. But *I* have the heart it takes to be Queen. Put me to shore, and I'll follow them on my own."

Giraldus growled in frustration. He knew that her threat

was very real and that short of binding her from shoulder to foot and keeping her that way, nothing he could do would stop her now. All he could do was leave her or go with her . . . he gestured for the men to keep going.

Aurya was not prepared for the sight that awaited just within the cavern's dome. When she saw the hollow pillars of stone, heard the crescendoing cries of the fledglings and parent birds echoing off the high ceilings, she knew that this, not Yembo, was the place of Tambryn's scroll. She had been on the wrong path from the beginning.

She said nothing of this to Giraldus. It did not matter—she was on the right path now.

But not if they did not hurry. Up ahead the thread of magic light was dimming. Soon, Aurya feared, she would lose sight of it completely.

"Over there." She pointed to where the thread led to the riverside. The raft followed its direction. Even so, the light of the thread was growing dimmer with each breath she took.

"Hurry!" she cried.

When they reached the bank, she did not wait to be handed to dry land, but scrambled ashore on her own. Not waiting for the others, she started running down the passage ahead. It was long, and for now, straight. Piles of luminous stones held off the darkness, but she took no time to wonder at them. With each step, her guide was growing fainter.

She found the stored boats of The Others and had to climb over them. *Fools,* she thought, *if they believe that will stop me.* But, once past the boats, the thread she had been following stopped. Aurya closed her eyes for a moment, spending some of her remaining strength to try and *feel* the presence of the mage . . . trying to *feel* anyone or anything ahead in this underground. But there was nothing. It was as if the passageway led straight into a realm of complete *emptiness*.

Then she noticed it. The fire that was her power, that burned as much a part of her as her own breath, was gone, extinguished. It was as if her heartbeat had stopped. After almost a lifetime with its presence, she now felt empty, defenseless—and utterly lost.

Only courage and pride kept her in control. She heard the sound of the men's feet running toward her. As soon as Giraldus was again at her side, she pointed down the passage ahead of them.

"That way," she said in a voice resounding with the confidence she did not feel, and she led the way forward.

Lysandra felt as if she could have slept the clock round, awakened to eat, and then gone back to sleep some more. But circumstances were not wishes, and just over four hours after she collapsed, she heard Renan calling her name.

"Lysandra," he said again, "wake up. There isn't much time. They're coming."

His words dispelled the last of her sleep. She sat up as quickly as her protesting muscles would allow.

"Where are they?" Her voice was thick and hoarse with too little rest.

"Close," he replied, "but Eiddig has everyone ready. Here." He placed a small bowl in her hands. "It's a balm the Cryf healers sent. It works wonders. And there's some food and drink waiting."

She nodded, bringing the balm to her nose. She could smell peppermint, which would be cool and soothing to her tired muscles, but the strong scent kept her from telling what else it contained. *No matter*, she thought absently as she began to slather it on, first her sore arms and then her tired legs. *I can find out later.*

The peppermint immediately began its work, making her body feel more refreshed than it was. The sudden coolness and slight tingling also helped clear her mind. Tired though she was, she could think again.

She heard Renan doing something a few feet away. "Here," he said. "I've brought you a plate. But you'll have to hurry—Eiddig is waiting."

Lysandra ate as quickly as she could, aware of strength returning to her body with each mouthful. Finally finished, she held out one hand and felt Cloud-Dancer take his usual place. Then she held out the other hand to Renan.

"Lead the way," she said. "I'm ready."

He gave her hand a little squeeze and together they left the sleeping cave, heading for the huge, central meeting cavern where Eiddig waited.

The distance did not feel as long this time as it had during their previous stay. When they stepped from the passage into the huge open area Eiddig came hurrying toward them with amazing speed in one so old.

The Cryf Guide placed his palm, fingers pointing upward, against Lysandra's forehead in the greeting he had used several times before.

"The Divine truly hath guided thy footsteps, Healer," he said. "Renan-Sant and our son of the Twelfth Clan, Talog, have told us of thy plight. Fear not, for the Cryf are prepared and are strong in battle. By the Will and Bidding of the Divine, we shall protect thee, who art Prophecy's Hand, and She-Who-Is-Wisdom."

Lysandra was suddenly frightened for the Cryf. In their own way, they were more unworldly then even Selia. Did they know whom they were offering to fight—not just Giraldus and his soldiers, but the Lady Aurya and her magic?

"I . . . we . . . thank you, Eiddig-Sant, and all of the Cryf, for your many kindnesses," she searched for the right words. "The Up-worlders who are coming are dangerous, Eiddig-Sant. There is one who has great power."

He held up his hand. "Talog hath told us all, Healer. Thou must cease thy fear and trust in the Divine. All shall be well."

Just then a runner dashed into the cavern. He ran up to Eiddig and spoke a few quick words in their own language. Eiddig nodded, then he turned and gestured to the other Cryf in the cavern. Within seconds, Lysandra's *Sight* showed there was no one but the Cryf Guide, the two humans, and a wolf left to be seen.

Eiddig then addressed Renan. "Take the Healer to the place prepared, as I did show unto thee," he said. "Thou shalt watch and know what must be done."

"The Divine be with thee," Renan answered. "Come away, Lysandra."

"We can't just leave him," she protested. "He can't face Giraldus alone, and especially he can't just wait there for Lady Aurya. What if her magic *does* work here? You're the only hope then. You can't just go hide."

"Lysandra," he said sternly, "it's already settled . . . and I won't be hiding, not exactly. Please, come. You need to be with Selia right now. She *needs* you."

Just then, she heard the running footsteps—booted footsteps—heading their way.

"Damn," Renan muttered, pulling her along.

Calling to Cloud-Dancer, Lysandra ran to keep up with Renan. But she sent her *Sight* backward into the cavern. The last thing she *saw* before rounding a bend was Eiddig, sitting on a great stone in the center of the cavern floor, his gnarled hands loosely gripping his great staff and a gentle smile on his face, waiting alone to meet the foe.

The men ran with swords drawn; Aurya came with her head held high. She carried no sword, but a long dagger hung from her belt where she could easily draw it. Thus far, she had used it only for such chores as slicing meat, knowing that her magic was her greatest protection.

Now her magic was gone and the dagger's weight had become a comfort. With each step down the long, dim, twisting passage, she told herself that her magic would return any second. To believe otherwise was for her to invite the defeat of madness.

They hurried on, following the directions she gave as if she still saw the thread before her. She did not know why she chose the branch she took each time the passage separated, but their only choice was to continue onward. She knew that she was lost and could not have found her way back to the river. They were either going to find the child and its protectors—or they were going to find their deaths, lost in darkness beneath the mountains.

But from up ahead, the light grew stronger and the passage opened into another great cavern, as big as the one at the entrance to the underground. Aurya crouched at the opening. Giraldus was next to her again and together they studied what lay ahead, looking for signs of danger.

All they saw was a strange old . . . man? . . . sitting alone on a rock, holding a tall, elaborate staff in his gnarled hands.

Giraldus did not wait for Aurya's directions. He strode forward, leading his men and letting Aurya follow as she would.

The wizened creature before them looked up as they

approached. As they drew close, Aurya doubted it was a man after all. Then it smiled oddly at them and spoke.

"Ah, ye have arrived and finally," it said. "Your coming hath been expected."

"Expected for what, old one?" Giraldus asked haughtily. He raised his sword. "Did you expect this, too? Give us the child you're hiding, or you'll feel the bite of it."

The old one kept smiling. "Ye are given a choice," he said, "and in that choosing doth your destiny lie. Lay down your weapons and depart from here in peace, and ye shall all be shown the path back unto the Upworld—"

Giraldus laughed, stopping the old one's words. He brought his sword up to the creature's throat.

"Do as I say, old one—or your life ends now."

The words were barely out of his mouth when, suddenly, all around the cavern floor and up on the many rough-hewn shelves that encircled it, others of these strange creatures stood. In their hands they carried weapons of sharpened pikes, of picks and axes, of broadbladed knives and long-handled large-headed hammers. They began to surge forward, emitting a weird high-pitched wail that made Aurya want to cover her ears.

Around her, the men cringed at the sound as they went into fighting stance. The old one still had not moved. He just kept smiling.

"Lay aside your weapons now," he said, "and ye shall suffer no injury. It is your last warning."

"No," Aurya screamed. Even as the first of the soldiers' swords rang out in contact with his attackers, she drew her dagger and lunged, plunging it into the chest of the old one. His body crumpled while the swarm of creatures crashed in upon them.

* * *

In the cave where she was waiting, Lysandra screamed. Sitting with Selia she was using her *Sight* to watch the cavern and Eiddig. She *saw* the sudden frenzy of Aurya's attack, her dagger rise and plunge into Eiddig.

Once again, what she *saw* was blood and death.

Lysandra was no longer aware of the young woman sitting next to her, whose hands she had been holding. She was only aware of the bloody horror she was witnessing.

Though hopelessly outnumbered, Giraldus, Aurya, and their band of soldiers would not give up. The number of Cryf coming at them only spurred them to greater destruction. Swords and daggers met picks and axes, turned aside pikes. The Cryf, though strong, were not trained to fighting. Swords cut and stabbed, sliced and parried. The hard-packed earth of the cavern floor soon became soaked with stains of blood.

Blood was everywhere. It filled Lysandra's *Sight*. It ran from swords, dripped from axes and pikes. It gushed from wounds, mortal and glancing. It flew in great drops through the air, sent flying by swords raised to strike yet again and pooled beneath the bodies of the fallen.

The soldiers would not give up. One of them fell, then another; their wounds only made the others fight harder. It was a scene from hell, both pitiful and horrific.

Although screams welled in Lysandra's throat, they did not again pass her lips. She was struggling to *see* into the melee, to find Talog and Renan, and to know they were yet all right.

The *Sight* before her, *within* her, seemed to move in slow motion. The fallen of both sides were being trampled by the vast numbers of the onslaught. Giraldus's band could not win; they must know that. *Give up*, Lysandra's mind urged them. *Let the killing stop.*

He could not have heard her—yet seconds later, the Baron raised his weapon in surrender. Beside him, Lysandra *saw* Aurya turn on him, screaming her frenzied demand for more bloodshed. She raised her bloody dagger to him, but Giraldus disarmed her before she could strike, throwing her weapon to the ground.

Hatred distorted Aurya's beautiful face, twisting it into a mask that looked barely human. Lysandra had never witnessed such hatred, with eyes of her body or of her mind.

Only three of Giraldus's party still stood: Giraldus, Aurya, and one other—a soldier whose years and experience showed on his face. They were held fast while ropes were brought to bind them.

Lysandra stood. "I have to go to the wounded," she said to Selia. "Stay here until—"

Just then, Renan burst through the entrance of the cave. He was disheveled and dirty, covered with sweat and blood. But most of the blood was not his own. He bore one wound in his left arm, where the point of a soldier's sword had caught him, but bleeding had already stopped.

"It's over," he told them breathlessly.

"We know," Lysandra replied, standing very still. She wanted to run to him, throw her arms around him and assure herself that he was truly all right. The intensity of the desire shocked and frightened her.

But Cloud-Dancer had no such hesitation. He ran to Renan, nearly knocking the man over with enthusiasm. Renan laughed. Lysandra could hardly believe her ears . . . after all that her *Sight* had just witnessed, this man was able to *laugh*.

But the laughter died quickly. "The Cryf need both of you. Lysandra, the Elders have asked for you to come care for Eiddig. They fear he may not survive. And Selia, for you they have waited a long time."

"For me?" Selia said, her voice filled with new uncertainties. "But I don't know what to do."

Lysandra reached out and took the young woman's hands, holding them as she had all those miles ago in Caerryck. Their minds touched, opened, merged. They were Wisdom and Prophecy. Just as Wisdom had brought Prophecy forth, now Prophecy helped Wisdom to understand that they were both called by a Power far greater than themselves.

Are you ready now? Lysandra asked her.

Will I ever be? Selia answered.

Yes, Lysandra told her. *I did not think I would be, but now I understand. Trust the Wisdom within you, Selia. It is your Truth, and in your Truth is Life.*

Lysandra felt rather than heard the younger woman's acceptance. Together they followed Renan back to the Great Cavern and the path that had begun and awaited them there.

In the silences of the convent, Selia's habit of silence had been received as the assumption of true vocation. But she had known herself for a coward who sought the life of a Religious as an escape from the world.

She still felt like a coward as she walked beside Lysandra—the blind woman who had risked everything and traveled the length of a kingdom to find her. For her sake, for the sake of all those who believed in her though they did not know her and now had fought to keep her safe, she would try to be something greater than she had ever thought herself to be.

The scene when they entered the cavern was far more terrible than Selia had imagined. Although Lysandra had told her what her *Sight* revealed, the descriptions did not prepare Selia for the agony that was reality.

The smell of blood and death was everywhere, filling her lungs with each breath. The whimpers of the dying, the cries of the wounded, filled her with a pity that made bile gush up in the back of her throat. She turned and spewed the contents of her stomach on the cavern floor.

Shaking slightly, she followed Renan and Lysandra to the center of the cavern floor, where Giraldus, Aurya, and the remaining soldier stood bound amid the assembled Cryf. Healers were moving amidst the bodies of the fallen, closing the eyes of the dead and ministering to the living.

The Cryf parted to let Selia and the others through. Lysandra gave a cry, then hurried over to the body of Eiddig, the old Guide who had greeted her arrival with such joy. Remembering his solemn touch upon her forehead, the expression in his ancient eyes that went far beyond welcome to the wonder and elation of faith fulfilled, Selia felt anger rising within her, filling her the same way that nausea had just moments before.

She turned on Giraldus and Aurya. Truth—the first of her gifts and the grounding of her Wisdom—revealed them to her in all their greed and ambition. She saw the blackness of their hearts and of their intentions.

The light of her Truth touched it all. She understood, finally, what Lysandra had meant when she said to trust the Wisdom. With the first absolute certainty of her life, she spoke.

"You had best pray that the old one lives," she told the prisoners. "*You* have brought this destruction here and if he dies, you die."

"And who are you," Aurya snarled when the others remained quiet, "to think to pass judgment on *me*?"

Selia drew herself up, looking into the eyes of this woman who had sought a child she could use and control.

"*I* am the Font of Wisdom," Selia said. In that single moment of true acceptance, clarity descended and embraced her, and she truly became what she had finally declared herself to be.

Chapter thirty-five

Lysandra had Eiddig carried to his chamber. The Cryf Healers rushed to have everything waiting for her. They settled their Guide on his sleeping shelf and stepped back to let Lysandra work. She found the audience disconcerting, but as she knelt by Eiddig's side, it was the fear of failure that momentarily overwhelmed her. This was not like setting an animal's bone or soothing the cough of a crofter's winter cold.

Eiddig's wound had been temporarily staunched. Before Lysandra removed the dressing, she turned to the array of medicines on the table next to her. Using her senses of touch, smell, and taste, she began to arrange everything the way she needed. She feared the wound would bleed again once she removed the dressing. She did not want to chance the old one becoming too weak from loss of blood to recover because she had to grope around to find the right herb.

Finally satisfied, she was ready to set to work. But first she laid her hand on top of Eiddig's, which was gnarled and twisted with age and reminded Lysandra of some of the trees they had seen in Rathreagh. But though Eiddig's hands might appear misshapen, to Lysandra they were beautiful, for they were hands that had been used in faithful service. Remembering the gentle touch of his palm on her forehead, Lysandra silently promised both herself and Eiddig that she would try to live her life and use her hands only in the same way.

Drawing a deep breath, Lysandra carefully lifted the dressing away from Eiddig's wound, trying not to cause him any more pain than she must. Mercifully, the old one had lost consciousness before he was moved, but even so he moaned slightly as Lysandra gently examined the inside of the wound with her fingers and her *Sight*.

Aurya's dagger had missed his heart, nor had the blade cut any of the main blood vessels leading into or away from that central organ. Lysandra considered that to be nothing short of miraculous. But the wound was serious, *mortally* serious if Lysandra could not stop the blood now oozing from the secondary veins. If it continued, it would fill his chest cavity until his heart could not beat and his lungs could not expand with breath.

She took only a few seconds for her examination. Her hands shook slightly as she reached for the first of the medicines she had laid within reach. Although all living creatures shared some things in common, there were also differences in treating their ills. Praying that she had made the right choices and that she could work quickly enough, she washed the wound with a strong infusion of agrimony, burdock, and juniper—the best herbs to clean a wound of the dangerous humors that could bring infection. Then, into a decoction of shepherd's purse, she added finely ground milfoil and mountain daisy, herbs that stopped bleeding.

Eiddig moaned again as Lysandra applied this mixture as deeply into the wound as she could. Then she reached for the one thing that had come from her own possessions rather than the Cryf's stores. It was a small folded wallet of carefully collected and preserved spider's silk. This was Eiddig's best chance. The adhesive properties of the spider's silk would bind the bleeding edges, filling in the wound and slowly dissolving as healthy tissue grew again.

Once that was done, Lysandra quickly slathered a salve of purple coneflower onto the outer area of the wound, to fight both the pain and the possibility of putrefaction. Only then did she apply an outer dressing. It, too, was made from Cryf supplies. The inner layer was of that wondrous soft material she had never before encountered, the same material that covered their beds and turned hard stone shelves into nests of comfort. It was then bound in place with strips of sturdy, tightly woven cloth that Lysandra was certain would not shift or stretch.

There, she thought as she sat back, *I have done all that I can.*

But she knew that was not yet—not quite—true. There was one more thing she could try although, briefly, her mind recoiled from the thought. She told herself that the Cryf probably had medicines within their stores, white willow bark or pain-in-poppy, that would help ease pain; as a healer, Lysandra knew that pain could be friend, warning a body of danger or forcing the stillness necessary for healing to occur. But pain itself, especially in the aged, could also be an enemy. If severe or prolonged enough, it could weaken the body's reserves and prevent healing.

Would the Cryf medicines be enough for Eiddig? Of that she was not so sure. She knew so little about the Cryf—and she had never before encountered a being as old as Eiddig. The Cryf Guide was one hundred forty years, by his own reckoning, and even if the work she had just done healed the flesh, the prolonged pain of the injury might well be enough to kill the old one. She knew she had to try to do for Eiddig what she had done for Talog the first time he saw the sun; she had to try to take the old one's pain.

It was not easy to make herself so vulnerable. But, she asked herself, how could she not do this for Eiddig when he and his people had risked their lives to protect her and Selia? And how could she ask Selia to give herself, her gifts, to save the kingdom if she was not willing to do the same to save one being?

Lysandra laid her hands once more on Eiddig's chest, covering his wound gently. Once more fear coursed through her. What if she had failed? What if she found that all her efforts had come to naught and Eiddig was dying beneath her hands? How could she live with that knowledge?

It is better not to know, her fear whispered. *Turn away now. You've done enough.*

But of all the truths she had learned by this journey, the greatest was that *fear* was the ultimate enemy; *fear* was the enemy of life, of growth, of hope. It must be fought at every turn—and the greatest weapons against fear, the only weapons, were faith . . . and love.

Fear would not hold her captive again.

Slowly, Lysandra reached out with her *Sight.* Second by second, she deepened her focus upon him; layer by layer, she let her mind open, dropping the guarded veils that separated them. The fingers of her mind reached out to touch each nerve, each vein, each particle of injured flesh and wrap them with the energy of her healer's touch, the way the outer flesh was now bathed in healing herbs.

As she worked, she prepared herself for the flow of pain that would travel back from Eiddig into her. She had braced herself now and was ready for it, willing to feel whatever she must for the old one's sake. She could *see* the red and throbbing aura of pain beneath her mental fingers—but, seconds turned to minutes and still the pain did not come.

Instead, all through her mind, down her arm, and out the fingers of her hand that rested so lightly atop his bandaged wound, Lysandra felt a radiant warmth begin. It tingled with health and life. Slowly, it began to glow— golden at its heart, slowly shading to purest white. Then she *saw* the Light pouring into her, though its source was far beyond anything her *Sight* could touch. It grew stronger, brighter, and she *saw* it filling her, channeling down through her into Eiddig's torn body.

She was filled with an emotion that went far beyond wonder, far beyond awe. She felt she could bask in this golden white Light forever.

But that, it would not allow. It urged her to a thought that, like the Light, came from something outside herself, bringing a possibility she would never before have dared to consider. It compelled her to deepen her touch still more, to open her mind, her heart—her soul—to the gift the Light was still waiting to impart.

She did not act at once, but explored the thought hesitantly. How could she dare? Yet in that same instant she knew she had to try. Drawing a deep breath, she let it out slowly. Once more, she drew air in, held it—and let go of that last guard behind which she held herself. As the breath slowly left her body, she opened her innermost mind and heart to the Light, to become the instrument of whatever it chose.

The Light pouring through her hands grew brighter, almost too bright for her *Sight* to look upon, and yet neither could she look away. Her thoughts reached out and touched the piercing depth of Eiddig's wound.

Still urged and guided by this great and unknown force, Lysandra dared to picture true healing taking place. As her mind conjured forth the picture, her *Sight* looked upon the reality. Beneath her hand and within her *Sight*, she watched in awe as Eiddig's body responded.

With the speed of her thoughts, the brilliant Light went where she directed, touched and surrounded, filled and permeated Eiddig's wound. Lysandra *saw* and felt, used, and was used by, the Light until the oozing of blood completely stopped, until severed blood vessels were made whole, throbbing nerves soothed and rejoined, tissue drew together, healed.

Slowly, the warmth in her arms and hands began to fade. The Light dimmed. It did not leave her, but rather seemed to grow smaller and smaller, contracting into a tiny seed no bigger than a grain of sand. Just as the Light had begun at a place far beyond where her *Sight* could reach, so now it entered and planted itself as a seed within her soul.

Humbled and amazed, she could hardly think what this might mean. Would this new and wondrous occurrence ever happen again, or was it a gift granted for the sake of Eiddig and the Cryf? Did she dare to hope . . . to *believe* . . . that it might be part of what she had felt awaken within her at the moment when Wisdom and Prophecy had touched?

Then, like a silent benediction, the Light that was now

within her whispered again. The Truth enfolded her in preternatural arms, and she knew.

Eiddig was healed—and finally, after ten years of grief and guilt and silent sorrow, so was she.

She lifted her hands from the old one's chest. A wave of fatigue washed through her, reminding her that no Gift comes without a cost. But even as it closed in with sudden, nearly crushing severity, she knew that no price was too great to pay to be able to truly *heal*.

As she worked, Lysandra had forgotten about the others in the chamber. As she fell back on her heels, her arms limp at her sides now, the healers came forward in a rush to aid her. She was grateful for the strong hands beneath her elbows, helping her to stand again, then keeping her from falling as yet another wave of weariness overwhelmed her.

What had they seen? she wondered. Had the Light and warmth, so much a part of the inner *Sight* of her experience, been visible outside her body?

If it was, the other healers said nothing. Through their silence, Lysandra could feel their anxiety.

"Eiddig-Sant will be well," she assured them. "All he needs now is sleep."

They began to speak quickly to one another in their own language. Then the one who appeared to be their leader stepped forward. She was an older female whose reddish brown hair bore two long streaks of white that began at her temples and ran all the way past her waist.

Until that moment, Lysandra had felt only reserve from this particular Cryf. Now she touched her palm to Lysandra's forehead, hand flat and fingers pointed upward in the gesture Lysandra had learned was the Cryf salute of both blessing and respect.

"I be Averill," she said, taking a step back and studying Lysandra's face as she spoke. "I be First Healer of the Cryf, and I beg of thee forgiveness. With an unkind heart looked I upon thee, seeing only that thou wast Up-worlder and disdaining to see the Hand of the Divine upon thee. Eiddig, whom thou hast healed today, is Guide of the Cryf—and also my brother. The debt I owe thee is thus twice great. We, the healers of the Cryf, ask that thou accept a place amongst our number, and I, who am First Mother of my Clan, do name thee unto our own. Thou art Up-world *and* Cryf. It is but small payment on so great a debt, but if thou wilt accept, then I do rename thee. Thou shalt here and forever be known as *Alysesgwyn Tangwystlwinn*. In the words of the Cryf, this meaneth 'She of Noble-Strength, our Peace-pledged Friend'—for thou hast healed the heart of distrust and become the bridge betwixt thy world and the Realm of the Cryf. Wilt thou so honor us by thy acceptance of these words?"

"It is I who am honored," Lysandra replied, "and I do accept, with gratitude."

Touched though she was, Lysandra knew that her strength was nearing its end. Her head was beginning to spin, making the room tilt as she struggled not to lose consciousness.

Without further words, the Cryf healers lifted her and she was carried in procession back to what she had come to think of as her own chamber. By the time she was laid upon the soft nesting material that covered the stone shelf, she was already asleep.

While Lysandra was busy with Eiddig, Renan withdrew from company. His heart had cried out in horror when he had seen the water turn red as he washed the blood and grime of battle from himself. He had known then that he must be alone.

He left Selia in the company of Talog and the Cryf Elders. Now he sat beside the deep pool that was the birthplace of the Great River. Eiddig had called it the Heart of the Realm; Renan had somehow been drawn to it as the best place to examine his own heart.

So far, his thoughts had run in inconclusive circles. He was not certain whether he had been here too long or not nearly long enough. Minutes felt like hours and hours passed like minutes, and still the same unanswered questions filled his soul.

All Renan could see in himself was fault. He had been so sure of himself, so full of pride—not only when he had left Ballinrigh, presuming to be guide to the amazing woman whose strength of spirit dwarfed his own, but for the last twenty years. He had thought that a single, private vow, spoken as a few words in the solitude of his own mind, would change who he was inside.

Now, his vow to eschew magic was broken. He had taken up arms . . . and he had killed. The vows of his priesthood were intact of deed—but were they true of heart? Who was he now? *What* was he now? He had thought his life long settled, but now he saw that the answers he thought he possessed were just products of his own arrogance of spirit. He had become a priest for the wrong reasons; he had thought the Church would protect him from himself. It was an act of cowardice, of running away instead of the running *toward* of true Religious vocation.

And now, he asked himself, *what do I have now?* His only reply was silence, and at that moment Renan truly knew himself to be a soul adrift.

Then, as his thoughts began again their round, into the silence came the sound of a footstep. Renan turned to see Lysandra leaning on the arm of Talog. Her face had the white, pinched look of one who has given everything and beyond.

The sight filled Renan with guilt. Lysandra should be in her home, safe, cared for—loved, by someone who *could* love her, who *would* keep her safe. Instead, she had found herself on the brink of death, pursued by an enemy whose magic was as black as her heart, and had rallied time and again to pour out her strength in the aid of others . . . including himself.

As he looked at her, Renan was afraid of the harm he might have done her. But most of all, he was afraid of his feelings. Like the double death of a two-edged sword suspended over his heart, he feared to leave his current life and offer his love to her—and he feared a future without her.

Lysandra turned to Talog and whispered something Renan could not hear. The young Cryf nodded solemnly, then turned and left her standing alone.

"Renan?" she said softly, her voice husky with fatigue.

"I'm over here."

"You'll have to keep talking," she said with a slight smile. "My *Sight* is taking a rest. It's been through rather a lot in the last few days."

"You should be resting as well," Renan replied. "Your *Sight* is not the only part of you that has been through a lot."

"I have rested. In fact, I just awakened a short time ago. Talog said you had been here since after the battle. I thought you might want someone to talk to."

Lysandra was close enough now for Renan to gently grasp her outstretched hand.

"Where's Cloud-Dancer?" he asked, realizing how alone and vulnerable she looked without the wolf beside her.

"I left him with Selia while she talks with the Elders.
I thought she could use his company."

"How's Eiddig?" Renan asked as Lysandra settled beside him. "Is he—"

Again she gave him that small smile, a smile Renan
was uncertain how to read. "He'll be fine after more rest."

Renan could not ignore how *right* it felt to have Lysandra next to him. His questions quieted when she was near.
He fought the urge to put an arm around her and hold
her warmth against his body. Renan had always been content with his vow of celibacy. Many of his brother priests,
he knew, laid it aside as an outdated formality, part of the
service of ordination but no more practical in everyday
life than the ornate stoles and robes they wore for Mass.

Renan had been proud—ah, there was his pride again—
that he had never had such feelings. Nor was what he felt
toward Lysandra so base. He was in love with her, love
born out of friendship and admiration, out of respect that
deepened with every hour he spent in her company. It was
a love that wanted to protect not possess—to know and
share her mind, her heart, her dreams, her soul, not just
her body, and to give all of who he was in return.

It was a love such as he had, long ago, hoped someday to find—and now was forbidden, and afraid, to feel.

"Eiddig is fine," Lysandra said again, "and Talog, and
Selia. But you are not. What is it, Renan, that troubles
you so much? Please let me help."

"Let me help," Renan repeated softly. "Do you know,
Lysandra, I think those are the three most important words
we can say to one another. All the really important words
are simple like that. But they can also be the hardest ones
to answer."

Lysandra did not reply, but it was not an empty silence
she offered him. It was filled with encouragement and ac-

ceptance, a gift and a kindness he had only to open his heart to receive.

"Tell me, Lysandra," he said, "is there any prophecy in your *Sight* for me? Can you see my road ahead?"

Lysandra closed her eyes. Renan could feel the stillness that descended upon her as she waited, trying, as always, to do her best to answer the needs of another. But the questions of his life were not answered that easily.

Finally, Lysandra shook her head. "I'm sorry," she said. "I can *see* that you are at a crossroads, but only your own heart can tell you which path you should take."

Renan gave a small, mirthless smile. "That is no comfort," he said.

"It was not meant to be," was her reply.

Lysandra placed a hand upon his arm in a touch that was both firm and gentle, a healer's touch. She left it there for a long moment. Then she stood to leave.

"Renan," she said, "I do not know what decision you should make or which path is the right one for your future. But remember that every choice carries its own price and its own reward. Look at both of them honestly, without fear or judgment, and your answer will become clear."

Lysandra turned and called for Talog. The young Cryf stepped from the passage and came forward to take Lysandra's arm. She gave Renan one more brief touch upon his shoulder, then walked away. There was no need for more words. He knew that whichever way his decision took him, their paths would remain interwoven and their friendship would continue unscathed.

Chapter Thirty-six

The next morning, all of the Twelve Clans of the Cryf gathered in the Great Cavern, completely packing both the floor and all of the many ridges that ran in circles nearly to the ceiling. A dais had been raised in the center of the floor so that all might witness what was to come. Lysandra stood beside Selia as they waited for Baron Giraldus, Lady Aurya, and their remaining comrade, Sergeant Maelik, to be brought from where the Cryf were holding them prisoner.

Renan sat a little removed from them, still battling with the questions and decisions that had kept him several more hours beside the pool of the Great River. Lysandra longed to ease the burden she could feel he carried—though its cause was something he still would not speak of and until he was ready, she would not pry.

What she had told him yesterday was true; he was at a crossroads, and he, alone, must decide which path to follow. What she had not said was that whichever way he chose would be hard and full of danger to both body and spirit. There was darkness ahead for Renan. But Lysandra knew with the surety of breath that she would try to help him through until he could find the Light once more.

Lysandra heard a sound at the back of the cavern. It

slowly grew and she realized it was the sound of greetings, of joy and amazement. She did not need her *Sight* to tell her that Eiddig was slowly making his way through the crowd of his people. With her *Sight,* however, she examined her past patient as he walked—perhaps a little more stiffly and slowly than was his usual wont, but steadily, leaning heavily on the arm of Talog, his heir-apparent.

The Elder Guide's strength was returning and to Lysandra's healer's *Sight,* it looked as if Eiddig would carry the staff for many years yet.

When Eiddig reached the dais and walked up the ramp to stand before the assembled Cryf, the cavern erupted in noise. Every man, woman, and child there sent forth their strangely joyful, chirping cry at the sight of their beloved Guide restored and whole before them. Eiddig raised his arms, staff in hand, and stood for a moment looking as if he would embrace them all.

Then, while the cheering cry continued, he came over to Lysandra and once more touched her forehead in salute. "My life is thine, Healer," he said, though Lysandra had trouble hearing him above the din. "The Hand of the Divine is truly upon thee, and thou hast blessed us by thy presence here. Among the Cryf is thy home ever found. Thy name shall be honored and remembered with the hope of thy return unto us."

Lysandra, not knowing what to say or how to speak above the cries that continued to echo through the cavern, bowed to the Guide. Whatever his words, *she* was the one who had been blessed in this place. Eiddig, Talog—and all the Cryf—had been part of the reawakening of her heart.

Eiddig blessed each of them in turn, starting with Cloud-Dancer. Laying a hand upon his head, the Guide spoke to the wolf in the Cryf language. The words did not matter; the gesture was understood by all.

Eiddig then went to Renan. Lysandra did not know what passed between them, but she could *see* that the Guide's words touched Renan's heart. She hoped that somehow they also eased some of the burden her friend still carried.

Then Eiddig came to Selia, who was standing to Lysandra's right. Once more the Guide saluted her, touching palm to forehead.

"Thou art the Font of Wisdom," Lysandra heard him say. "It is now thy time. Let go the fears of thy childhood, for they have no more substance than smoke upon the wind. Art thou ready to step into the future? The Hand of the Divine is open and the Heart of the Divine waits for thee to speak the words of Truth."

"I am ready," Selia answered.

Lysandra's heart swelled at Selia's words. Though softly spoken, they were full of confidence and acceptance. Although Eiddig had been the one wounded, it was all the rest of them whose hearts had been most truly healed.

At a gesture from Eiddig, the Up-world prisoners were brought forth. The sight of them caused the cry in the cavern to change. It suddenly sounded as if some great beast growled, preparing to strike, and Lysandra felt the hair on her arms and the back of her neck rise in response.

The growl changed to silence at another gesture from Eiddig. The prisoners stood at the base of the dais, and though their hands were bound behind them, there was no submission in their eyes.

Selia, you are so young to face such a difficult moment, Lysandra thought. *I wish I could help you—but none of us can. However long it takes to gain the throne, this*

*is where your reign begins, and whatever happens now
will forever mark what is to follow.*

Although she had not spoken aloud, Selia turned and
looked at her. Their eyes locked for a long moment.
Sighted and blind, each *saw* the other—mind, heart, and
soul. In that instant, the last of Lysandra's doubts vanished. Selia had within her the heart—and the *Wisdom*—
to be a great ruler. She was truly the hope for Aghamore's
future.

Lysandra gave Selia a little nod. The younger woman
stepped forward and looked down at the prisoners. They
stared back defiantly, no contrition or plea for mercy on
any of the three faces. Lysandra was certain they expected
a sentence of death, and she wondered again what Selia
would do.

"Baron Giraldus of Kilgarriff," Selia began, her voice
carrying through the thick, expectant silence, "Lady Aurya
Treasigh, also of Kilgarriff, Sergeant Wylbeorn Maelik, I
offer you a chance to speak before sentence is passed."

She waited. For a moment the silence continued until,
finally, Aurya took a single step forward. Her eyes burned
with hatred as she looked not only at Selia but, one by
one, at each of her companions.

"Sentence?" she said at last, disdain heavy in the word.
"From you? These—creatures—here might hold you in
regard, but I do not. You are *nothing*, and the words you
say here *mean* nothing."

"They may mean nothing," Selia answered softly, "but
by them you will live. Hear then the sentence that shall
rule your life. It shall be in this place and among these
people that your lives shall be lived—not as rulers, as
you thought to force upon the land, but as servants. By your
hands were many lives taken from the Cryf. Now your
hands and your lives shall be given to serve those whom

you have wronged. You shall never leave this Realm, never again see the sun or walk among the trees. And never again shall you have the chance to do harm to those who looked to you for care. As you once sought to rule, now you shall be ruled; as you sought to control, so shall your lives now be in the control of others—and in the mercy of their hearts shall your joys or sorrows be found."

Lysandra was impressed by Selia's judgment. It was both wise and just. The Cryf were the only ones safe from Aurya's magic, and Lysandra found herself hoping that their other strengths and virtues might someday impress themselves upon the prisoners. Then would judgment be turned to redemption and Wisdom's mercy be revealed.

She hoped—but she did not believe.

A great cheer went up through the crowd of Cryf. Then, as the Cryf guards began to lead the prisoners away, Aurya shook off her captor's hands and turned to face Selia once more.

"They told me your name is Selia," she said. "I shall remember it. Be warned, Selia-who-thinks-to-be-Queen. I will get free—and then you shall pay for this moment and for every one hereafter. There shall be a blood feud between your House and mine. It matters not how much time it takes. My House shall avenge this moment until your House or time comes to an end."

With that, Aurya turned and walked regally from the cavern.

Lysandra's heart felt a sudden chill as her *Sight* turned prophetic with its new power. She was certain someday they would all face Aurya again—and, like this one, the encounter would be marked in blood.

Now that the sentencing was over, the moment of farewell was upon them. It was time to leave this strange and beautiful Realm for the Up-world that was their home.

There was still a task ahead that would demand all they had to give and more, for they must still find the way to save Aghamore and see Selia safely on the throne. For one moment longer, everyone on the dais stood in silence, none wanting to be the first to say good-bye. Then Eiddig once more stepped forward. He gestured and a young Cryf of perhaps ten years old came to the Guide, carrying a box of polished agate.

The old one lifted the hinged lid. From it he withdrew a necklace: a bright shard of amethyst, long as a man's finger, blazed on a silver chain, embedded with tiny rubies. This he gave to Selia, speaking so only she could hear. When he finished, she bowed her head and stepped back, nor did she raise her head again while the old one continued.

From the box he withdrew a second necklace. A golden topaz, two inches long, hung suspended from a braided rope of gold. This Eiddig put around Renan's neck, once more speaking to him alone. Like Selia, Renan accepted the Guide's words with thoughtful solemnity.

Eiddig drew a final necklace from the box. This one had a heart of lapis lazuli wrapped in a net of thinnest gold. At the top a fire opal caught the light with sparks of red and gold. The chain on which it hung was woven with threads of silver and gold. Lysandra was stunned by the beauty of it.

Eiddig put it around her neck and brought his head close to her ear. "Blue is the Healer's Stone," he said, "and the opal burneth with the fire of Prophecy. Use thy gifts well, Lysandra-Sant, for they are not of thy choosing, but of the Divine's. In thy time of need, these stones shall serve thee. For thine ears alone have these words been given. May they guide thee well.

"In Sight is Blindness and in Blindness, Vision. Illu-

sion is often found within and beareth the face of longing. Therefore, be thou certain of what thou seekest. Beware the whispered lie that ringeth of truth. Doubt thou
the child and trust the woman, trust thou the child and
doubt the woman—remember all are One in the Heart of
the Divine."

Lysandra found nothing but confusion in Eiddig's
words and if the other messages were as cryptic as this,
she could understand why Renan and Selia stood with
their heads bowed.

Eiddig stepped back. He touched his palm to Lysandra's forehead. "Farewell, Lysandra-Sant," he said, "and
to thee, Cloud-Dancer, whose heart is Loyalty. Remember thy home is now also among the Cryf and return to
us."

Eiddig was tiring visibly. Lysandra wanted to ask him
what his words had meant but she knew, as they all did,
the time had come to go. And she suspected that even if
they were to stay, Eiddig would offer no explanations. If
the words were for her ears alone, then she, alone, must
find their meaning.

After Talog escorted Eiddig to the foot of the dais, he
then lifted the belongings Lysandra and the others had left
in their sleeping chambers.

"Come," he told them. "The Cryf shall escort you on
your way."

"Talog," Lysandra said, "come with us, continue to help
us. Our task is not completed yet."

"My task be here," he replied, "but when She-Who-Is-
Wisdom cometh at last unto her throne, I shall come."

There was nothing more to say. Talog saluted each in
turn as they walked from the dais. They left the Great
Cavern, taking the passage that would lead them once

more to the hidden entrance between this Realm and the land above.

The passageway was lined with Cryf. All the way back through the caverns and tunnels, they were never alone. Finally, they stood once more upon the stone ledge that was the way out. Renan was the first to leave, then Selia. But before Lysandra followed them, she turned and looked back, letting her *Sight* embrace these beings whose strangeness had turned to beauty in her heart.

She raised her hand in a silent farewell. Then, to the sound of the Cryf's shrill cry, she placed it once more on Cloud-Dancer's head and followed the others into the Upworld.

Epilogue

In Ummara, cathedral city of the province of Kilgarriff, Elon was celebrating a Solemn High Mass of Thanksgiving. It was the first Sunday since his return from Ballinrigh and the mighty cathedral was filled to overflowing. Billows of incense flowed from the huge thurible swinging from the transept crossbeam, swung on its chain by the two robed acolytes given that duty today. Now, pulled up out of the way, it still rolled out billows of scented smoke that gathered like a bank of fog along the vaulted and corbelled ceiling.

The smaller, handheld thurible had been handed to him at the appropriate moments throughout the Mass so that he could cense the altar, paraments and vessels, the dean, deacons, and acolytes in symbolic purification at various times during the Mass. Elon was grateful for the smell of the incense, masking the odor of so many human bodies jammed into the cathedral on a warm and sunny day.

With so many concelebrants eager to take over the job, Elon rarely bothered himself with sermons anymore. Happily, the days of that particular responsibility had passed, though many other duties had taken its place. Nor were the papers in his hand a lapse into that old pattern. As in every other parish and cathedral throughout the kingdom over the next weeks, he carried the proclamation sent out by the College of Bishops, the proclamation he had helped draft, announcing the Church's choice and support of Giraldus DeMarcoe, Baron of Kilgarriff, as the next High King of Aghamore.

Elon mounted the narrow stairs that led into the elevated pulpit. Raised on high this way, he could be seen and heard even by those crowded into the back of the nave and overflowing into the narthex. As he looked out over the sea of upturned faces, Elon could imagine all the faces in Aghamore turned and waiting for this statement of guidance from their spiritual leaders. All except two—the two most important ones.

Aurya and Giraldus had still not returned. They could still lose everything he had gained. *The story of your pilgrimage will not hold forever. A few more weeks at most—and then the vultures will close in. They are already circling. If you don't have the child by now, then you've failed . . . and I must find another path to the Archbishop's throne.*

And he would, he thought with unwavering determination as he cleared his throat and prepared to speak. He could feel the anticipation pouring from the people below—and he was now ready to give them what they had come to hear.

"It is a great day for all the people of Aghamore," he began, "but especially so for us, the people of Kilgarrif. . . ."

It took them nine days to reach the Great Forest and another two before they reached Lysandra's cottage. She was weary beyond measure with all this traveling, but what she felt as they walked beneath the canopy of branches now leafed out in the full glory of new growth and breathed the air that to Lysandra seemed sweeter than anywhere else in the kingdom transcended joy.

She was *home*.

They had bypassed Ballinrigh completely as they traveled south. Although they all knew that they would eventually have to return to the capital, they first had to form a plan. Neither Renan nor Selia were ready to face what entering Ballinrigh represented. Decisions must be made and changes take place once they began to walk the path ahead; these they would face soon enough and for the rest of their lives. But first they needed to rest—and Lysandra just wanted to get back to her own cottage, her own bed, her own *life* at least for a little while.

It was full dark when they arrived, but Lysandra needed neither her *Sight* nor Cloud-Dancer's vision to know how it looked and where everything would be. Her mind—and her heart—saw all that was needed.

Lysandra let Renan set a fire to chase the chill from the cottage while she visited each room, as if to assure herself that everything was as it should be. Cloud-Dancer followed her, his happy prancing telling its own tale of homecoming.

She walked around her cottage, grazing the walls and furniture with light, unrealized caresses. She had not known until she walked through the door, how tightly held her heart had been or how heavily the longing to return had weighed upon her soul. From the moment she entered the forest, the bands around her heart had begun to loosen, and now, finally, the weight had lifted and she breathed free at last.

Despite the darkness, she felt compelled to walk one time through her garden, stopping briefly to sit upon the stone bench that marked its center and listen to the sounds that were unlike any heard in all her travels. These, too, were part of being home. She needed not *Sight* to recognize them all: the owl that lived in the hollowed spur of the larch that had fallen five years ago, the scurry of badgers and foxes whose kits must be half-grown by now, the startled scamper of mice and other prey, and the sudden sharp call of birds shaken from somnolence by the activity below. Nowhere else, in all of Aghamore, had the night sounded so sweet, so full, so *right*.

Finally, with a sigh that breathed contentment into the night, Lysandra stood and turned again toward her home. Tomorrow she would return to her garden and tend the plants that were no doubt in need of care after her absence. But it would be a labor of joy and of love. Perhaps, too, she thought as she walked toward her door, she would begin teaching Renan about the herbs that he wanted to learn.

She was not forgetting the task that lay ahead for all of them, but its planning could be accomplished as well in the garden as in the cottage.

Once she was back indoors, they dined on the last of the food the Cryf had sent for their journey, washed down with mugs of chamomile tea. Then, finally, came sleep, and it came quickly and deeply for them all.

The moon had fully risen and was shining on the garden, turning the green to silver with its touch. No noise drifted out from the closed shutters of the cottage; even the sounds of the forest had grown silent once again.

But the garden was not empty. At its center, on the little stone bench that Lysandra had earlier occupied, sat the spectral vision of a man. He was outlined in a gentle aura of green, and his clothes appeared the worn, much-mended habit of a monk. On his lined and ancient, bearded face, was a knowing smile as he sat looking at the cottage.

Finally, he nodded as if satisfied with what he saw and what he knew to be inside. Then he stood and began to walk the garden paths, stopping to touch the plants as if greeting old friends. When he reached the garden gate, he turned and looked back at the cottage yet again. Once more the knowing smile; again the nod. Then he passed through the gate and out into the forest.

But the green did not immediately fade from the garden air. It rose gently from beneath the bench, as if something there responded to his presence. Now that he was gone the light slowly faded, taking its secret with it.

Appendices

Provinces and Houses:

Founded by King Liam Roetah I, the Kingdom of Aghamore, which means "The Great Field," is divided into The Nine Provinces. These Provinces were ruled by Liam's sons, now by their descendants, and the Houses each bear their founder's name.

Urlar is the central and capital Province; it was inherited by Liam II, who became High King upon his father's death. The Provinces are counted in this order:

Urlar, "the level place," First Province and House, House of Roetah;

Tievebrack, "the speckled hillside," Second Province and House, House of Gathelus

Kilgarriff, "the rough wood," Third Province and House, House of Lidahanes

Dromkeen, "the beautiful ridge," Fourth Province and House, House of Caethal

Camlough, "the crooked lake," Fifth Province and House, House of Nuinseann

Sylaun, "place of sallows," Sixth Province and House, House of Niamh

Farnagh, "place of alders," Seventh Province and House, House of Ragenald

Lininch, "the half island," Eighth Province and House, House of Baoghil

Rathreagh, "the gray fort," Ninth Province and House, House of Cionaod

Barons of Aghamore:

Urlar: Central and Capital Province, direct rule of the High King

Tievebrack: Baron Phelan Gradaigh, House of Gathelus

Kilgarriff: Baron Giraldus DeMarcoe, House of Lidahanes

Dromkeen: Baron Curran OhUigio, House of Caethal

Camlough: Baron Oran Keogh, House of Nuinseann

Sylaun: Baron Ardal Mulconry, House of Niamh

Farnagh: Baron Thady Cathain, House of Ragenald

Lininch: Baron Einar Maille, House of Baoghil

Rathreagh: Baron Hueil Ruairc, House of Cionaod

Bishops of Aghamore

Urlar: Archbishop Colm apBeirne

Tievebrack: Bishop Mago Reamonn

Kilgarriff: Bishop Elon Gallivin

Dromkeen: Bishop Awnan Baroid

Camlough: Bishop Dwyer Tuama

Sylaun: Bishop Gairiad apMadain

Farnagh: Bishop Tavic Laighin

Lininch: Bishop Sitric Annadh

Rathreagh: Bishop Bresal Ciardha

Pronunciation Guide to Cryf Words: The Cryf language is phonetic; if a letter is there, it is pronounced. The Cryf alphabet and sounds are as follows:

A, soft as in apple
B, as in boy
C, always hard, as in cat
Ch, breathy back of the throat sound as in Scottish *loch*
D, as in dog
Dd, soft 'th' as in bath
E, long "A" sound, as in able
F, "v" sound, as in very
Ff, "f" sound as in friend
G, hard, as in goat
H, as in heard
I, hard "e," as in east
L, as in long
Ll, breathy sound made by placing tongue behind front teeth and blowing air out the sides

M, as in man
N, as in nice
O, long as in open
P, as in peace
R, rolled
S, as in safe
T, as in toy
Th, long, as in bathe
U, soft "e", as in every
W, double "oo" sound, as in moon
Y, soft "i" sound, as in inch

Acknowledgments

Writing is, by its very nature, a solitary profession. No one else can pick up the pen for me or turn the idea in my mind into written form. But outside that immediate solitary circle, there exists a web of support without which this writer could not function. It is, therefore, from the deepest truth of my heart that I give my respect, my gratitude, and my affection to all those who have granted me the gift to call them *Friend*.

I wish I could name you all, individually, but that is something time and page constraints will not allow. However, there are a precious few I must acknowledge, for without them this book would not exist:

To Jenn, my wonderful agent, who is a joy both to work with and to know;

To Betsy, my equally wonderful editor, who applies her skill to give encouragement—and humility;

To Kata, healer and compassion-made-flesh, who has gotten me through some difficult times and whose skill at the healing arts is out-measured only by the beauty of her soul;

To Steve B., whose concern, encouragement, and respect are precious jewels I treasure more than I can say;

To Mike and Ellen, who have helped me with both friendship and information;

To Diana, whose gifts of music and laughter bring me much needed respite;

To Lori, Tristan, and Mario, for all the friendship, pets, purrs, moments of silence and of companionship;

And to those whose presence gives purpose, strength, and joy not only to my work, but to my life:

To Donna, dearest friend of my heart, who reads and rereads, shares the triumphs and disasters, the laughter and the sorrows, and who, through the years, has given me more than any paper has room to hold or any words the skill to express;

To Mary, who also reads and rereads, who has blessed my life in countless ways for over four decades, and is the living proof that a sister can also be a dear and beloved friend;

And most of all, always and all ways, to Stephen, husband, truly the other half of my soul, without whom all that I am would not exist—the past two decades are only the beginning, for only an eternity can hold my love for you.

To all of you, named and unnamed, you are the steady rock upon which the house of my life is built. I give you all my continual and everlasting thanks . . . and all my love.

-R-

REBECCA V. NEASON is the author of the bestselling STAR TREK: The Next Generation novel, *Guises of the Mind*, as well as two HIGHLANDER novels, *The Path* and *Shadow of Obsession*. She also has published numerous non-fiction articles which, along with her poetry, have been featured in regional, national and international publications. In 1988 she was awarded a Certificate of Recognition for Outstanding Literary Merit by the Pacific Northwest Writers Conference, and she is a graduate of the Clarion West Writers Workshop. A frequent speaker at science fiction conventions, Ms. Neason also lectures on pre-Christian through Medieval British History, Middle English, and the development of English as a written language.

Ms. Neason lives on ten wooded acres in rural Washington, sharing her home and her life with a husband and a large number of cats and dogs, all of whom are rescues—a cause to which Ms. Neason is extremely dedicated.

ESSENTIAL
WITCH WORLD

The Key of the Keplian
Andre Norton and Lyn McConchie
(0-446-60220-5)

✦

The Magestone
Andre Norton and Mary H. Schaub
(0-446-60222-1)

✦

The Warding of Witch World
Andre Norton
(0-446-60369-4)

✦

Ciara's Song: A Chronicle of Witch World
Andre Norton and Lyn McConchie
(0-446-60644-8)

AT BOOKSTORES EVERYWHERE FROM WARNER ASPECT

VISIT WARNER ASPECT ONLINE!

THE WARNER ASPECT HOMEPAGE
You'll find us at: www.twbookmark.com then by clicking on Science Fiction and Fantasy.

NEW AND UPCOMING TITLES
Each month we feature our new titles and reader favorites.

AUTHOR INFO
Author bios, bibliographies and links to personal websites.

CONTESTS AND OTHER FUN STUFF
Advance galley giveaways, autographed copies, and more.

THE ASPECT BUZZ
What's new, hot and upcoming from Warner Aspect: awards news, bestsellers, movie tie-in information . . .